Pirate penguin vs Ninja chicken

Escape from Skull-Fragment Island!

PIRATE PENGUIN vs NINJA CHICKEN

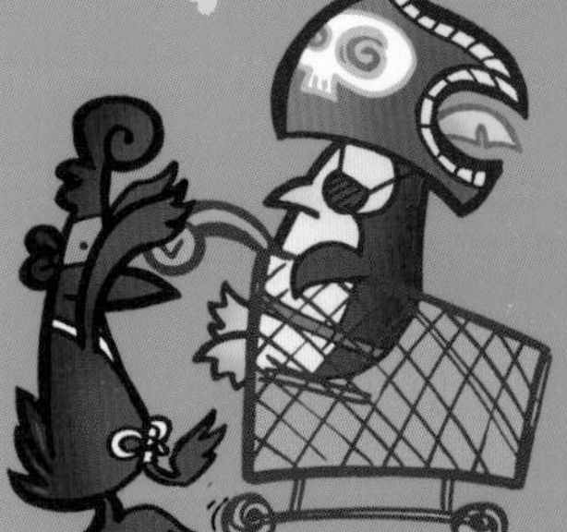

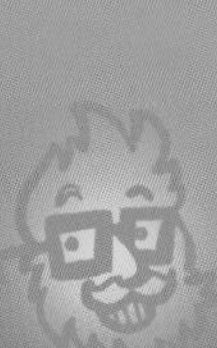

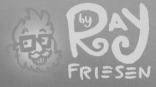

by RAY FRIESEN

Other Books by Ray Friesen

PPvsNC: Troublems With Frenemies
Lookit! A Cheese Related Mishap
Lookit! YARG!
Another Dirt Sandwich
Cupcakes of Doom!
Lookit! Piranha Pancakes
Fairy Tales I Just Made Up!

Pirate Penguin Vs Ninja Chicken
Book Two: Escape From Skull-Fragment Island
www.PiratePenguinVsNinjaChicken.com

ISBN 978-1-60309-367-5

Published by Top Shelf Productions,
PO Box 1282, Marietta, GA 30061-1282, USA.
Top Shelf Productions is an imprint of IDW Publishing,
a division of Idea and Design Works, LLC. Offices:
2765 Truxtun Road, San Diego, CA 92106. Top Shelf Productions, the Top Shelf logo, Idea and Design Works, and the IDW
logo are registered trademarks of Idea and Design Works, LLC.

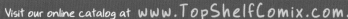

Editor-in-Chief: Chris Staros.

Printed in Korea

19 18 17 16   5 4 3 2 1

Visit our online catalog at www.TopShelfComix.com.

Smooching Consultation: Michelle Harshberger
Coloring Minion: Joe Heath, www.MintyPineapple.com
Font-ification by Missy Meyer
Production Baby: Wellington Emmet

Unwitting Pirate Models: Scott F, Fred H, Scratch S, Mike S,
Joe H, Ben P, Chris H, Rob W, Chelcat X, Sarah E, Kakapo J, Lexi F.
Catering by the Salty Things Corporation of America

Edited by Zac Boone.

TABLE of CONTENTS

Now stop reading this Table of Contents and go comic it up!

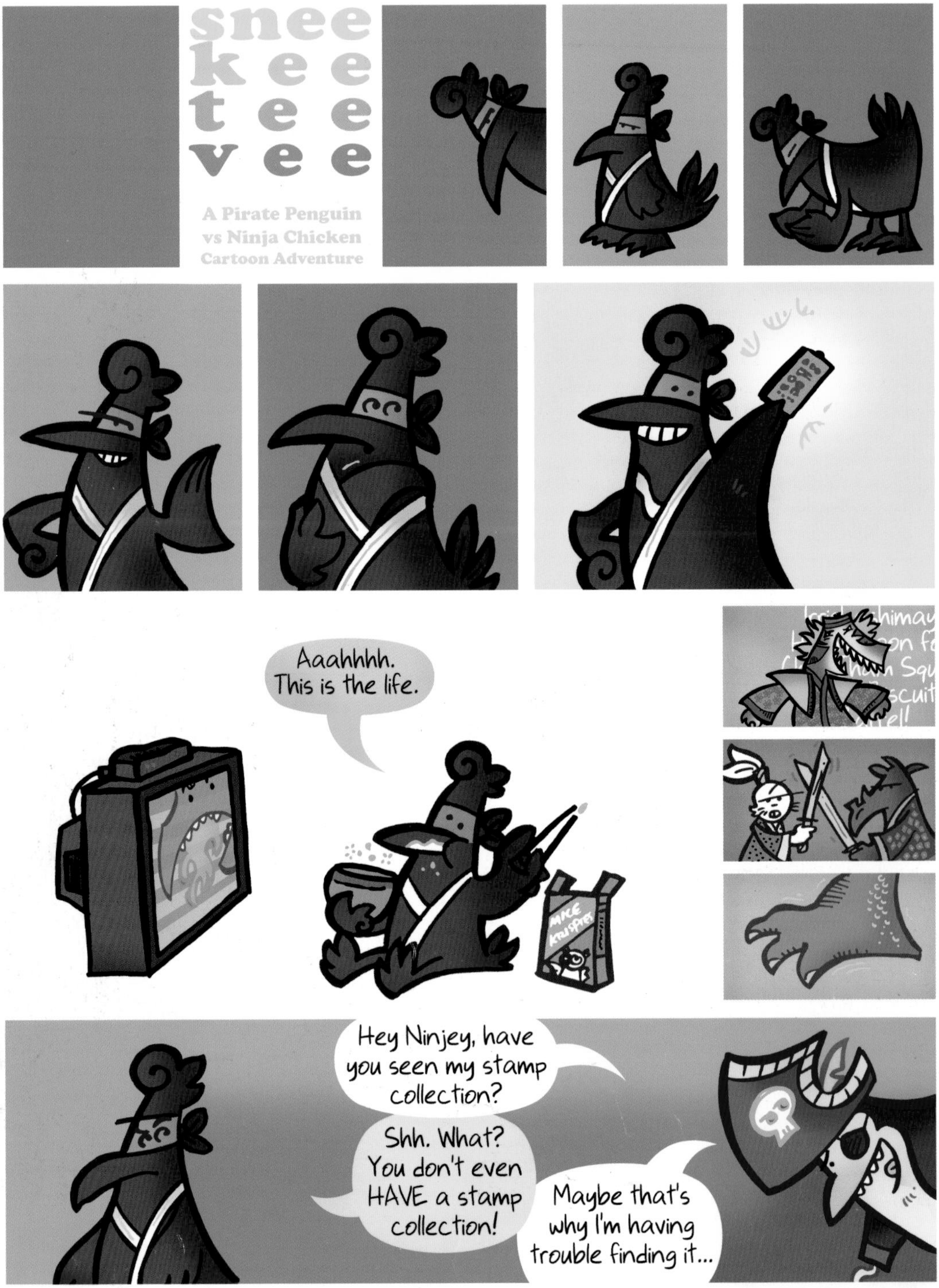

sneekee teevee
A Pirate Penguin vs Ninja Chicken Cartoon Adventure
Aaahhhh. This is the life.
Hey Ninjey, have you seen my stamp collection?
Shh. What? You don't even HAVE a stamp collection!
Maybe that's why I'm having trouble finding it...

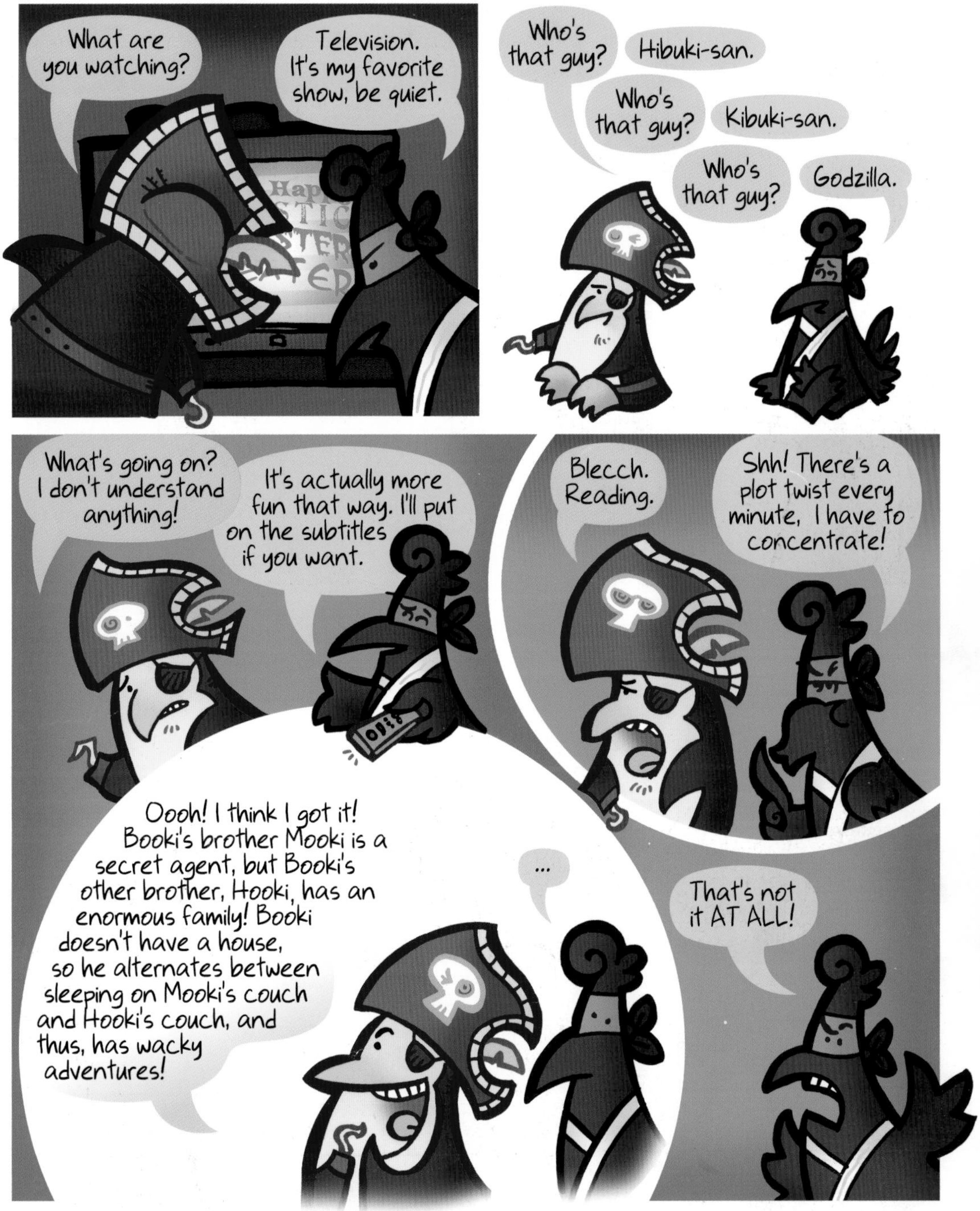
What are you watching?
Television. It's my favorite show, be quiet.
Who's that guy?
Hibuki-san.
Who's that guy?
Kibuki-san.
Who's that guy?
Godzilla.
What's going on? I don't understand anything!
It's actually more fun that way. I'll put on the subtitles if you want.
Blecch. Reading.
Shh! There's a plot twist every minute, I have to concentrate!
Oooh! I think I got it! Booki's brother Mooki is a secret agent, but Booki's other brother, Hooki, has an enormous family! Booki doesn't have a house, so he alternates between sleeping on Mooki's couch and Hooki's couch, and thus, has wacky adventures!
...
That's not it AT ALL!

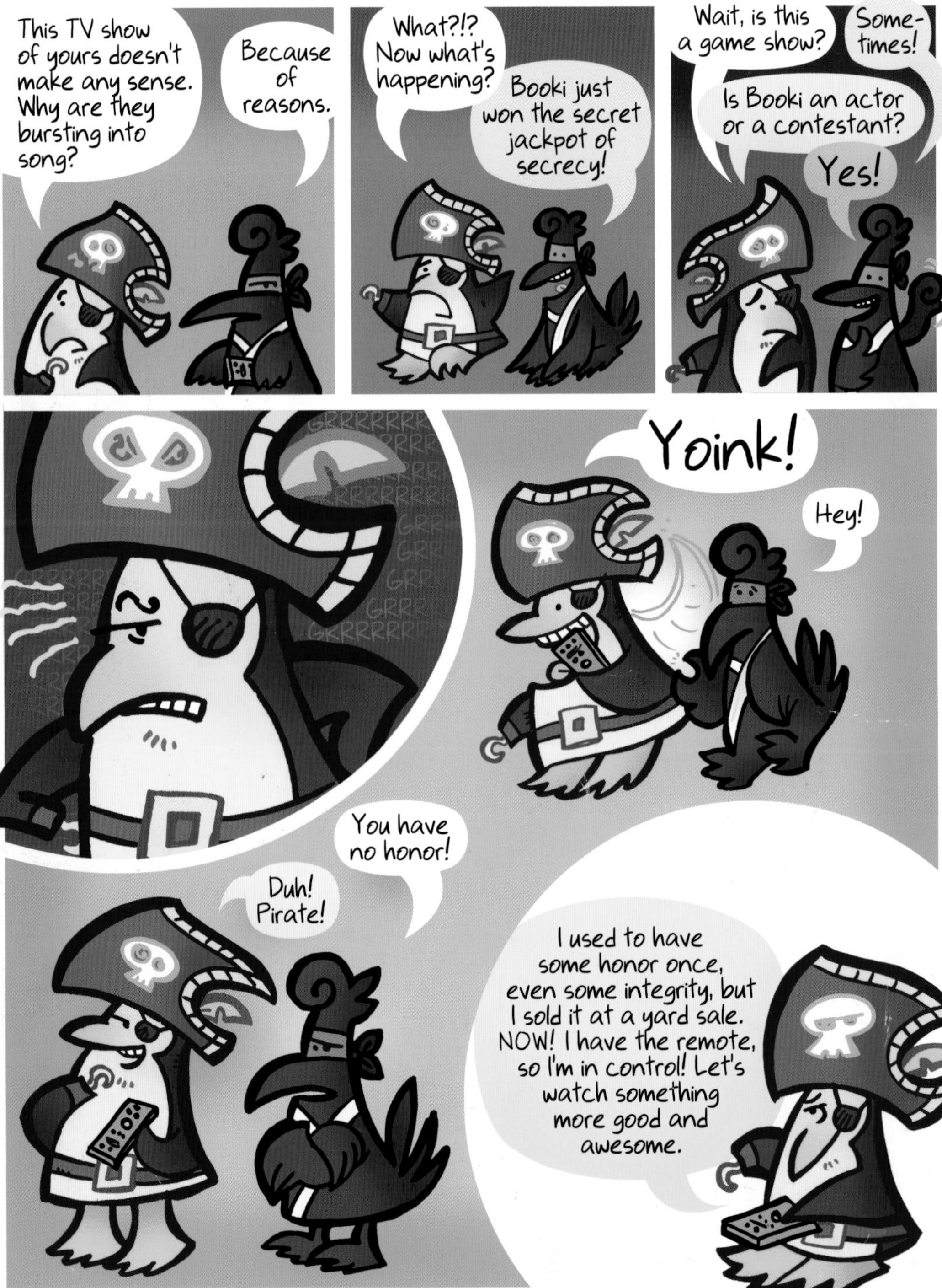
This TV show of yours doesn't make any sense. Why are they bursting into song?
Because of reasons.
What?!? Now what's happening?
Booki just won the secret jackpot of secrecy!
Wait, is this a game show?
Some-times!
Is Booki an actor or a contestant?
Yes!
GRRRRRR
Yoink!
Hey!
You have no honor!
Duh! Pirate!
I used to have some honor once, even some integrity, but I sold it at a yard sale. NOW! I have the remote, so I'm in control! Let's watch something more good and awesome.

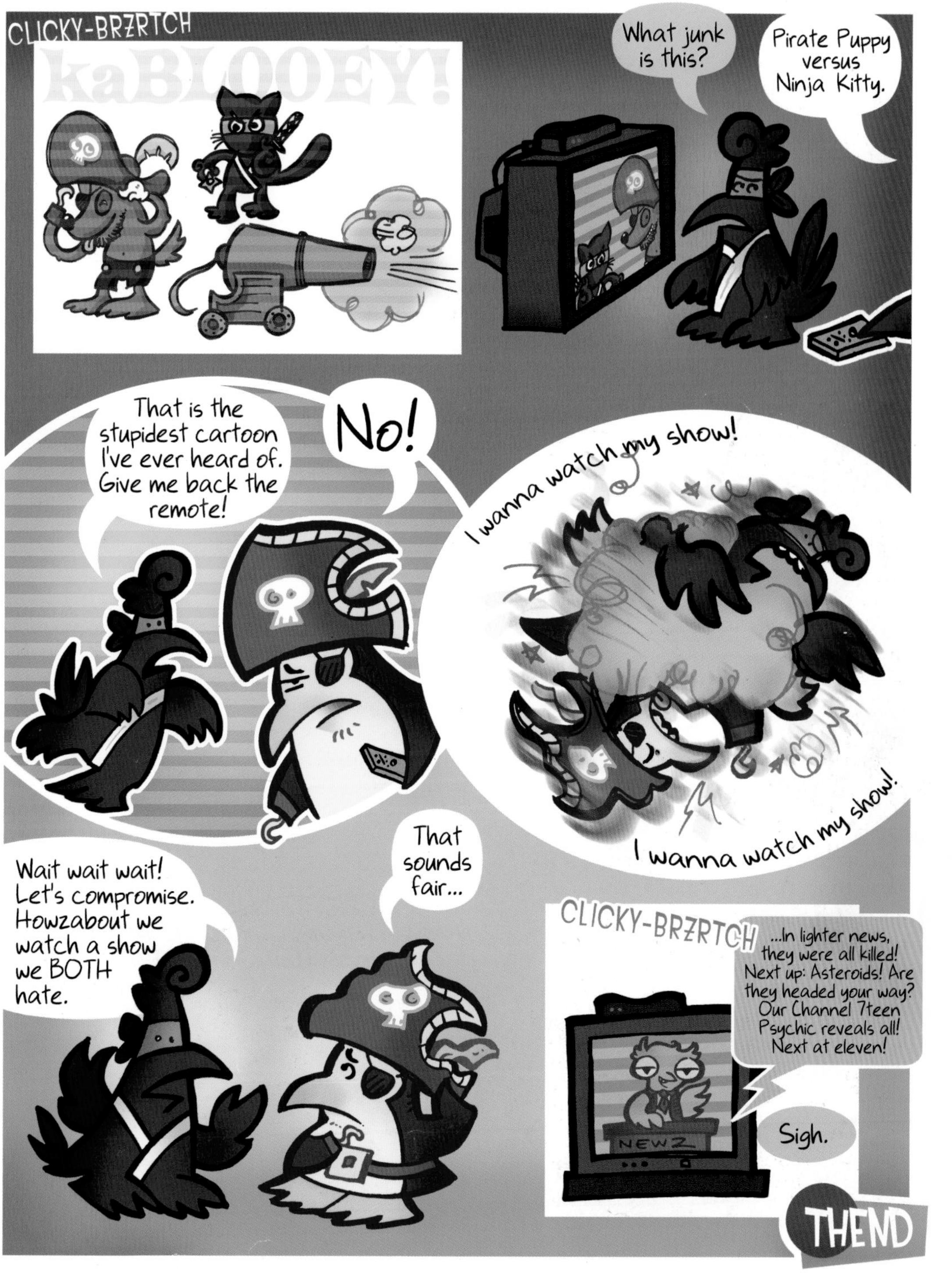
CLICKY-BRZRTCH
kaBLOOEY!
What junk is this?
Pirate Puppy versus Ninja Kitty.
That is the stupidest cartoon I've ever heard of. Give me back the remote!
No!
I wanna watch my show!
I wanna watch my show!
Wait wait wait! Let's compromise. Howzabout we watch a show we BOTH hate.
That sounds fair...
CLICKY-BRZRTCH
...In lighter news, they were all killed! Next up: Asteroids! Are they headed your way? Our Channel 7teen Psychic reveals all! Next at eleven!
NEWZ
Sigh.
THEND

Horsin' around

A Pirate Penguin vs Ninja Chicken Cartoon Adventure

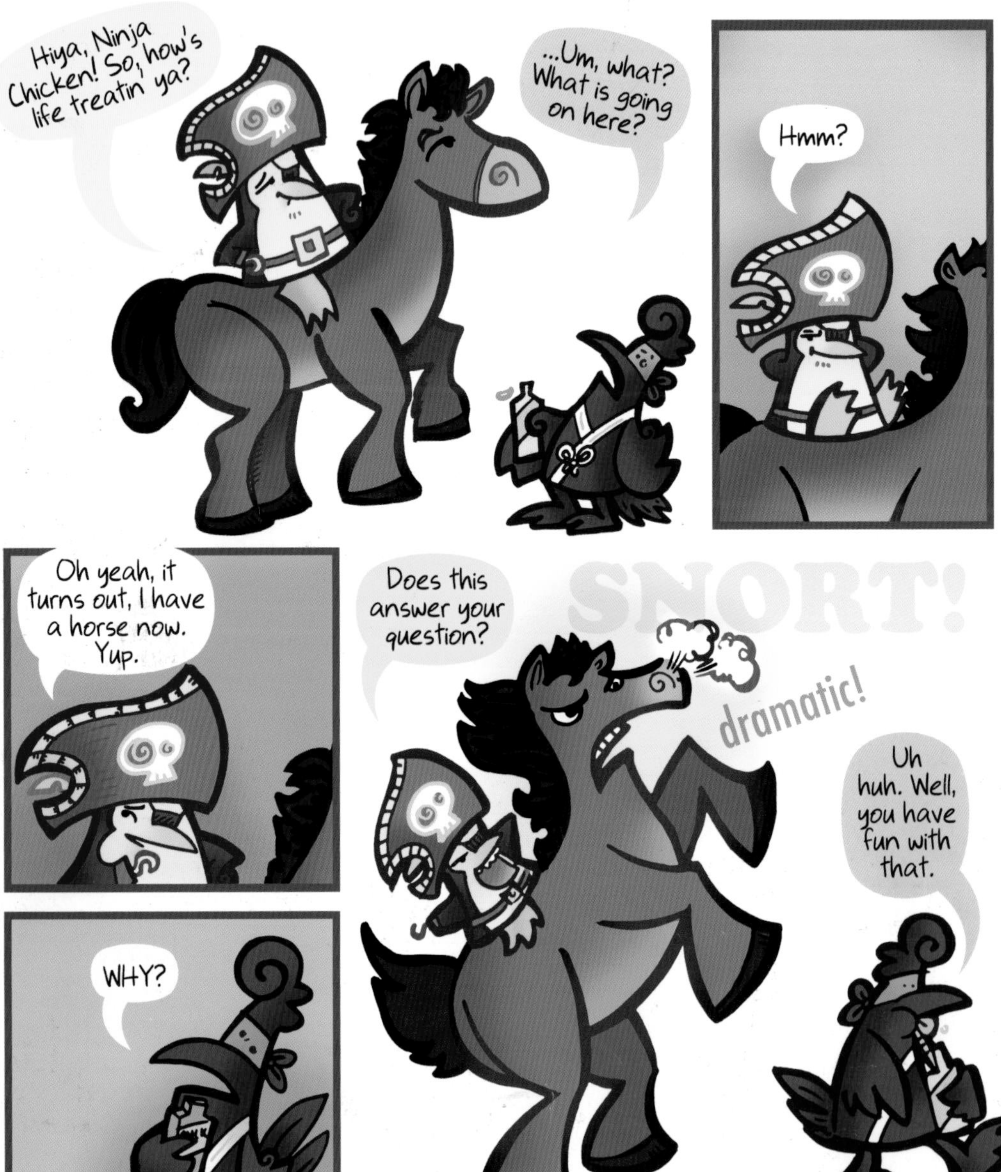
Hiya, Ninja Chicken! So, how's life treatin' ya?
...Um, what? What is going on here?
Hmm?
Oh yeah, it turns out, I have a horse now. Yup.
WHY?
Does this answer your question?
SNORT!
dramatic!
Uh huh. Well, you have fun with that.

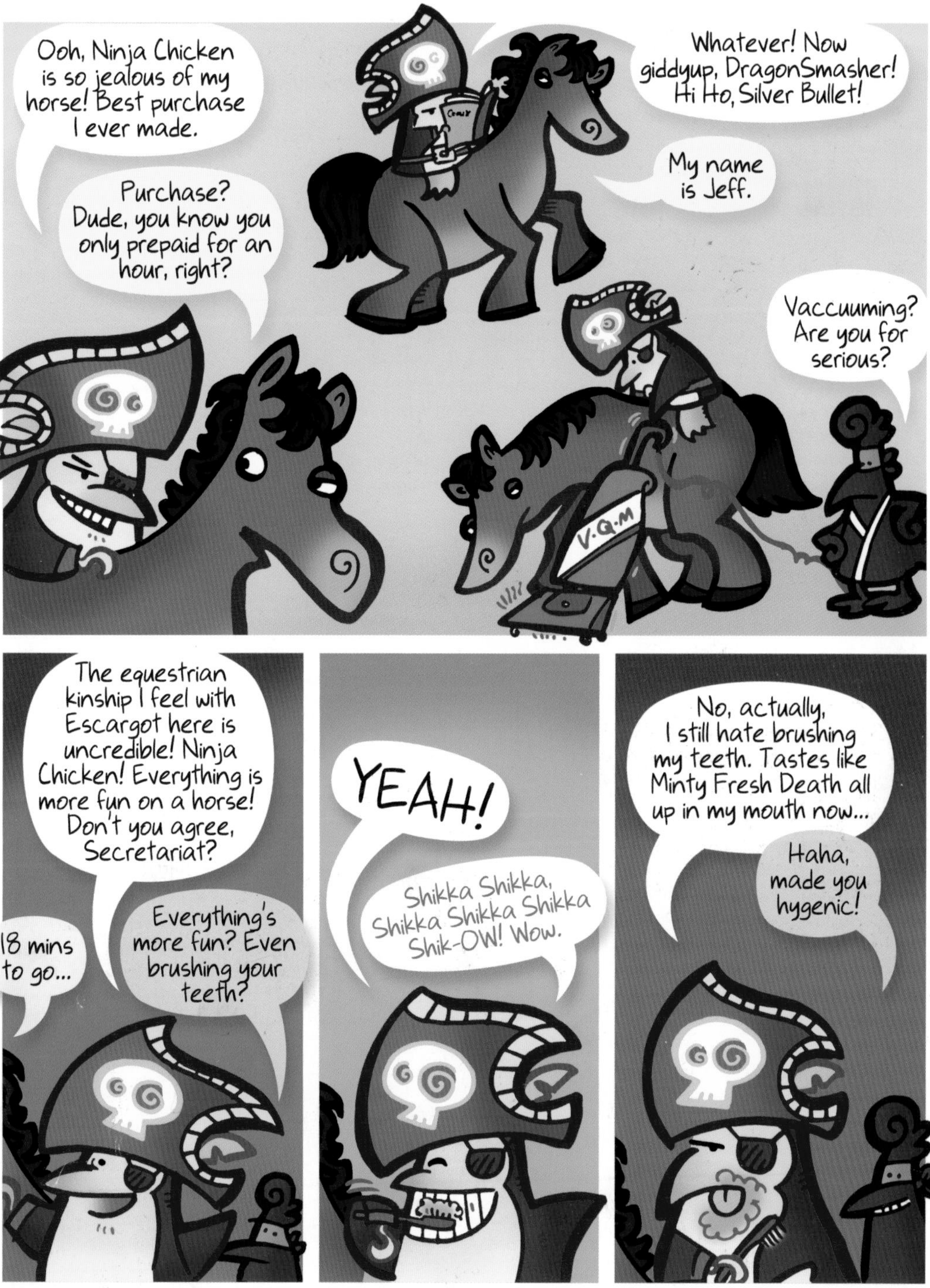

Ooh, Ninja Chicken is so jealous of my horse! Best purchase I ever made.
Whatever! Now giddyup, DragonSmasher! Hi Ho, Silver Bullet!
My name is Jeff.
Purchase? Dude, you know you only prepaid for an hour, right?
Vaccuuming? Are you for serious?
V.Q.M
The equestrian kinship I feel with Escargot here is uncredible! Ninja Chicken! Everything is more fun on a horse! Don't you agree, Secretariat?
18 mins to go...
Everything's more fun? Even brushing your teeth?
YEAH!
Shikka Shikka, Shikka Shikka Shikka Shik-OW! Wow.
No, actually, I still hate brushing my teeth. Tastes like Minty Fresh Death all up in my mouth now...
Haha, made you hygenic!

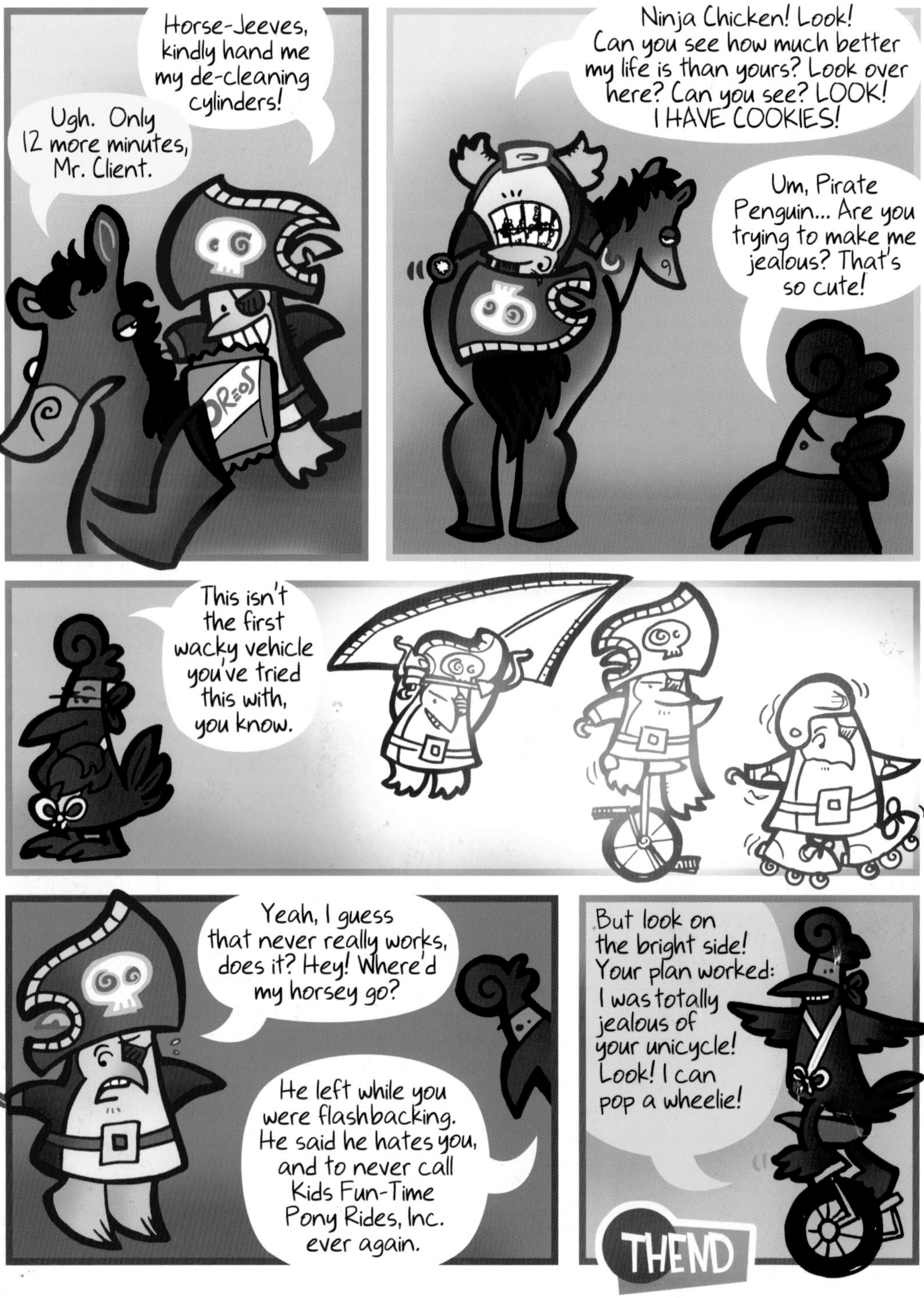
Horse-Jeeves, kindly hand me my de-cleaning cylinders!
Ugh. Only 12 more minutes, Mr. Client.
OREOS
Ninja Chicken! Look! Can you see how much better my life is than yours? Look over here? Can you see? LOOK! I HAVE COOKIES!
Um, Pirate Penguin... Are you trying to make me jealous? That's so cute!
This isn't the first wacky vehicle you've tried this with, you know.
Yeah, I guess that never really works, does it? Hey! Where'd my horsey go?
He left while you were flashbacking. He said he hates you, and to never call Kids Fun-Time Pony Rides, Inc. ever again.
But look on the bright side! Your plan worked: I was totally jealous of your unicycle! Look! I can pop a wheelie!
THEND

The LOW-PRICED CONSUMER GOODS of DEATH

A PIRATE PENGUIN VS NINJA CHICKEN CARTOON ADVENTURE

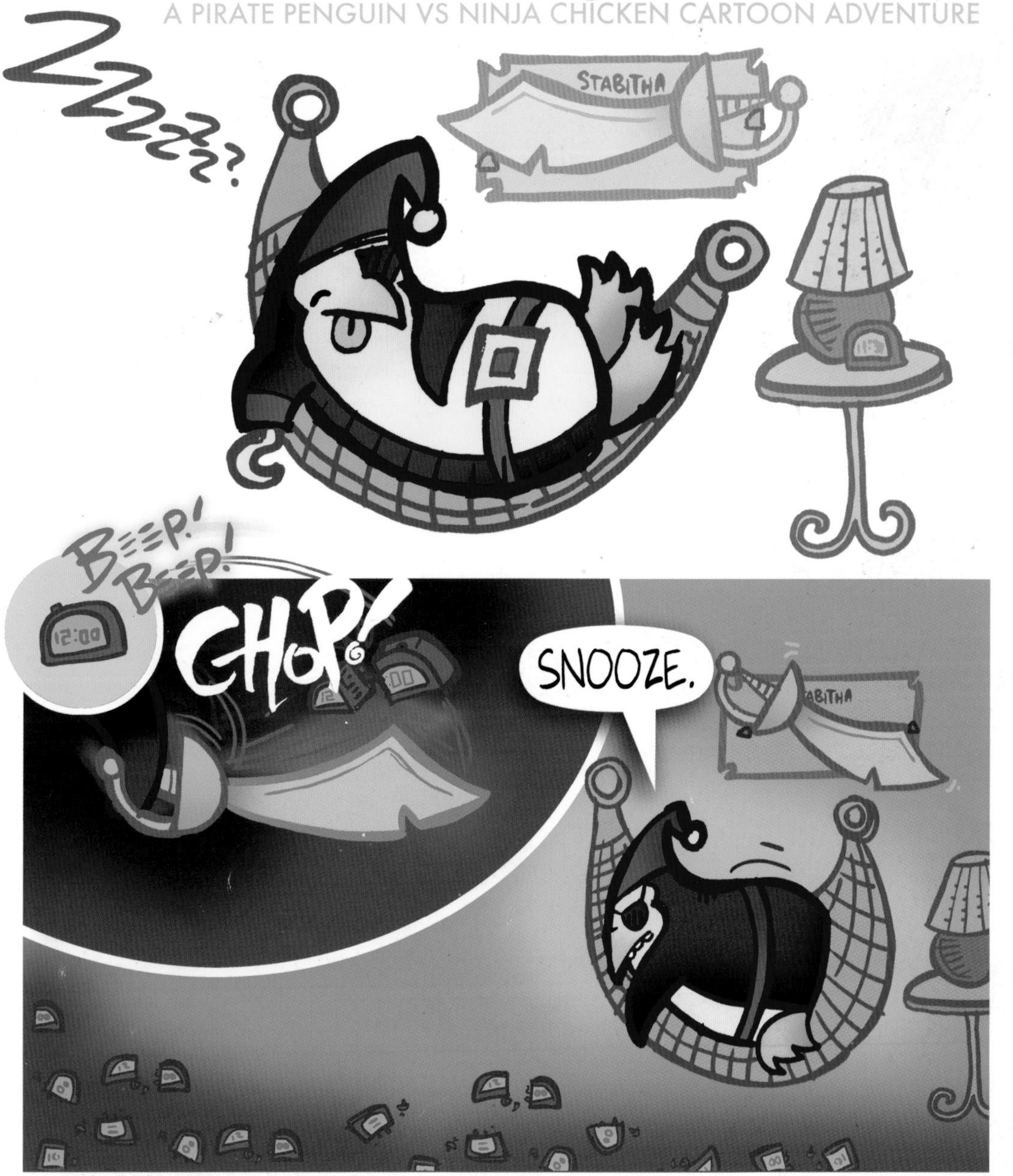

STABITHA
BEEP! BEEP!
12:00
CHOP!
SNOOZE.

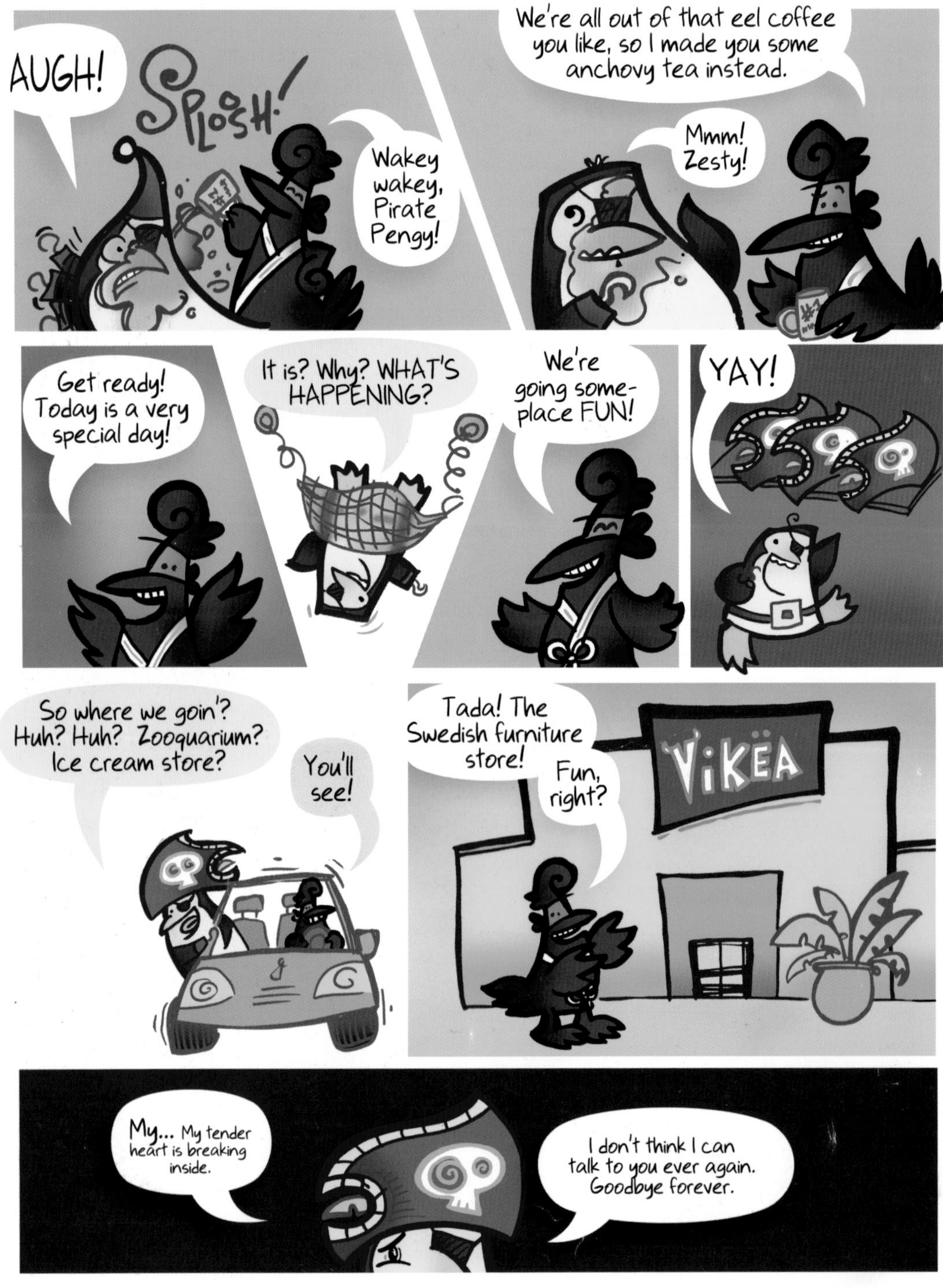
AUGH!
SPLOOSH!
Wakey wakey, Pirate Pengy!
We're all out of that eel coffee you like, so I made you some anchovy tea instead.
Mmm! Zesty!
Get ready! Today is a very special day!
It is? Why? WHAT'S HAPPENING?
We're going some-place FUN!
YAY!
So where we goin'? Huh? Huh? Zooquarium? Ice cream store?
You'll see!
Tada! The Swedish furniture store!
Fun, right?
ViKËA
My... My tender heart is breaking inside.
I don't think I can talk to you ever again. Goodbye forever.

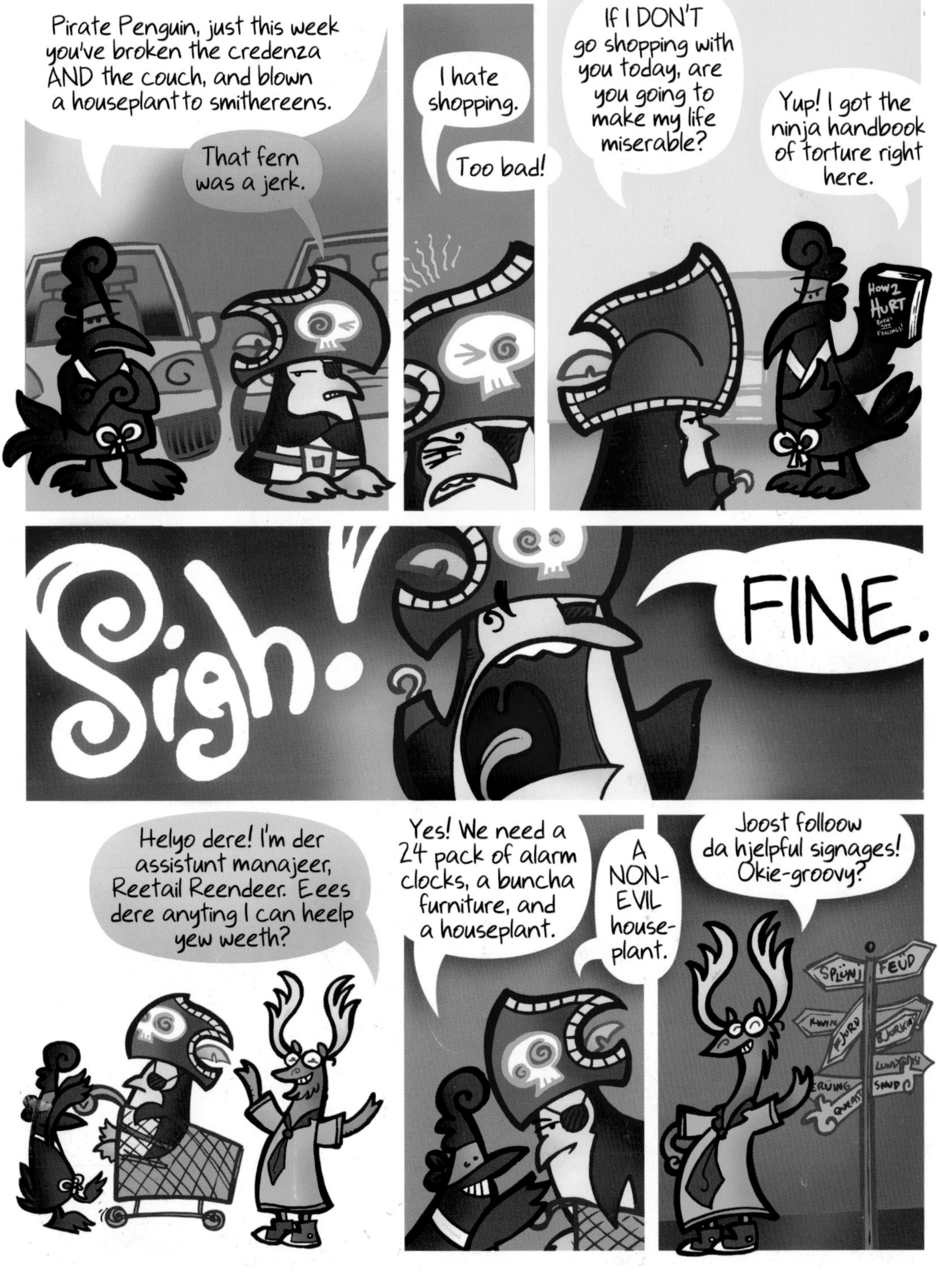
Pirate Penguin, just this week you've broken the credenza AND the couch, and blown a houseplant to smithereens.
That fern was a jerk.
I hate shopping.
Too bad!
If I DON'T go shopping with you today, are you going to make my life miserable?
Yup! I got the ninja handbook of torture right here.
HOW 2 HURT
Sigh!
FINE.
Helyo dere! I'm der assistunt manajeer, Reetail Reendeer. Eees dere anyting I can heelp yew weeth?
Yes! We need a 24 pack of alarm clocks, a buncha furniture, and a houseplant.
A NON-EVIL house-plant.
Joost folloow da hjelpful signages! Okie-groovy?
FEÜD

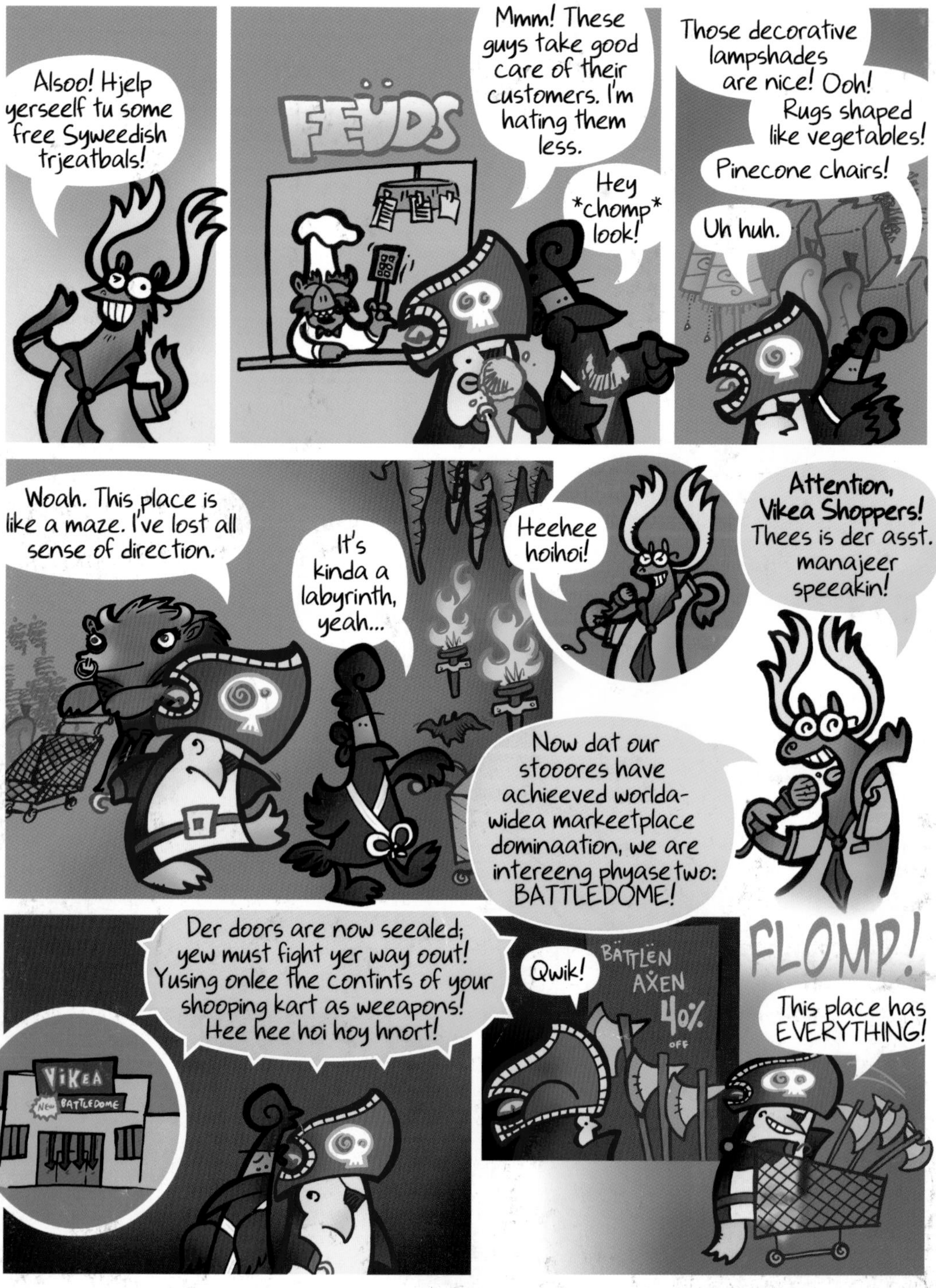

Alsoo! Hjelp yerseelf tu some free Syweedish trjeatbals!
FEÜDS
Mmm! These guys take good care of their customers. I'm hating them less.
Hey *chomp* look!
Those decorative lampshades are nice! Ooh!
Rugs shaped like vegetables!
Pinecone chairs!
Uh huh.
Woah. This place is like a maze. I've lost all sense of direction.
It's kinda a labyrinth, yeah...
Heehee hoihoi!
Attention, Vikea Shoppers! Thees is der asst. manajeer speeakin!
Now dat our stooores have achieeved worlda-widea markeetplace dominaation, we are intereeng phyase two: BATTLEDOME!
Der doors are now seealed; yew must fight yer way oout! Yusing onlee the contints of your shooping kart as weeapons! Hee hee hoi hoy hnort!
VIKEA
New BATTLEDOME
Qwik!
BÄTTLËN AXEN 40% OFF
FLOMP!
This place has EVERYTHING!

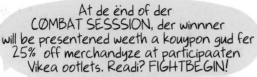
At de ënd of der COMBAT SESSSION, der winnner will be presentened weeth a kouypon gud fer 25% off merchandyze at participaaten Vikea ootlets. Readi? FIGHTBEGIN!

Weird. Would they really...

RAWR! There can be ONLY ONE!

GEEZ, Grandma!

Grapple!

SPIN!

Clank!

TWuRL

WARNIG!!!!!!!!!!!!

Um, guys? watch out for the...

Wait, why is there a cliff in a furniture store?

ARNIG!!! !!!!!!!!!

AUGH!

Pirate Penguin? Old lady? Hello?

WARNIG !!!!!!!!

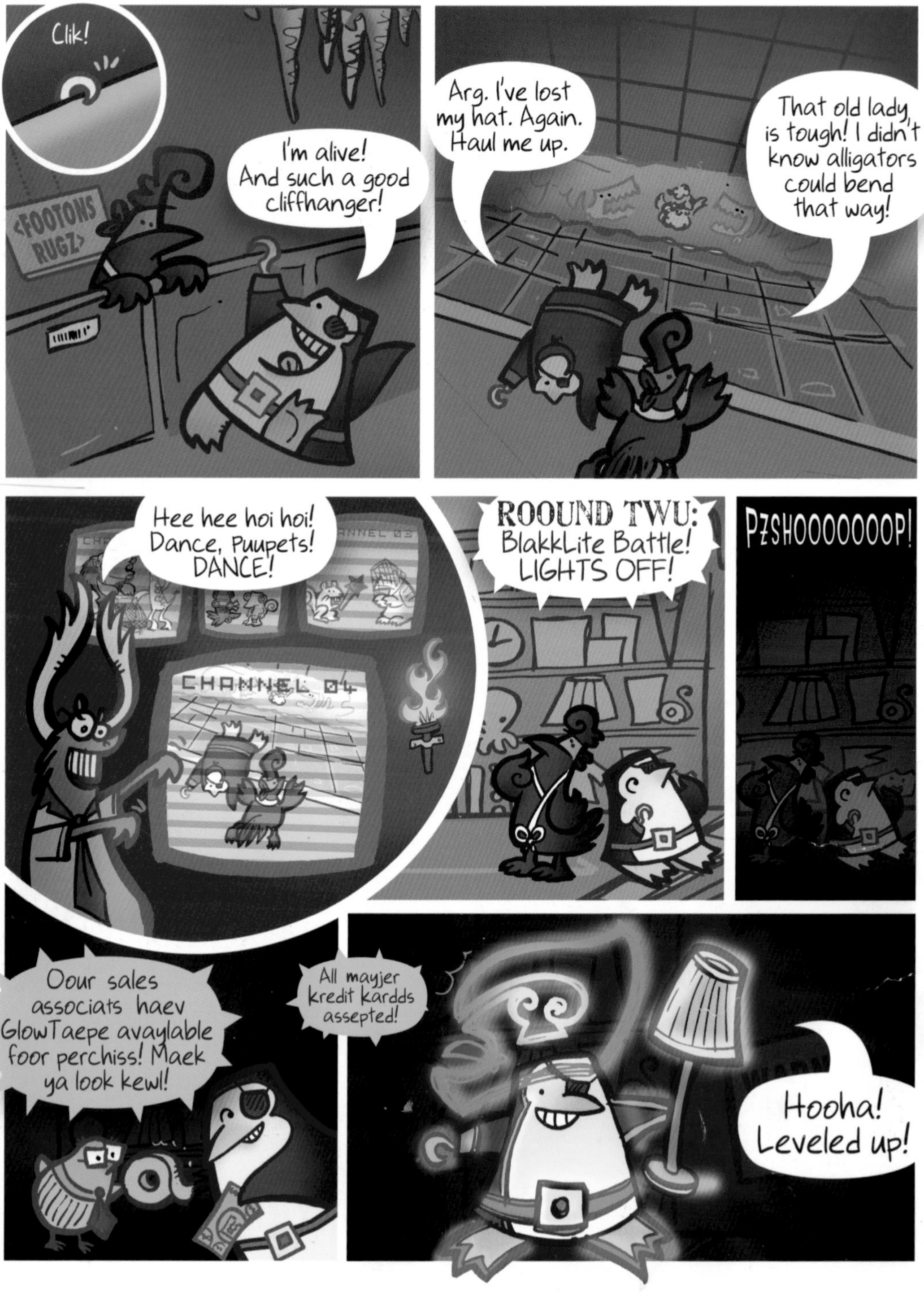
Clik!
I'm alive! And such a good cliffhanger!
<FOOTONS RUGZ>
Arg. I've lost my hat. Again. Haul me up.
That old lady is tough! I didn't know alligators could bend that way!
Hee hee hoi hoi! Dance, Puupets! DANCE!
CHANNEL 03
CHANNEL 04
ROOUND TWU: BlakkLite Battle! LIGHTS OFF!
PZSHOOOOOOOP!
Oour sales associats haev GlowTaepe avaylable foor perchiss! Maek ya look kewl!
All mayjer kredit kardds assepted!
Hooha! Leveled up!

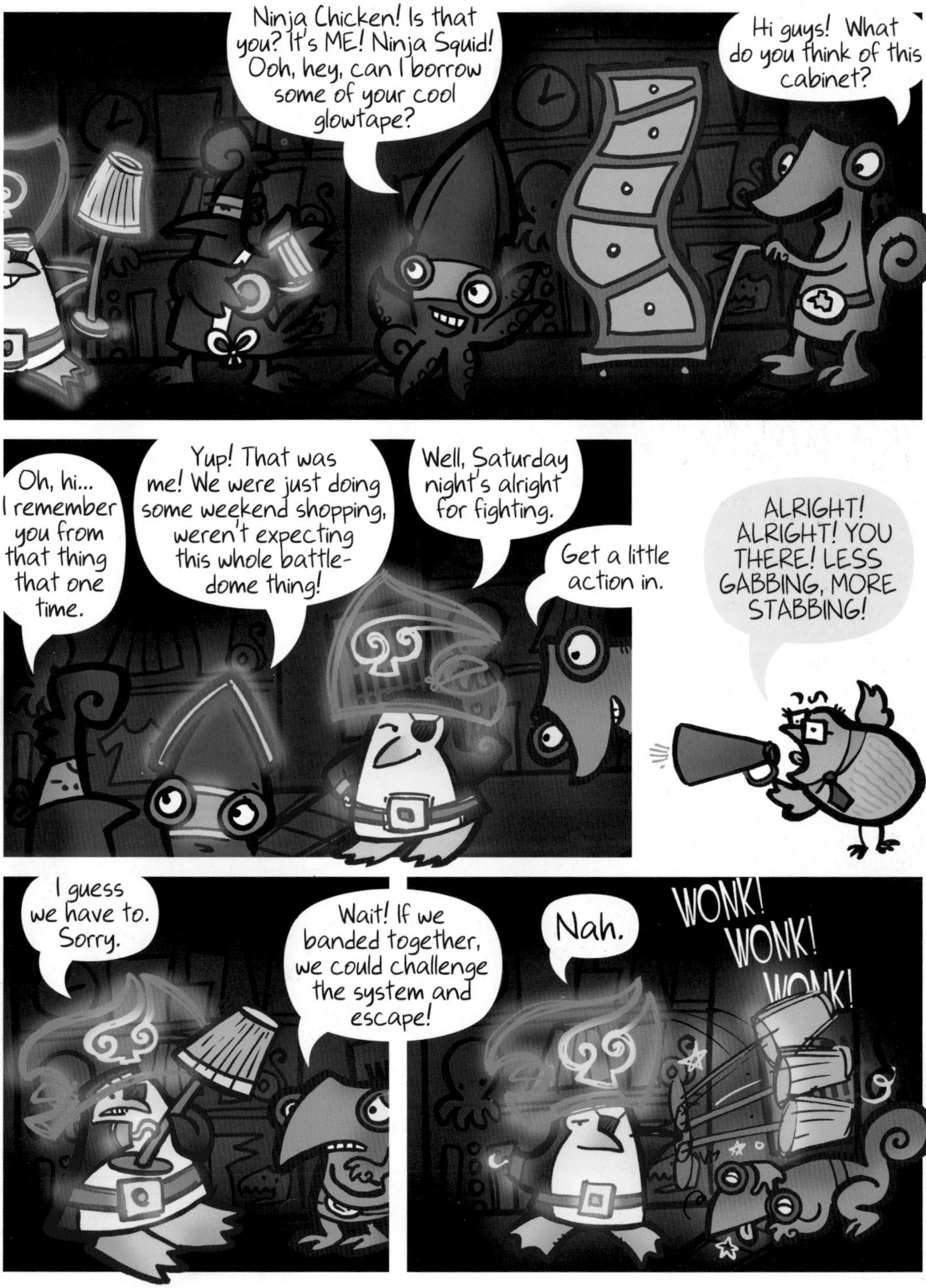
Ninja Chicken! Is that you? It's ME! Ninja Squid! Ooh, hey, can I borrow some of your cool glowtape?
Hi guys! What do you think of this cabinet?
Oh, hi... I remember you from that thing that one time.
Yup! That was me! We were just doing some weekend shopping, weren't expecting this whole battle-dome thing!
Well, Saturday night's alright for fighting.
Get a little action in.
ALRIGHT! ALRIGHT! YOU THERE! LESS GABBING, MORE STABBING!
I guess we have to. Sorry.
Wait! If we banded together, we could challenge the system and escape!
Nah.
WONK!
WONK!
WONK!

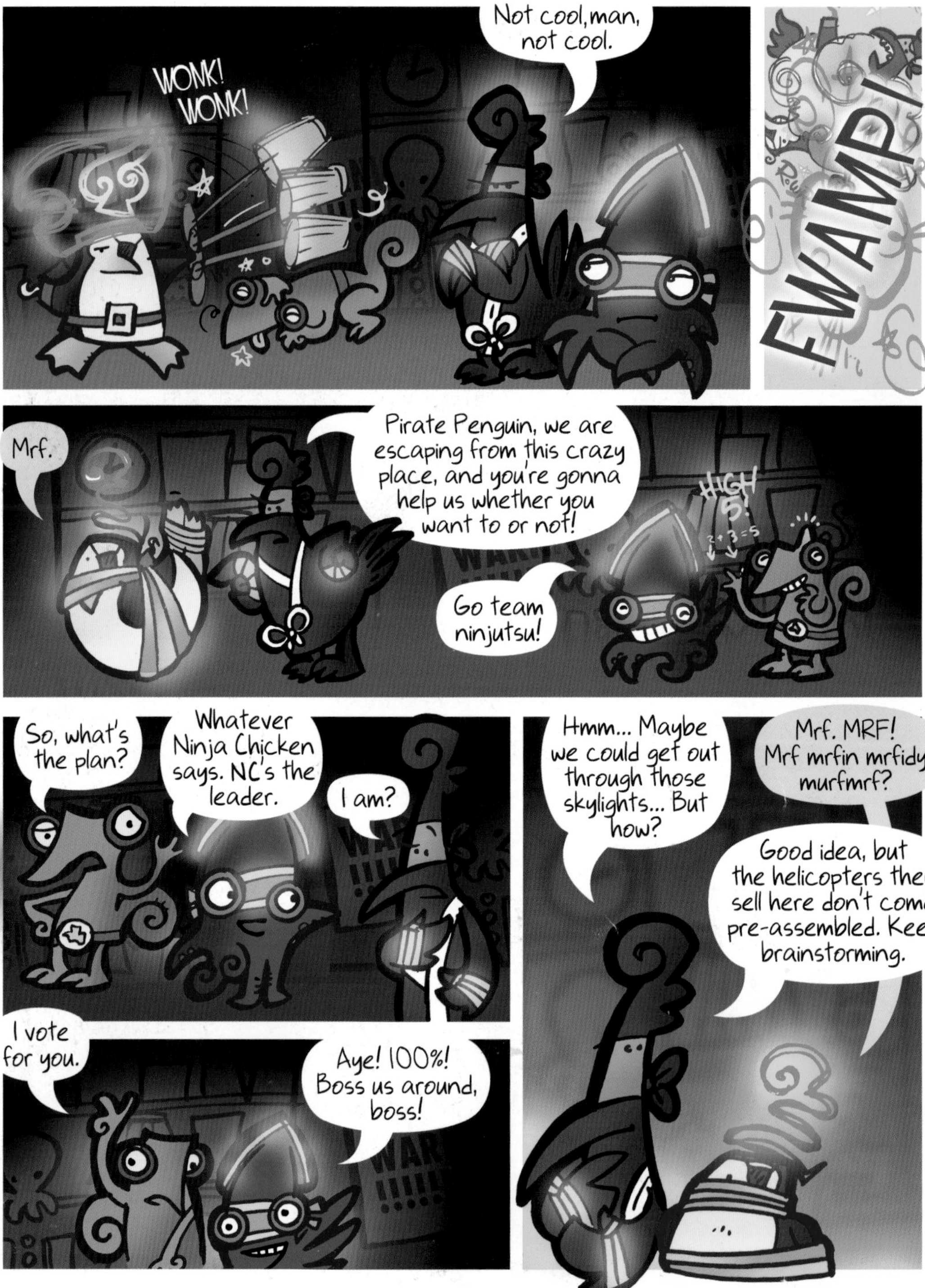
WONK!
WONK!
Not cool, man, not cool.
FWAMP!
Mrf.
Pirate Penguin, we are escaping from this crazy place, and you're gonna help us whether you want to or not!
HIGH 5!
2 + 3 = 5
Go team ninjutsu!
So, what's the plan?
Whatever Ninja Chicken says. NC's the leader.
I am?
I vote for you.
Aye! 100%! Boss us around, boss!
Hmm... Maybe we could get out through those skylights... But how?
Mrf. MRF! Mrf mrfin mrfidy murfmrf?
Good idea, but the helicopters they sell here don't come pre-assembled. Keep brainstorming.

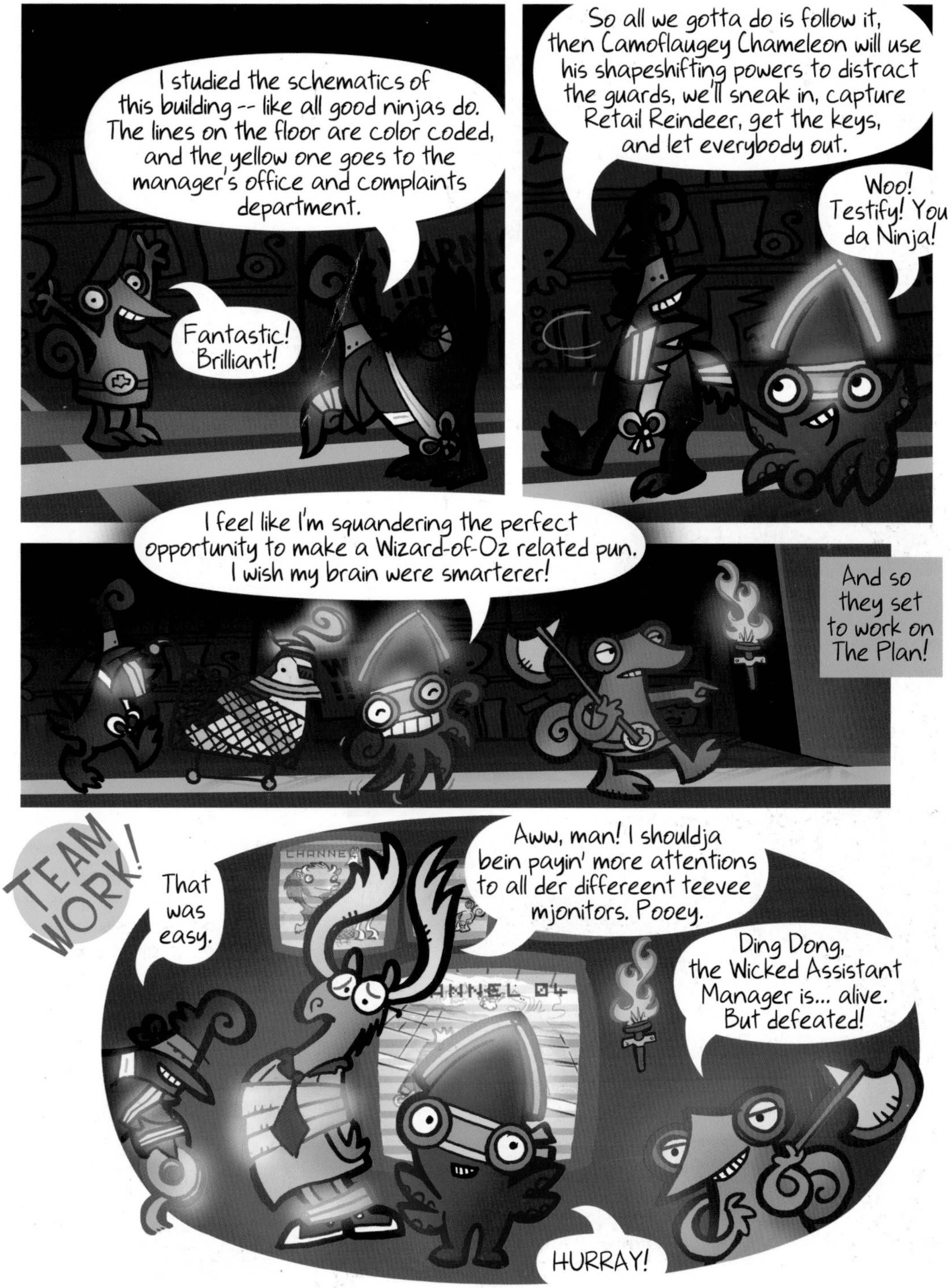

I studied the schematics of this building -- like all good ninjas do. The lines on the floor are color coded, and the yellow one goes to the manager's office and complaints department.
Fantastic! Brilliant!
So all we gotta do is follow it, then Camoflaugey Chameleon will use his shapeshifting powers to distract the guards, we'll sneak in, capture Retail Reindeer, get the keys, and let everybody out.
Woo! Testify! You da Ninja!
I feel like I'm squandering the perfect opportunity to make a Wizard-of-Oz related pun. I wish my brain were smarterer!
And so they set to work on The Plan!
TEAM WORK!
That was easy.
Aww, man! I shouldja bein payin' more attentions to all der differeent teevee mjonitors. Pooey.
CHANNEL 04
Ding Dong, the Wicked Assistant Manager is... alive. But defeated!
HURRAY!

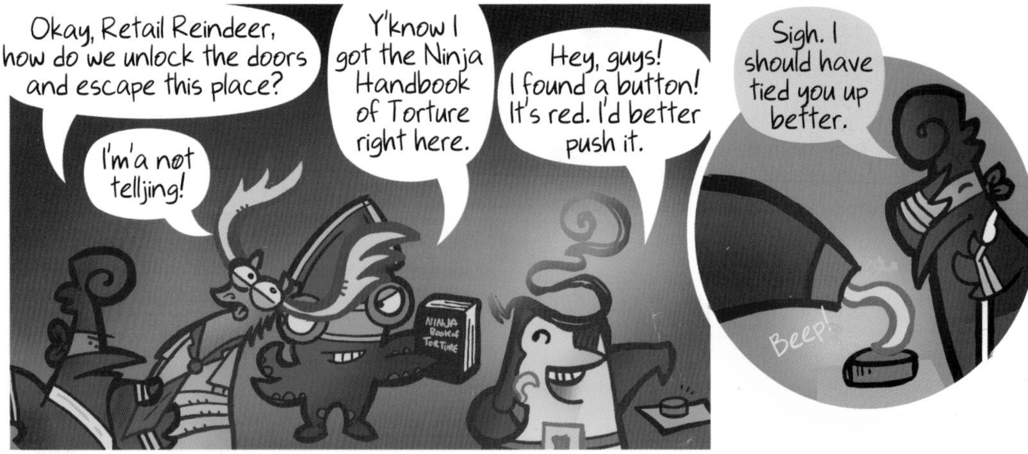
Okay, Retail Reindeer, how do we unlock the doors and escape this place?
I'm'a not telljing!
Y'know I got the Ninja Handbook of Torture right here.
NINJA Book of TORTURE
Hey, guys! I found a button! It's red. I'd better push it.
Sigh. I should have tied you up better.
Beep!

ROOUND THRIE: VINTER VUNDERLANDT: SNOW GO!

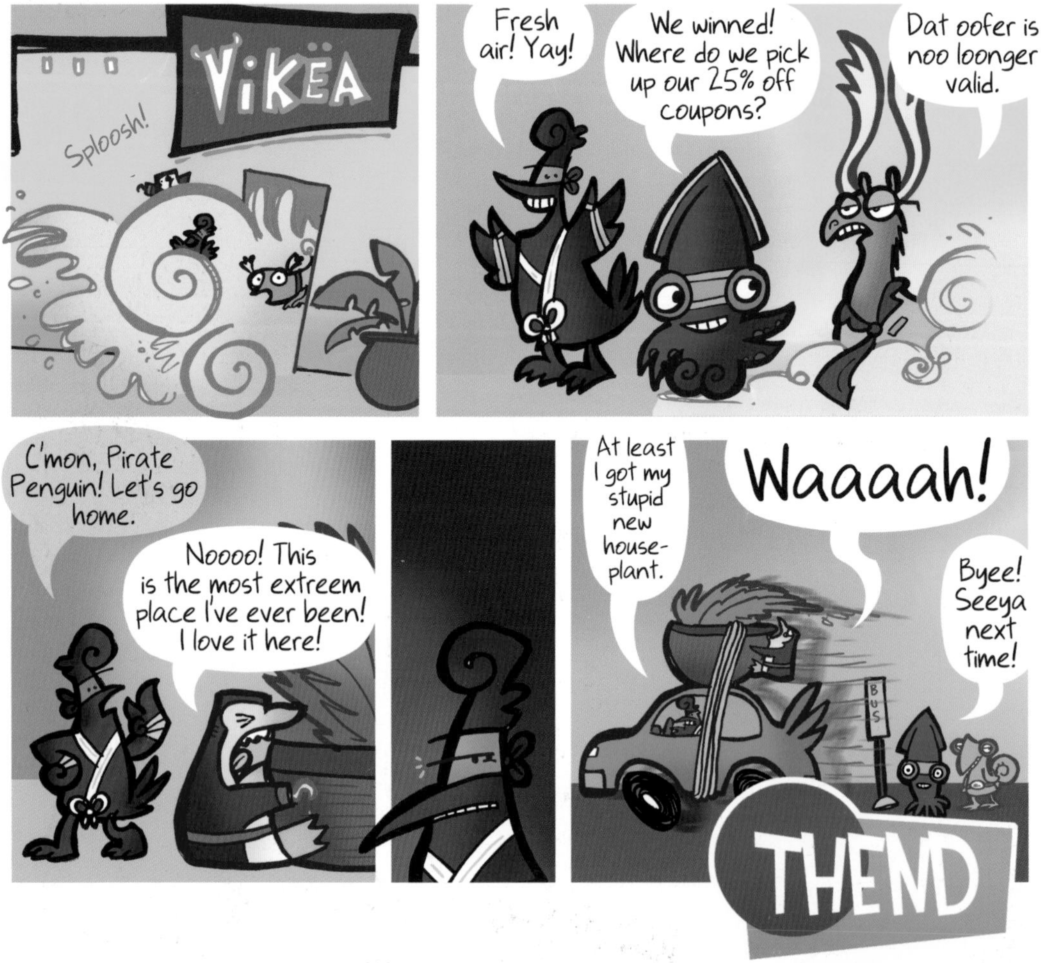
ViKËA
Sploosh!
Fresh air! Yay!
We winned! Where do we pick up our 25% off coupons?
Dat oofer is noo loonger valid.
C'mon, Pirate Penguin! Let's go home.
Noooo! This is the most extreem place I've ever been! I love it here!
At least I got my stupid new house-plant.
Waaaah!
Byee! Seeya next time!
BUS
THEND

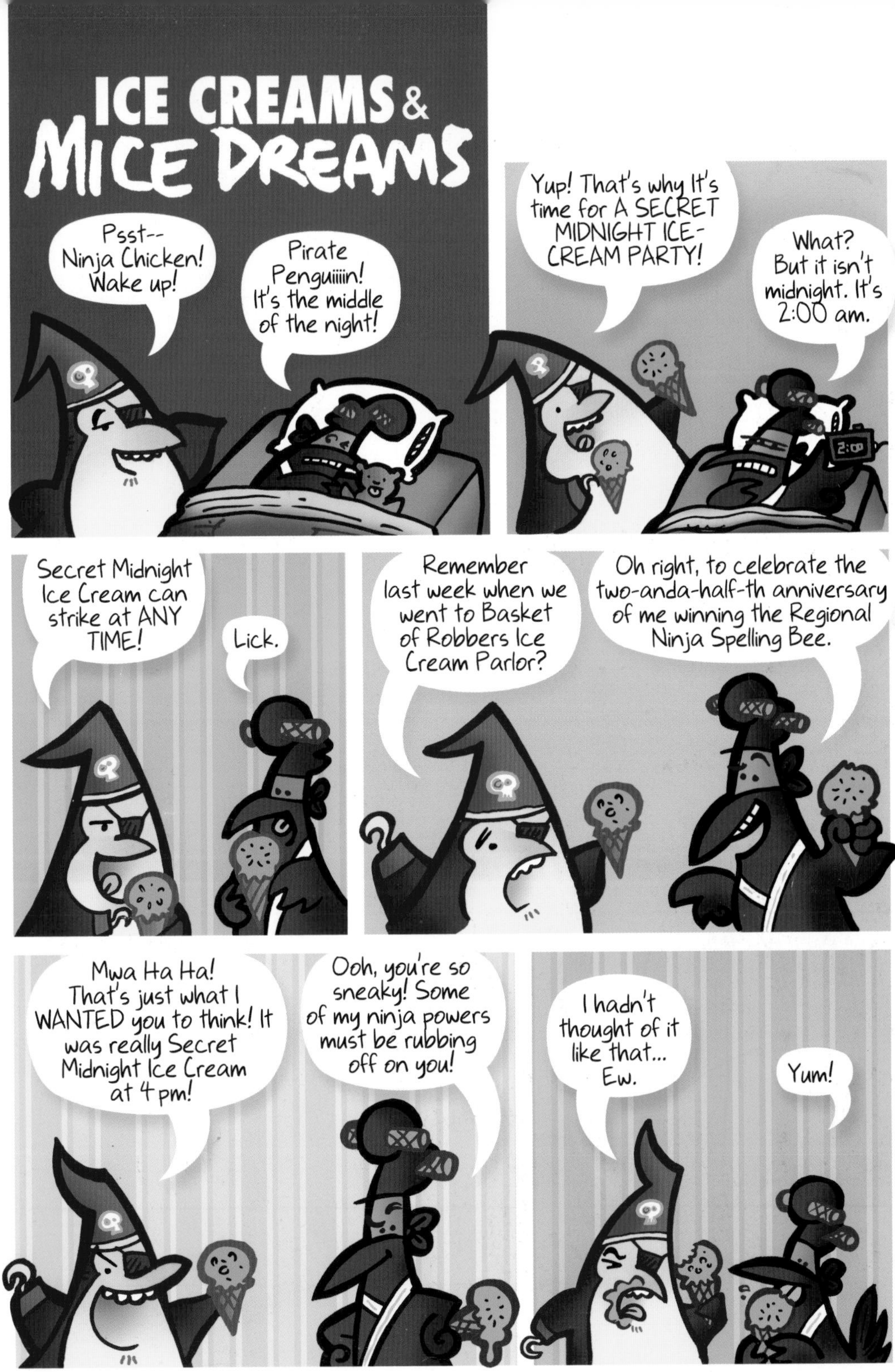
ICE CREAMS & MICE DREAMS
Psst-- Ninja Chicken! Wake up!
Pirate Penguiiiin! It's the middle of the night!
Yup! That's why It's time for A SECRET MIDNIGHT ICE-CREAM PARTY!
What? But it isn't midnight. It's 2:00 am.
2:00
Secret Midnight Ice Cream can strike at ANY TIME!
Lick.
Remember last week when we went to Basket of Robbers Ice Cream Parlor?
Oh right, to celebrate the two-anda-half-th anniversary of me winning the Regional Ninja Spelling Bee.
Mwa Ha Ha! That's just what I WANTED you to think! It was really Secret Midnight Ice Cream at 4 pm!
Ooh, you're so sneaky! Some of my ninja powers must be rubbing off on you!
I hadn't thought of it like that... Ew.
Yum!

This mintacinno is quite scrumptious! Secret Midnight Ice Cream was a good idea.

Thanks! I actually had an ulterior motive for giving you caffeine and keeping you up - I'm having some bad dreams, and I wanted to share the insomnia.

Oh, I don't ever have troubles sleeping! I just go into a zenjitsu trance of restfulness: OMMMM...

Wait! Lemme tell you about my dream! There was this mouse, that wasn't a mouse, and he was just staring at me for hours. What do you think that means?

ZzzZz

SNAP! SNIP! SNOP!

ZzzZz

Well then, fine, I'm gonna eat your ice cream.

ZzzZz   GRR!

ARG! Your grip is like steel! I caaaaan't... YAAAWN!

ZZZZZZsnurkz...

zzzheeheehee. LickLickLickzzz.

ZzzZz

AUGH!

THE ND

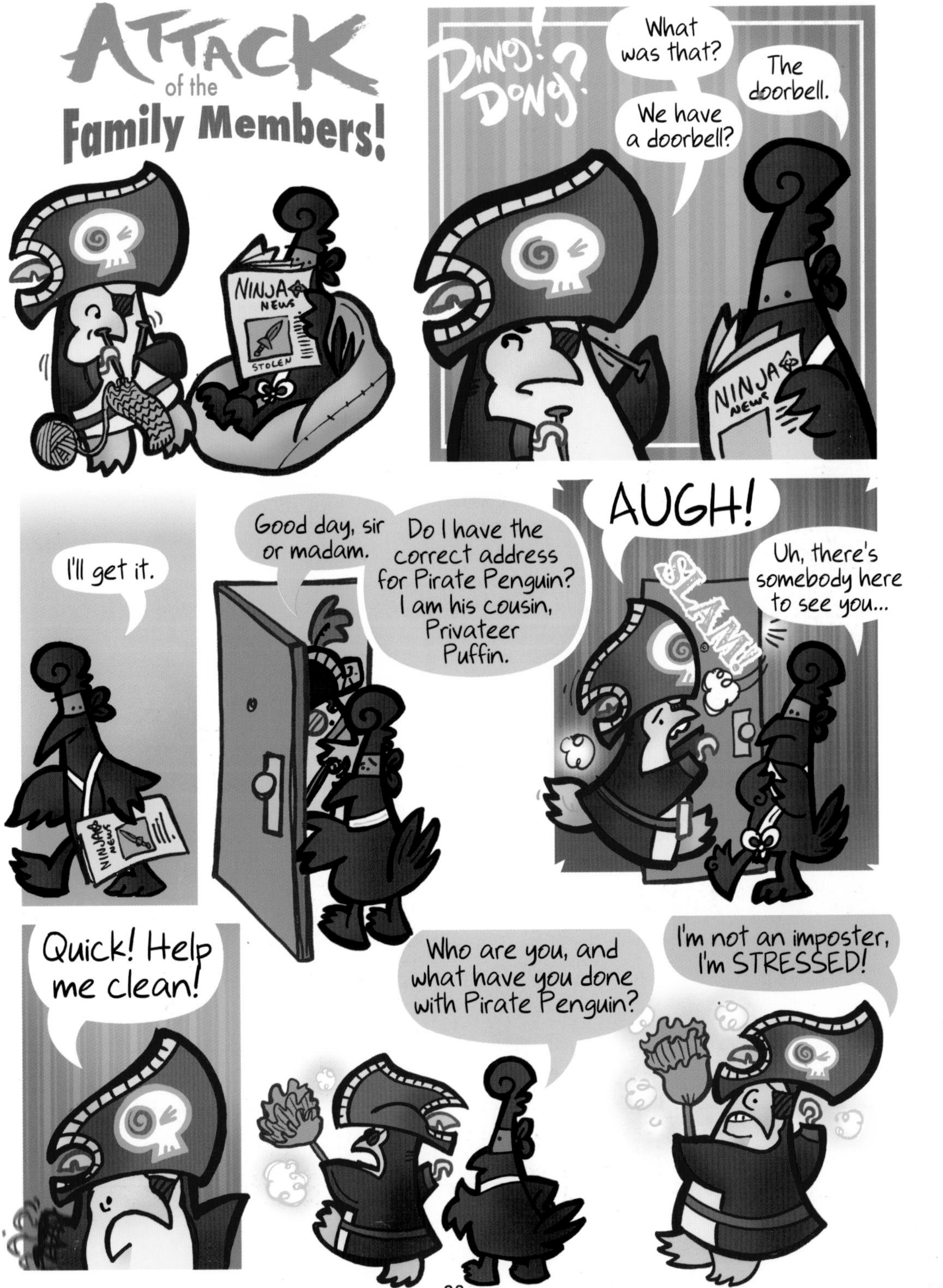
ATTACK of the Family Members!
NINJA NEWS
STOLEN
DING! DONG?
What was that?
The doorbell.
We have a doorbell?
NINJA NEWS
I'll get it.
NINJA NEWS
Good day, sir or madam.
Do I have the correct address for Pirate Penguin? I am his cousin, Privateer Puffin.
AUGH!
SLAM!
Uh, there's somebody here to see you...
Quick! Help me clean!
Who are you, and what have you done with Pirate Penguin?
I'm not an imposter, I'm STRESSED!

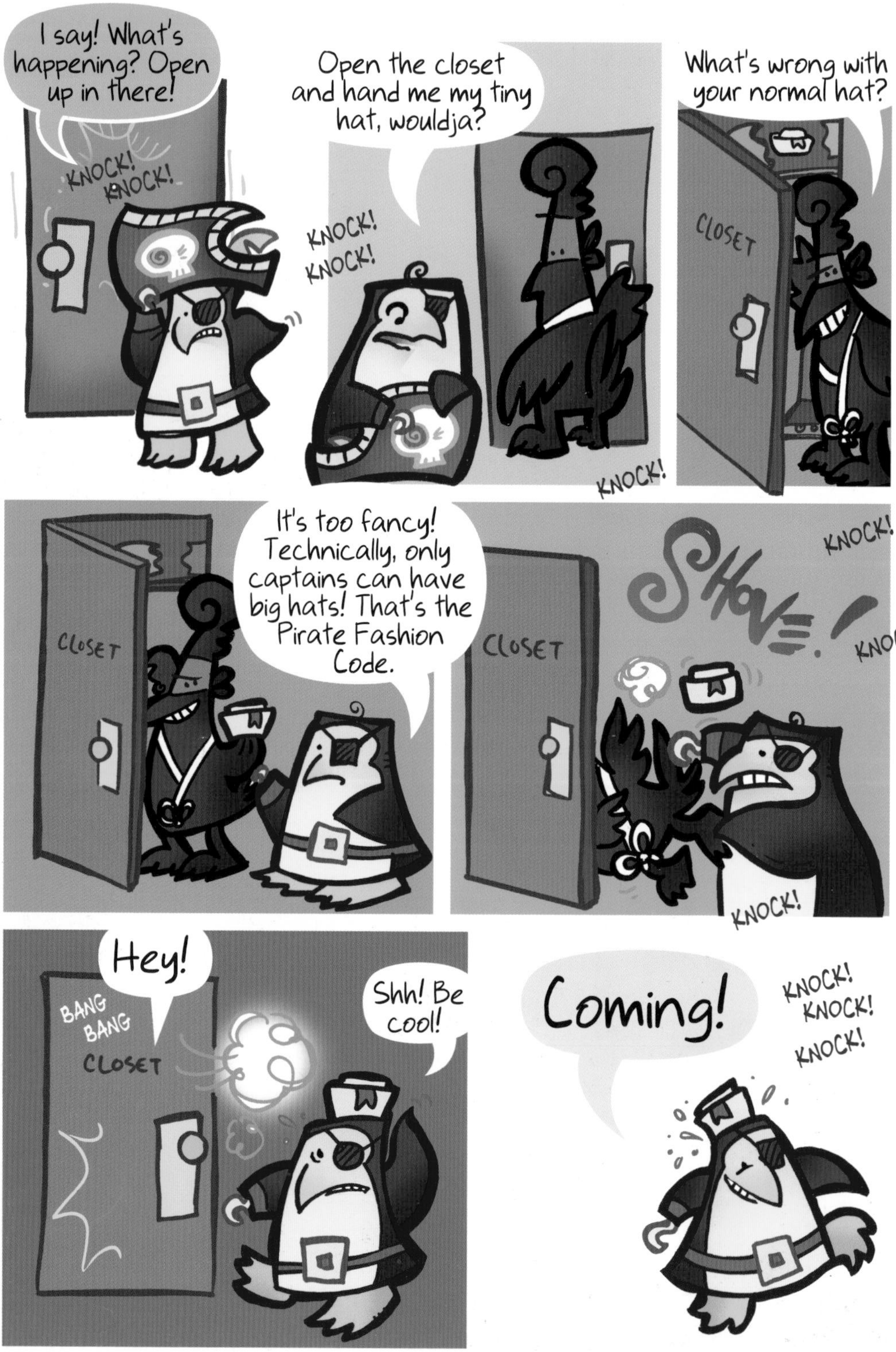
I say! What's happening? Open up in there!
KNOCK! KNOCK!
Open the closet and hand me my tiny hat, wouldja?
KNOCK! KNOCK!
What's wrong with your normal hat?
CLOSET
KNOCK!
CLOSET
It's too fancy! Technically, only captains can have big hats! That's the Pirate Fashion Code.
SHOVE!
KNOCK!
KNOCK!
CLOSET
KNOCK!
Hey!
BANG BANG
CLOSET
Shh! Be cool!
Coming!
KNOCK! KNOCK! KNOCK!

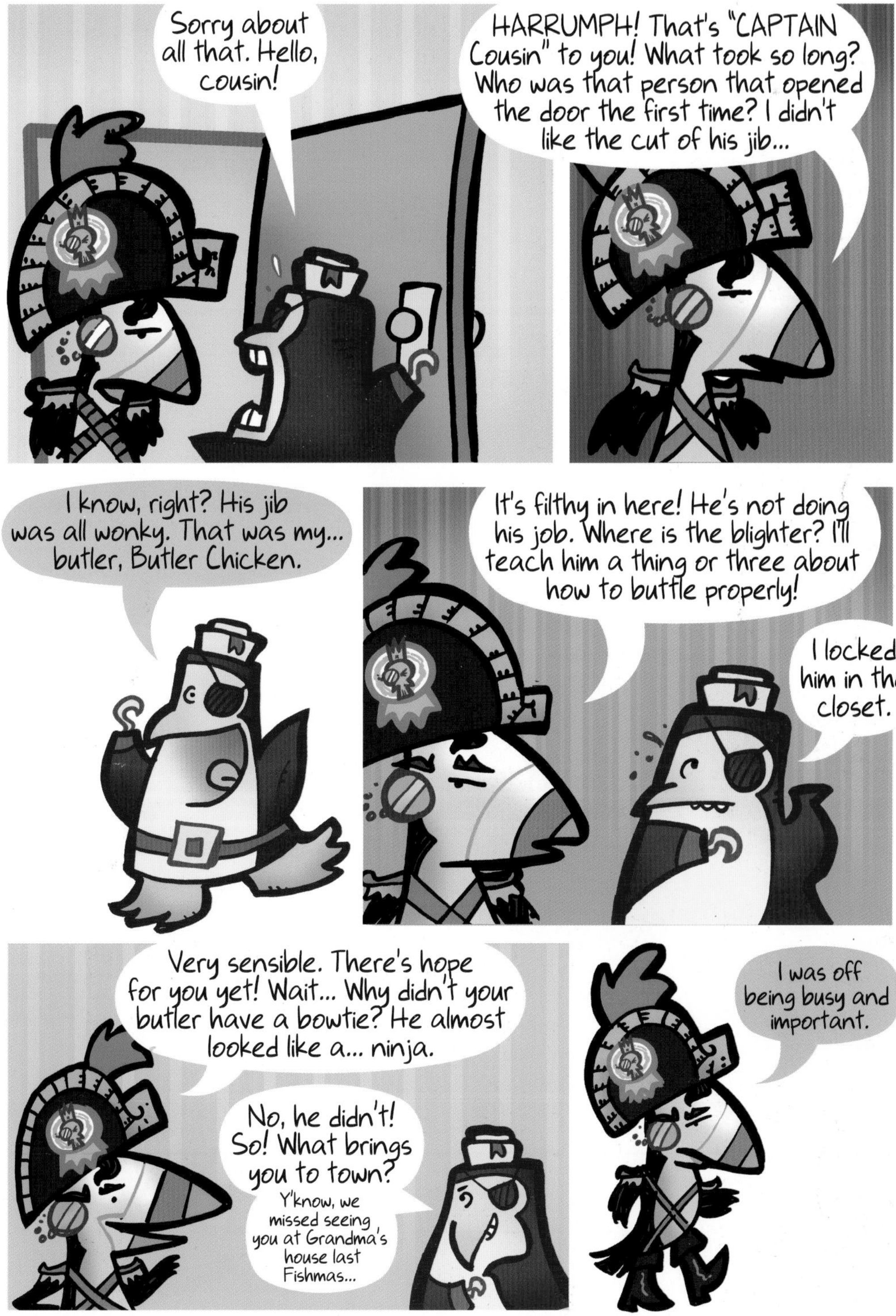
Sorry about all that. Hello, cousin!
HARRUMPH! That's "CAPTAIN Cousin" to you! What took so long? Who was that person that opened the door the first time? I didn't like the cut of his jib...
I know, right? His jib was all wonky. That was my... butler, Butler Chicken.
It's filthy in here! He's not doing his job. Where is the blighter? I'll teach him a thing or three about how to buttle properly!
I locked him in the closet.
Very sensible. There's hope for you yet! Wait... Why didn't your butler have a bowtie? He almost looked like a... ninja.
No, he didn't! So! What brings you to town?
Y'know, we missed seeing you at Grandma's house last Fishmas...
I was off being busy and important.

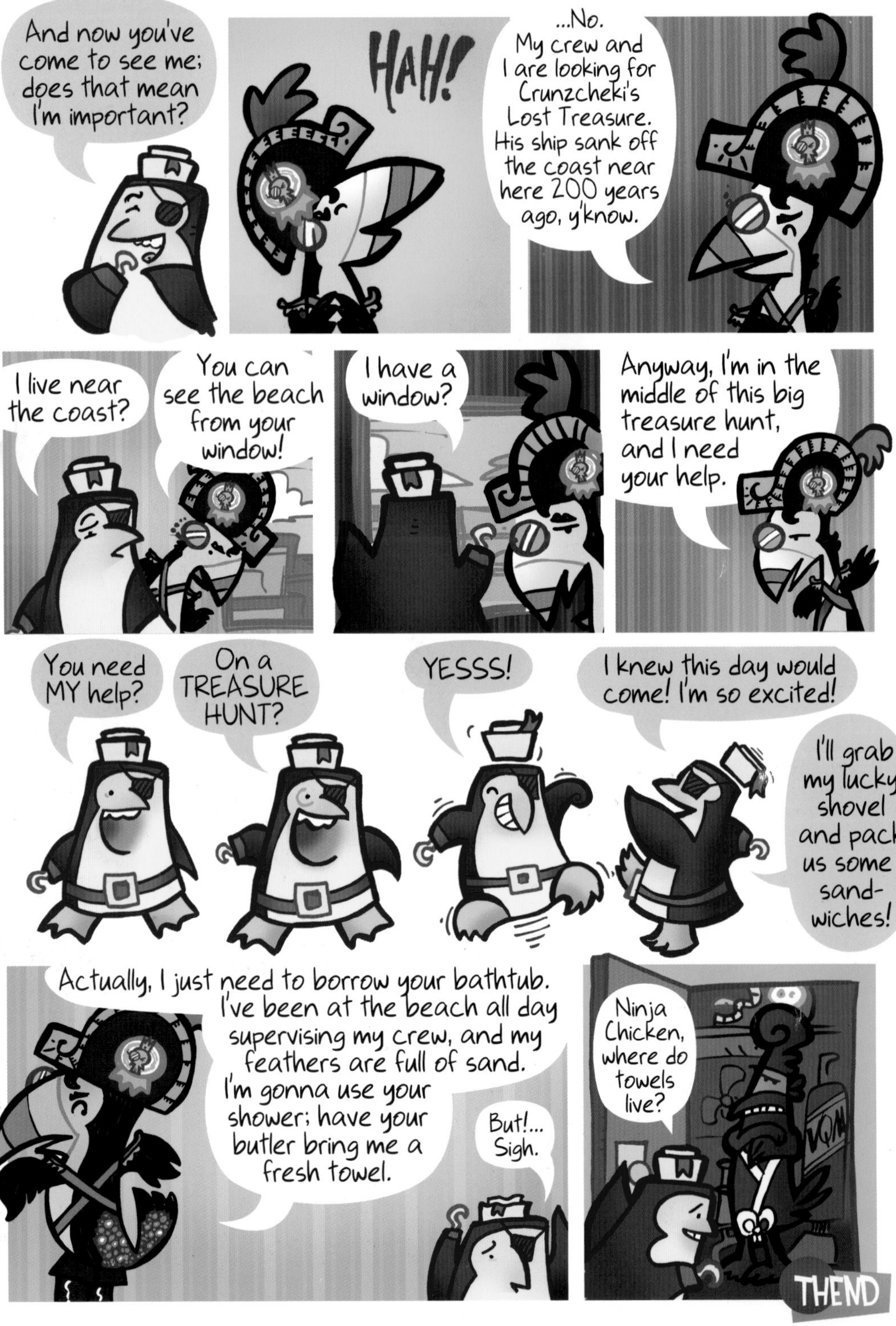

And now you've come to see me; does that mean I'm important?
HAH!
...No. My crew and I are looking for Crunzcheki's Lost Treasure. His ship sank off the coast near here 200 years ago, y'know.
I live near the coast?
You can see the beach from your window!
I have a window?
Anyway, I'm in the middle of this big treasure hunt, and I need your help.
You need MY help?
On a TREASURE HUNT?
YESSS!
I knew this day would come! I'm so excited!
I'll grab my lucky shovel and pack us some sand-wiches!
Actually, I just need to borrow your bathtub. I've been at the beach all day supervising my crew, and my feathers are full of sand. I'm gonna use your shower; have your butler bring me a fresh towel.
But!... Sigh.
Ninja Chicken, where do towels live?
THEND

Everyone's Favorite TV Quiz Show
QUESTIONY TIME!

I'm your host, Quizmaster Quetzel!

As you all know, I am THE MASTER of QUIZZING, and you will OBEY ME!

CLAP CLAP CLAP

MORE CLAPS!

CLAP CLAP CLAP CLAP CLAP CLAP CLAP CLAP CLAP CLAP CLAP CLAP CLAP CLAP CLAP CLAP CLAP CLAP

Let's meet tonight's contestants! I forgot their names...

Hi, I'm Ninja Chicken. Big fan of the show.

Pirate Penguin. Medium-sized fan of the show.

No comment.

What? I don't give out personal information.

Tonight's categories are:

SPACE
(The Final Frontier)

TEXAS

FANCY CHEESES

NO FAIR! Astronaut Armadillo's an expert on all those things, while I don't know anything about anything!

Who? Heh heh.

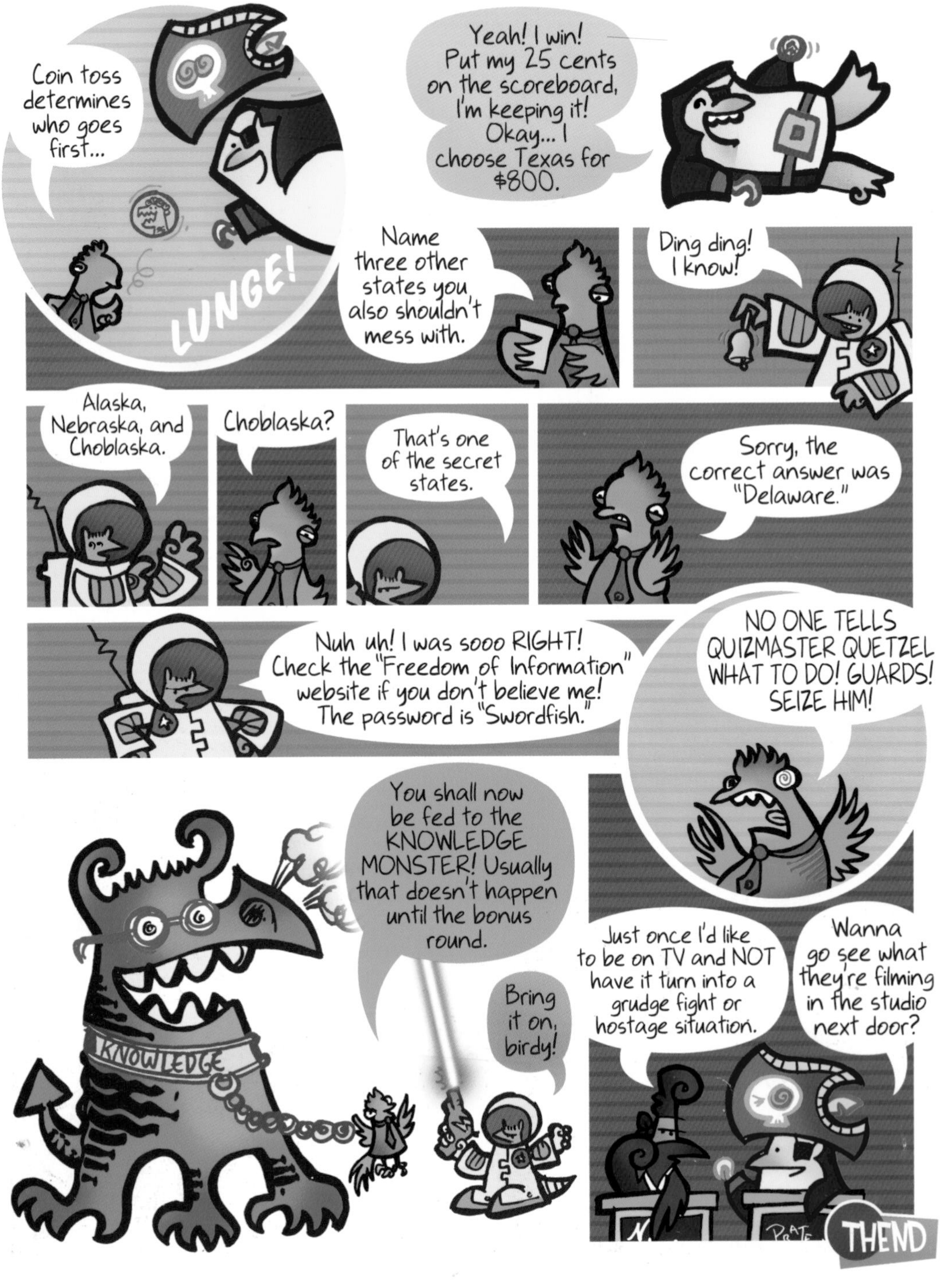

Coin toss determines who goes first...
LUNGE!
Yeah! I win! Put my 25 cents on the scoreboard, I'm keeping it! Okay... I choose Texas for $800.
Name three other states you also shouldn't mess with.
Ding ding! I know!
Alaska, Nebraska, and Choblaska.
Choblaska?
That's one of the secret states.
Sorry, the correct answer was "Delaware."
Nuh uh! I was sooo RIGHT! Check the "Freedom of Information" website if you don't believe me! The password is "Swordfish."
NO ONE TELLS QUIZMASTER QUETZEL WHAT TO DO! GUARDS! SEIZE HIM!
You shall now be fed to the KNOWLEDGE MONSTER! Usually that doesn't happen until the bonus round.
KNOWLEDGE
Bring it on, birdy!
Just once I'd like to be on TV and NOT have it turn into a grudge fight or hostage situation.
Wanna go see what they're filming in the studio next door?
THEND

FISH STORY

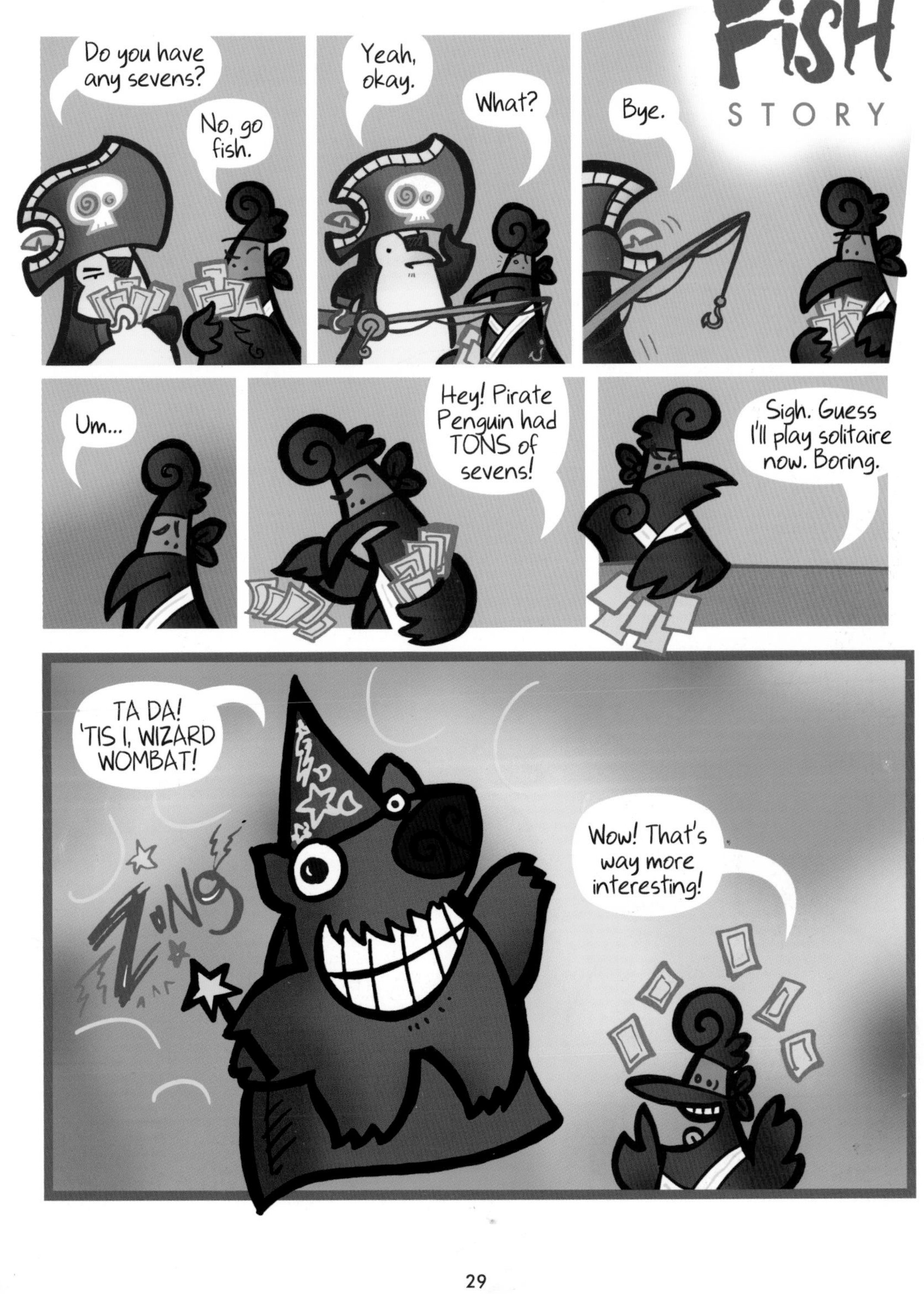

Do you have any sevens?
No, go fish.
Yeah, okay.
What?
Bye.
Um...
Hey! Pirate Penguin had TONS of sevens!
Sigh. Guess I'll play solitaire now. Boring.
TA DA! 'TIS I, WIZARD WOMBAT!
ZING
Wow! That's way more interesting!

O mighty and powerful Wizard Wombat! Are you here to grant my wishes and make all my dreams come true?

Um, SURE! If your dreams involve me drinking all your ginger ale, then TOTALLY!

Psst-- Hey, wanna see a card trick?

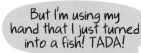

A magic card trick?

It's really more sleight of hand.

But I'm using my hand that I just turned into a fish! TADA!

Hello! I'm Freddie, the Feeble-Excuse Fish!

Wow! That was weirdmazing! So, what's the card trick?

That WAS it!

You didn't even touch the cards...

I bet you weren't expecting THAT!

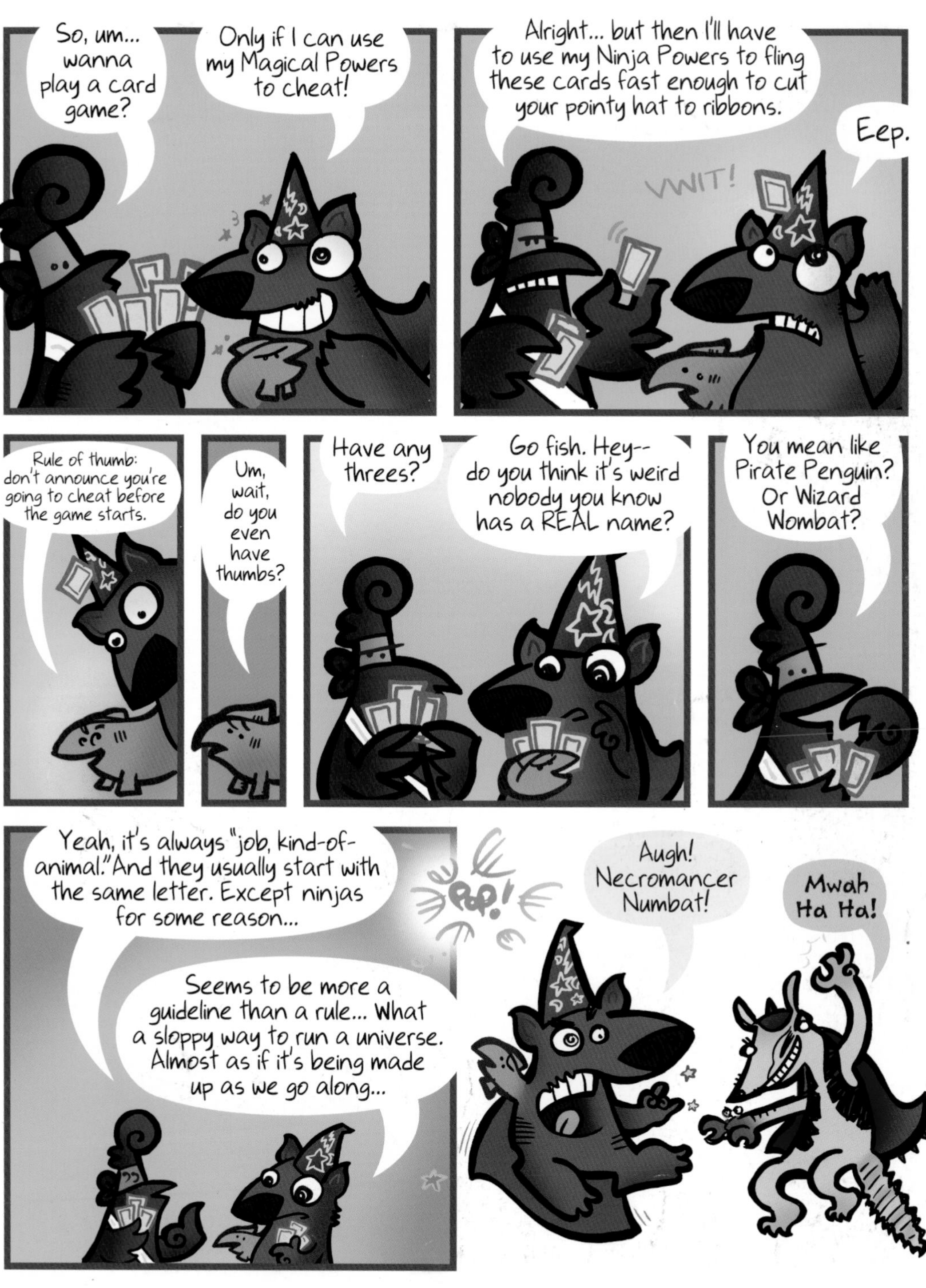

So, um... wanna play a card game?
Only if I can use my Magical Powers to cheat!
Alright... but then I'll have to use my Ninja Powers to fling these cards fast enough to cut your pointy hat to ribbons.
VWIT!
Eep.
Rule of thumb: don't announce you're going to cheat before the game starts.
Um, wait, do you even have thumbs?
Have any threes?
Go fish. Hey-- do you think it's weird nobody you know has a REAL name?
You mean like Pirate Penguin? Or Wizard Wombat?
Yeah, it's always "job, kind-of-animal." And they usually start with the same letter. Except ninjas for some reason...
Seems to be more a guideline than a rule... What a sloppy way to run a universe. Almost as if it's being made up as we go along...
POP!
Augh! Necromancer Numbat!
Mwah Ha Ha!

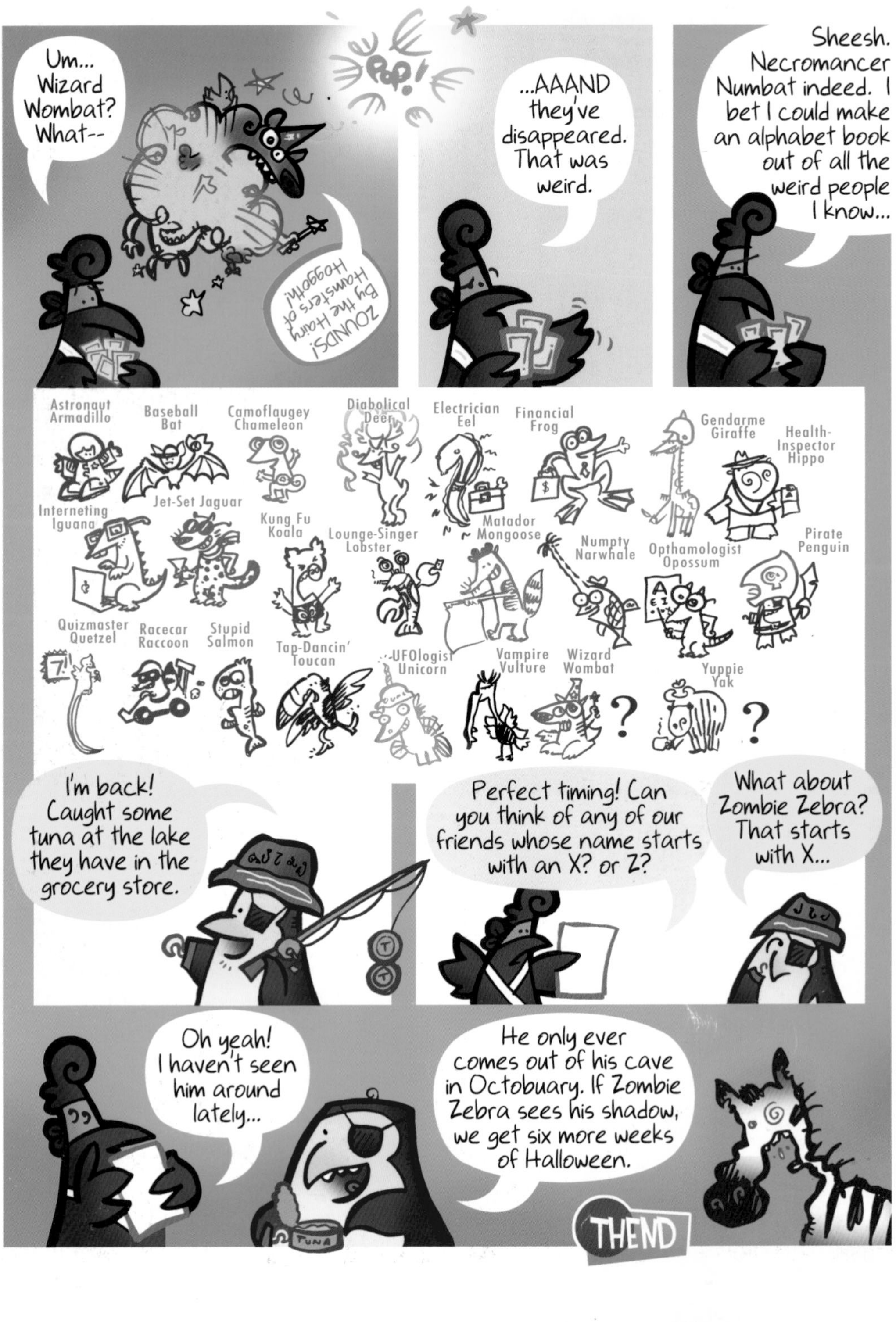
Um... Wizard Wombat? What--
POP!
ZOUNDS! By the Hairy Hamsters of Hoggoth!
...AAAND they've disappeared. That was weird.
Sheesh. Necromancer Numbat indeed. I bet I could make an alphabet book out of all the weird people I know...
Astronaut Armadillo
Baseball Bat
Camoflaugey Chameleon
Diabolical Deer
Electrician Eel
Financial Frog
Gendarme Giraffe
Health-Inspector Hippo
Interneting Iguana
Jet-Set Jaguar
Kung Fu Koala
Lounge-Singer Lobster
Matador Mongoose
Numpty Narwhale
Opthamologist Opossum
Pirate Penguin
Quizmaster Quetzel
Racecar Raccoon
Stupid Salmon
Tap-Dancin' Toucan
UFOlogist Unicorn
Vampire Vulture
Wizard Wombat
?
Yuppie Yak
?
I'm back! Caught some tuna at the lake they have in the grocery store.
Perfect timing! Can you think of any of our friends whose name starts with an X? or Z?
What about Zombie Zebra? That starts with X...
Oh yeah! I haven't seen him around lately...
He only ever comes out of his cave in Octobuary. If Zombie Zebra sees his shadow, we get six more weeks of Halloween.
TUNA
THEND

COSTUME **CONFUSERY** A Pirate **Penguin** vs **Ninja** Chicken

Cartoon Adventure

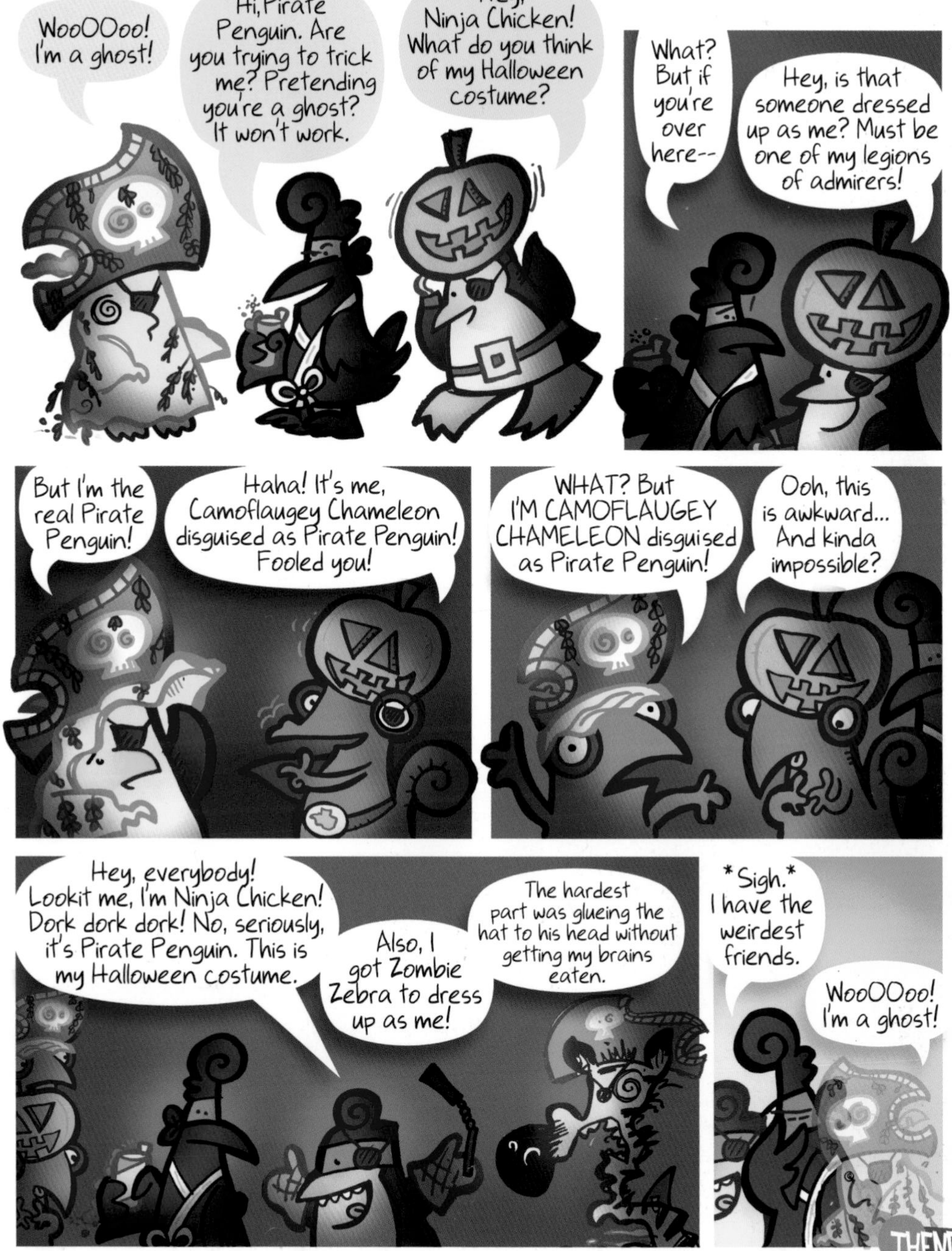
WooOOoo! I'm a ghost!
Hi, Pirate Penguin. Are you trying to trick me? Pretending you're a ghost? It won't work.
Hey, Ninja Chicken! What do you think of my Halloween costume?
What? But if you're over here--
Hey, is that someone dressed up as me? Must be one of my legions of admirers!
But I'm the real Pirate Penguin!
Haha! It's me, Camoflaugey Chameleon disguised as Pirate Penguin! Fooled you!
WHAT? But I'M CAMOFLAUGEY CHAMELEON disguised as Pirate Penguin!
Ooh, this is awkward... And kinda impossible?
Hey, everybody! Lookit me, I'm Ninja Chicken! Dork dork dork! No, seriously, it's Pirate Penguin. This is my Halloween costume.
Also, I got Zombie Zebra to dress up as me!
The hardest part was glueing the hat to his head without getting my brains eaten.
Sigh. I have the weirdest friends.
WooOOoo! I'm a ghost!
THEND

Pirate Penguin vs BABYSITTING

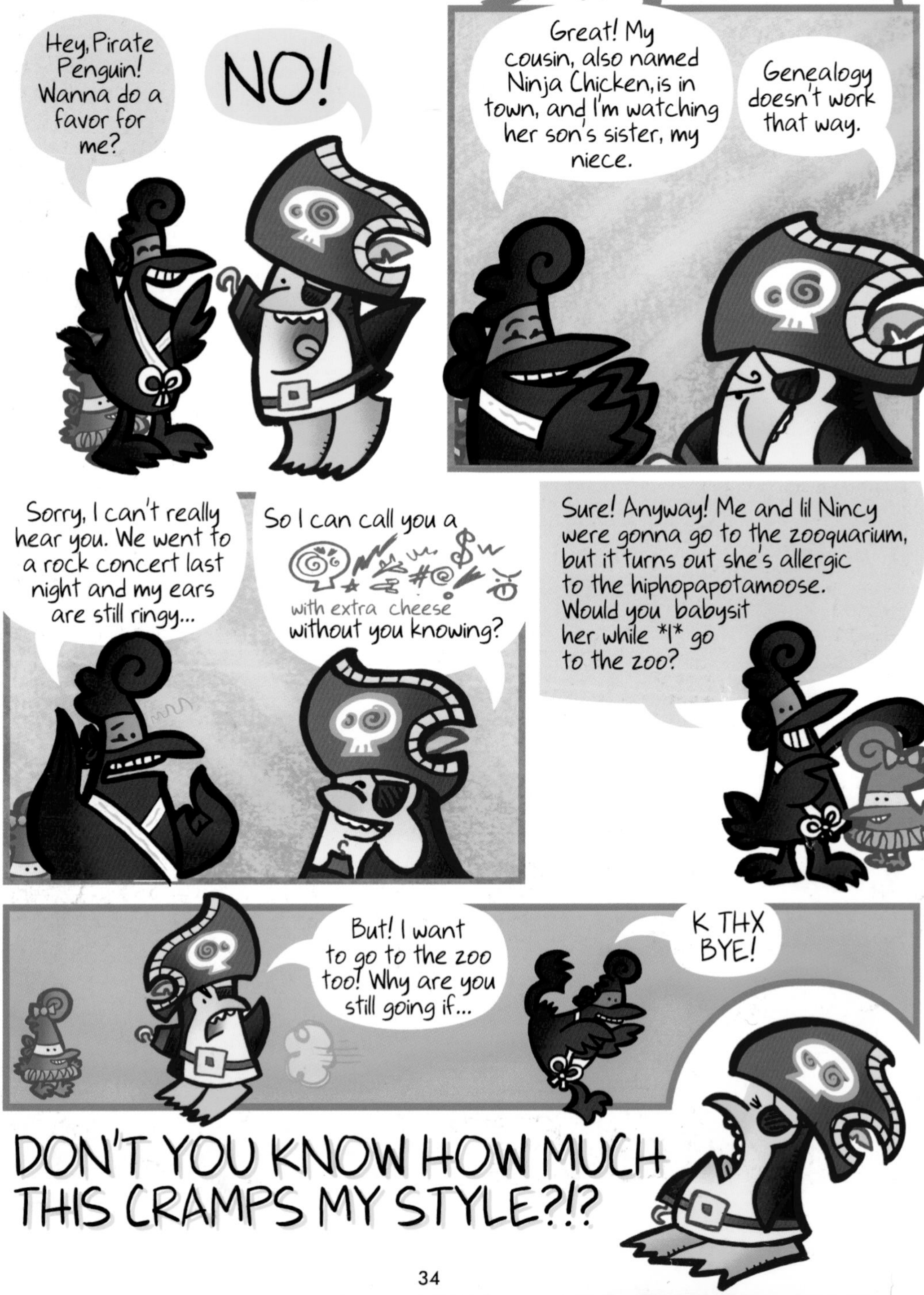

Hey, Pirate Penguin! Wanna do a favor for me?
NO!
Great! My cousin, also named Ninja Chicken, is in town, and I'm watching her son's sister, my niece.
Genealogy doesn't work that way.
Sorry, I can't really hear you. We went to a rock concert last night and my ears are still ringy...
So I can call you a
with extra cheese
without you knowing?
Sure! Anyway! Me and lil Nincy were gonna go to the zooquarium, but it turns out she's allergic to the hiphopapotamoose. Would you babysit her while *I* go to the zoo?
But! I want to go to the zoo too! Why are you still going if...
K THX BYE!
DON'T YOU KNOW HOW MUCH THIS CRAMPS MY STYLE?!?

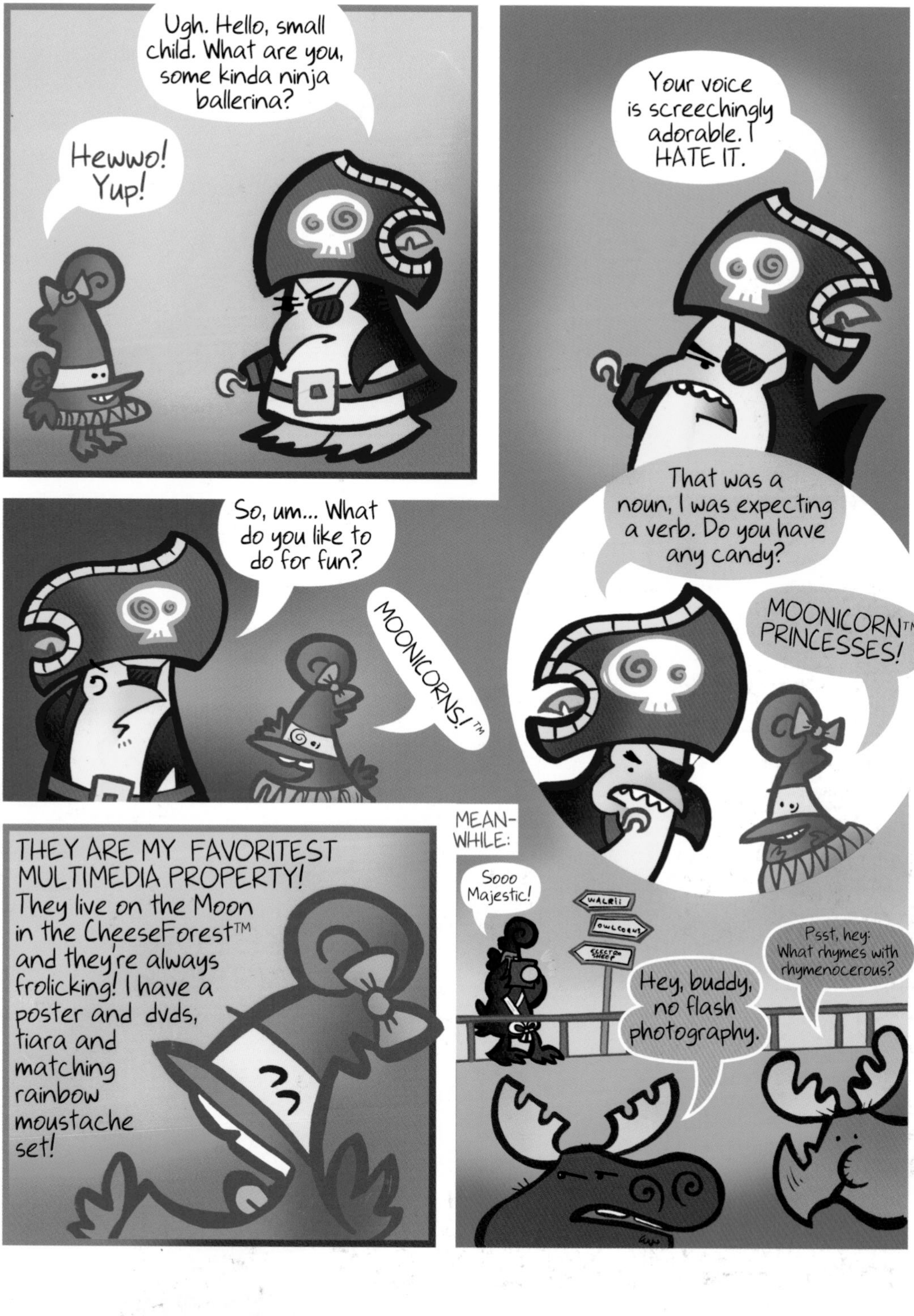
Ugh. Hello, small child. What are you, some kinda ninja ballerina?
Hewwo! Yup!
Your voice is screechingly adorable. I HATE IT.
So, um... What do you like to do for fun?
MOONICORNS!™
That was a noun, I was expecting a verb. Do you have any candy?
MOONICORN™ PRINCESSES!
THEY ARE MY FAVORITEST MULTIMEDIA PROPERTY! They live on the Moon in the CheeseForest™ and they're always frolicking! I have a poster and dvds, tiara and matching rainbow moustache set!
MEAN-WHILE:
Sooo Majestic!
Hey, buddy, no flash photography.
Psst, hey: What rhymes with rhymenocerous?

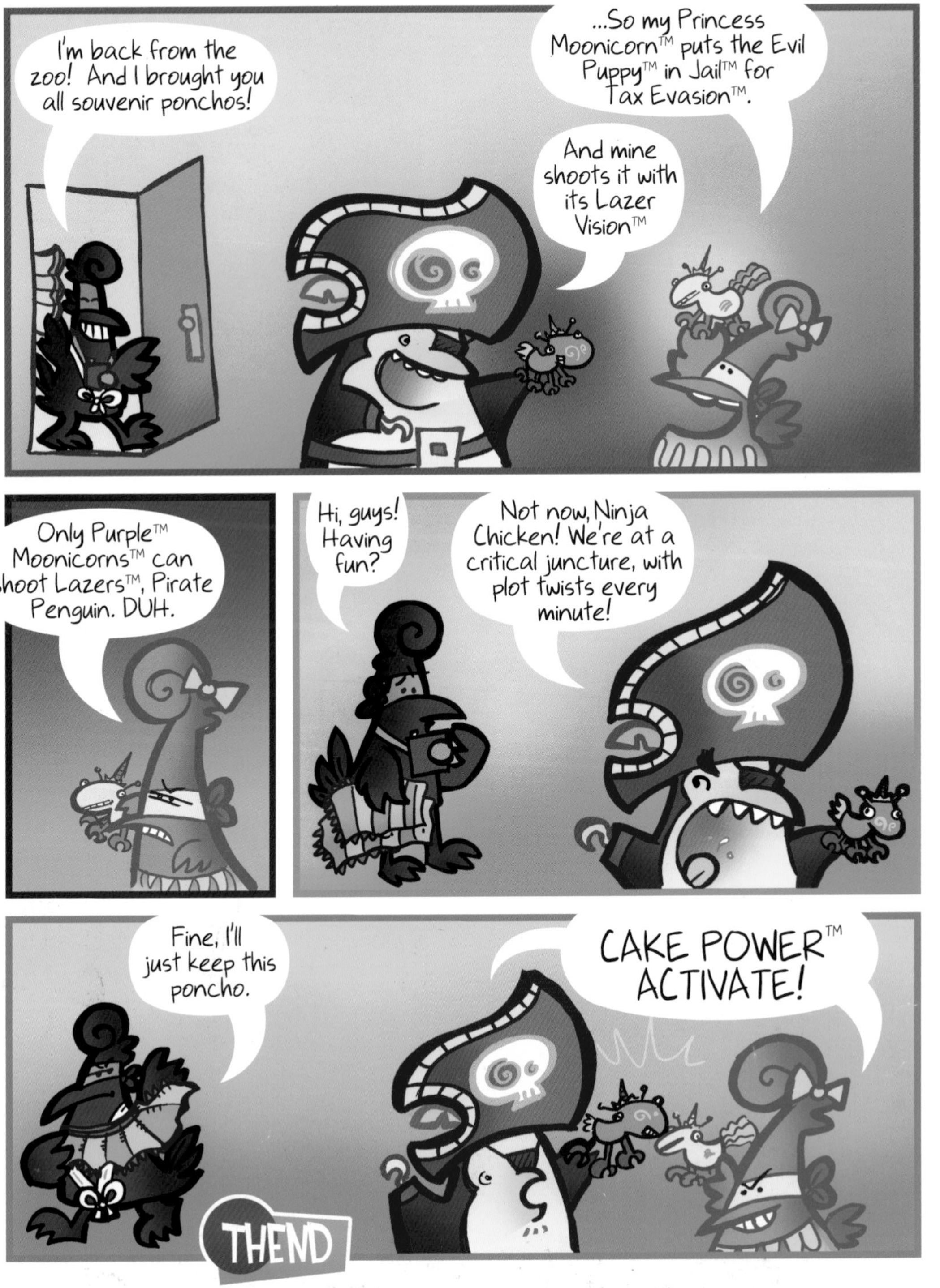
I'm back from the zoo! And I brought you all souvenir ponchos!
...So my Princess Moonicorn™ puts the Evil Puppy™ in Jail™ for Tax Evasion™.
And mine shoots it with its Lazer Vision™
Only Purple™ Moonicorns™ can shoot Lazers™, Pirate Penguin. DUH.
Hi, guys! Having fun?
Not now, Ninja Chicken! We're at a critical juncture, with plot twists every minute!
Fine, I'll just keep this poncho.
CAKE POWER™ ACTIVATE!
THEND

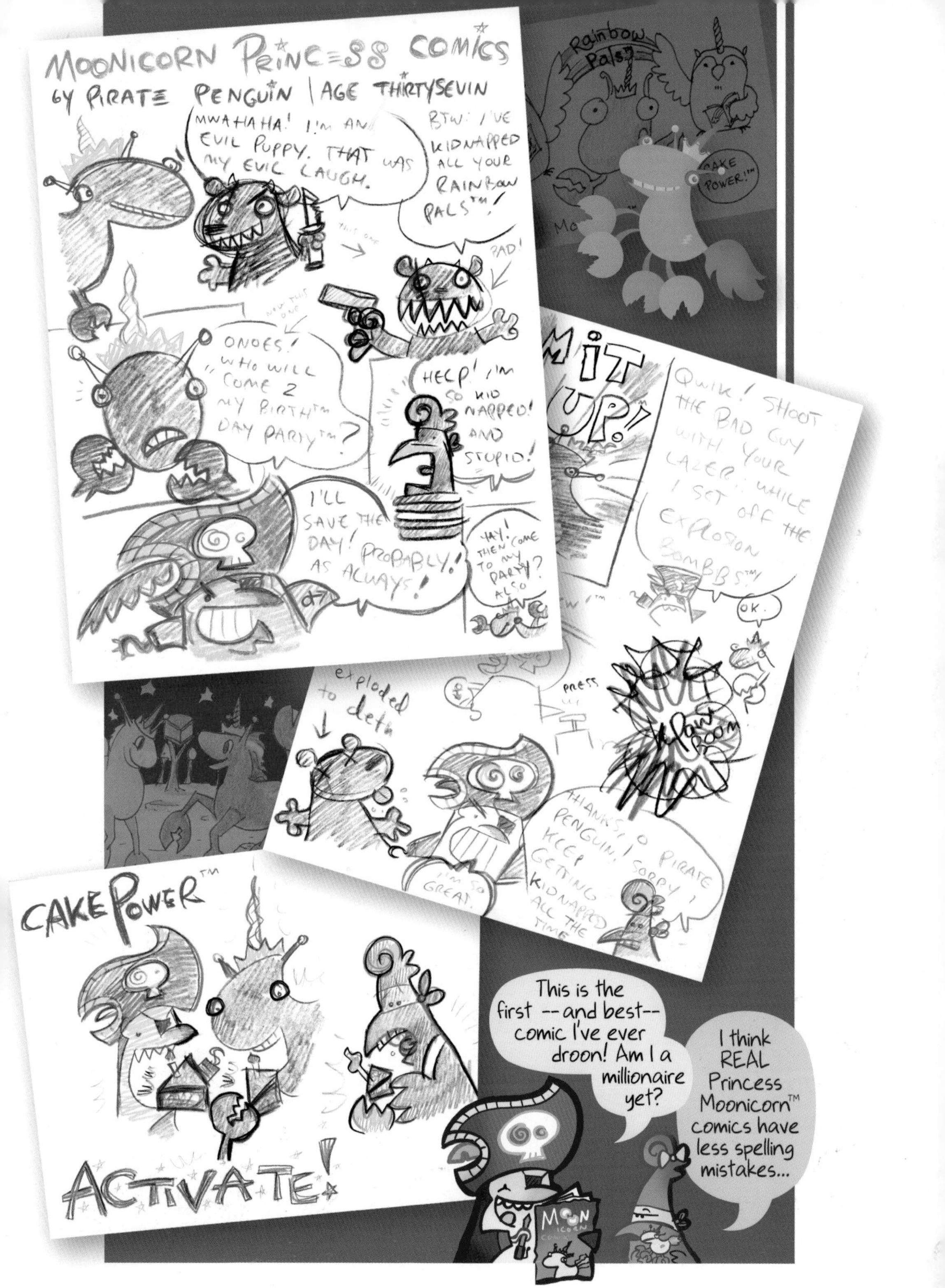

MOONICORN PRINCESS COMICS
by PIRATE PENGUIN | AGE THIRTYSEVIN
MWAHAHA! I'M AN EVIL PUPPY. THAT WAS MY EVIL LAUGH.
BTW: I'VE KIDNAPPED ALL YOUR RAINBOW PALS™!
BAD!
ONOES! WHO WILL COME 2 MY BIRTH™ DAY PARTY™?
HELP! I'M SO KID NAPPED! AND STUPID!
I'LL SAVE THE DAY! PROBABLY! AS ALWAYS!
YAY! THEN COME TO MY PARTY? ALSO
Rainbow Pals™
CAKE POWER!™
IT UP!
QWIK! SHOOT THE BAD GUY WITH YOUR LAZER! WHILE I SET OFF THE EXPLOSION BOMBBS™
OK.
exploded to deth
PRESS
KaPow BOOM
THANKS, O PIRATE PENGUIN! SORRY I KEEP GETTING KIDNAPPED ALL THE TIME
I'M SO GREAT.
CAKE POWER™
ACTIVATE!
This is the first --and best-- comic I've ever droon! Am I a millionaire yet?
I think REAL Princess Moonicorn™ comics have less spelling mistakes...

Pirate Penguin vs infomercials

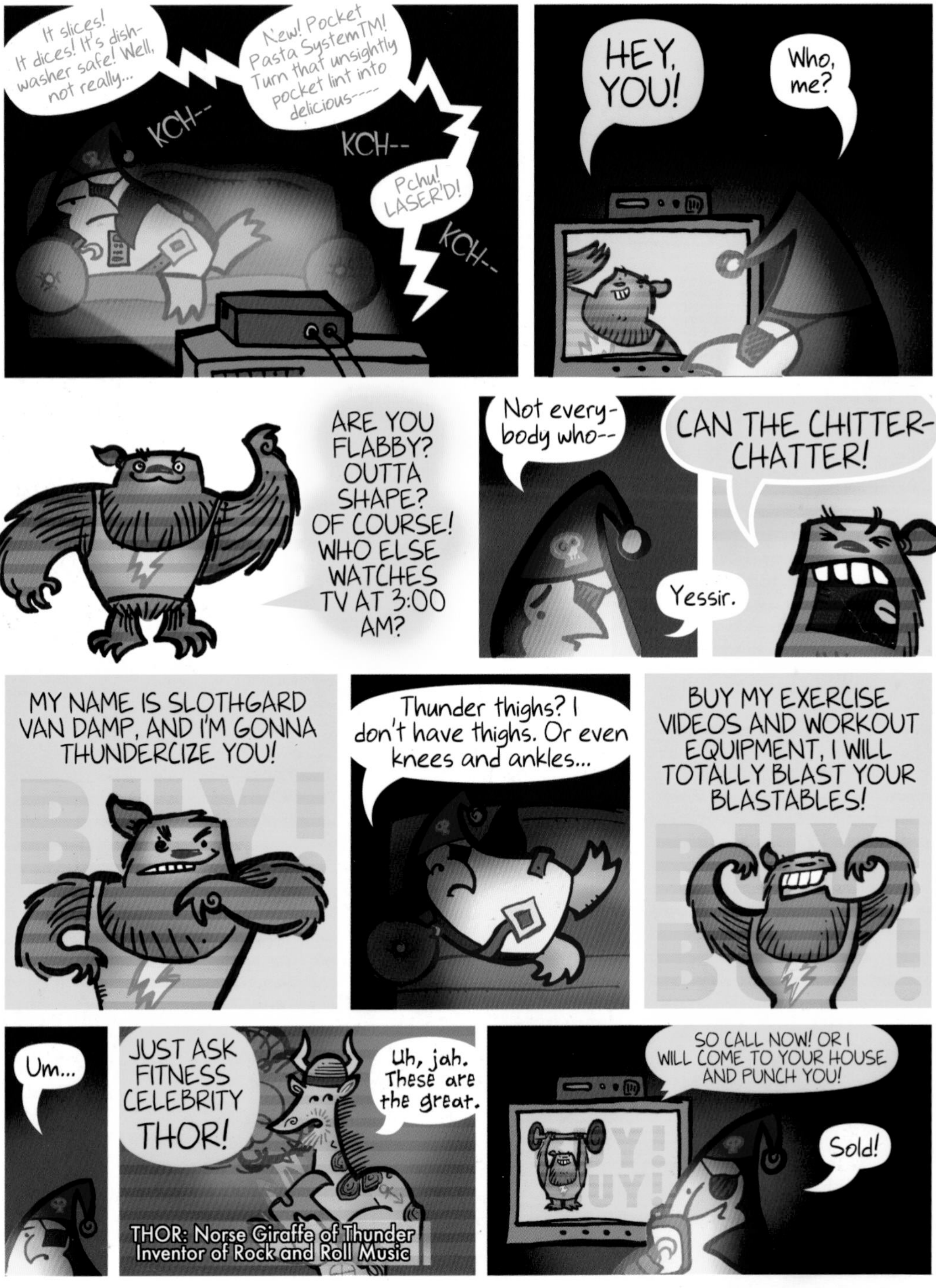
It slices! It dices! It's dish-washer safe! Well, not really...
New! Pocket Pasta SystemTM! Turn that unsightly pocket lint into delicious----
KCH--
KCH--
Pchu! LASER'D!
KCH--
HEY, YOU!
Who, me?
ARE YOU FLABBY? OUTTA SHAPE? OF COURSE! WHO ELSE WATCHES TV AT 3:00 AM?
Not every-body who--
CAN THE CHITTER-CHATTER!
Yessir.
MY NAME IS SLOTHGARD VAN DAMP, AND I'M GONNA THUNDERCIZE YOU!
BUY!
Thunder thighs? I don't have thighs. Or even knees and ankles...
BUY MY EXERCISE VIDEOS AND WORKOUT EQUIPMENT, I WILL TOTALLY BLAST YOUR BLASTABLES!
BUY! BUY!
Um...
JUST ASK FITNESS CELEBRITY THOR!
Uh, jah. These are the great.
THOR: Norse Giraffe of Thunder
Inventor of Rock and Roll Music
SO CALL NOW! OR I WILL COME TO YOUR HOUSE AND PUNCH YOU!
Sold!

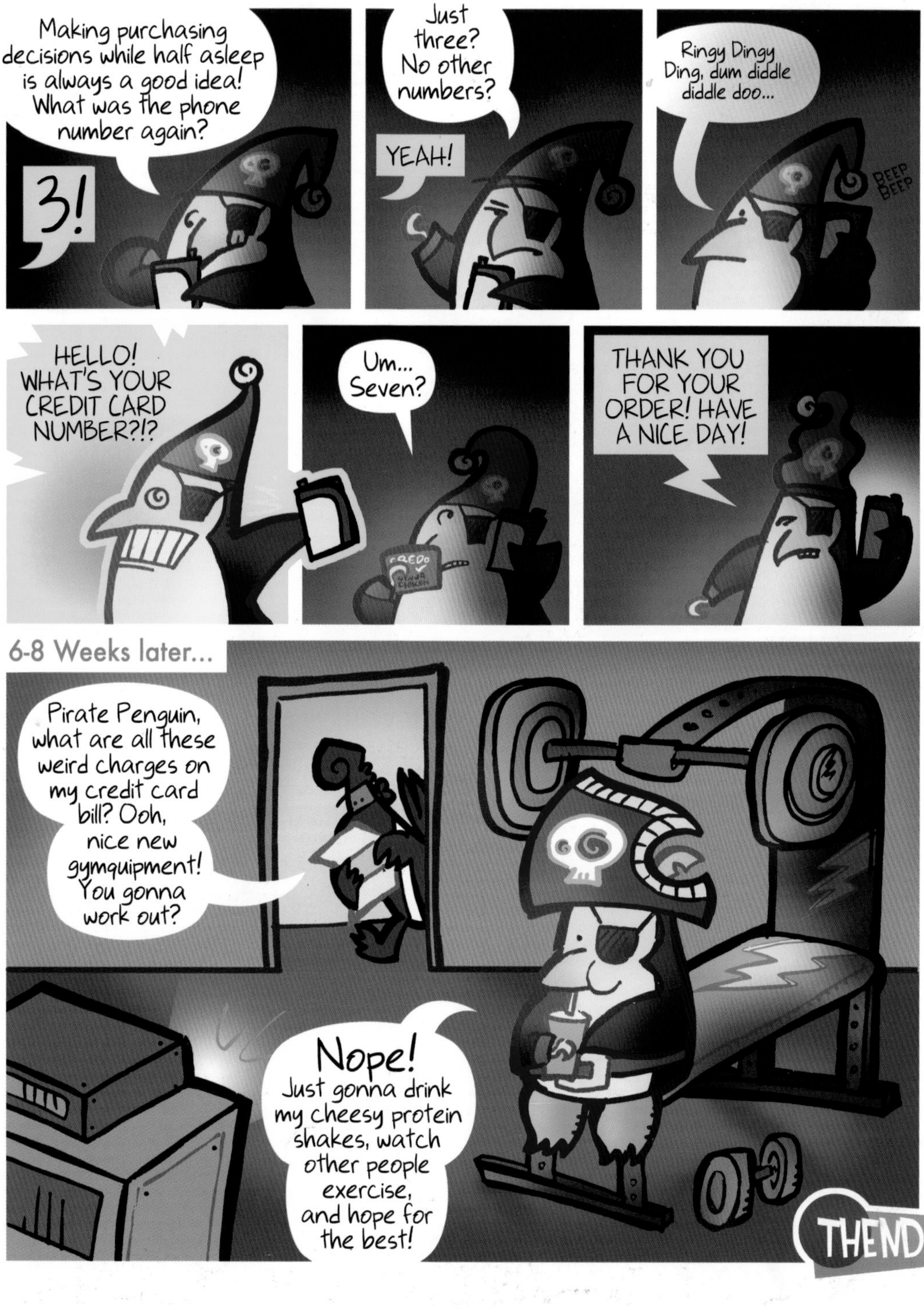
Making purchasing decisions while half asleep is always a good idea! What was the phone number again?
3!
Just three? No other numbers?
YEAH!
Ringy Dingy Ding, dum diddle diddle doo...
BEEP BEEP
HELLO! WHAT'S YOUR CREDIT CARD NUMBER?!?
Um... Seven?
THANK YOU FOR YOUR ORDER! HAVE A NICE DAY!
6-8 Weeks later...
Pirate Penguin, what are all these weird charges on my credit card bill? Ooh, nice new gymquipment! You gonna work out?
Nope! Just gonna drink my cheesy protein shakes, watch other people exercise, and hope for the best!
THEND

Pirate Penguin vs Ninja Chicken in: PEW PEW! PEW PEW PEW PEW! Pew!

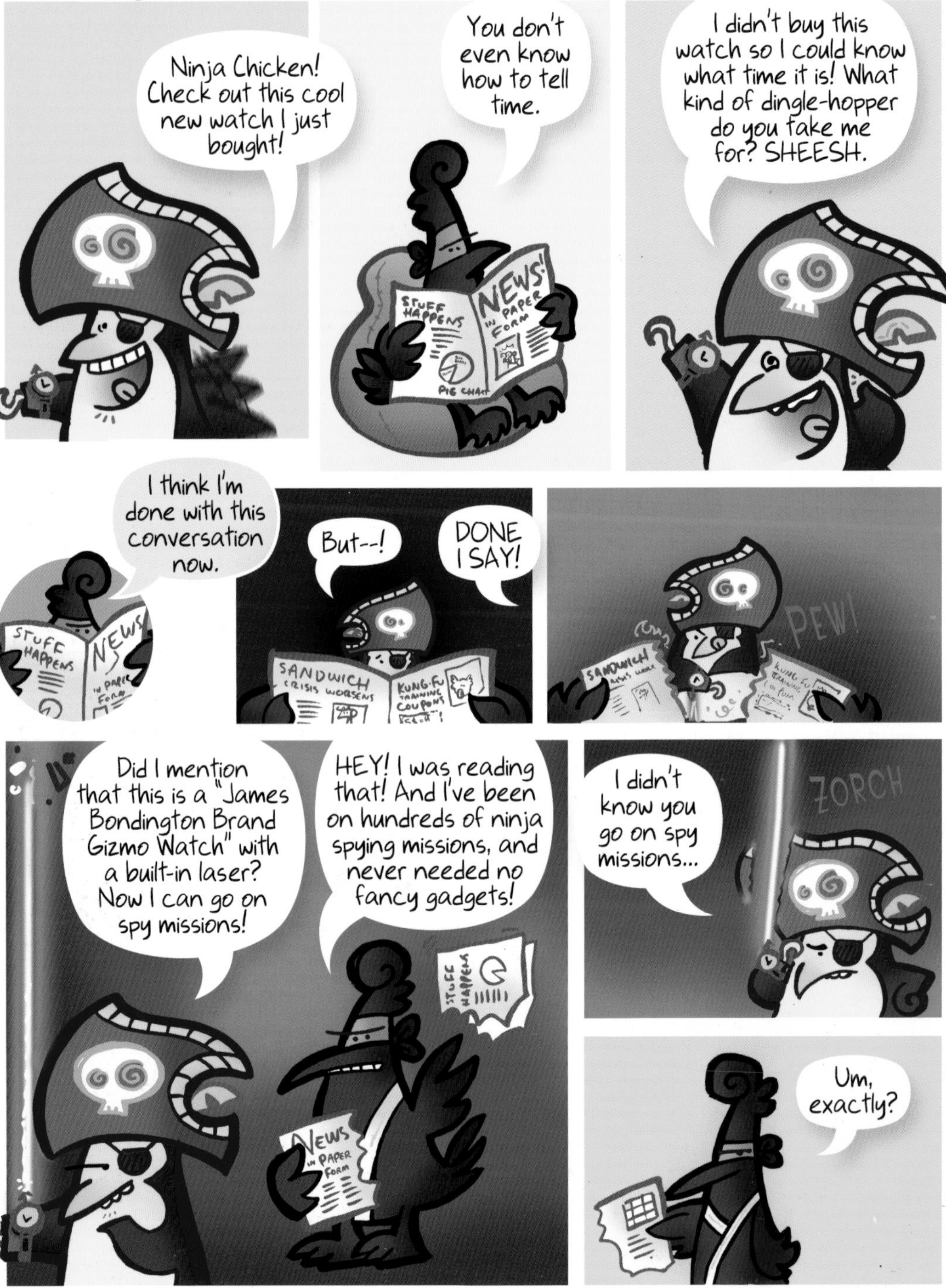
Ninja Chicken! Check out this cool new watch I just bought!
You don't even know how to tell time.
STUFF HAPPENS
NEWS! IN PAPER FORM
PIE CHART
I didn't buy this watch so I could know what time it is! What kind of dingle-hopper do you take me for? SHEESH.
I think I'm done with this conversation now.
STUFF HAPPENS
NEWS IN PAPER FORM
But--!
DONE I SAY!
SANDWICH CRISIS WORSENS
KUNG-FU TRAINING COUPONS
PEW!
Did I mention that this is a "James Bondington Brand Gizmo Watch" with a built-in laser? Now I can go on spy missions!
HEY! I was reading that! And I've been on hundreds of ninja spying missions, and never needed no fancy gadgets!
STUFF HAPPENS
NEWS IN PAPER FORM
I didn't know you go on spy missions...
ZORCH
Um, exactly?

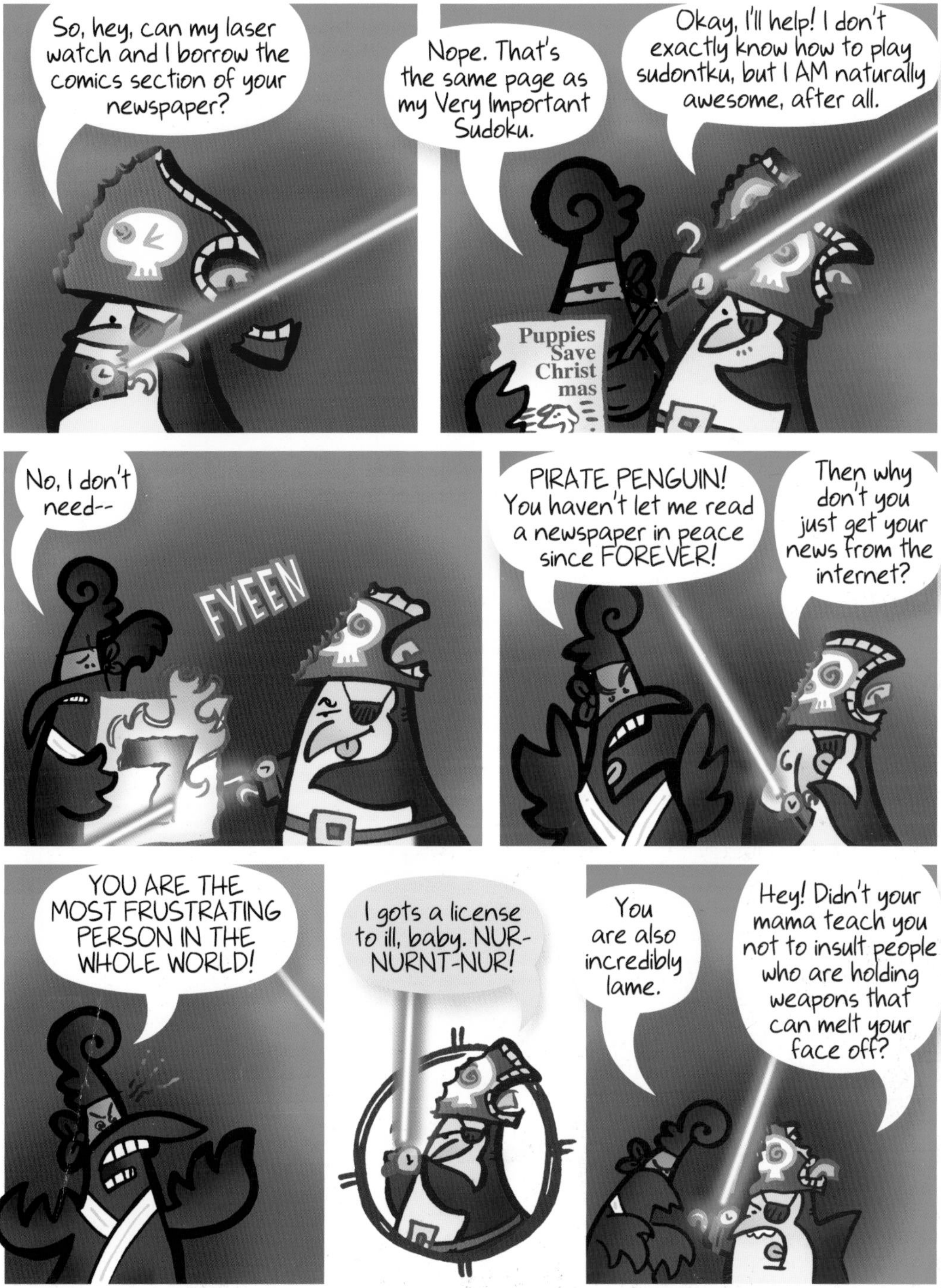
So, hey, can my laser watch and I borrow the comics section of your newspaper?
Nope. That's the same page as my Very Important Sudoku.
Okay, I'll help! I don't exactly know how to play sudontku, but I AM naturally awesome, after all.
Puppies Save Christ mas
No, I don't need--
FYEEN
PIRATE PENGUIN! You haven't let me read a newspaper in peace since FOREVER!
Then why don't you just get your news from the internet?
YOU ARE THE MOST FRUSTRATING PERSON IN THE WHOLE WORLD!
I gots a license to ill, baby. NUR-NURNT-NUR!
You are also incredibly lame.
Hey! Didn't your mama teach you not to insult people who are holding weapons that can melt your face off?

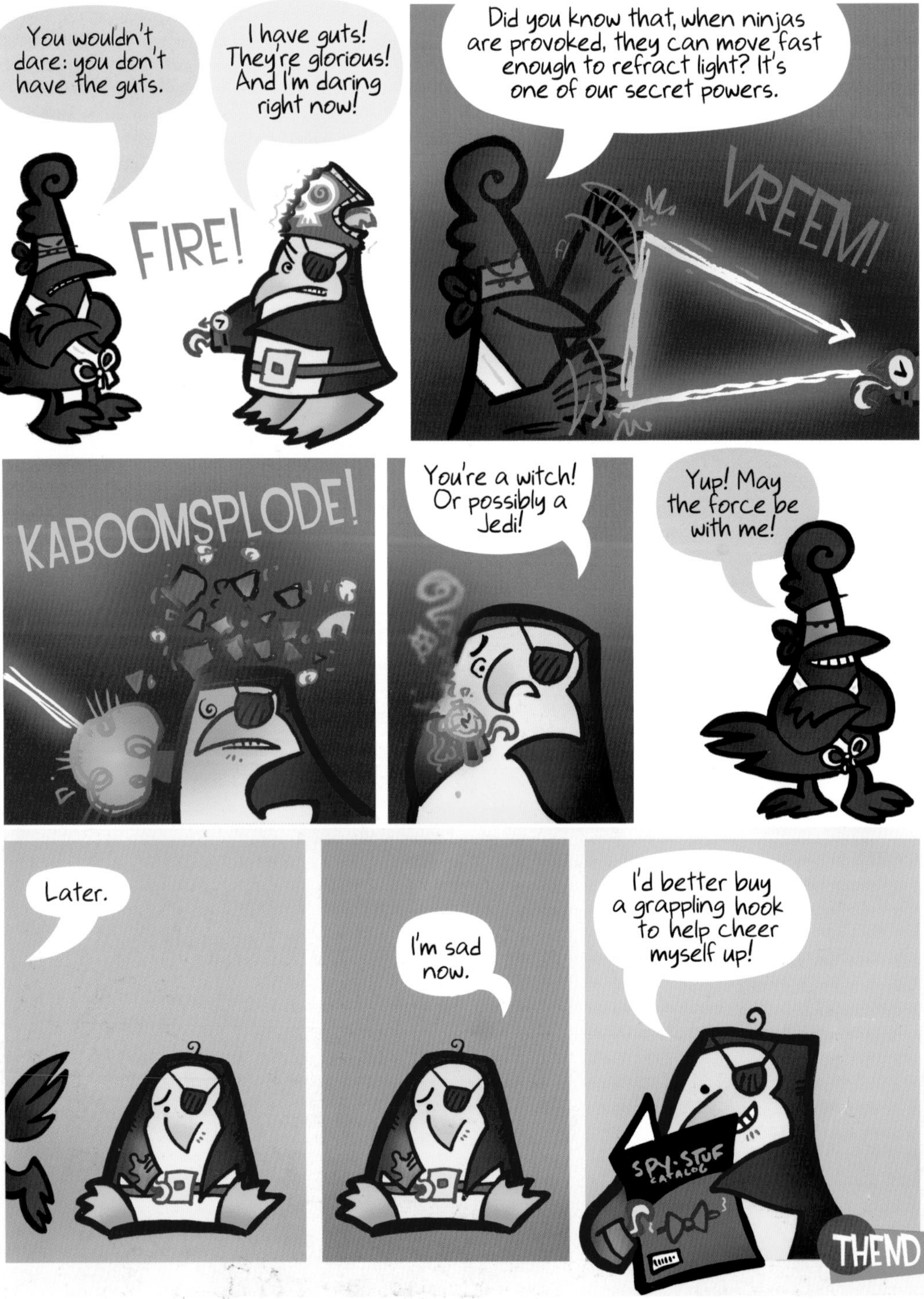
You wouldn't dare: you don't have the guts.
FIRE!
I have guts! They're glorious! And I'm daring right now!
Did you know that, when ninjas are provoked, they can move fast enough to refract light? It's one of our secret powers.
VREEM!
KABOOMSPLODE!
You're a witch! Or possibly a Jedi!
Yup! May the force be with me!
Later.
I'm sad now.
I'd better buy a grappling hook to help cheer myself up!
SPY-STUF CATALOG
THEND

AntiBacterial Refreshment

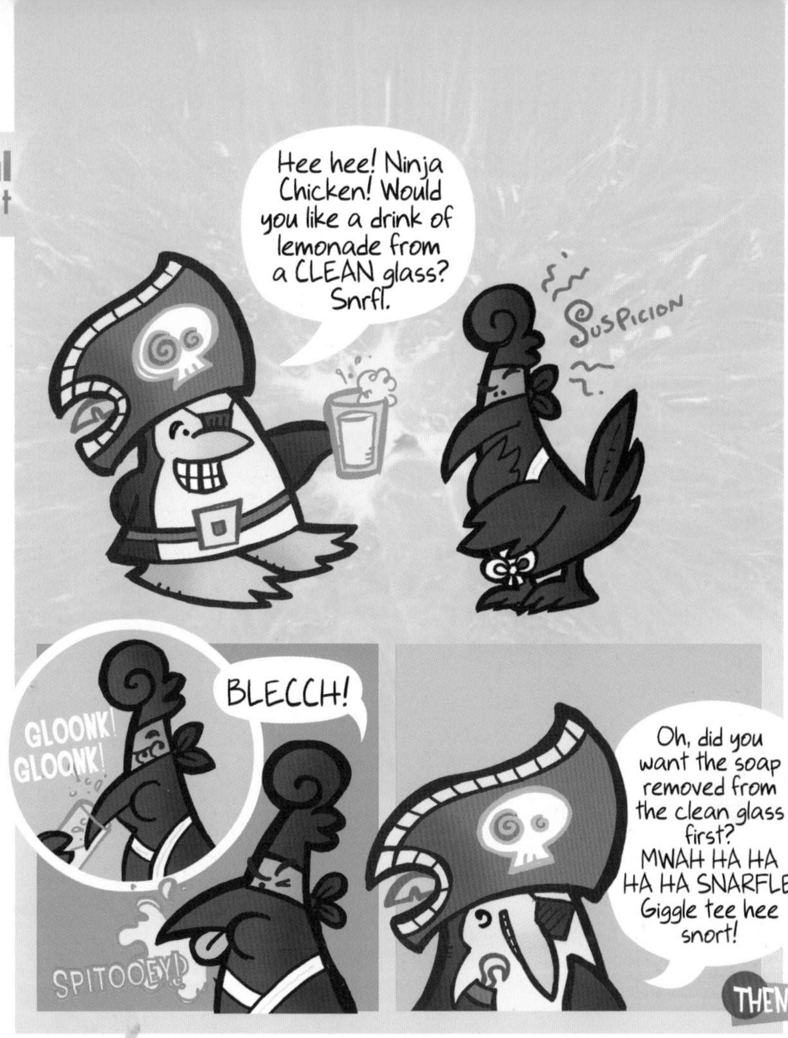
Hee hee! Ninja Chicken! Would you like a drink of lemonade from a CLEAN glass? Snrfl.
SUSPICION
GLOONK! GLOONK!
BLECCH!
SPITOOEY!
Oh, did you want the soap removed from the clean glass first? MWAH HA HA HA HA SNARFLE Giggle tee hee snort!
THEND

Unrelated Comics:

I May Not Know Art, But I Know What I Hate

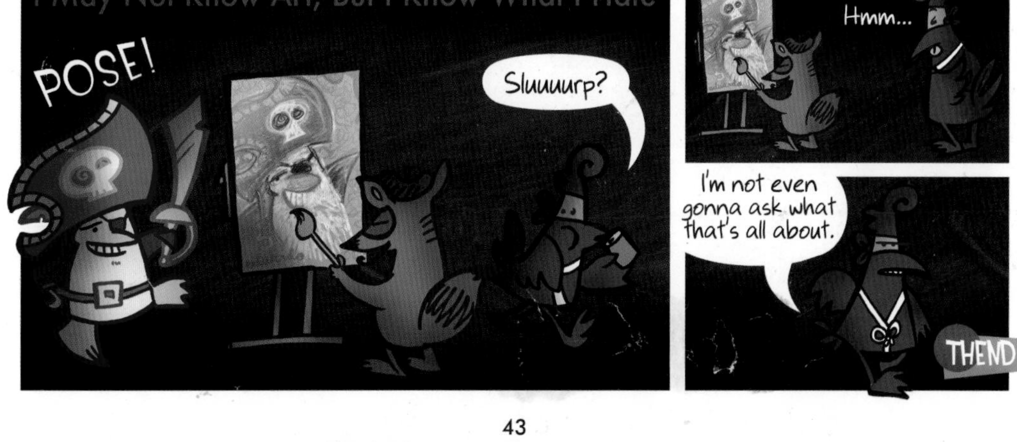
POSE!
Sluuuurp?
Hmm...
I'm not even gonna ask what that's all about.
THEND

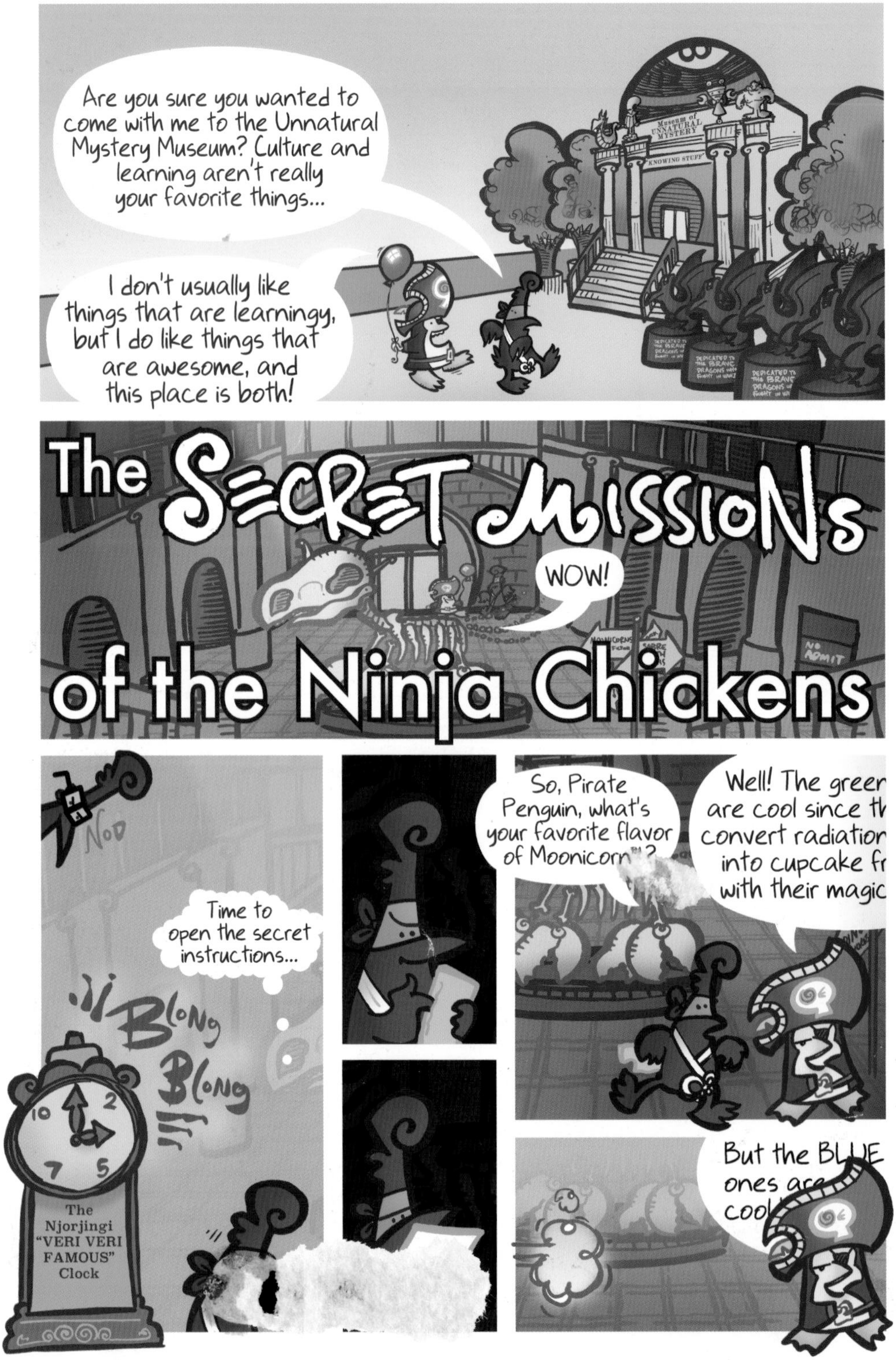
Are you sure you wanted to come with me to the Unnatural Mystery Museum? Culture and learning aren't really your favorite things...
Museum of UNNATURAL MYSTERY
KNOWING STUFF
I don't usually like things that are learningy, but I do like things that are awesome, and this place is both!
The SECRET MISSIONS of the Ninja Chickens
WOW!
NO ADMIT
NOD
Time to open the secret instructions...
BLONG
BLONG
The Njorjingi "VERI VERI FAMOUS" Clock
So, Pirate Penguin, what's your favorite flavor of Moonicorn
Well! The greer are cool since th convert radiatior into cupcake fr with their magic
But the BLUE ones are cool

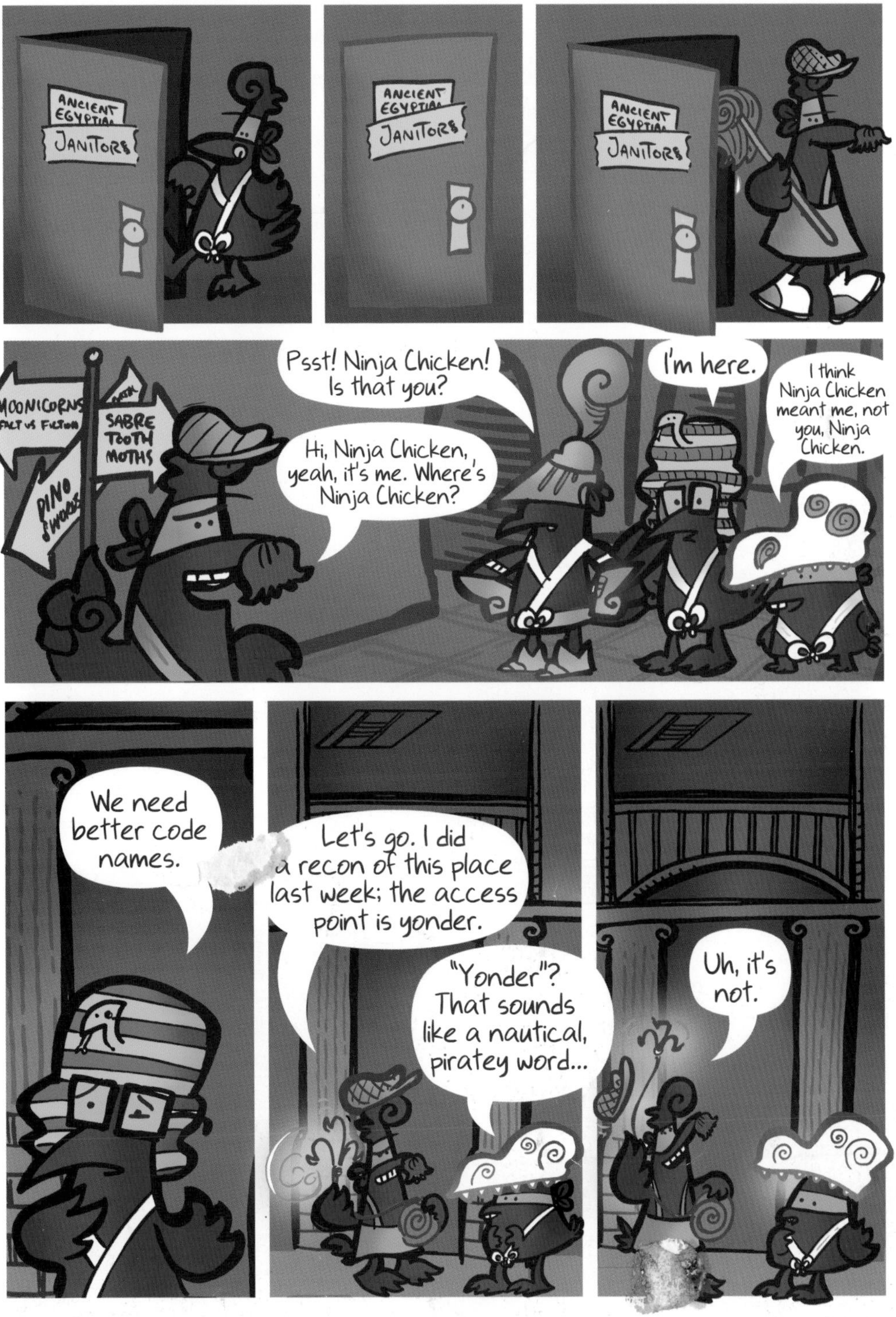
ANCIENT EGYPTIAN
JANITORS
ANCIENT EGYPTIAN
JANITORS
ANCIENT EGYPTIAN
JANITORS
MOONICORNS FACT vs FICTION
SABRE TOOTH MOTHS
DINO
Psst! Ninja Chicken! Is that you?
Hi, Ninja Chicken, yeah, it's me. Where's Ninja Chicken?
I'm here.
I think Ninja Chicken meant me, not you, Ninja Chicken.
We need better code names.
Let's go. I did a recon of this place last week; the access point is yonder.
"Yonder"? That sounds like a nautical, piratey word...
Uh, it's not.

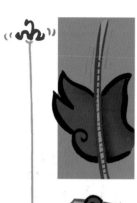

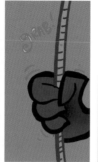

What are we gonna do about the security cameras?

True ninjas don't show up on film.

I didn't know that!

Why do you think we wear these stealth pajamas?

Fashion?

That too.

I'll just do a check for invisible lasers...

Right. Get ready.

CRACK

SECRET EXHIBITS

STAFF ONLY

SECRET EXHIBITS

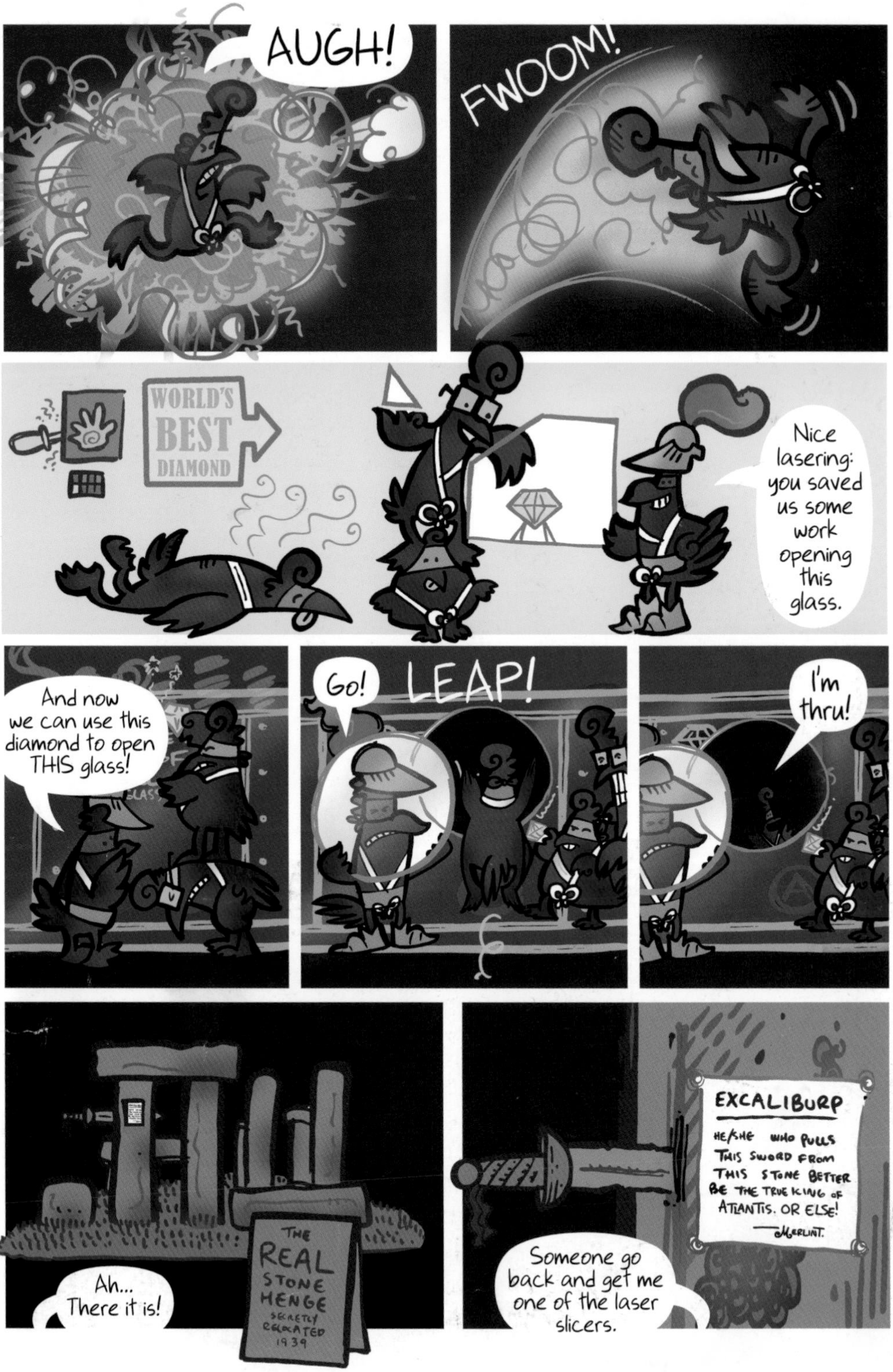
AUGH!
FWOOM!
WORLD'S BEST DIAMOND
Nice lasering: you saved us some work opening this glass.
And now we can use this diamond to open THIS glass!
Go!
LEAP!
I'm thru!
Ah... There it is!
THE REAL STONE HENGE SECRETLY RELOCATED 1939
EXCALIBURP
HE/SHE WHO PULLS THIS SWORD FROM THIS STONE BETTER BE THE TRUE KING OF ATLANTIS. OR ELSE!
—MERLINT.
Someone go back and get me one of the laser slicers.

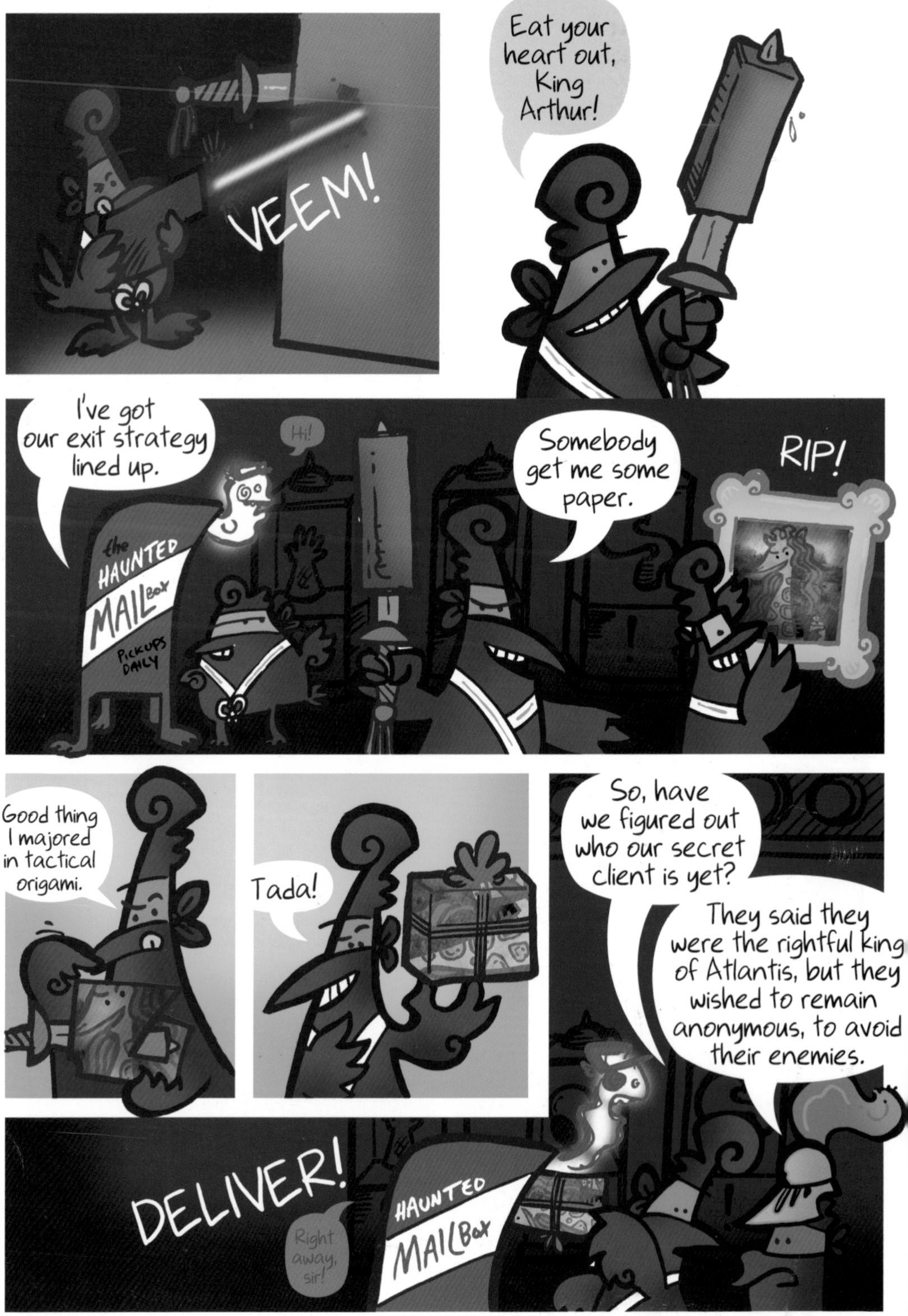
VEEM!
Eat your heart out, King Arthur!
I've got our exit strategy lined up.
Hi!
Somebody get me some paper.
RIP!
the HAUNTED MAILbox PICKUPS DAILY
Good thing I majored in tactical origami.
Tada!
So, have we figured out who our secret client is yet?
They said they were the rightful king of Atlantis, but they wished to remain anonymous, to avoid their enemies.
DELIVER!
Right away, sir!
HAUNTED MAILbox

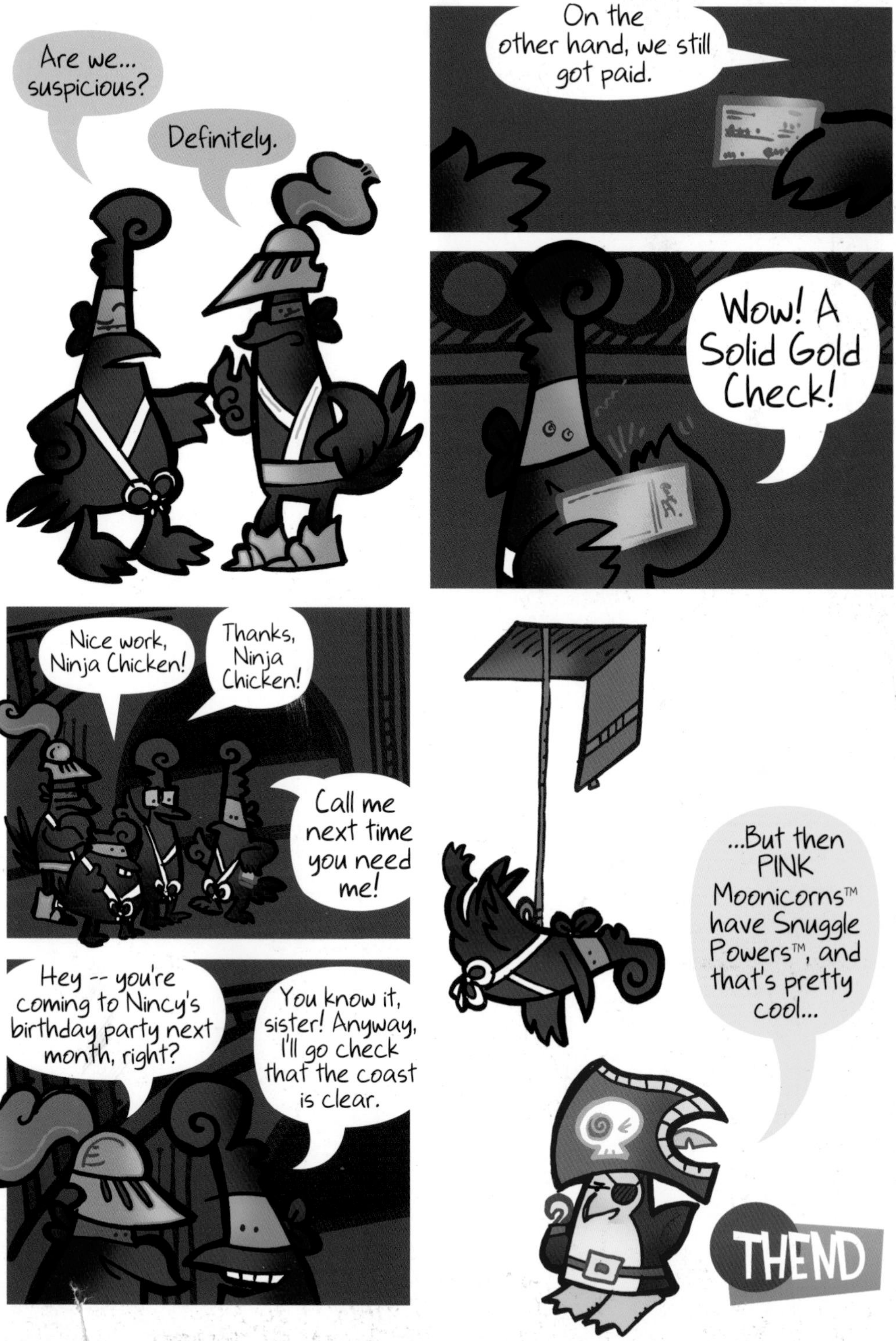
Are we... suspicious?
Definitely.
On the other hand, we still got paid.
Wow! A Solid Gold Check!
Nice work, Ninja Chicken!
Thanks, Ninja Chicken!
Call me next time you need me!
Hey -- you're coming to Nincy's birthday party next month, right?
You know it, sister! Anyway, I'll go check that the coast is clear.
...But then PINK Moonicorns™ have Snuggle Powers™, and that's pretty cool...
THE END

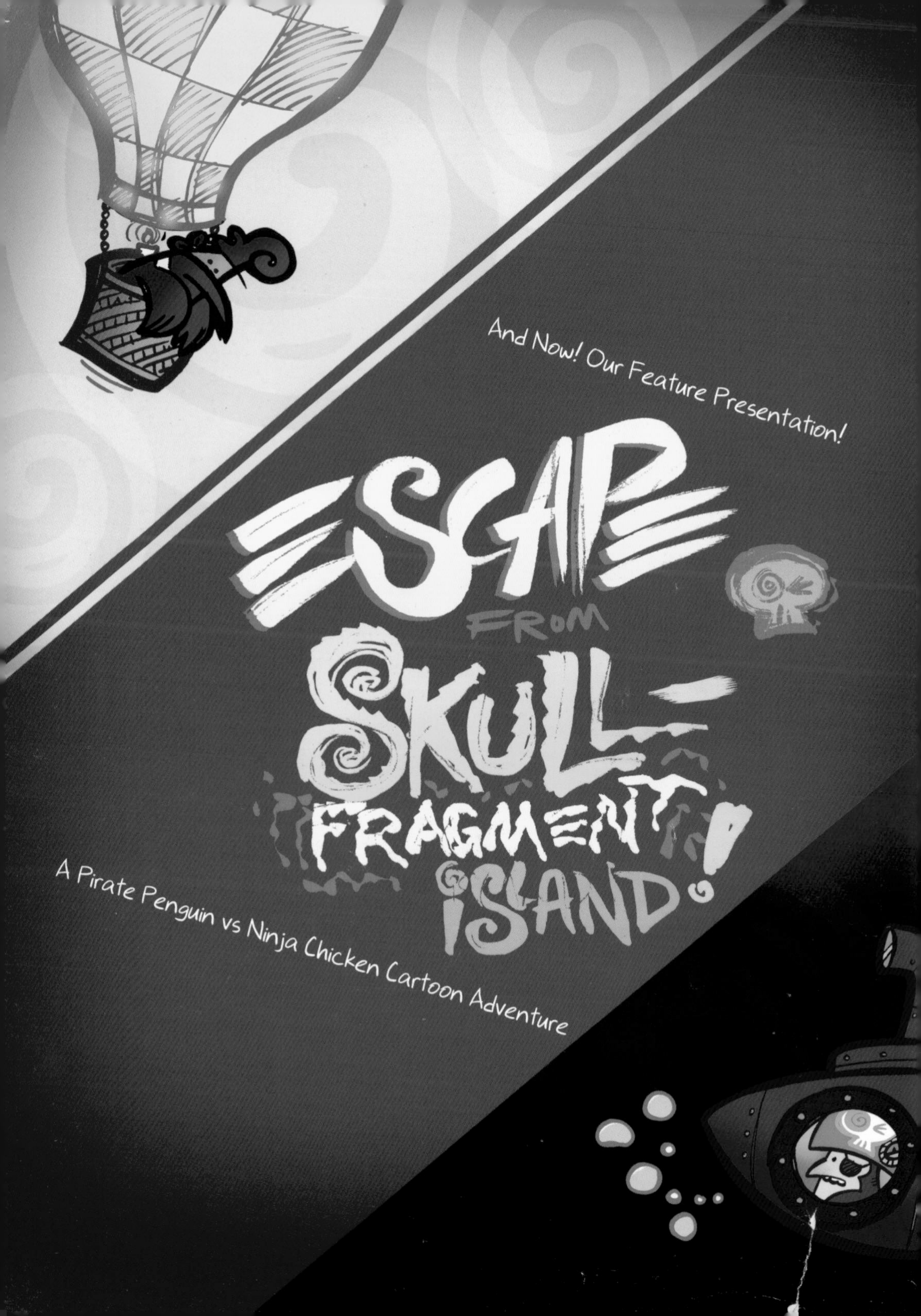
And Now! Our Feature Presentation!
ESCAPE
FROM
SKULL-
FRAGMENT
ISLAND!
A Pirate Penguin vs Ninja Chicken Cartoon Adventure

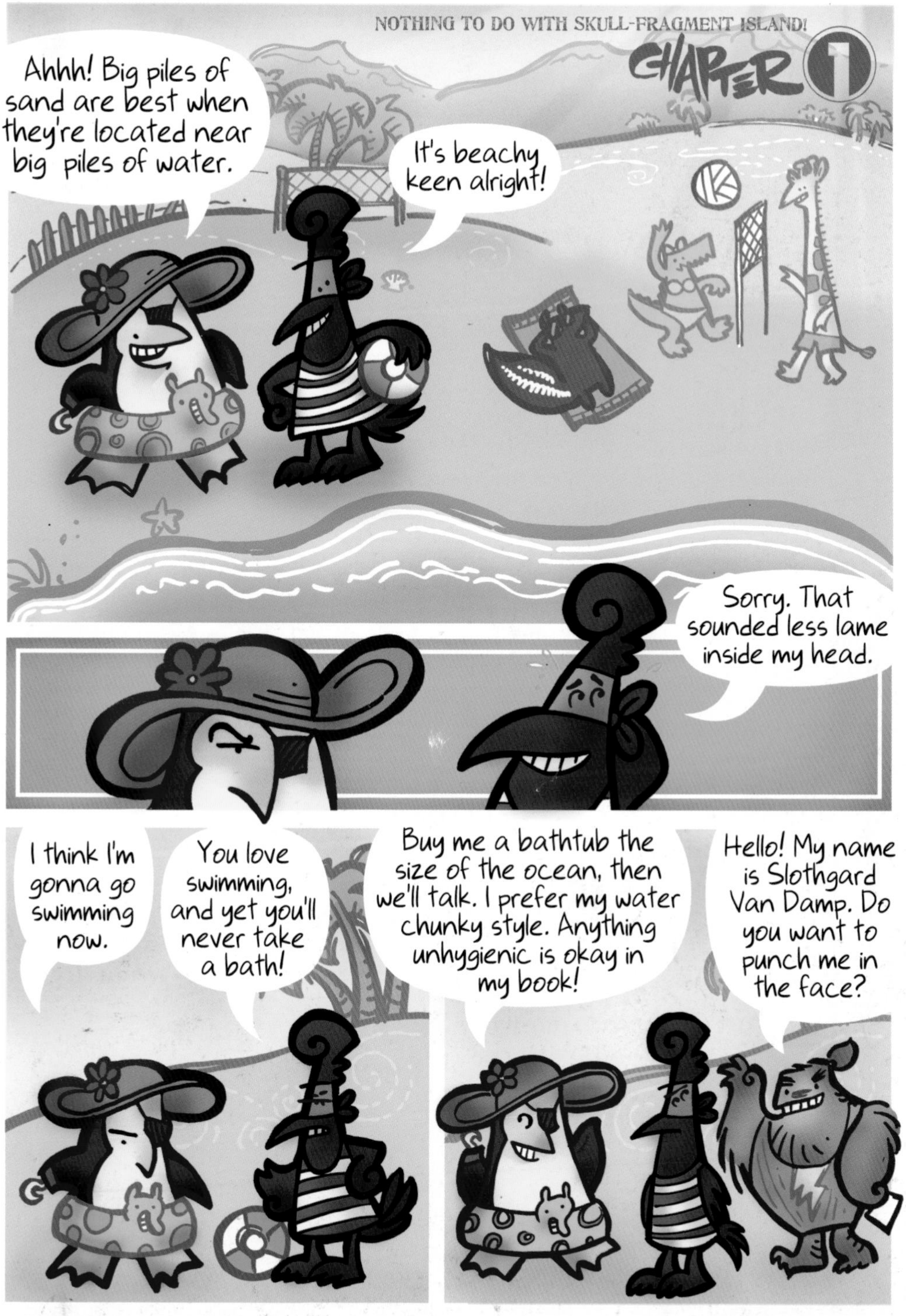
NOTHING TO DO WITH SKULL-FRAGMENT ISLAND!
CHAPTER 1
Ahhh! Big piles of sand are best when they're located near big piles of water.
It's beachy keen alright!
Sorry. That sounded less lame inside my head.
I think I'm gonna go swimming now.
You love swimming, and yet you'll never take a bath!
Buy me a bathtub the size of the ocean, then we'll talk. I prefer my water chunky style. Anything unhygienic is okay in my book!
Hello! My name is Slothgard Van Damp. Do you want to punch me in the face?

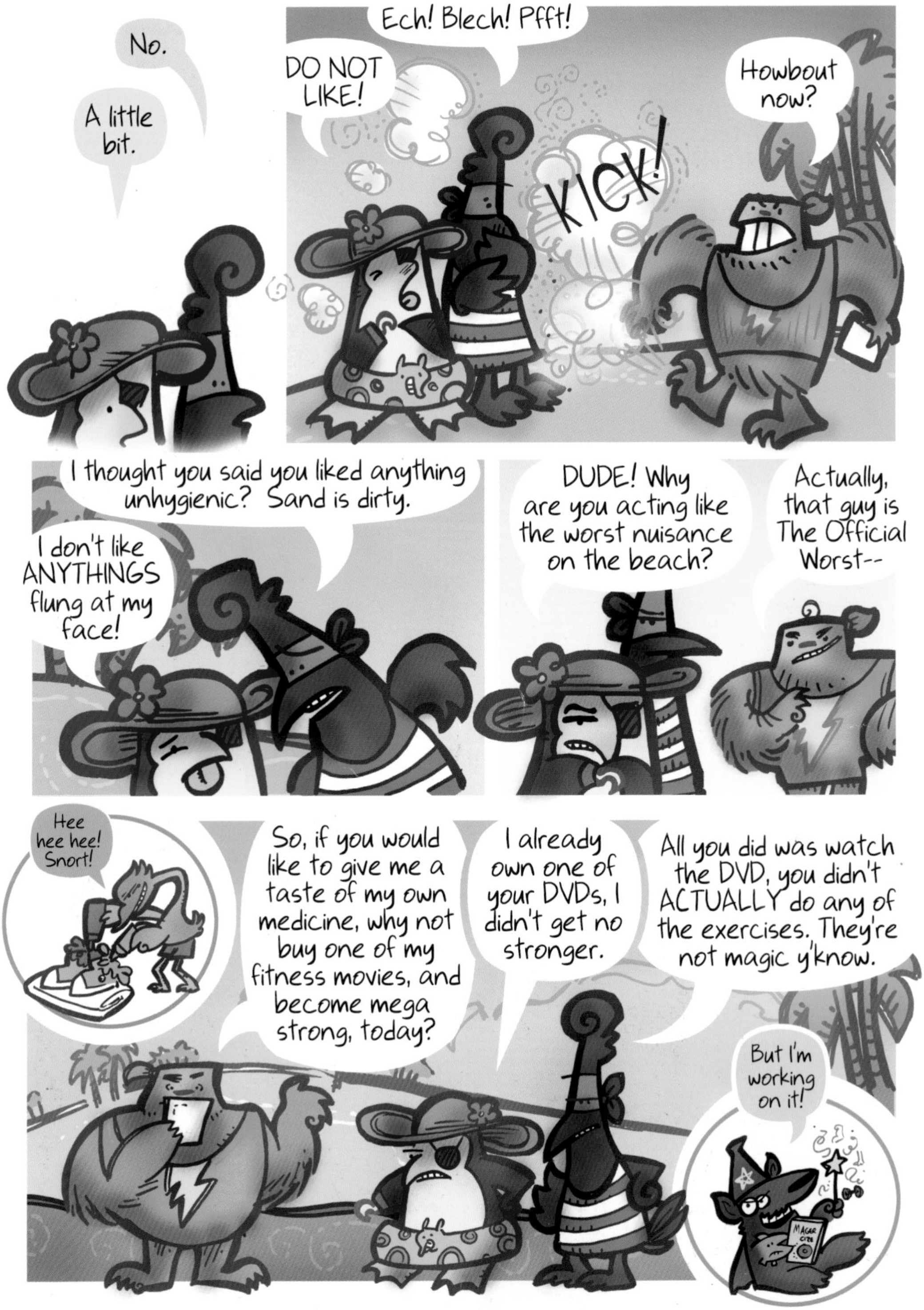
No.
A little bit.
Ech! Blech! Pfft!
DO NOT LIKE!
KICK!
Howbout now?
I thought you said you liked anything unhygienic? Sand is dirty.
I don't like ANYTHINGS flung at my face!
DUDE! Why are you acting like the worst nuisance on the beach?
Actually, that guy is The Official Worst--
Hee hee hee! Snort!
So, if you would like to give me a taste of my own medicine, why not buy one of my fitness movies, and become mega strong, today?
I already own one of your DVDs, I didn't get no stronger.
All you did was watch the DVD, you didn't ACTUALLY do any of the exercises. They're not magic y'know.
But I'm working on it!

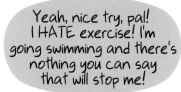

Yeah, nice try, pal! I HATE exercise! I'm going swimming and there's nothing you can say that will stop me!

Actually, swimming is the best form of excercise.

LALALA I'm pretending I can't hear you!

Run Run Run

≥SPLASH≤

Only $29.95, plus shipping and handling!

This is the worst sales method I've ever seen.

SWIMMING IN THE SAME OCEAN AS SKULL-FRAGMENT ISLAND!

CHAPTER 2

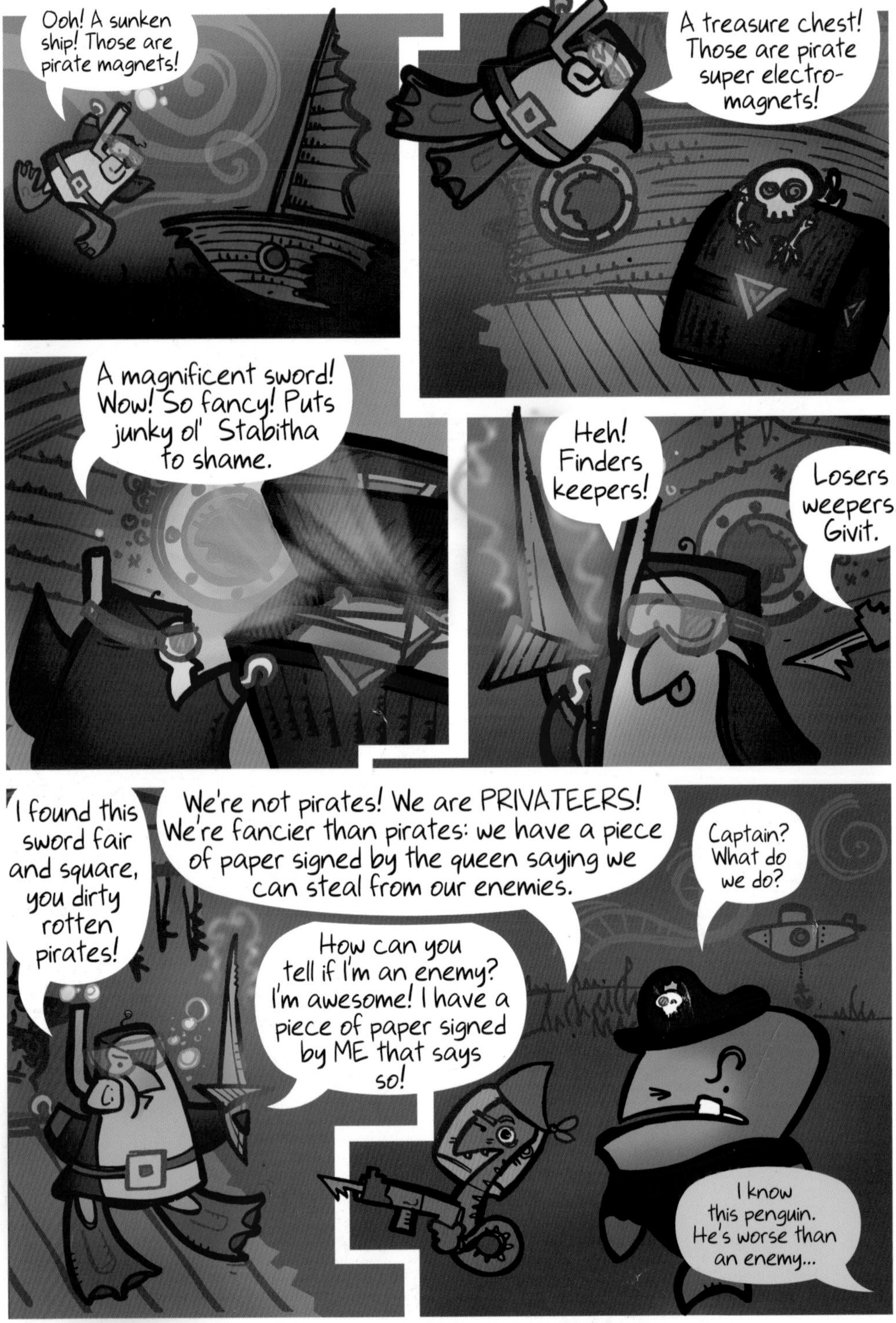
Ooh! A sunken ship! Those are pirate magnets!
A treasure chest! Those are pirate super electro-magnets!
A magnificent sword! Wow! So fancy! Puts junky ol' Stabitha to shame.
Heh! Finders keepers!
Losers weepers. Givit.
I found this sword fair and square, you dirty rotten pirates!
We're not pirates! We are PRIVATEERS! We're fancier than pirates: we have a piece of paper signed by the queen saying we can steal from our enemies.
Captain? What do we do?
How can you tell if I'm an enemy? I'm awesome! I have a piece of paper signed by ME that says so!
I know this penguin. He's worse than an enemy...

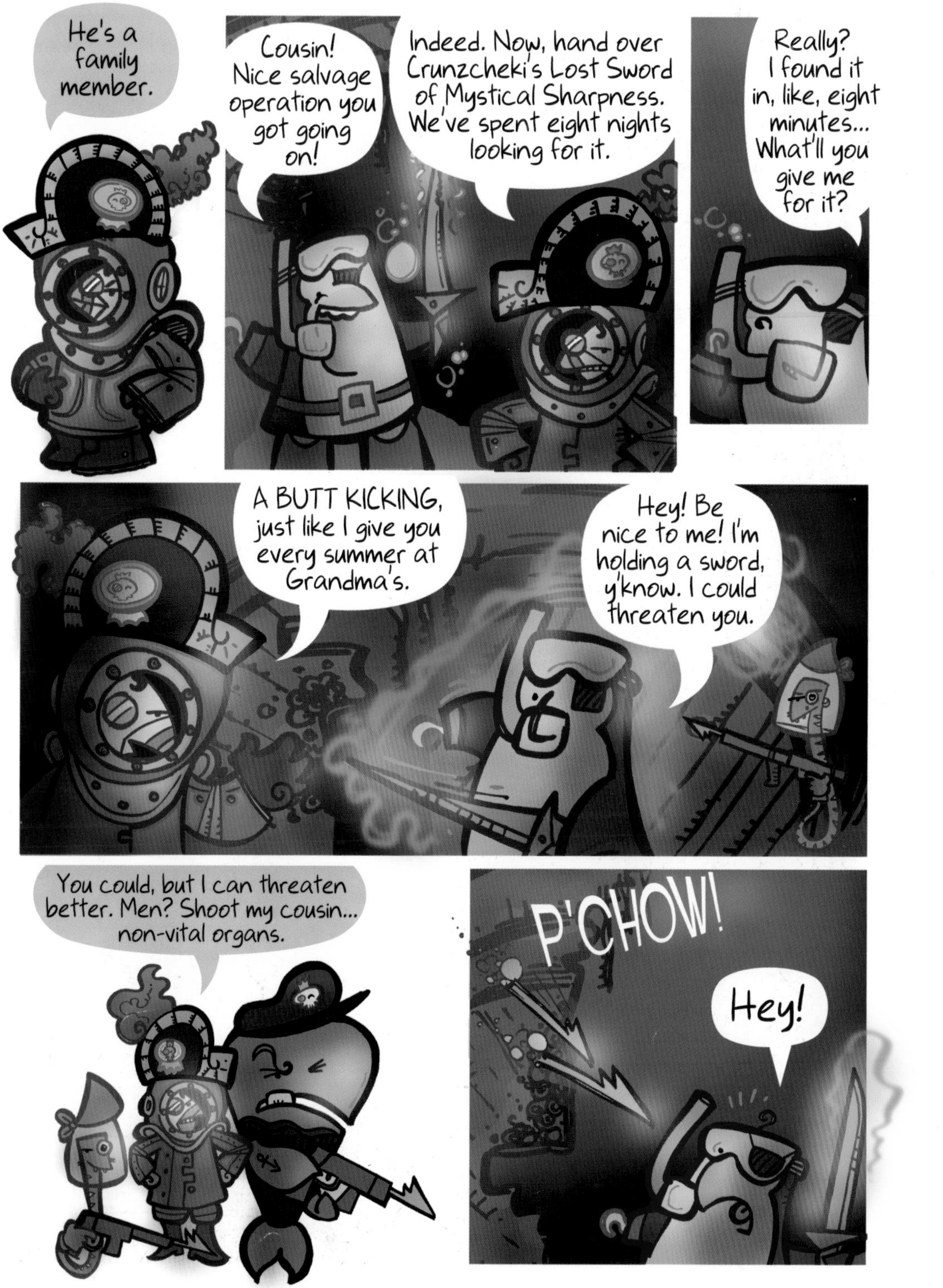
He's a family member.
Cousin! Nice salvage operation you got going on!
Indeed. Now, hand over Crunzcheki's Lost Sword of Mystical Sharpness. We've spent eight nights looking for it.
Really? I found it in, like, eight minutes... What'll you give me for it?
A BUTT KICKING, just like I give you every summer at Grandma's.
Hey! Be nice to me! I'm holding a sword, y'know. I could threaten you.
You could, but I can threaten better. Men? Shoot my cousin... non-vital organs.
P'CHOW!
Hey!

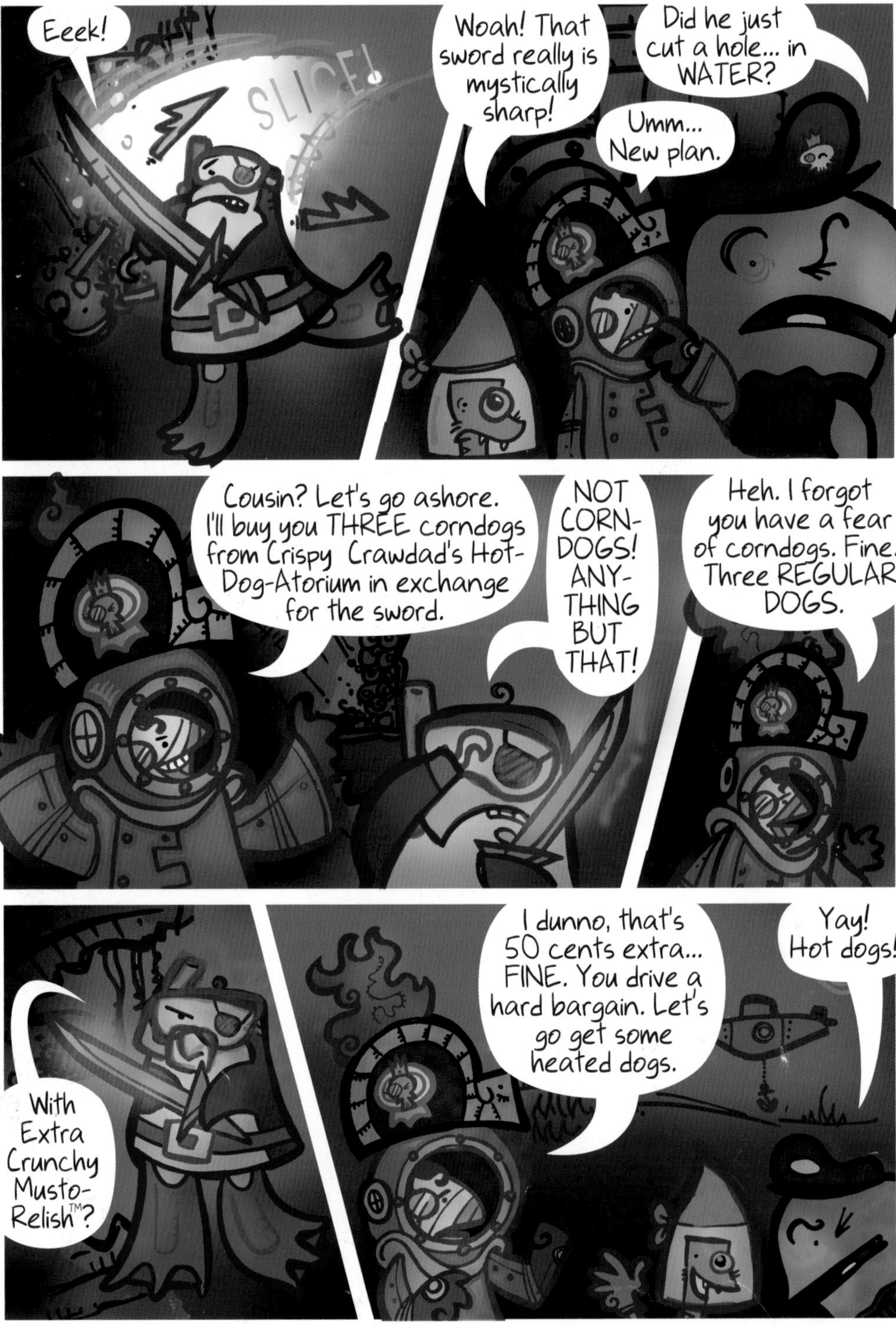

Eeek!
SLICE!
Woah! That sword really is mystically sharp!
Did he just cut a hole... in WATER?
Umm... New plan.
Cousin? Let's go ashore. I'll buy you THREE corndogs from Crispy Crawdad's Hot-Dog-Atorium in exchange for the sword.
NOT CORN-DOGS! ANY-THING BUT THAT!
Heh. I forgot you have a fear of corndogs. Fine. Three REGULAR DOGS.
With Extra Crunchy Musto-Relish™?
I dunno, that's 50 cents extra... FINE. You drive a hard bargain. Let's go get some heated dogs.
Yay! Hot dogs!

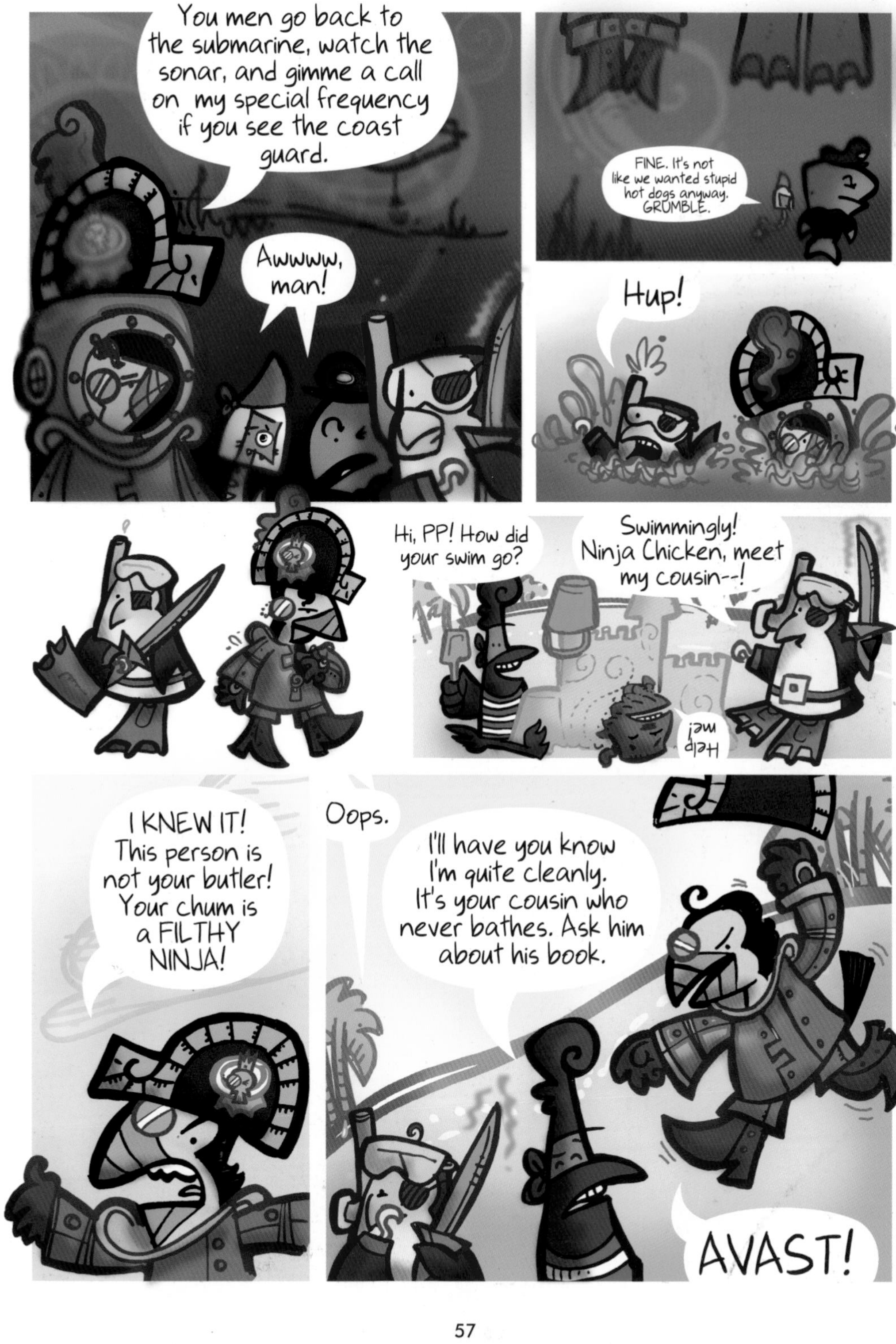
You men go back to the submarine, watch the sonar, and gimme a call on my special frequency if you see the coast guard.
Awwww, man!
FINE. It's not like we wanted stupid hot dogs anyway. GRUMBLE.
Hup!
Hi, PP! How did your swim go?
Swimmingly! Ninja Chicken, meet my cousin--!
Help me!
I KNEW IT! This person is not your butler! Your chum is a FILTHY NINJA!
Oops.
I'll have you know I'm quite cleanly. It's your cousin who never bathes. Ask him about his book.
AVAST!

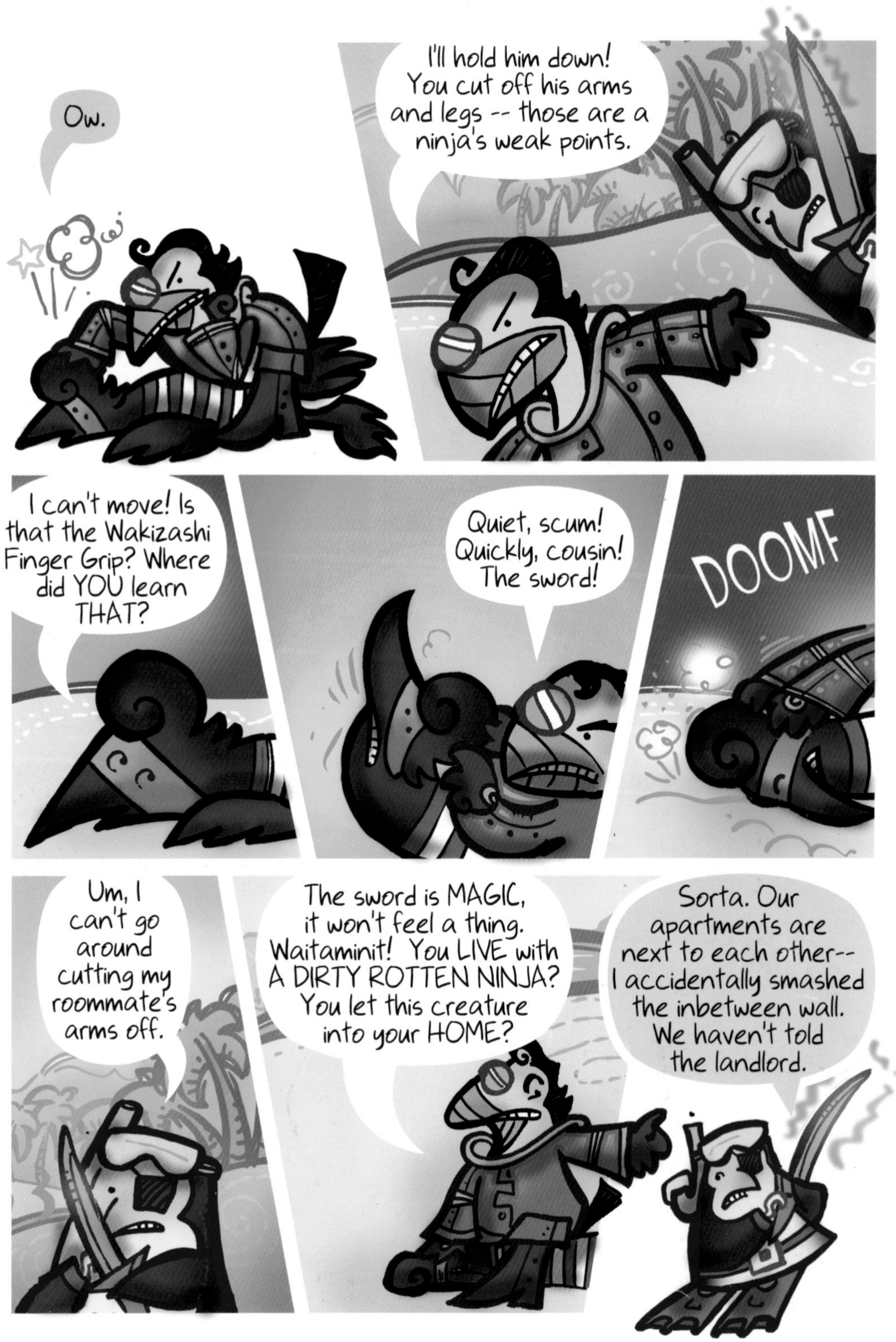
Ow.
I'll hold him down! You cut off his arms and legs -- those are a ninja's weak points.
I can't move! Is that the Wakizashi Finger Grip? Where did YOU learn THAT?
Quiet, scum! Quickly, cousin! The sword!
DOOMF
Um, I can't go around cutting my roommate's arms off.
The sword is MAGIC, it won't feel a thing. Waitaminit! You LIVE with A DIRTY ROTTEN NINJA? You let this creature into your HOME?
Sorta. Our apartments are next to each other-- I accidentally smashed the inbetween wall. We haven't told the landlord.

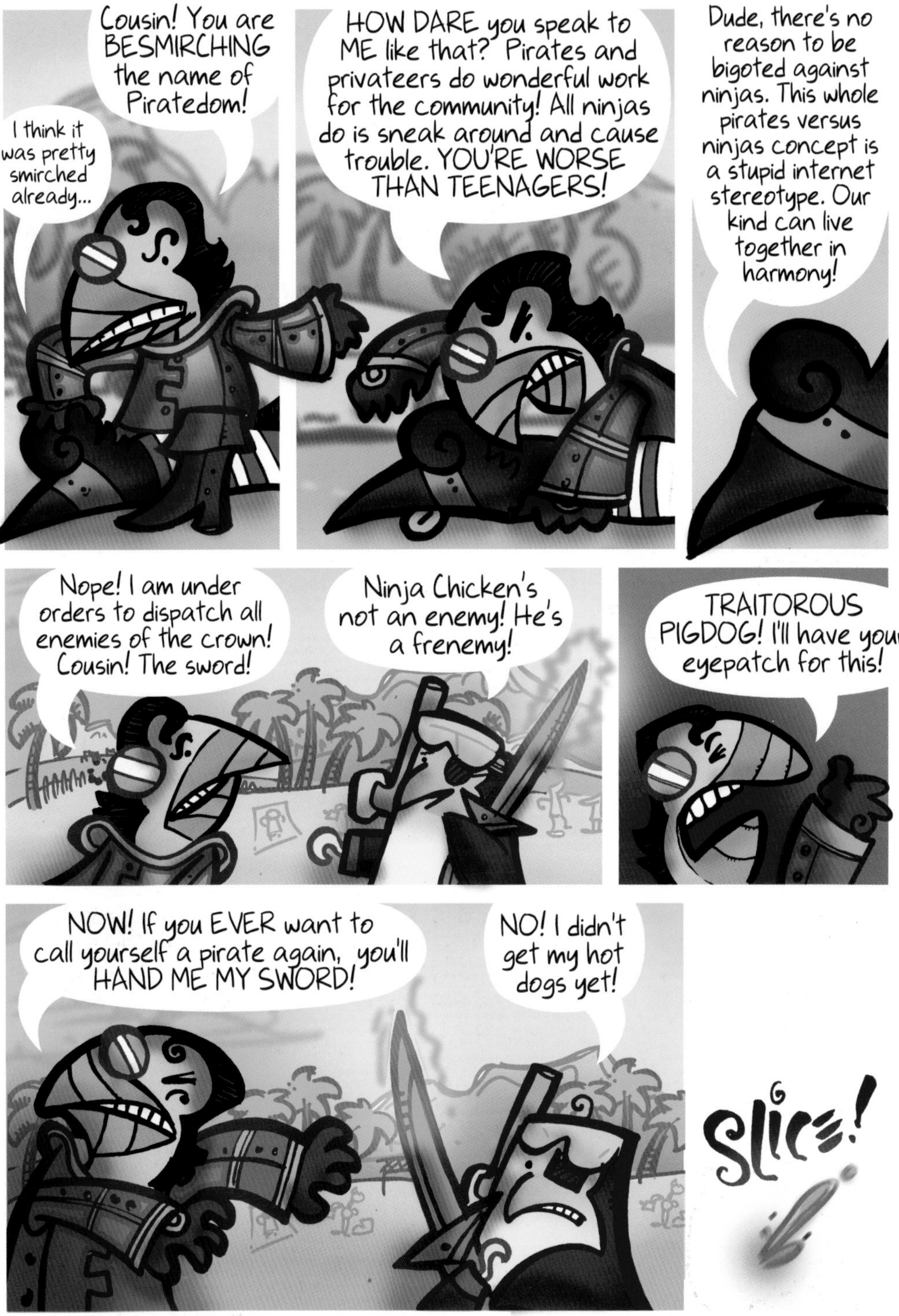
Cousin! You are BESMIRCHING the name of Piratedom!
I think it was pretty smirched already...
HOW DARE you speak to ME like that? Pirates and privateers do wonderful work for the community! All ninjas do is sneak around and cause trouble. YOU'RE WORSE THAN TEENAGERS!
Dude, there's no reason to be bigoted against ninjas. This whole pirates versus ninjas concept is a stupid internet stereotype. Our kind can live together in harmony!
Nope! I am under orders to dispatch all enemies of the crown! Cousin! The sword!
Ninja Chicken's not an enemy! He's a frenemy!
TRAITOROUS PIGDOG! I'll have your eyepatch for this!
NOW! If you EVER want to call yourself a pirate again, you'll HAND ME MY SWORD!
NO! I didn't get my hot dogs yet!
SLICE!

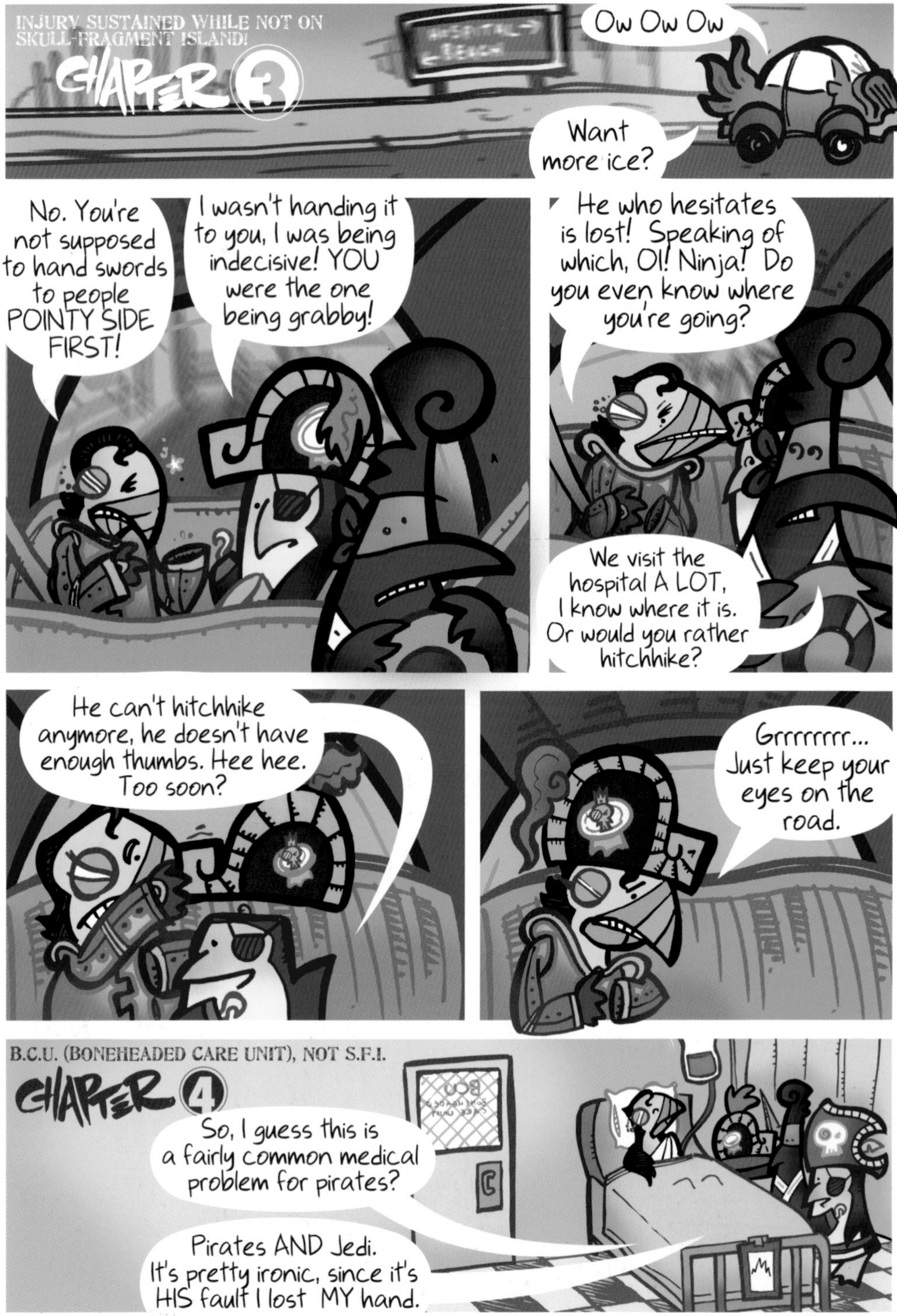
INJURY SUSTAINED WHILE NOT ON SKULL-FRAGMENT ISLAND!
CHAPTER 3
Ow Ow Ow
Want more ice?
No. You're not supposed to hand swords to people POINTY SIDE FIRST!
I wasn't handing it to you, I was being indecisive! YOU were the one being grabby!
He who hesitates is lost! Speaking of which, OI! Ninja! Do you even know where you're going?
We visit the hospital A LOT, I know where it is. Or would you rather hitchhike?
He can't hitchhike anymore, he doesn't have enough thumbs. Hee hee. Too soon?
Grrrrrrrr... Just keep your eyes on the road.
B.C.U. (BONEHEADED CARE UNIT), NOT S.F.I.
CHAPTER 4
So, I guess this is a fairly common medical problem for pirates?
Pirates AND Jedi. It's pretty ironic, since it's HIS fault I lost MY hand.

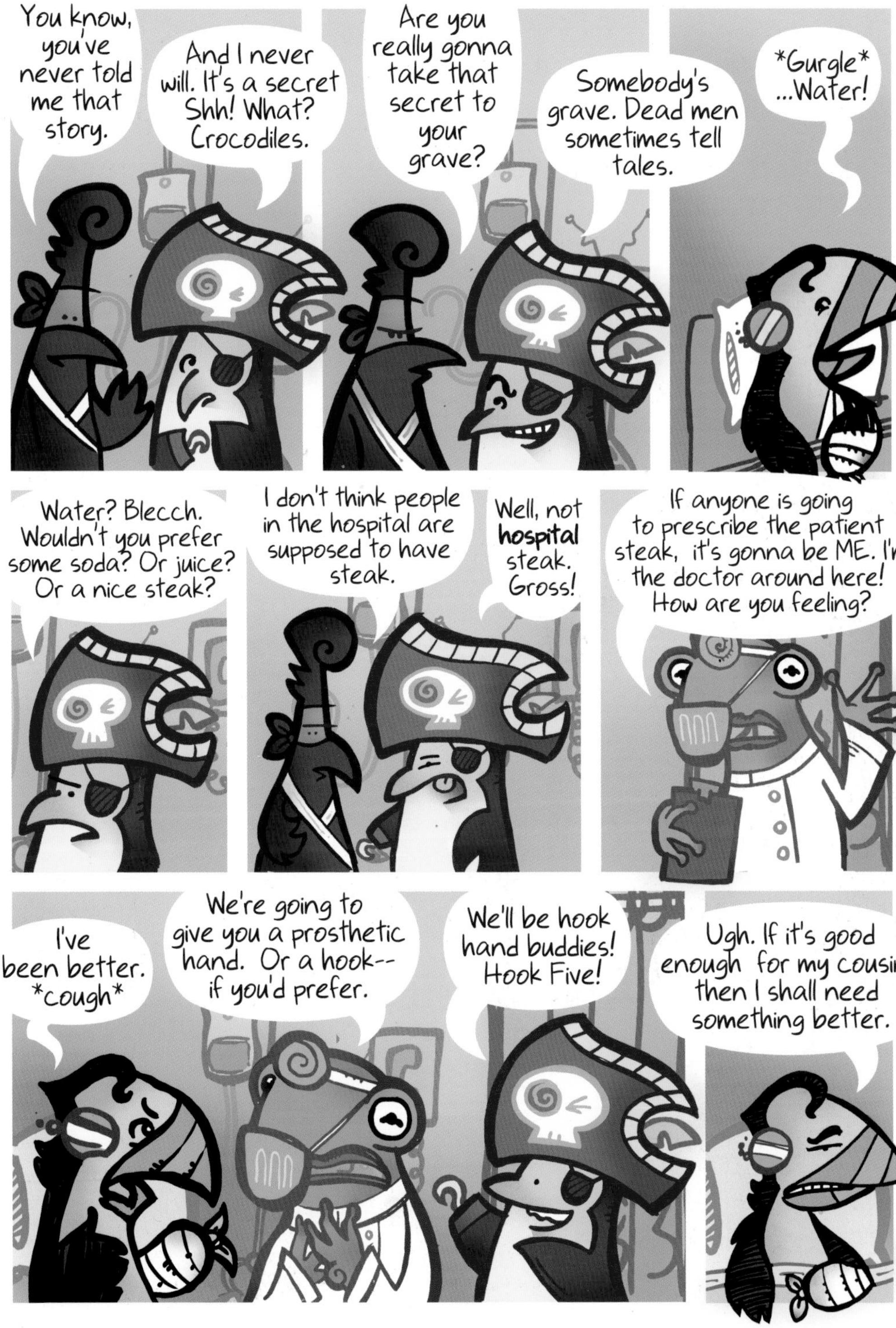

You know, you've never told me that story.
And I never will. It's a secret Shh! What? Crocodiles.
Are you really gonna take that secret to your grave?
Somebody's grave. Dead men sometimes tell tales.
Gurgle ...Water!
Water? Blecch. Wouldn't you prefer some soda? Or juice? Or a nice steak?
I don't think people in the hospital are supposed to have steak.
Well, not **hospital** steak. Gross!
If anyone is going to prescribe the patient steak, it's gonna be ME. I'm the doctor around here! How are you feeling?
I've been better. *cough*
We're going to give you a prosthetic hand. Or a hook-- if you'd prefer.
We'll be hook hand buddies! Hook Five!
Ugh. If it's good enough for my cousin, then I shall need something better.

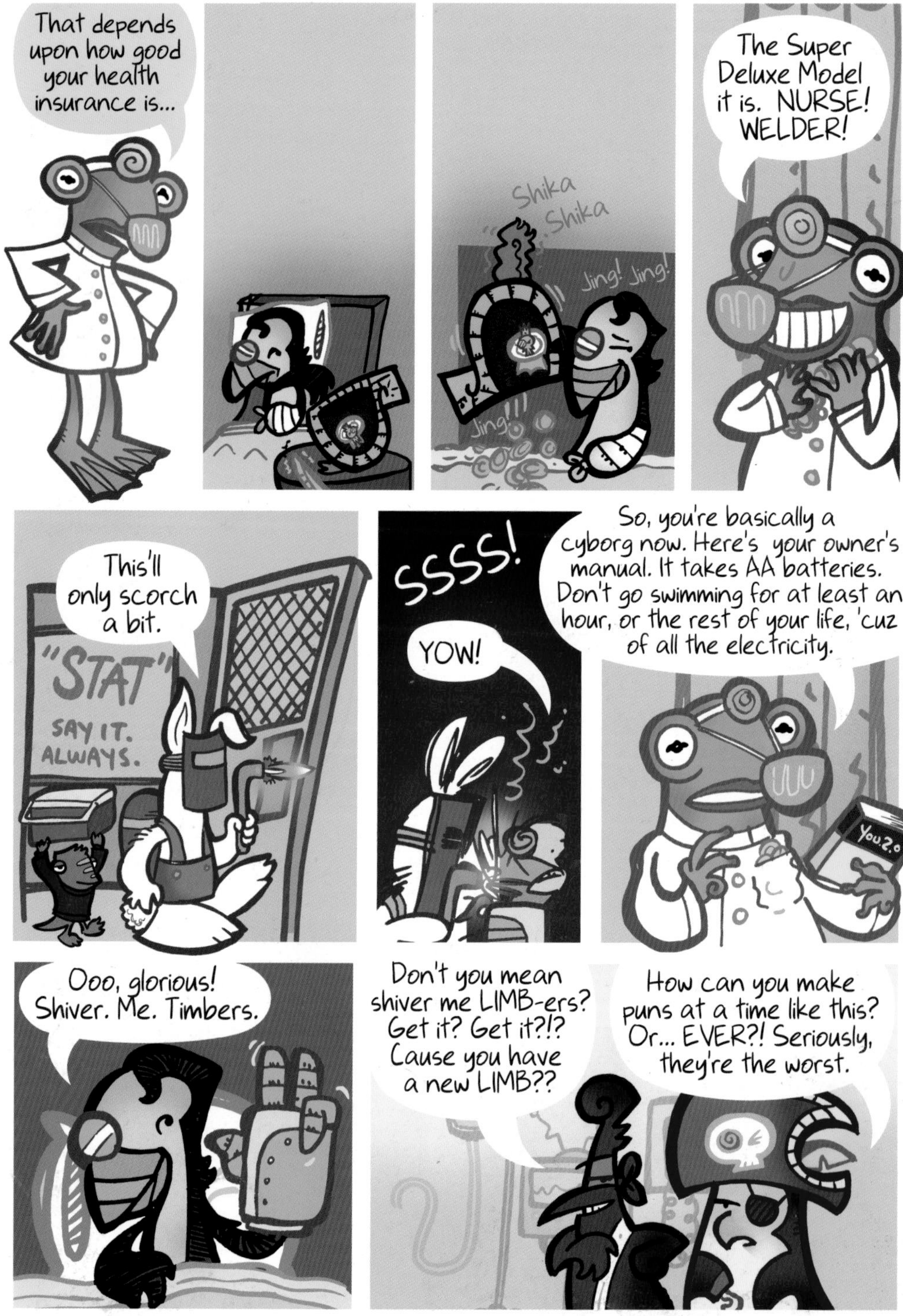
That depends upon how good your health insurance is...
Shika Shika
Jing! Jing!
Jing!
The Super Deluxe Model it is. NURSE! WELDER!
This'll only scorch a bit.
"STAT" SAY IT. ALWAYS.
SSSS!
YOW!
So, you're basically a cyborg now. Here's your owner's manual. It takes AA batteries. Don't go swimming for at least an hour, or the rest of your life, 'cuz of all the electricity.
You 2.0
Ooo, glorious! Shiver. Me. Timbers.
Don't you mean shiver me LIMB-ers? Get it? Get it?!? Cause you have a new LIMB??
How can you make puns at a time like this? Or... EVER?! Seriously, they're the worst.

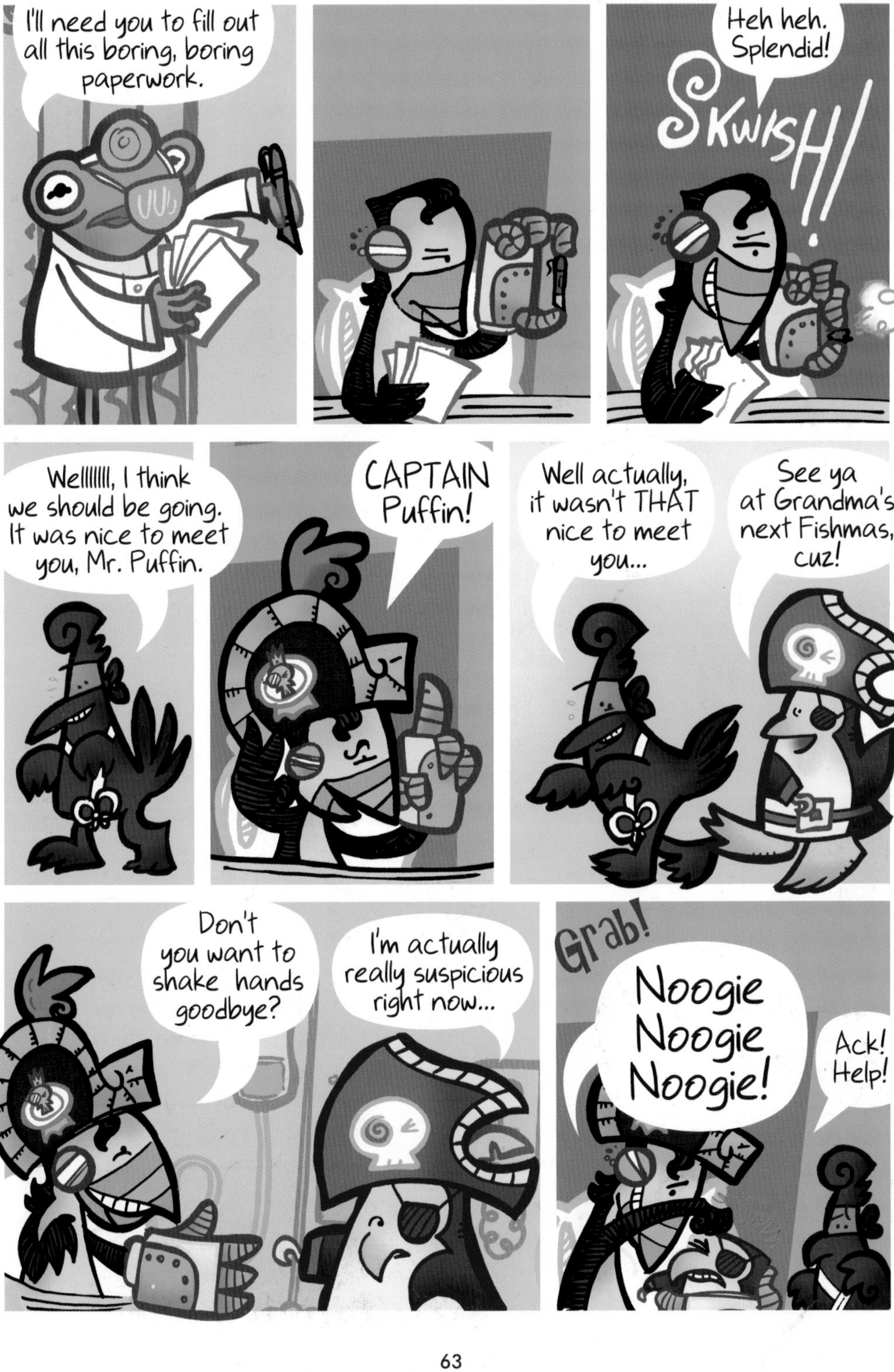
I'll need you to fill out all this boring, boring paperwork.
Heh heh. Splendid!
SKWISH!
Welllllll, I think we should be going. It was nice to meet you, Mr. Puffin.
CAPTAIN Puffin!
Well actually, it wasn't THAT nice to meet you...
See ya at Grandma's next Fishmas, cuz!
Don't you want to shake hands goodbye?
I'm actually really suspicious right now...
Grab!
Noogie Noogie Noogie!
Ack! Help!

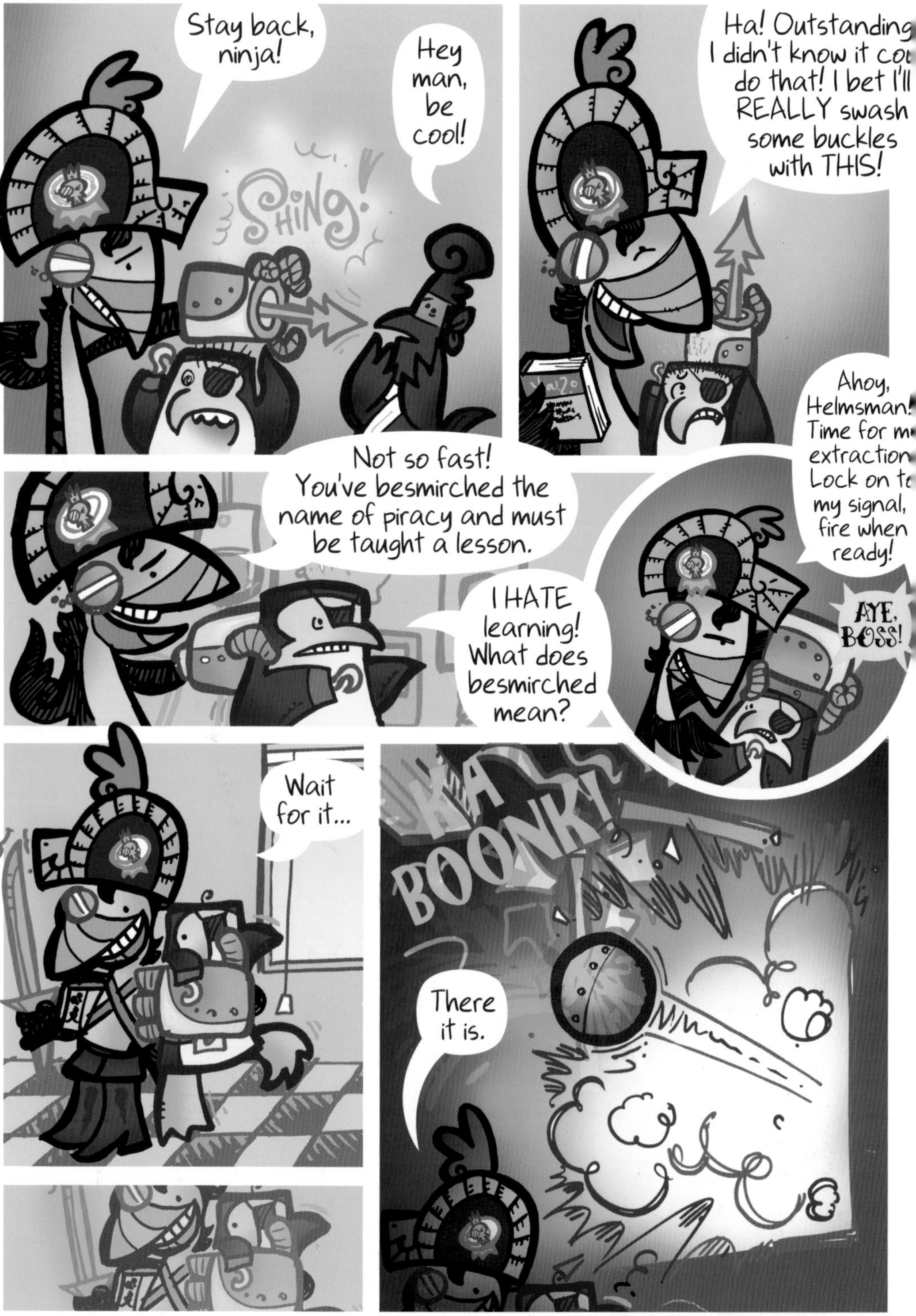
Stay back, ninja!
Hey man, be cool!
SHING!
Ha! Outstanding
I didn't know it co
do that! I bet I'll
REALLY swash
some buckles
with THIS!
Not so fast! You've besmirched the name of piracy and must be taught a lesson.
I HATE learning! What does besmirched mean?
Ahoy, Helmsman! Time for m
extraction
Lock on t
my signal, fire when ready!
AYE, BOSS!
Wait for it...
KA BOONK!
There it is.

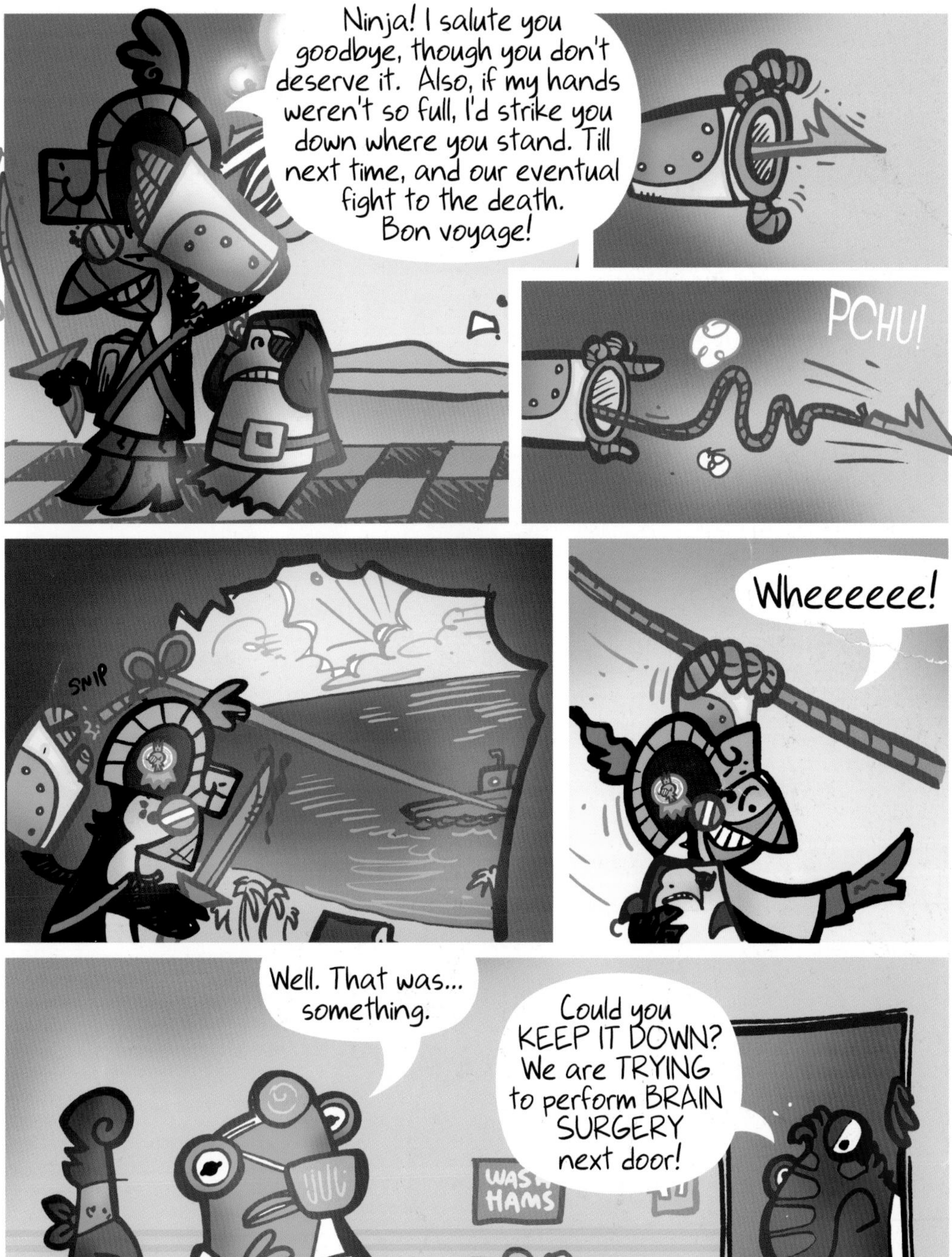

Ninja! I salute you goodbye, though you don't deserve it. Also, if my hands weren't so full, I'd strike you down where you stand. Till next time, and our eventual fight to the death. Bon voyage!
PCHU!
SNIP
Wheeeeee!
Well. That was... something.
Could you KEEP IT DOWN? We are TRYING to perform BRAIN SURGERY next door!
WASH HAMS
Oops.

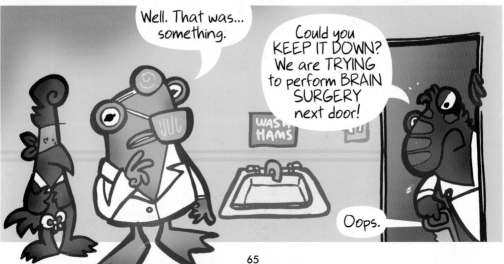

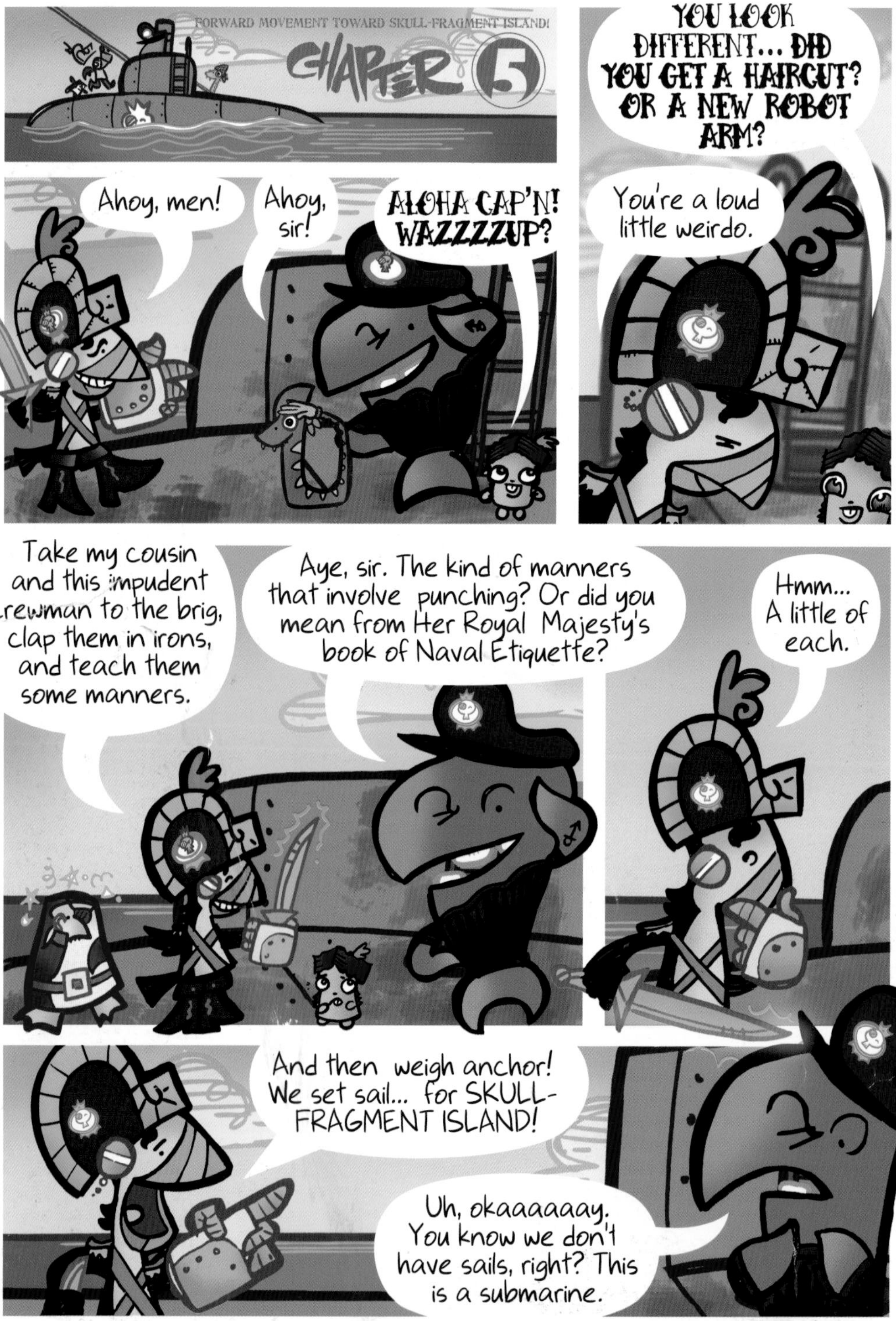
FORWARD MOVEMENT TOWARD SKULL-FRAGMENT ISLAND!
CHAPTER 5
YOU LOOK DIFFERENT... DID YOU GET A HAIRCUT? OR A NEW ROBOT ARM?
Ahoy, men!
Ahoy, sir!
ALOHA CAP'N! WAZZZZZUP?
You're a loud little weirdo.
Take my cousin and this impudent crewman to the brig, clap them in irons, and teach them some manners.
Aye, sir. The kind of manners that involve punching? Or did you mean from Her Royal Majesty's book of Naval Etiquette?
Hmm... A little of each.
And then weigh anchor! We set sail... for SKULL-FRAGMENT ISLAND!
Uh, okaaaaaaay. You know we don't have sails, right? This is a submarine.

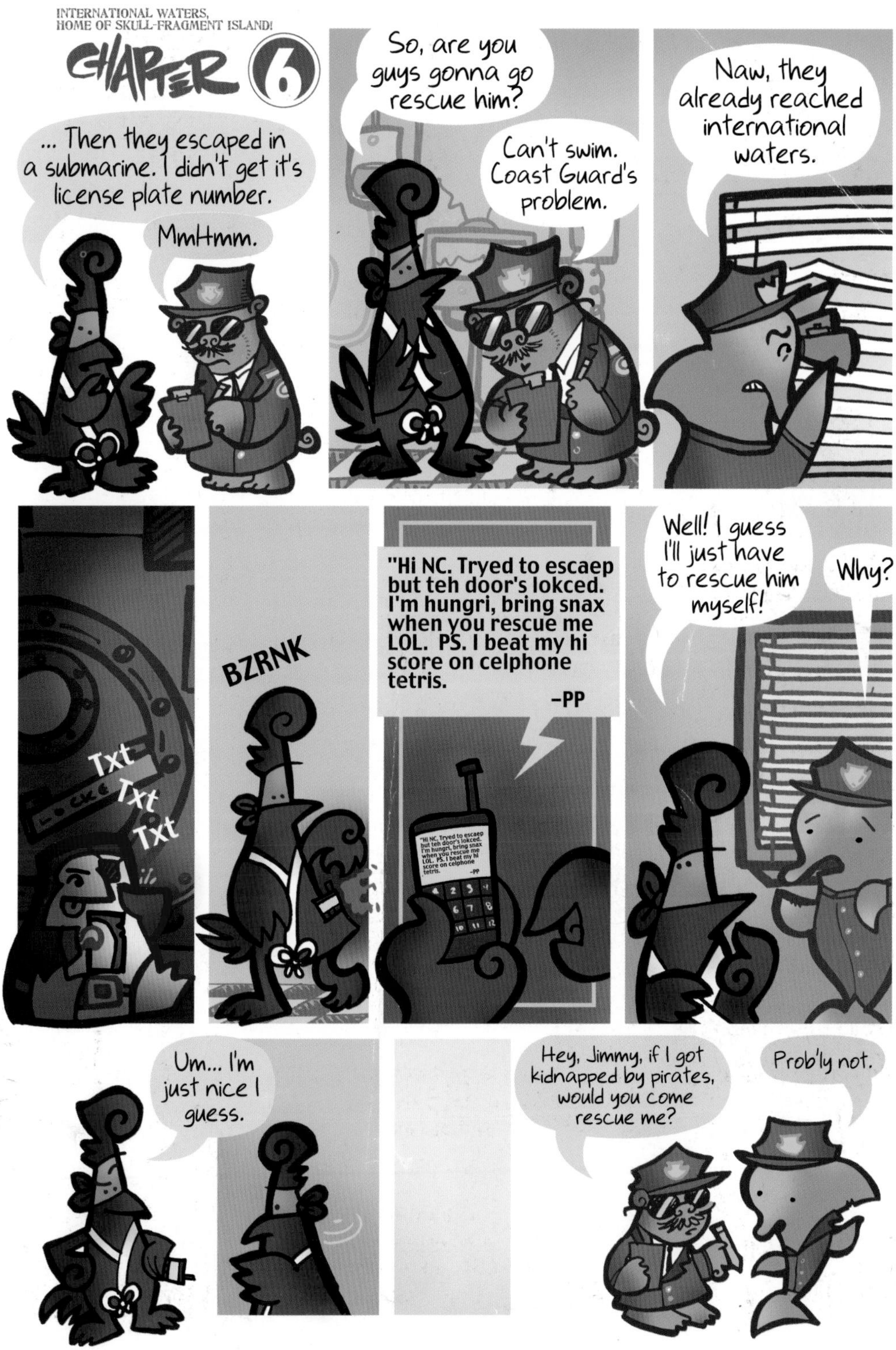
INTERNATIONAL WATERS, HOME OF SKULL-FRAGMENT ISLAND!
CHAPTER 6
... Then they escaped in a submarine. I didn't get it's license plate number.
MmHmm.
So, are you guys gonna go rescue him?
Can't swim. Coast Guard's problem.
Naw, they already reached international waters.
Txt Txt Txt
BZRNK
"Hi NC. Tryed to escaep but teh door's lokced. I'm hungri, bring snax when you rescue me LOL. PS. I beat my hi score on celphone tetris.
-PP
Well! I guess I'll just have to rescue him myself!
Why?
Um... I'm just nice I guess.
Hey, Jimmy, if I got kidnapped by pirates, would you come rescue me?
Prob'ly not.

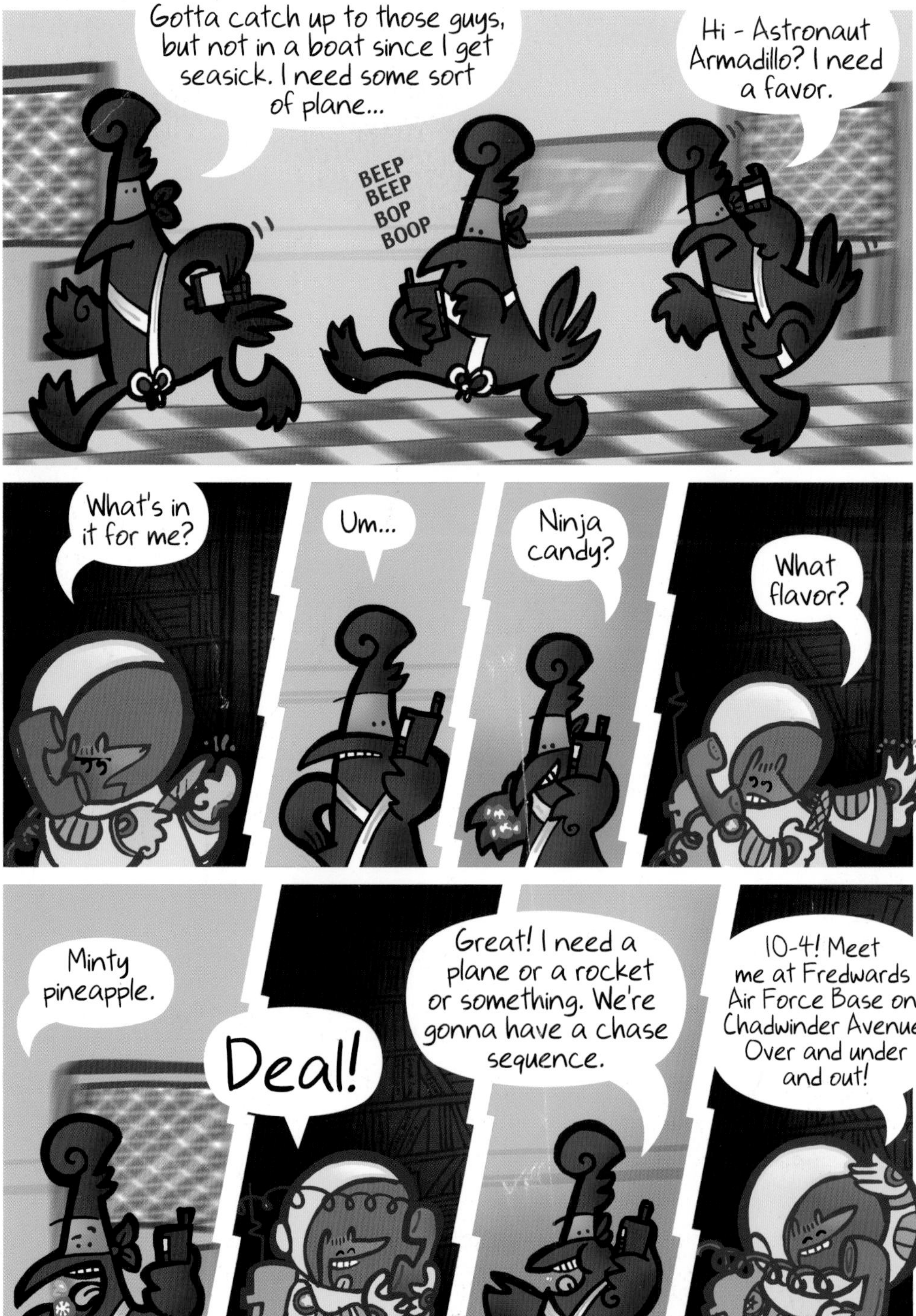
Gotta catch up to those guys, but not in a boat since I get seasick. I need some sort of plane...
BEEP BEEP BOP BOOP
Hi - Astronaut Armadillo? I need a favor.
What's in it for me?
Um...
Ninja candy?
What flavor?
Minty pineapple.
Deal!
Great! I need a plane or a rocket or something. We're gonna have a chase sequence.
10-4! Meet me at Fredwards Air Force Base on Chadwinder Avenue. Over and under and out!

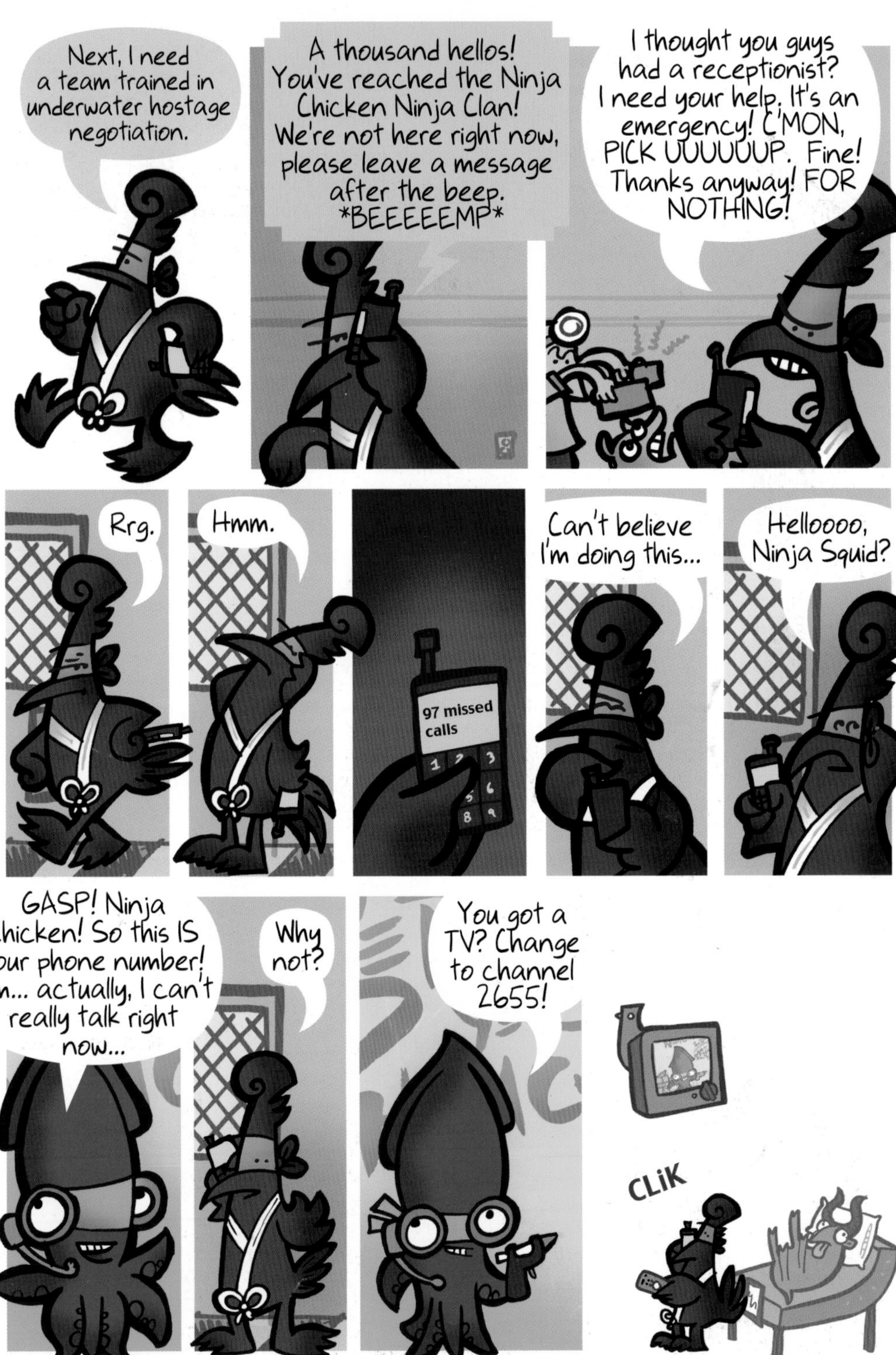
Next, I need a team trained in underwater hostage negotiation.
A thousand hellos! You've reached the Ninja Chicken Ninja Clan! We're not here right now, please leave a message after the beep. *BEEEEEMP*
I thought you guys had a receptionist? I need your help. It's an emergency! C'MON, PICK UUUUUUP. Fine! Thanks anyway! FOR NOTHING!
Rrg.
Hmm.
97 missed calls
Can't believe I'm doing this...
Helloooo, Ninja Squid?
GASP! Ninja Chicken! So this IS your phone number! Um... actually, I can't really talk right now...
Why not?
You got a TV? Change to channel 2655!
CLiK

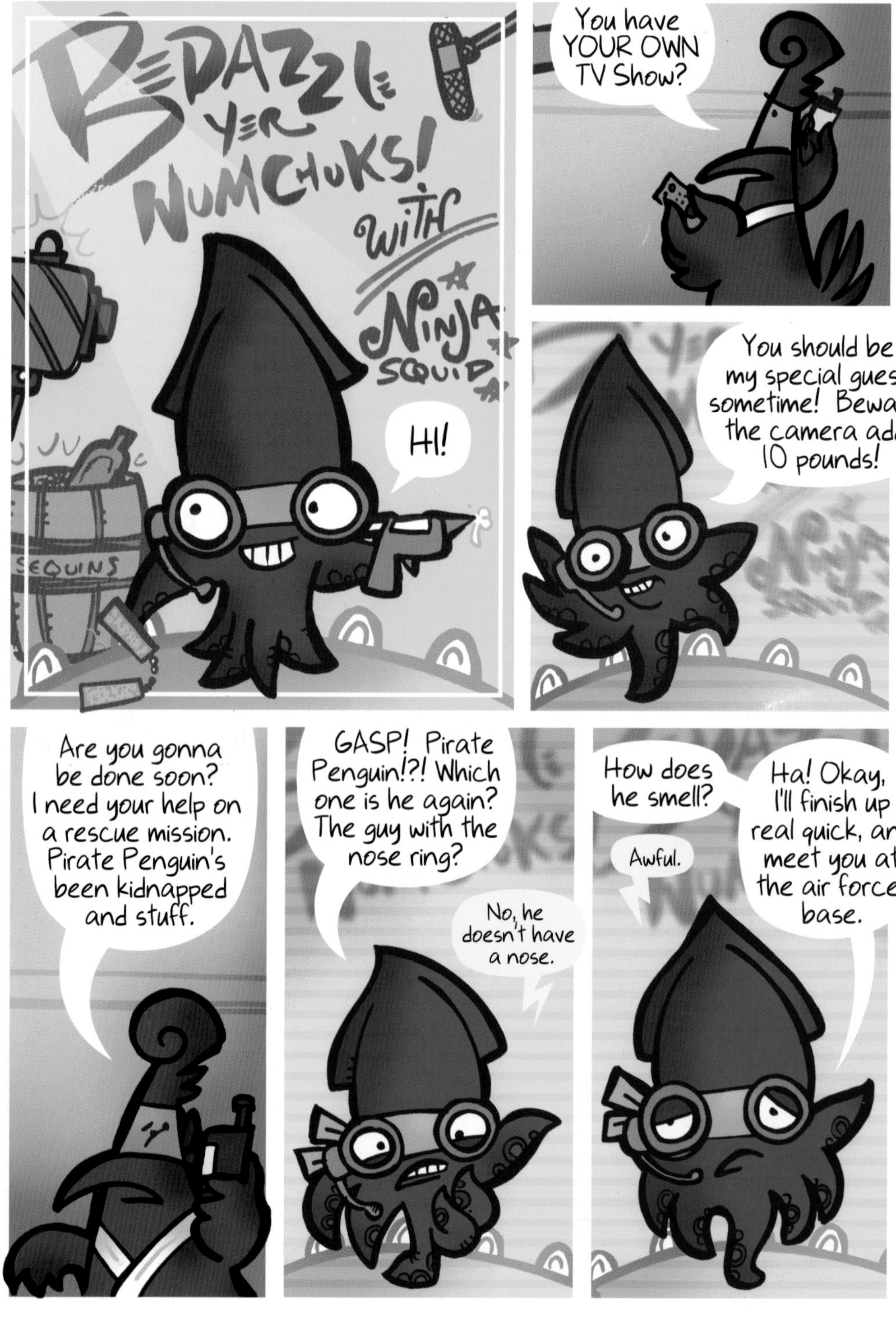
BEDAZZLE YER NUMCHUKS! WITH NINJA SQUID
HI!
SEQUINS
You have YOUR OWN TV Show?
You should be my special guest sometime! Beware the camera adds 10 pounds!
Are you gonna be done soon? I need your help on a rescue mission. Pirate Penguin's been kidnapped and stuff.
GASP! Pirate Penguin!?! Which one is he again? The guy with the nose ring?
No, he doesn't have a nose.
How does he smell?
Awful.
Ha! Okay, I'll finish up real quick, and meet you at the air force base.

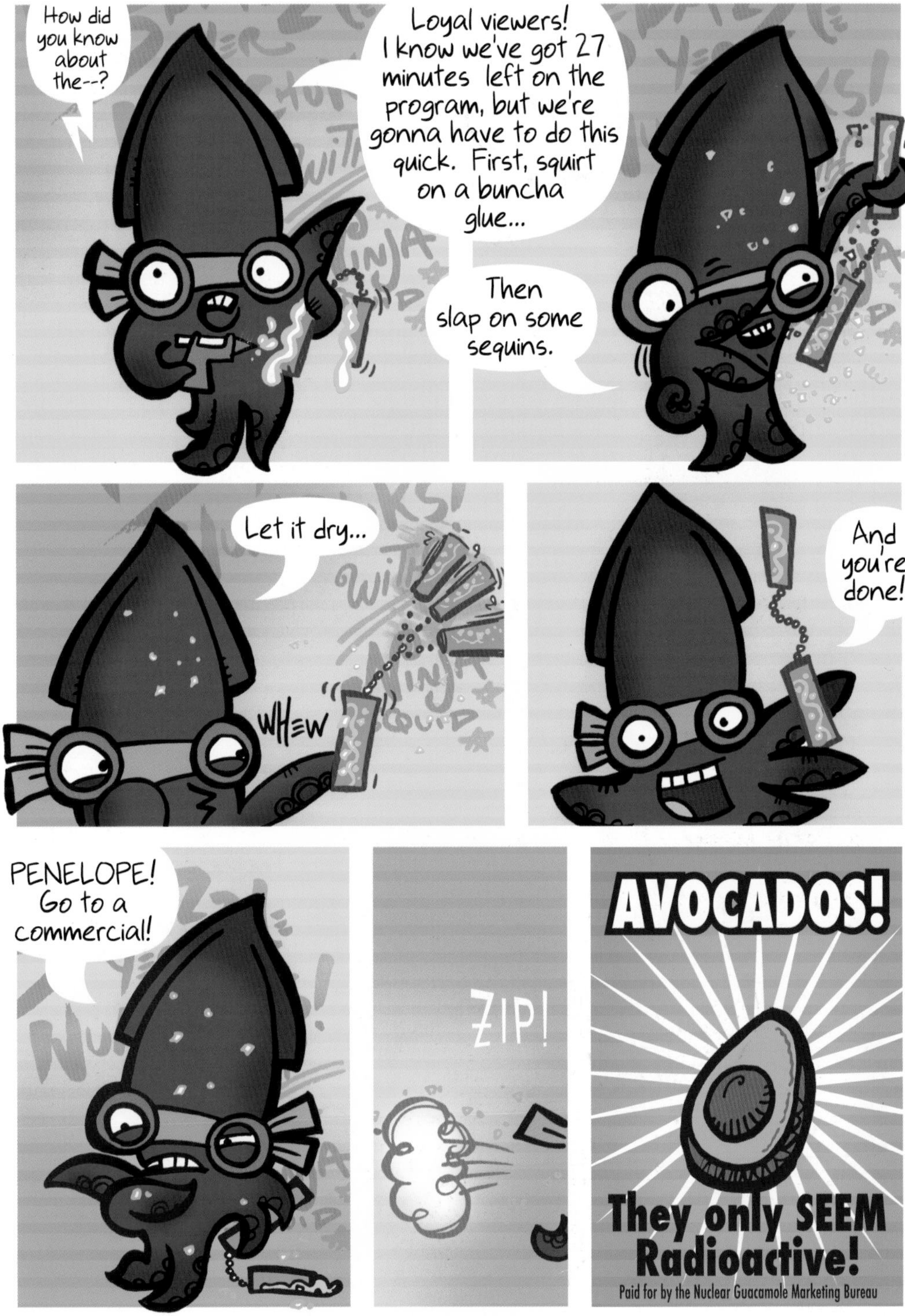
How did you know about the--?
Loyal viewers! I know we've got 27 minutes left on the program, but we're gonna have to do this quick. First, squirt on a buncha glue...
Then slap on some sequins.
Let it dry...
WHEW
And you're done!
PENELOPE! Go to a commercial!
ZIP!
AVOCADOS!
They only SEEM Radioactive!
Paid for by the Nuclear Guacamole Marketing Bureau

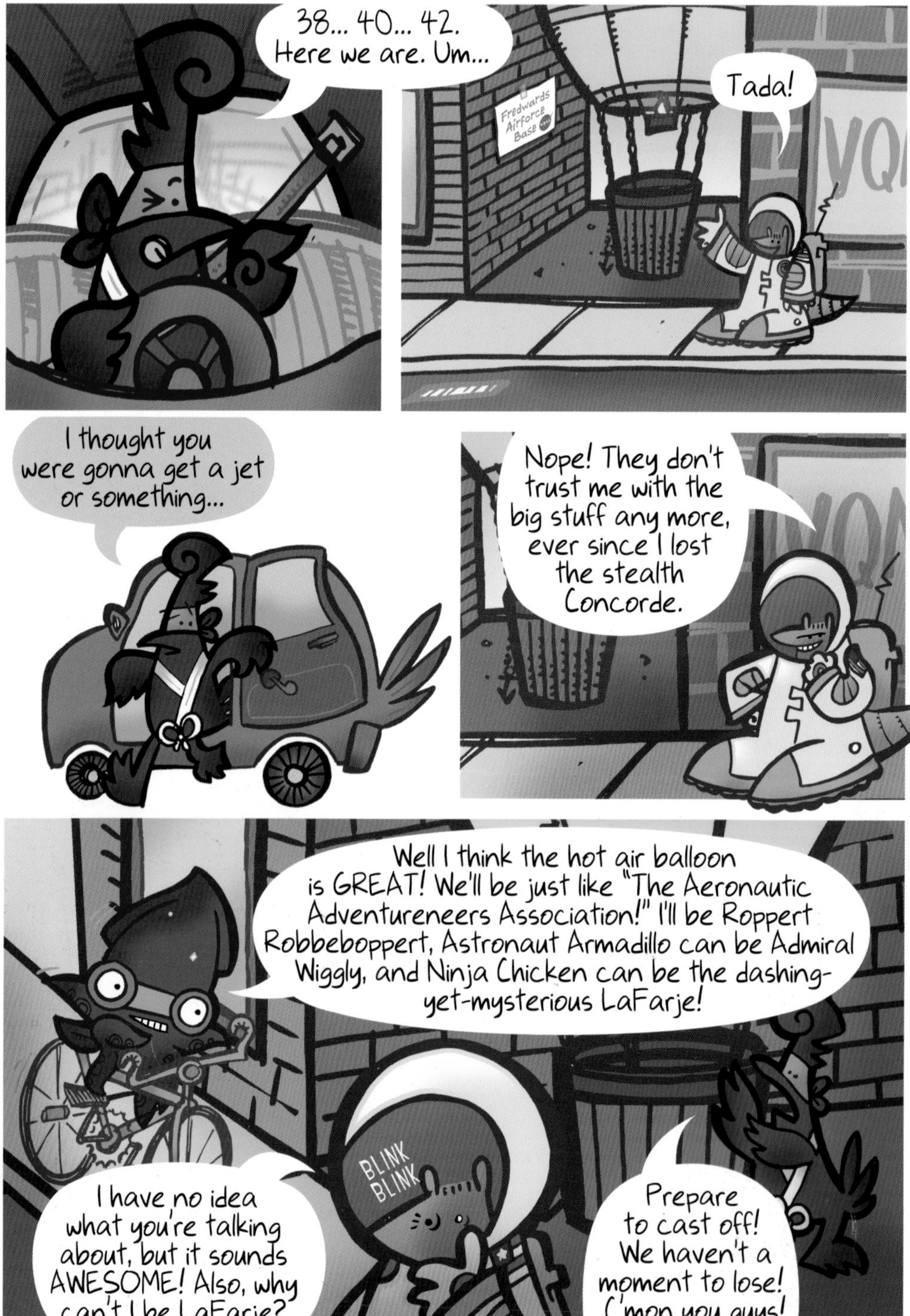
38... 40... 42.
Here we are. Um...
Fredwards Airforce Base
Tada!
I thought you were gonna get a jet or something...
Nope! They don't trust me with the big stuff any more, ever since I lost the stealth Concorde.
Well I think the hot air balloon is GREAT! We'll be just like "The Aeronautic Adventureneers Association!" I'll be Roppert Robbeboppert, Astronaut Armadillo can be Admiral Wiggly, and Ninja Chicken can be the dashing-yet-mysterious LaFarje!
BLINK BLINK
I have no idea what you're talking about, but it sounds AWESOME! Also, why can't I be LaFarje?
Prepare to cast off! We haven't a moment to lose! C'mon you guys!

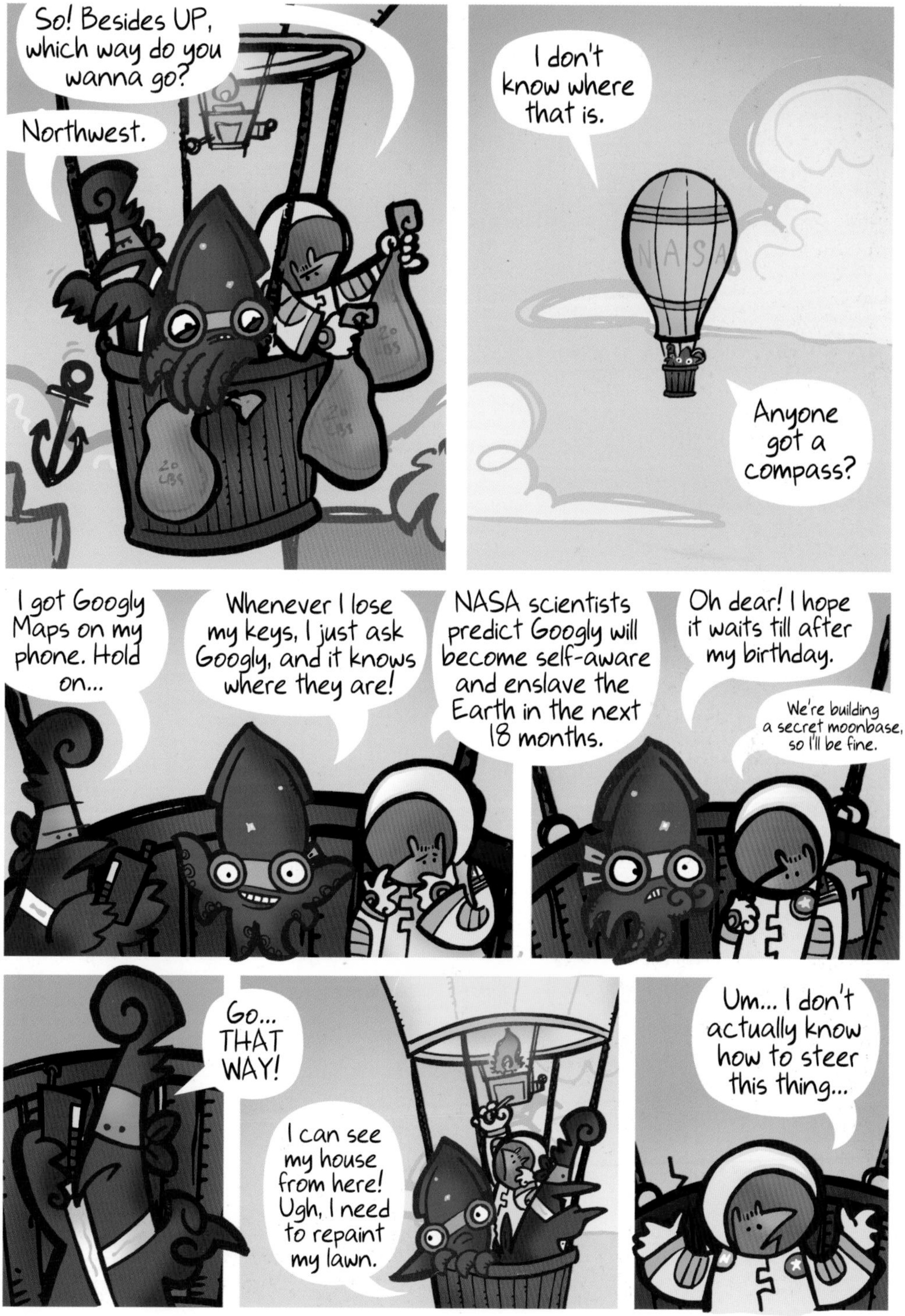
So! Besides UP, which way do you wanna go?
Northwest.
I don't know where that is.
NASA
Anyone got a compass?
I got Googly Maps on my phone. Hold on...
Whenever I lose my keys, I just ask Googly, and it knows where they are!
NASA scientists predict Googly will become self-aware and enslave the Earth in the next 18 months.
Oh dear! I hope it waits till after my birthday.
We're building a secret moonbase, so I'll be fine.
Go... THAT WAY!
I can see my house from here! Ugh, I need to repaint my lawn.
Um... I don't actually know how to steer this thing...

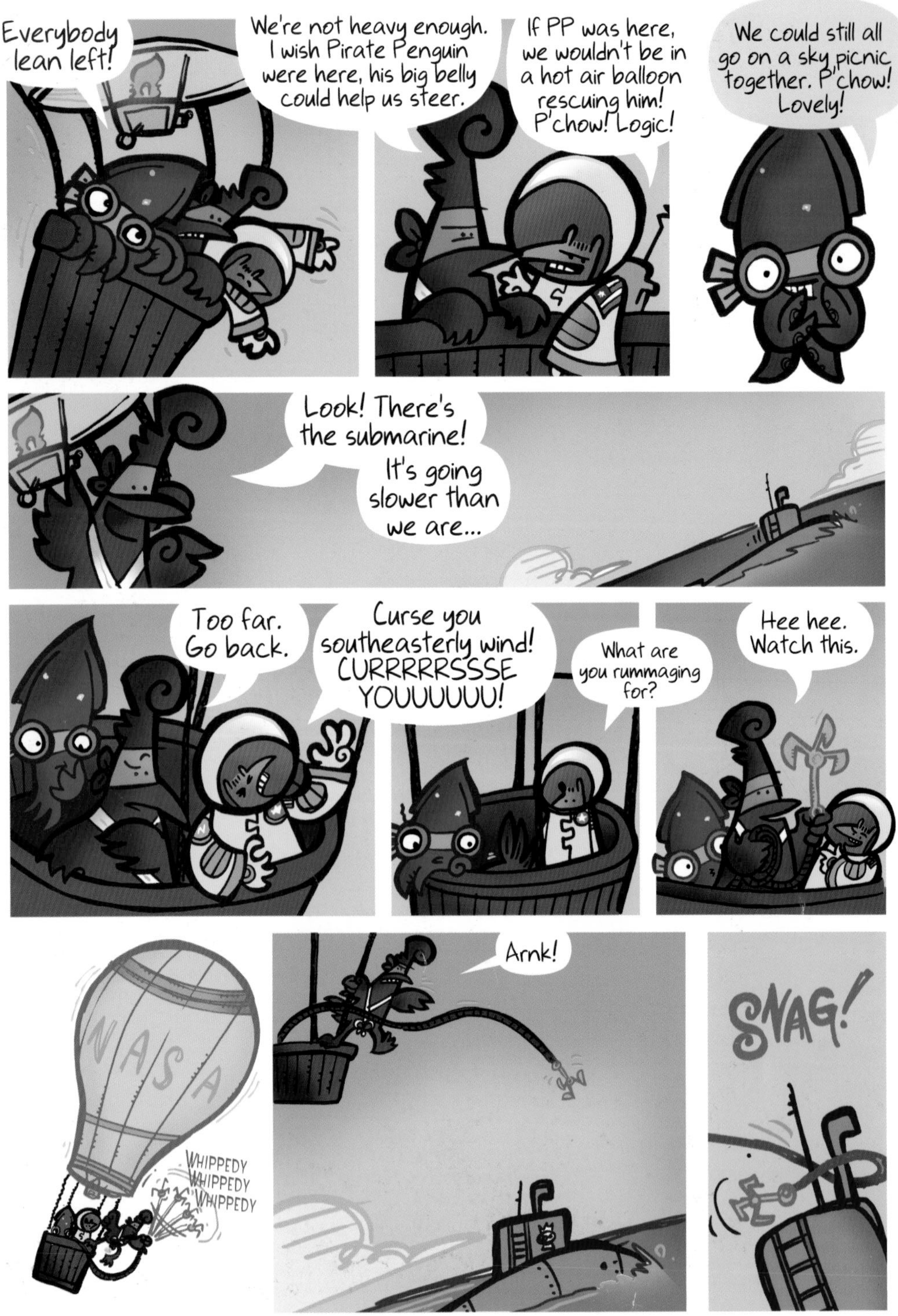
Everybody lean left!
We're not heavy enough. I wish Pirate Penguin were here, his big belly could help us steer.
If PP was here, we wouldn't be in a hot air balloon rescuing him! P'chow! Logic!
We could still all go on a sky picnic together. P'chow! Lovely!
Look! There's the submarine!
It's going slower than we are...
Too far. Go back.
Curse you southeasterly wind! CURRRRRSSSE YOUUUUUU!
What are you rummaging for?
Hee hee. Watch this.
NASA
WHIPPEDY WHIPPEDY WHIPPEDY
Arnk!
SNAG!

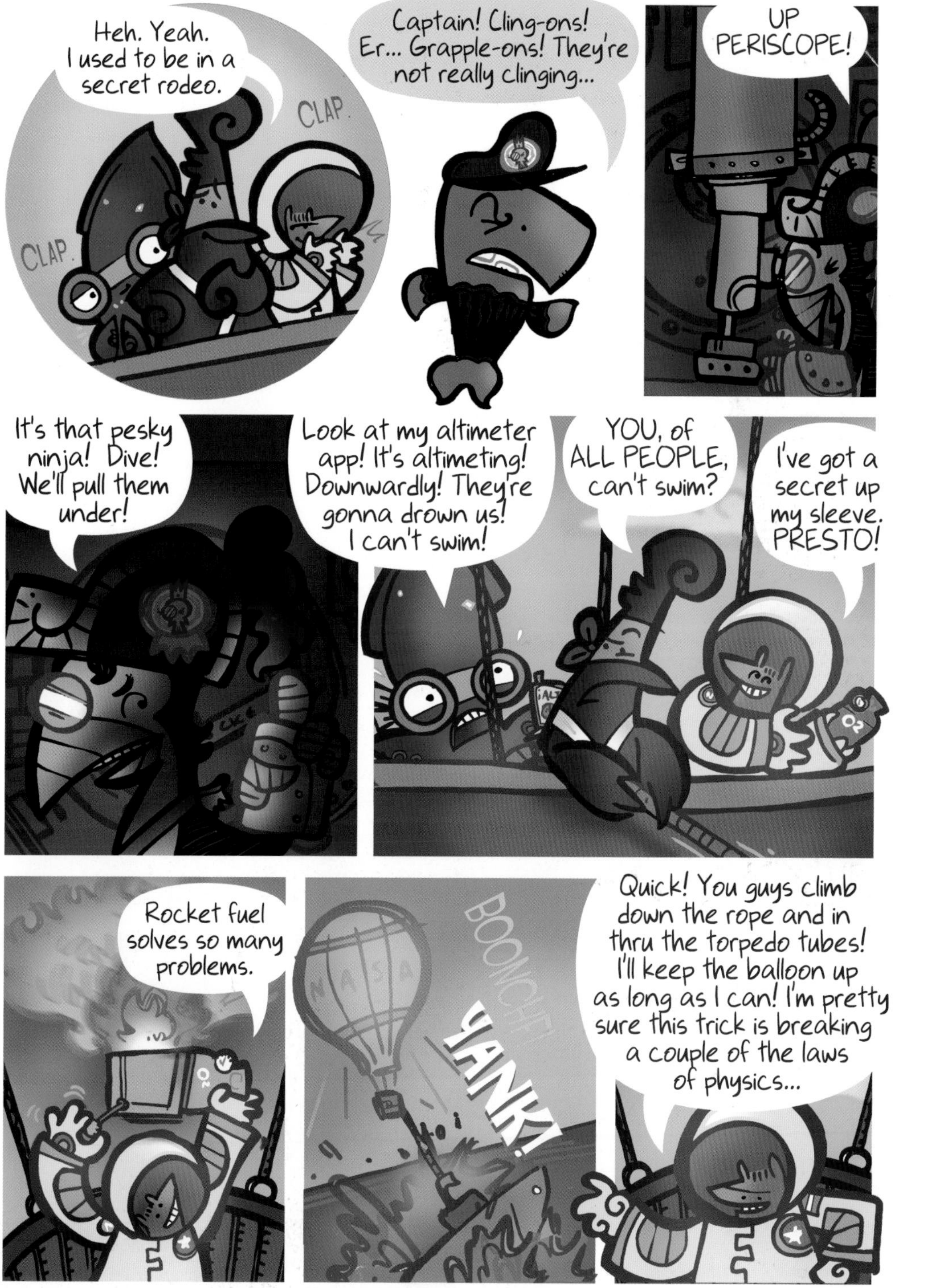
Heh. Yeah. I used to be in a secret rodeo.
CLAP.
CLAP.
Captain! Cling-ons! Er... Grapple-ons! They're not really clinging...
UP PERISCOPE!
It's that pesky ninja! Dive! We'll pull them under!
Look at my altimeter app! It's altimeting! Downwardly! They're gonna drown us! I can't swim!
YOU, of ALL PEOPLE, can't swim?
I've got a secret up my sleeve. PRESTO!
Rocket fuel solves so many problems.
BOONCHH!
YANK!
Quick! You guys climb down the rope and in thru the torpedo tubes! I'll keep the balloon up as long as I can! I'm pretty sure this trick is breaking a couple of the laws of physics...

But...!

NOW!

It's been an honor serving with you, sir!

It sure has! I'm pretty great.

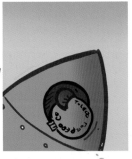

CRASH!

FLOMP

GASP!

Yes! I can breathe underwater! Finally!

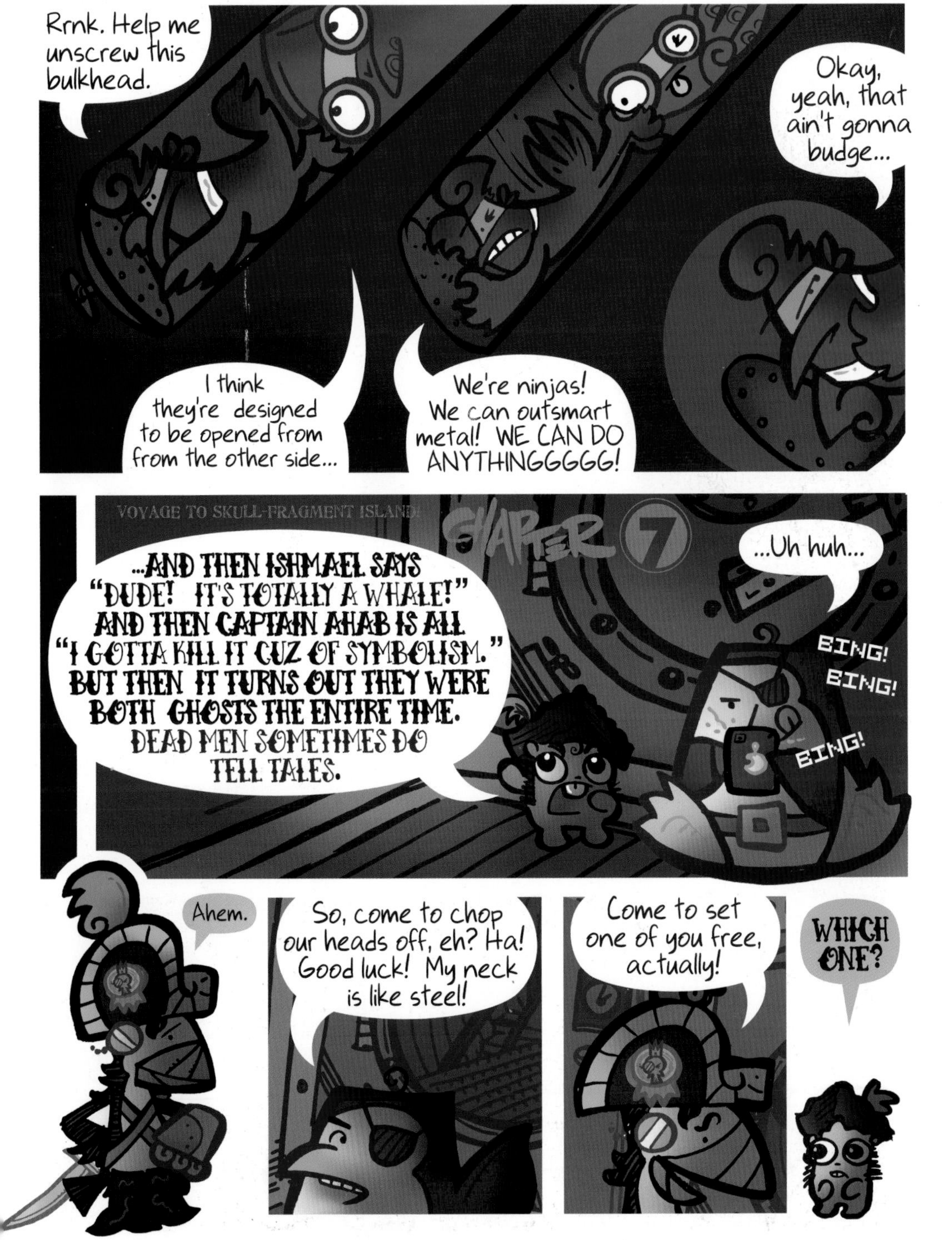
Rrnk. Help me unscrew this bulkhead.
Okay, yeah, that ain't gonna budge...
I think they're designed to be opened from from the other side...
We're ninjas! We can outsmart metal! WE CAN DO ANYTHINGGGGG!
VOYAGE TO SKULL-FRAGMENT ISLAND!
CHAPTER 7
...AND THEN ISHMAEL SAYS "DUDE! IT'S TOTALLY A WHALE!" AND THEN CAPTAIN AHAB IS ALL "I GOTTA KILL IT CUZ OF SYMBOLISM." BUT THEN IT TURNS OUT THEY WERE BOTH GHOSTS THE ENTIRE TIME. DEAD MEN SOMETIMES DO TELL TALES.
...Uh huh...
BING!
BING!
BING!
Ahem.
So, come to chop our heads off, eh? Ha! Good luck! My neck is like steel!
Come to set one of you free, actually!
WHICH ONE?

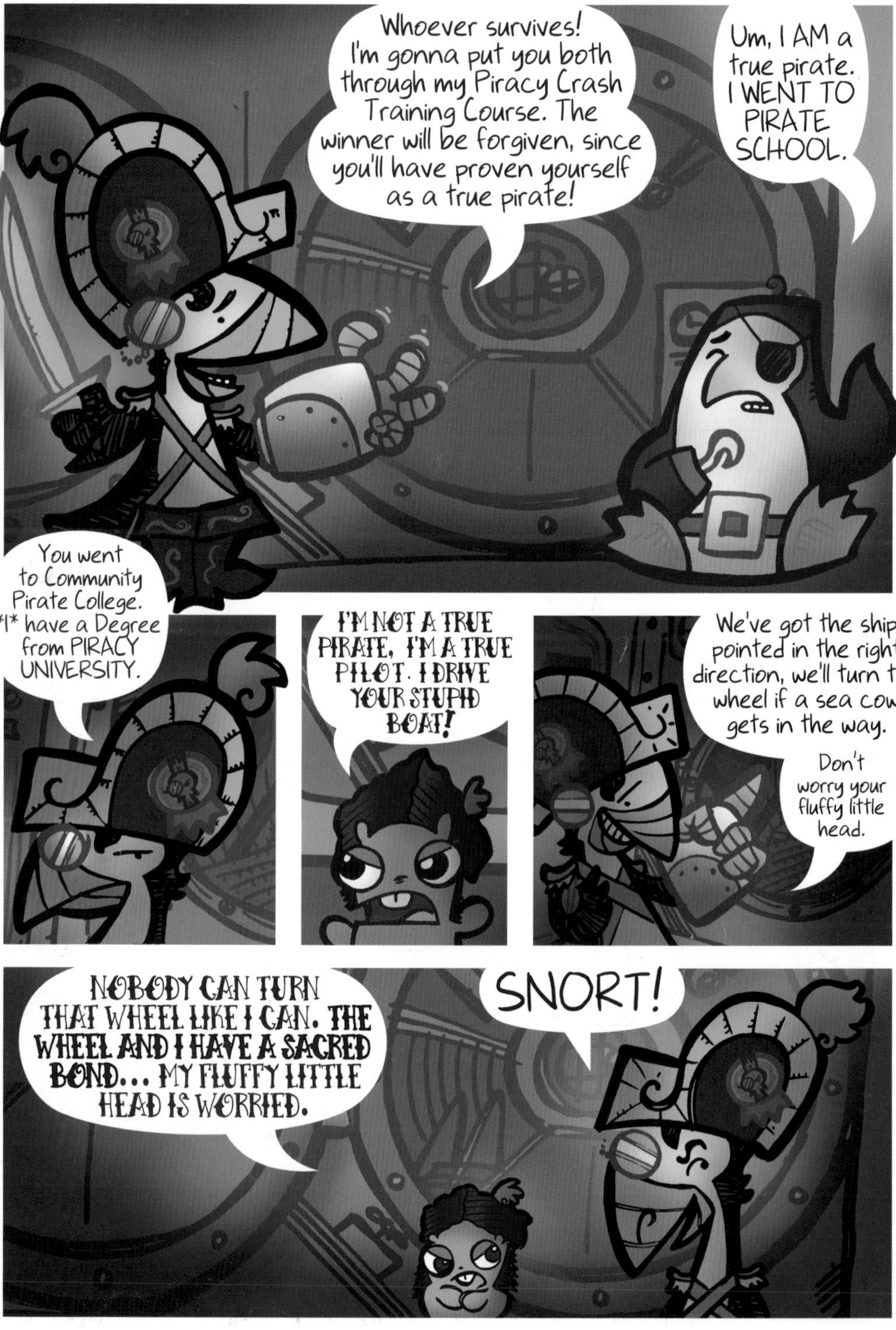
Whoever survives! I'm gonna put you both through my Piracy Crash Training Course. The winner will be forgiven, since you'll have proven yourself as a true pirate!
Um, I AM a true pirate. I WENT TO PIRATE SCHOOL.
You went to Community Pirate College. *I* have a Degree from PIRACY UNIVERSITY.
I'M NOT A TRUE PIRATE, I'M A TRUE PILOT. I DRIVE YOUR STUPID BOAT!
We've got the ship pointed in the right direction, we'll turn the wheel if a sea cow gets in the way.
Don't worry your fluffy little head.
NOBODY CAN TURN THAT WHEEL LIKE I CAN. THE WHEEL AND I HAVE A SACRED BOND... MY FLUFFY LITTLE HEAD IS WORRIED.
SNORT!

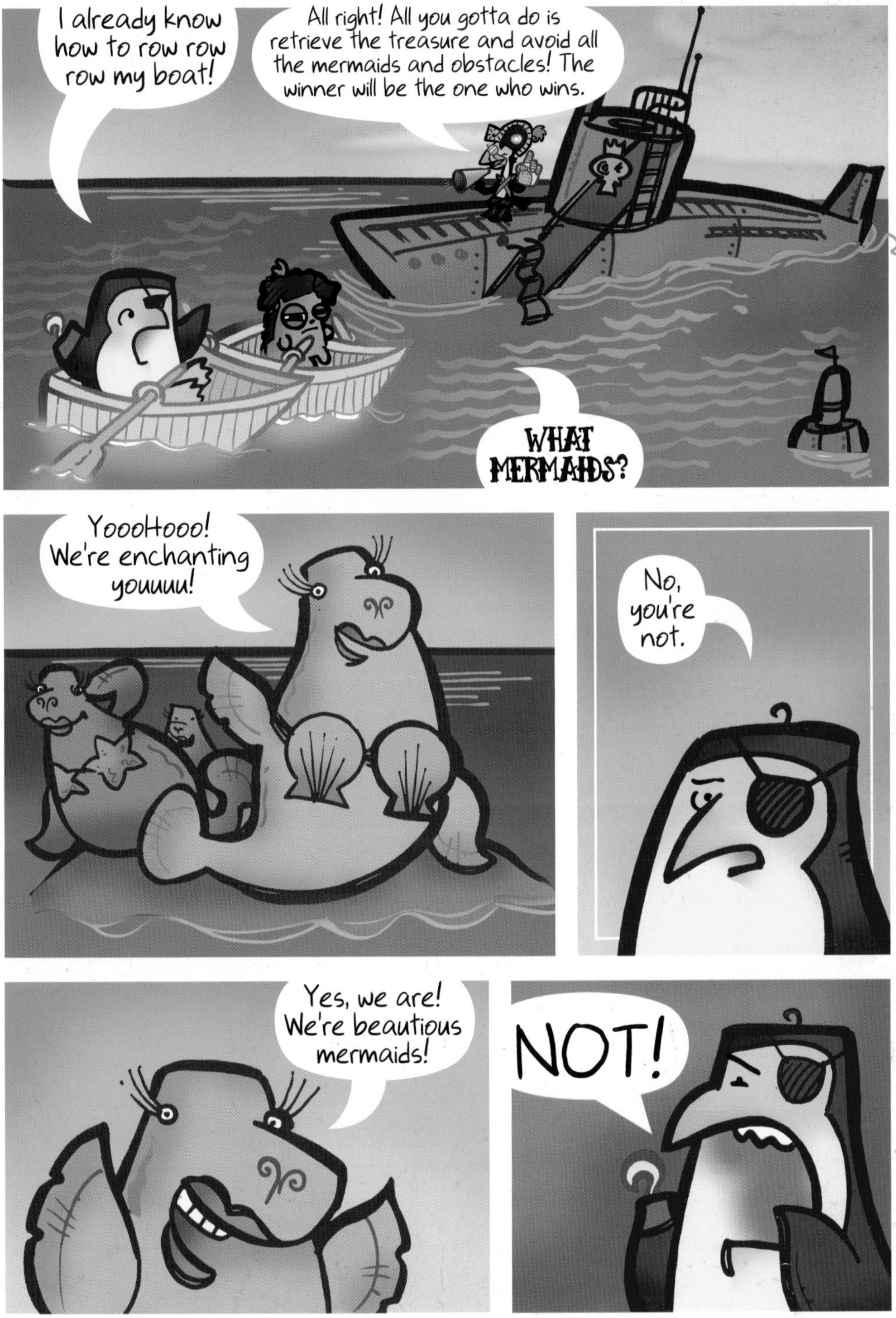

I already know how to row row row my boat!
All right! All you gotta do is retrieve the treasure and avoid all the mermaids and obstacles! The winner will be the one who wins.
WHAT MERMAIDS?
YoooHooo! We're enchanting youuuu!
No, you're not.
Yes, we are! We're beautious mermaids!
NOT!

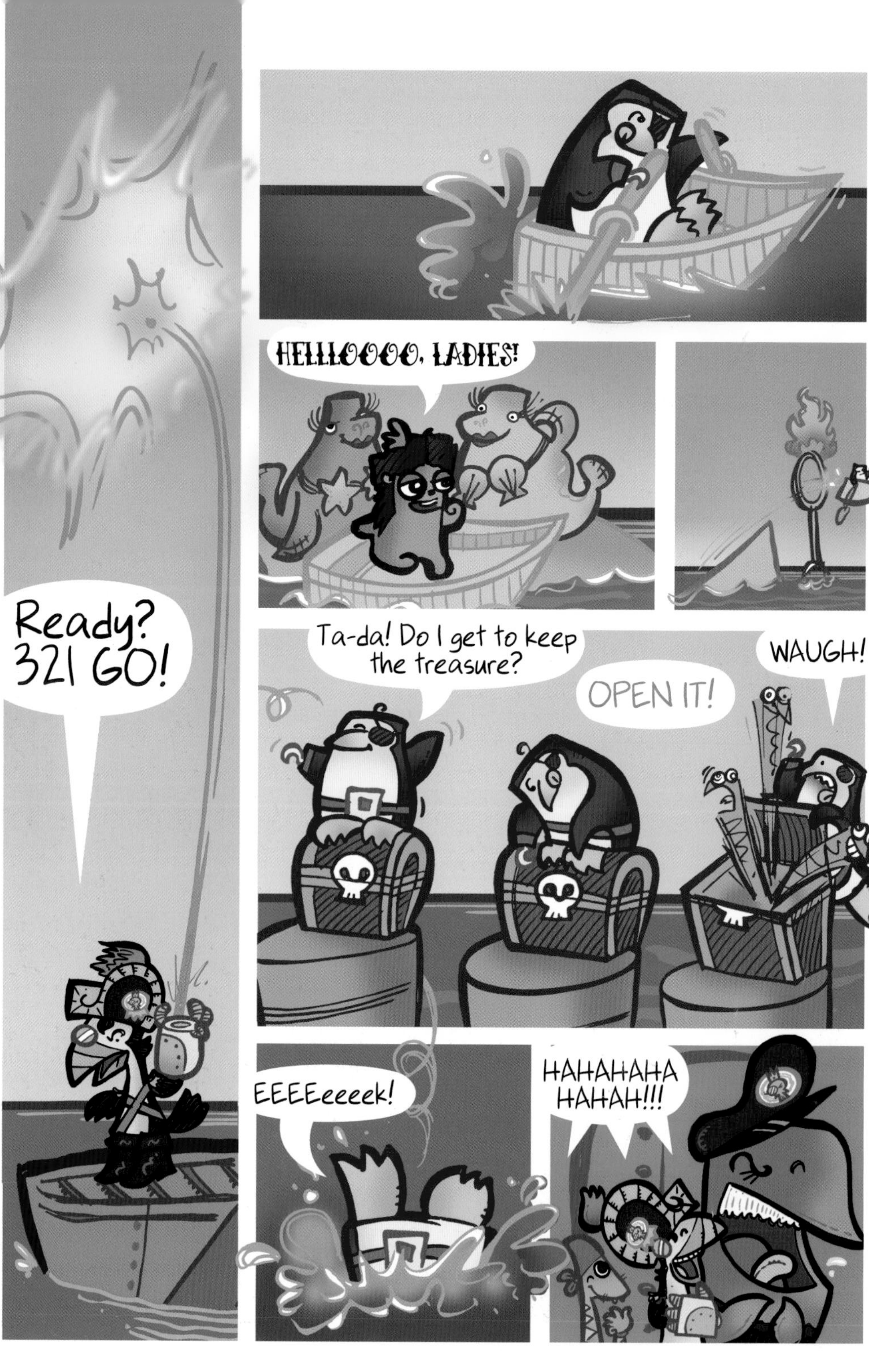
Ready? 321 GO!
HELLLOOOO, LADIES!
Ta-da! Do I get to keep the treasure?
OPEN IT!
WAUGH!
EEEEeeeek!
HAHAHAHA HAHAH!!!

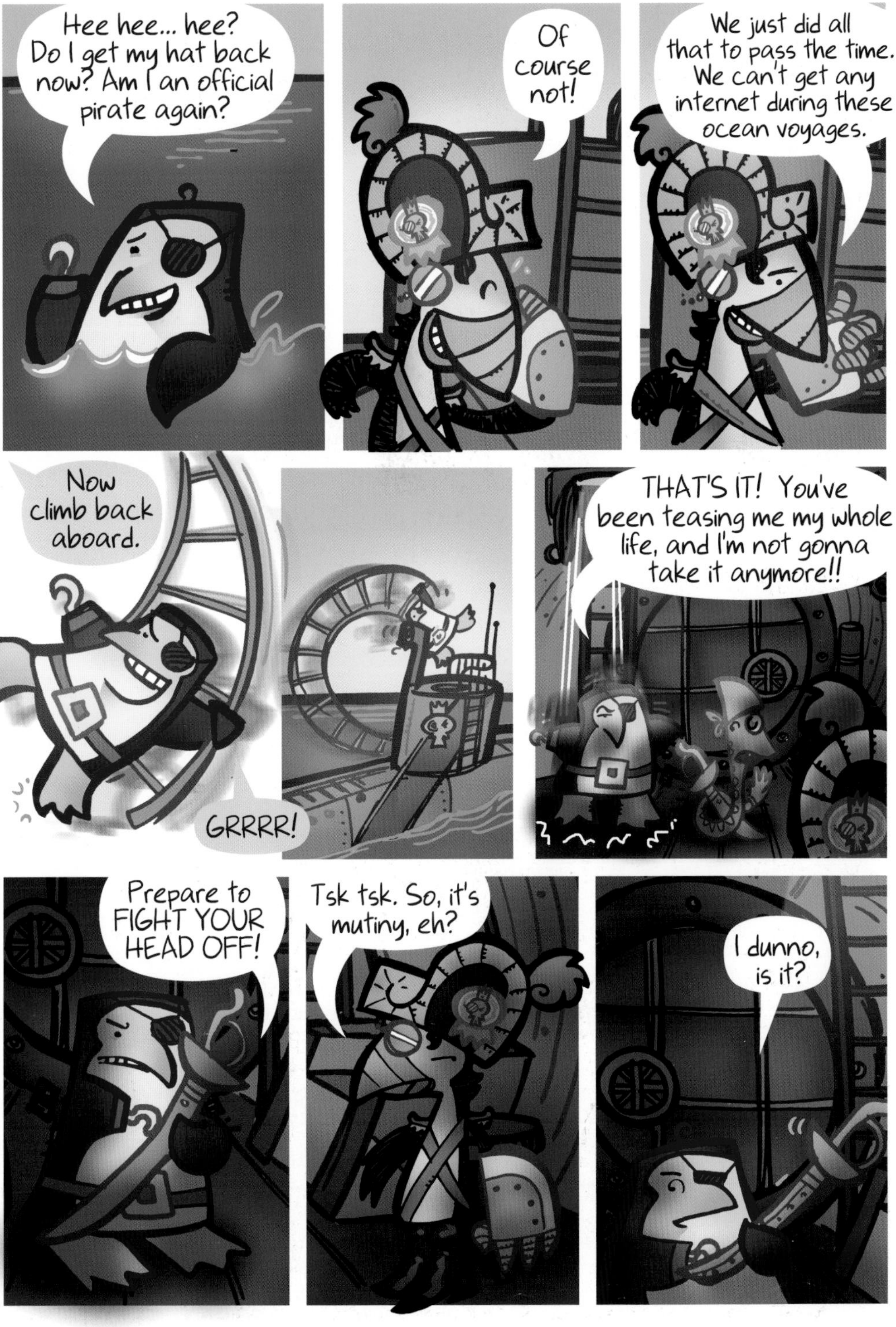
Hee hee... hee? Do I get my hat back now? Am I an official pirate again?
Of course not!
We just did all that to pass the time. We can't get any internet during these ocean voyages.
Now climb back aboard.
GRRRR!
THAT'S IT! You've been teasing me my whole life, and I'm not gonna take it anymore!!
Prepare to FIGHT YOUR HEAD OFF!
Tsk tsk. So, it's mutiny, eh?
I dunno, is it?

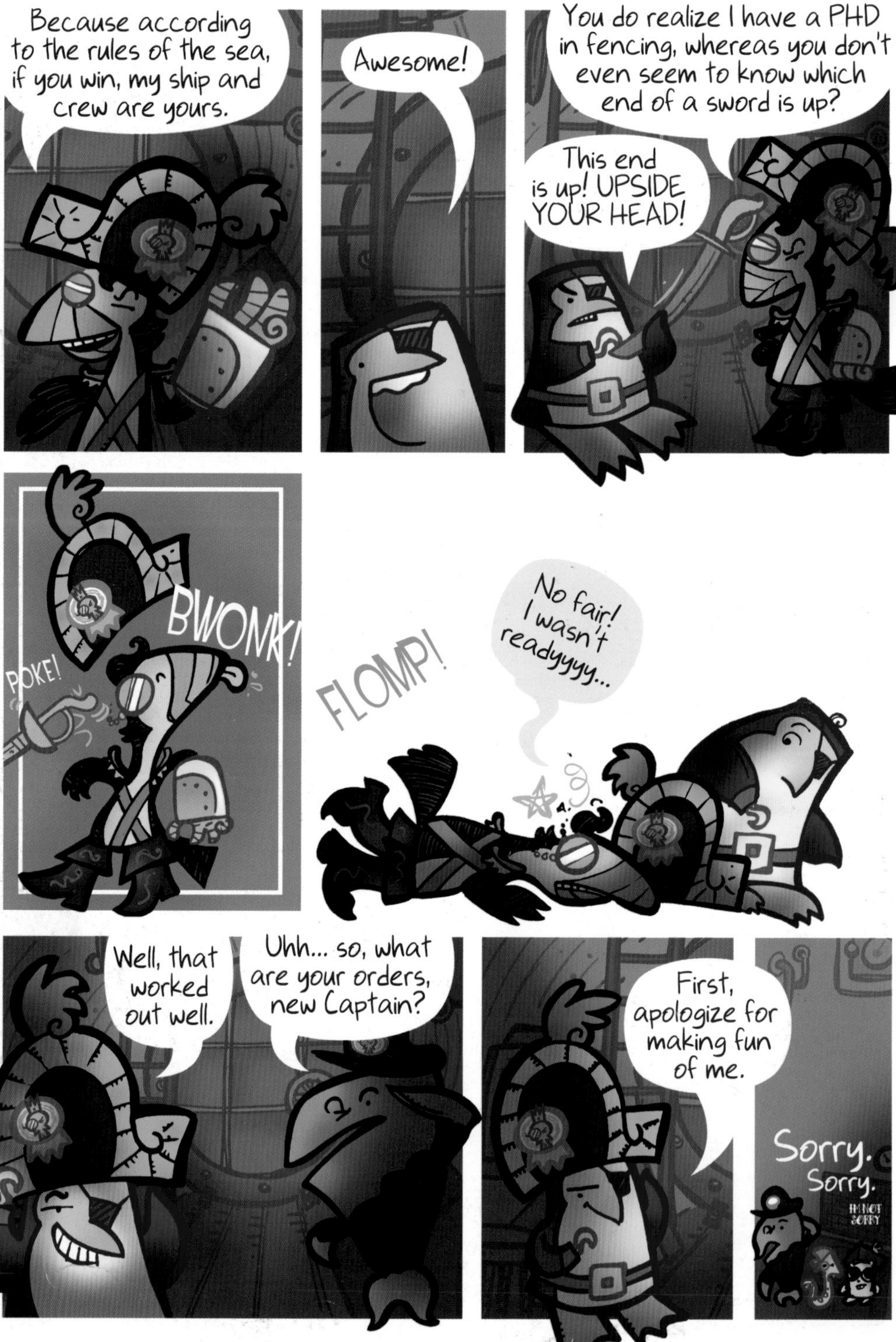
Because according to the rules of the sea, if you win, my ship and crew are yours.
Awesome!
You do realize I have a PHD in fencing, whereas you don't even seem to know which end of a sword is up?
This end is up! UPSIDE YOUR HEAD!
POKE!
BWONK!
FLOMP!
No fair! I wasn't readyyyy...
Well, that worked out well.
Uhh... so, what are your orders, new Captain?
First, apologize for making fun of me.
Sorry.
Sorry.
I'M NOT SORRY

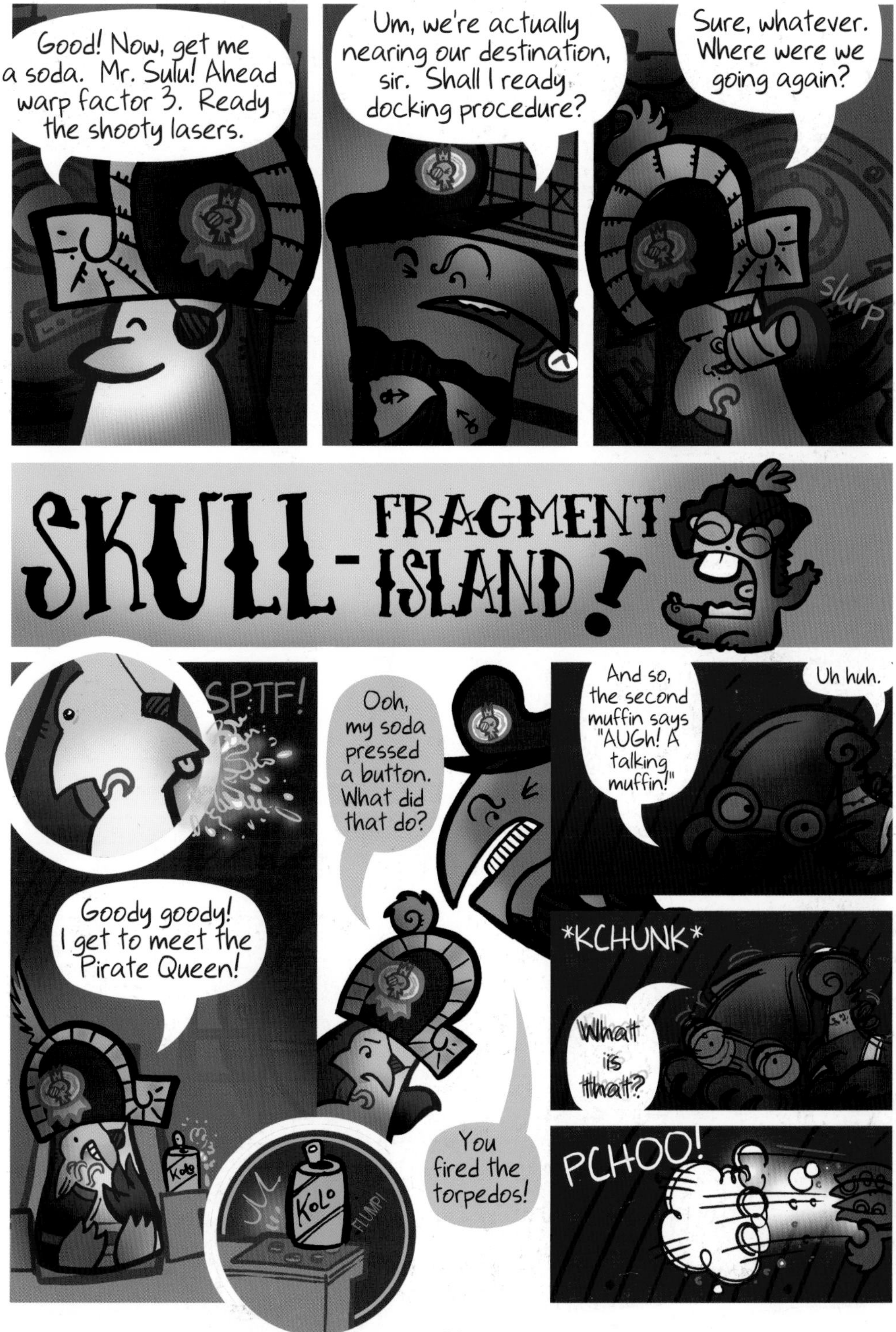
Good! Now, get me a soda. Mr. Sulu! Ahead warp factor 3. Ready the shooty lasers.
Um, we're actually nearing our destination, sir. Shall I ready docking procedure?
Sure, whatever. Where were we going again?
slurp
SKULL-FRAGMENT-ISLAND!
SPTF!
Ooh, my soda pressed a button. What did that do?
And so, the second muffin says "AUGH! A talking muffin!"
Uh huh.
Goody goody! I get to meet the Pirate Queen!
KoLo
FLUMP!
You fired the torpedos!
KCHUNK
What is that?
PCHOO!

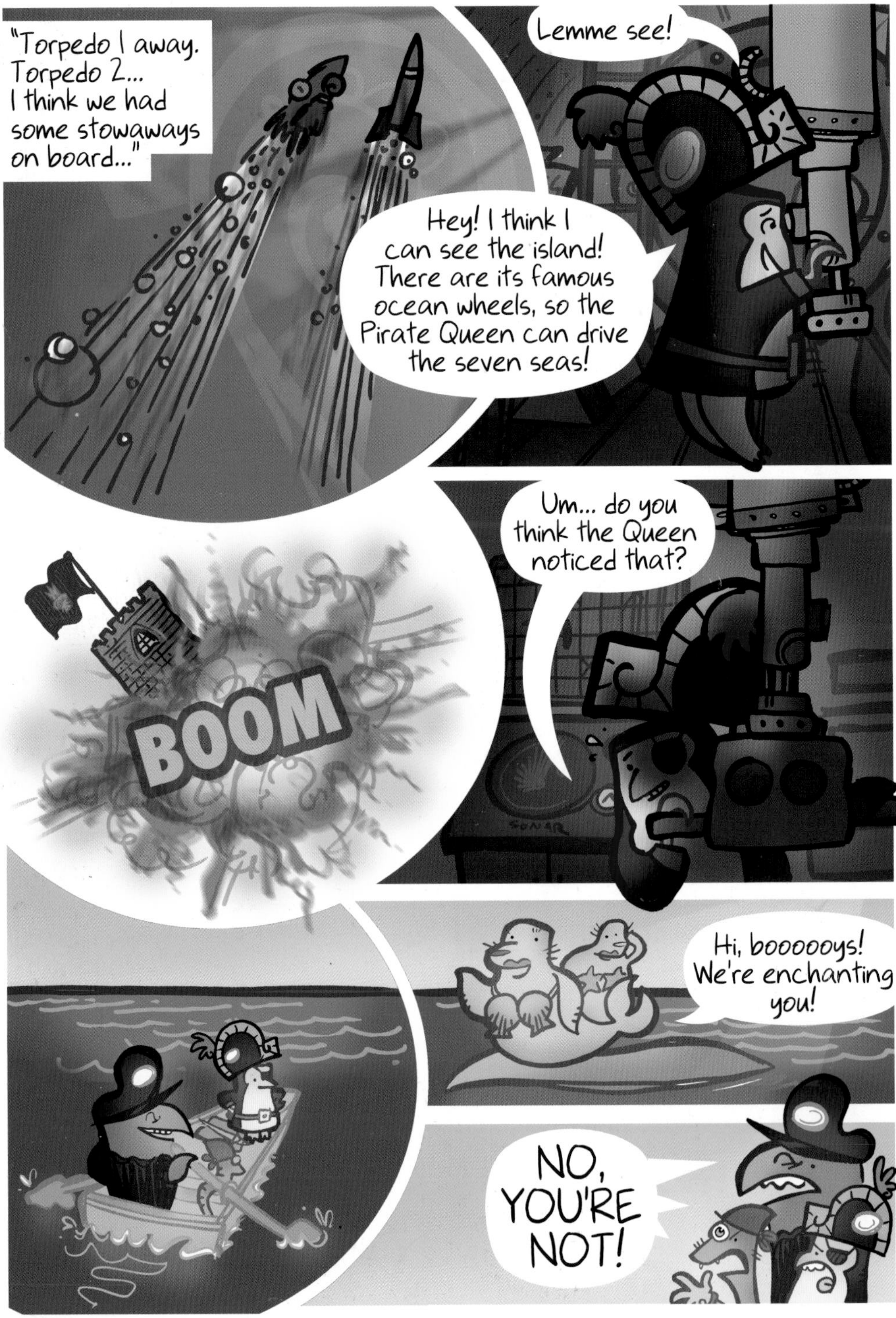
"Torpedo 1 away. Torpedo 2... I think we had some stowaways on board..."
Lemme see!
Hey! I think I can see the island! There are its famous ocean wheels, so the Pirate Queen can drive the seven seas!
Um... do you think the Queen noticed that?
BOOM
SONAR
Hi, boooooys! We're enchanting you!
NO, YOU'RE NOT!

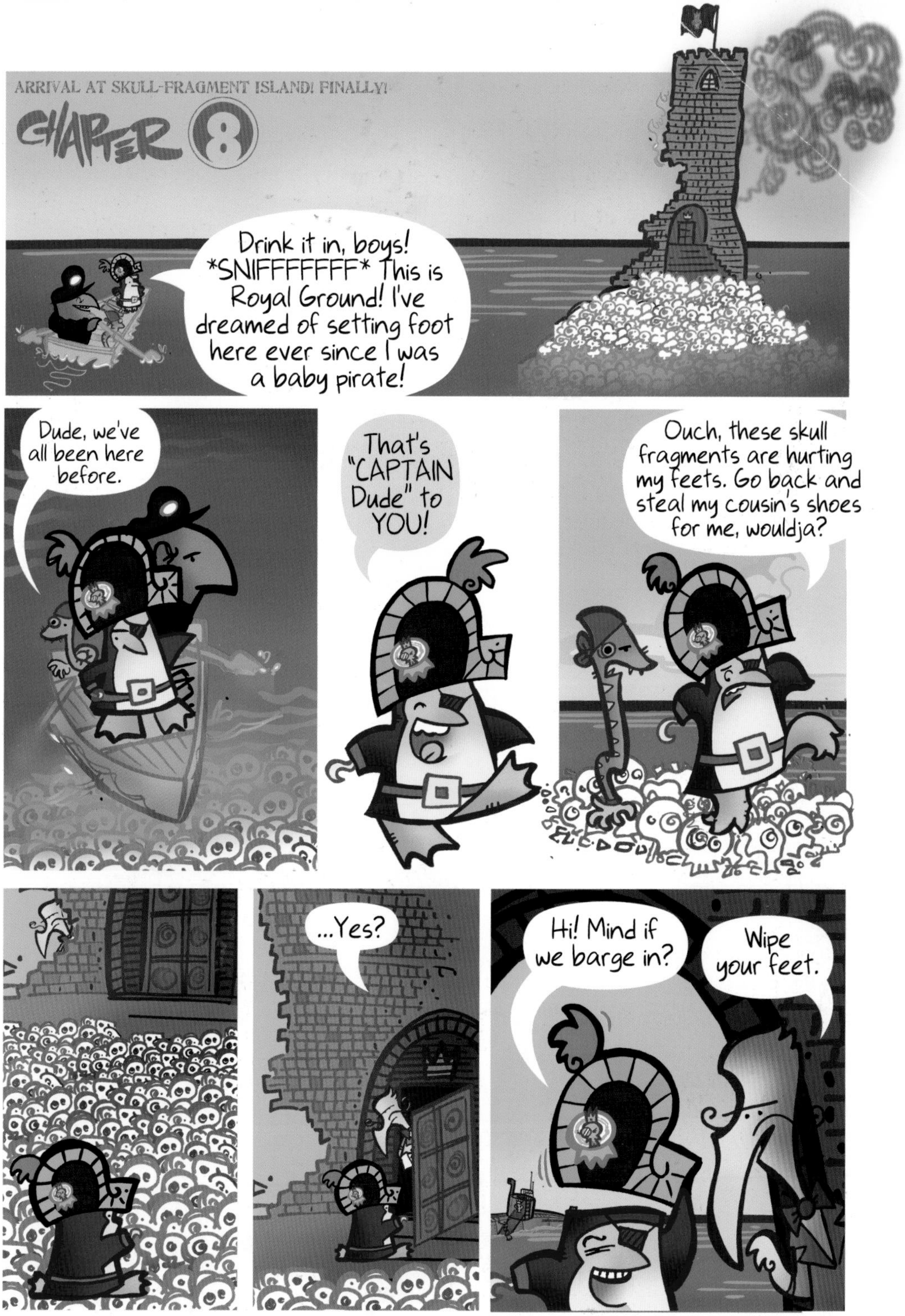
ARRIVAL AT SKULL-FRAGMENT ISLAND! FINALLY!
CHAPTER 8
Drink it in, boys! *SNIFFFFFFFF* This is Royal Ground! I've dreamed of setting foot here ever since I was a baby pirate!
Dude, we've all been here before.
That's "CAPTAIN Dude" to YOU!
Ouch, these skull fragments are hurting my feets. Go back and steal my cousin's shoes for me, wouldja?
...Yes?
Hi! Mind if we barge in?
Wipe your feet.

Oog.

Don't you just hate the ocean? Where are we? How's my hair? What's the plan?

I think we gotta climb this tower. Then we make up the plan as we go along based on whatever kind of stuff happens.

Ok.

So what's the deal with this bad guy we're supposed to fight?

He's got a big black hat and epaulettes, and a whadayacallit-- thing over one eye.

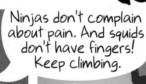

Ooow! I cut my finger on this stupid brick!

Ninjas don't complain about pain. And squids don't have fingers! Keep climbing.

I'd rather take the stairs.

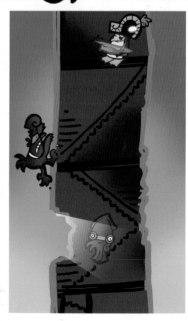

86

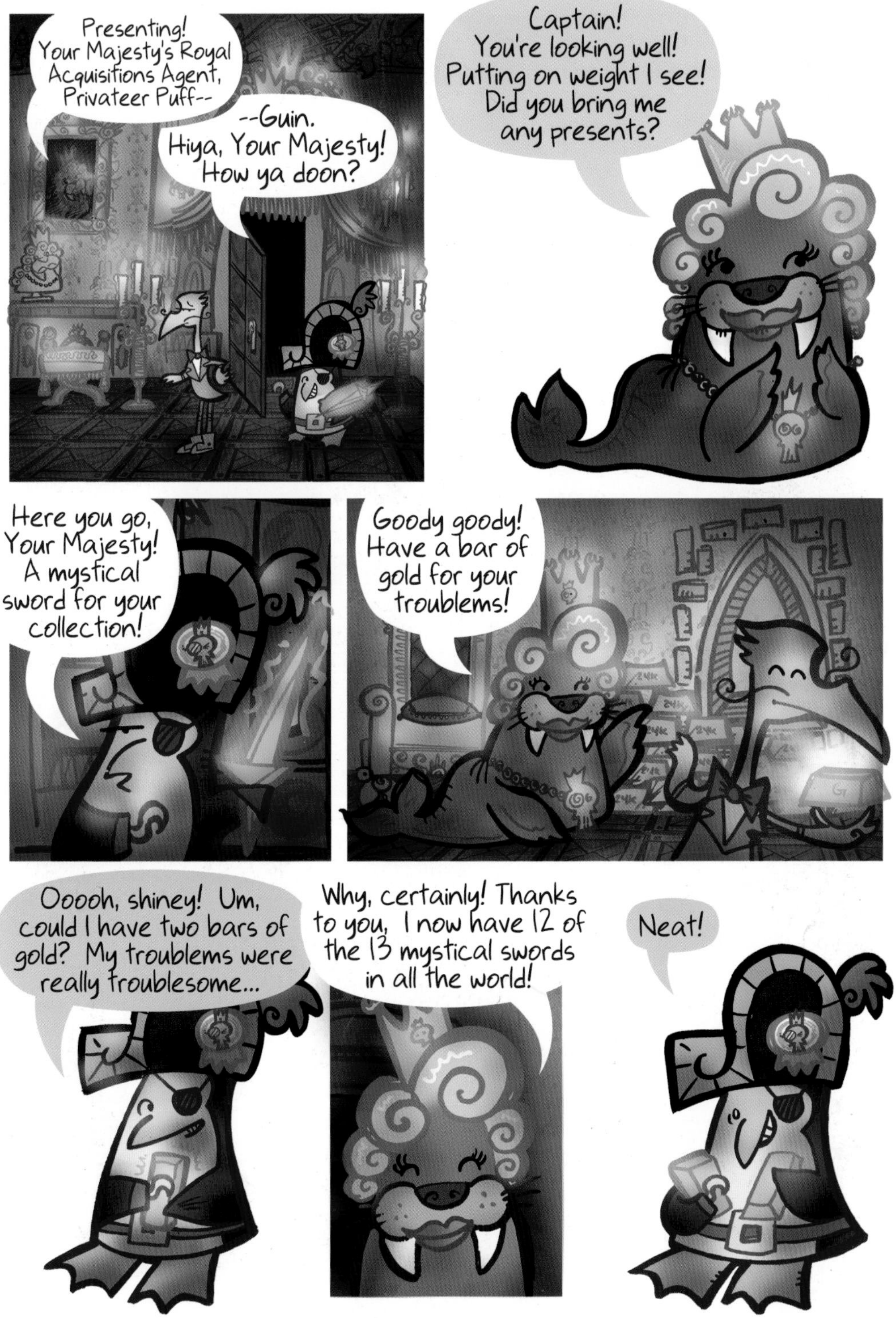

Presenting! Your Majesty's Royal Acquisitions Agent, Privateer Puff--
--Guin. Hiya, Your Majesty! How ya doon?
Captain! You're looking well! Putting on weight I see! Did you bring me any presents?
Here you go, Your Majesty! A mystical sword for your collection!
Goody goody! Have a bar of gold for your troublems!
24K
Ooooh, shiney! Um, could I have two bars of gold? My troublems were really troublesome...
Why, certainly! Thanks to you, I now have 12 of the 13 mystical swords in all the world!
Neat!

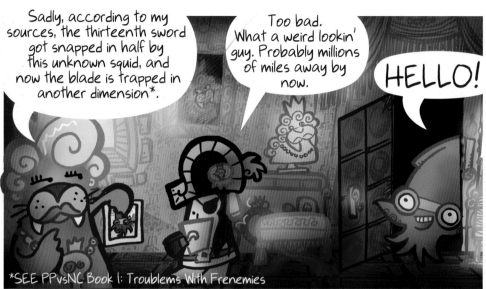

Sadly, according to my sources, the thirteenth sword got snapped in half by this unknown squid, and now the blade is trapped in another dimension*.

Too bad. What a weird lookin' guy. Probably millions of miles away by now.

HELLO!

*SEE PPvsNC Book I: Troublems With Frenemies

Wug.

Oi! Leggo my boots!

Sorry, Captain, new Captain's orders. Gotta steal your shoes.

How loyal are you to him?

Not very.

Good. Unclap my irons and round up the crew: we're gonna remutiny.

You're not in irons.

He just left me on the floor? Tsk tsk. My cousin has no standards.

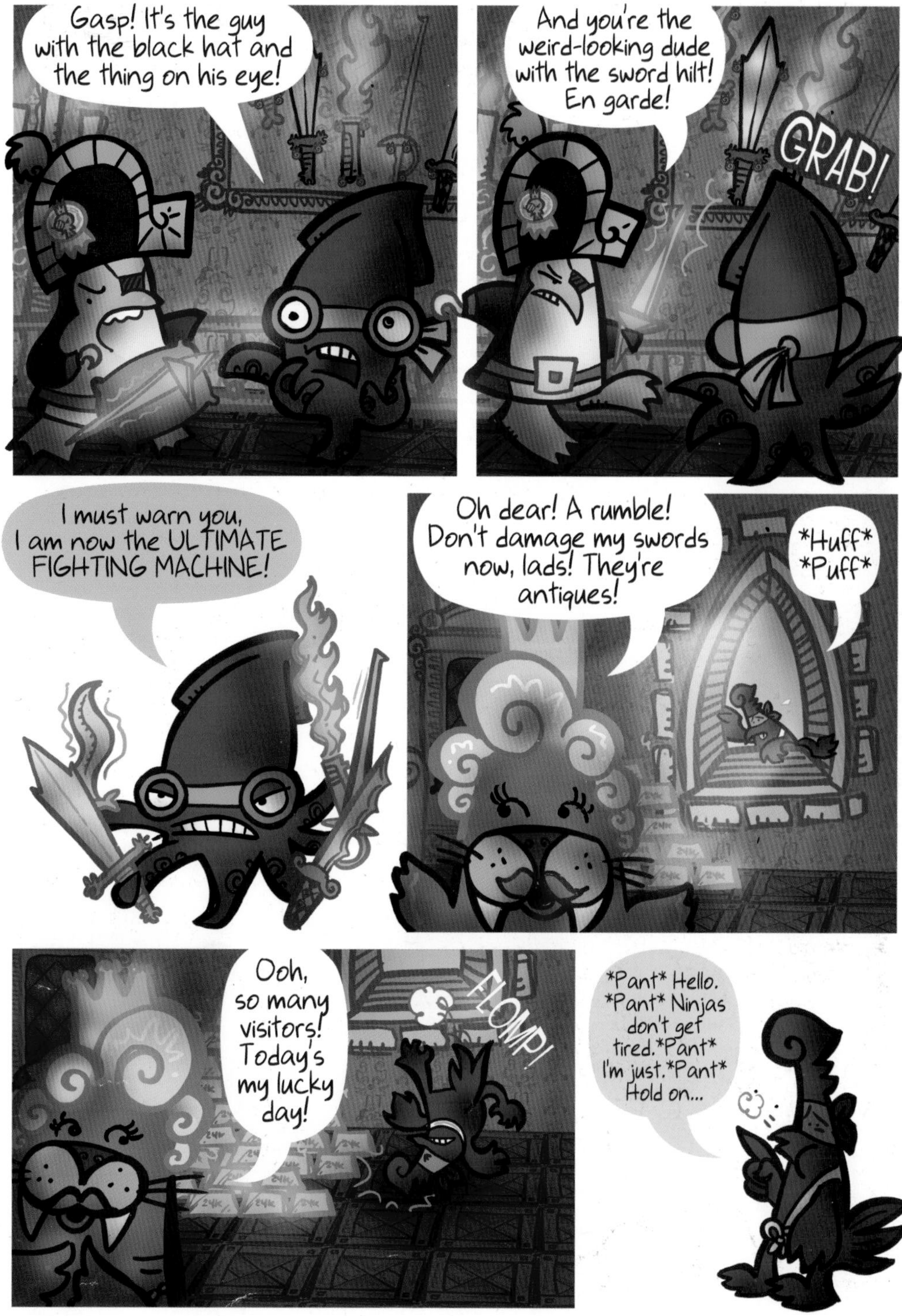

Gasp! It's the guy with the black hat and the thing on his eye!
And you're the weird-looking dude with the sword hilt! En garde!
GRAB!
I must warn you, I am now the ULTIMATE FIGHTING MACHINE!
Oh dear! A rumble! Don't damage my swords now, lads! They're antiques!
Huff *Puff*
Ooh, so many visitors! Today's my lucky day!
FLOMP!
Pant Hello. *Pant* Ninjas don't get tired. *Pant* I'm just. *Pant* Hold on...

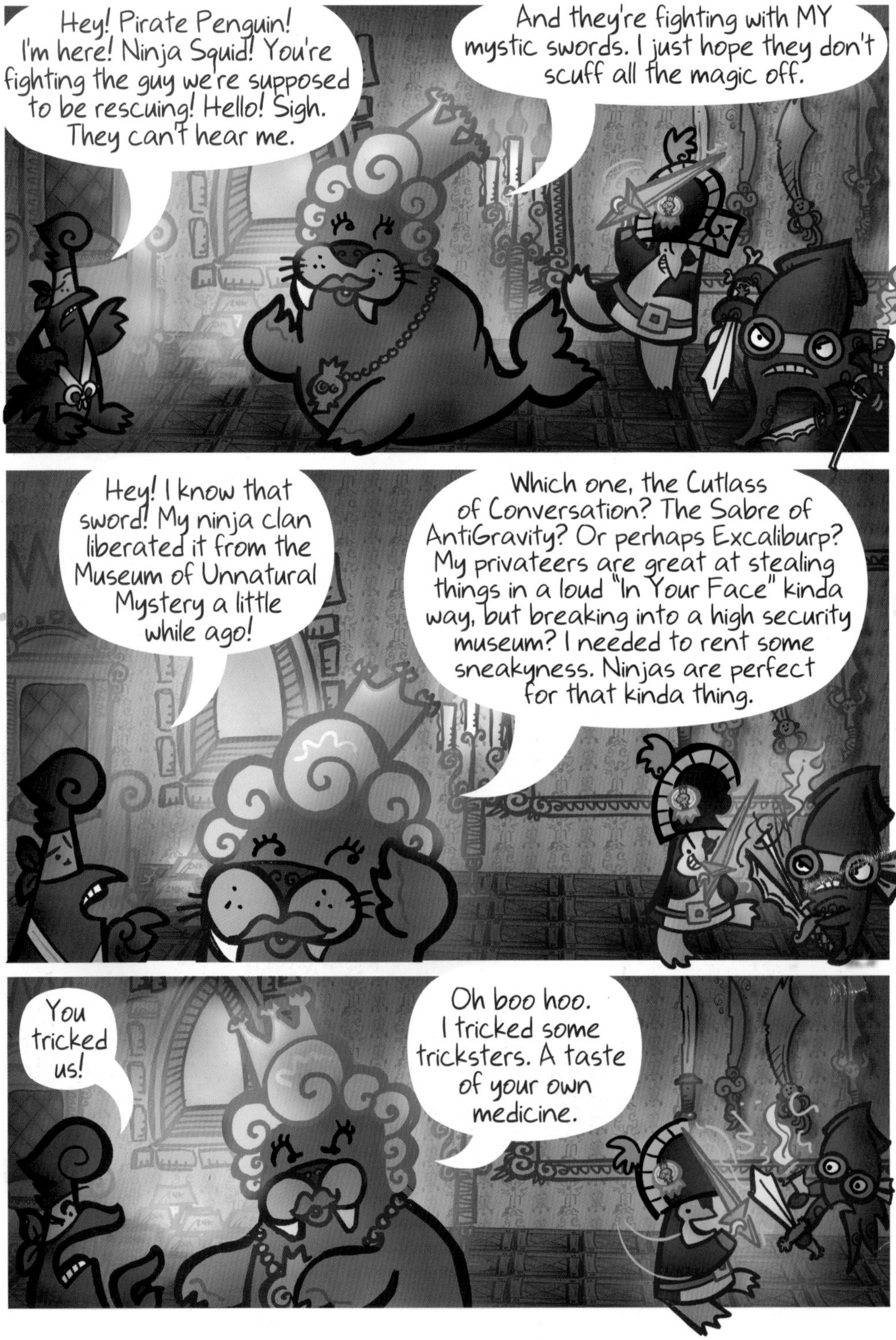
Hey! Pirate Penguin! I'm here! Ninja Squid! You're fighting the guy we're supposed to be rescuing! Hello! Sigh. They can't hear me.
And they're fighting with MY mystic swords. I just hope they don't scuff all the magic off.
Hey! I know that sword! My ninja clan liberated it from the Museum of Unnatural Mystery a little while ago!
Which one, the Cutlass of Conversation? The Sabre of AntiGravity? Or perhaps Excaliburp? My privateers are great at stealing things in a loud "In Your Face" kinda way, but breaking into a high security museum? I needed to rent some sneakyness. Ninjas are perfect for that kinda thing.
You tricked us!
Oh boo hoo. I tricked some tricksters. A taste of your own medicine.

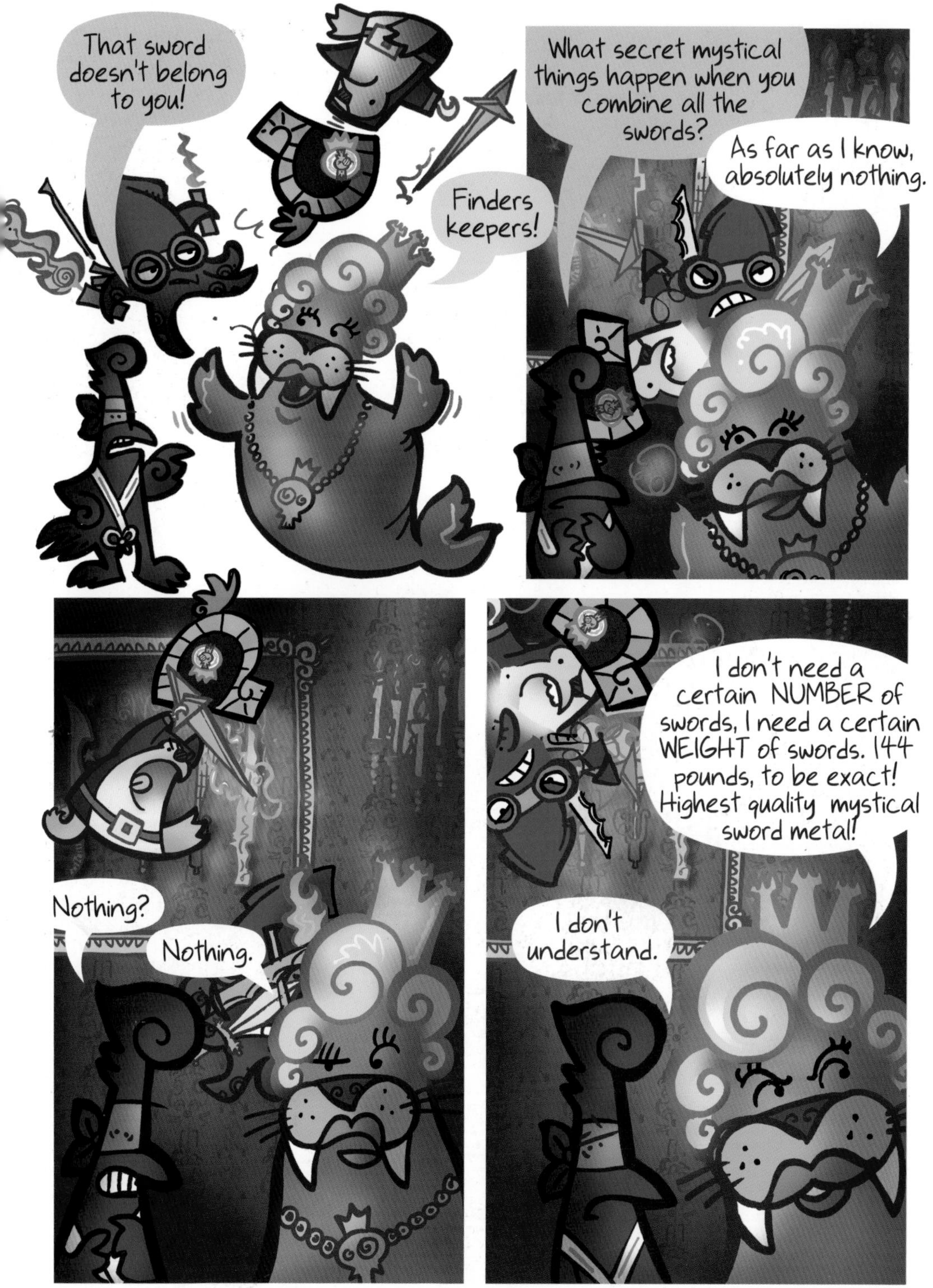
That sword doesn't belong to you!
Finders keepers!
What secret mystical things happen when you combine all the swords?
As far as I know, absolutely nothing.
Nothing?
Nothing.
I don't need a certain NUMBER of swords, I need a certain WEIGHT of swords. 144 pounds, to be exact! Highest quality mystical sword metal!
I don't understand.

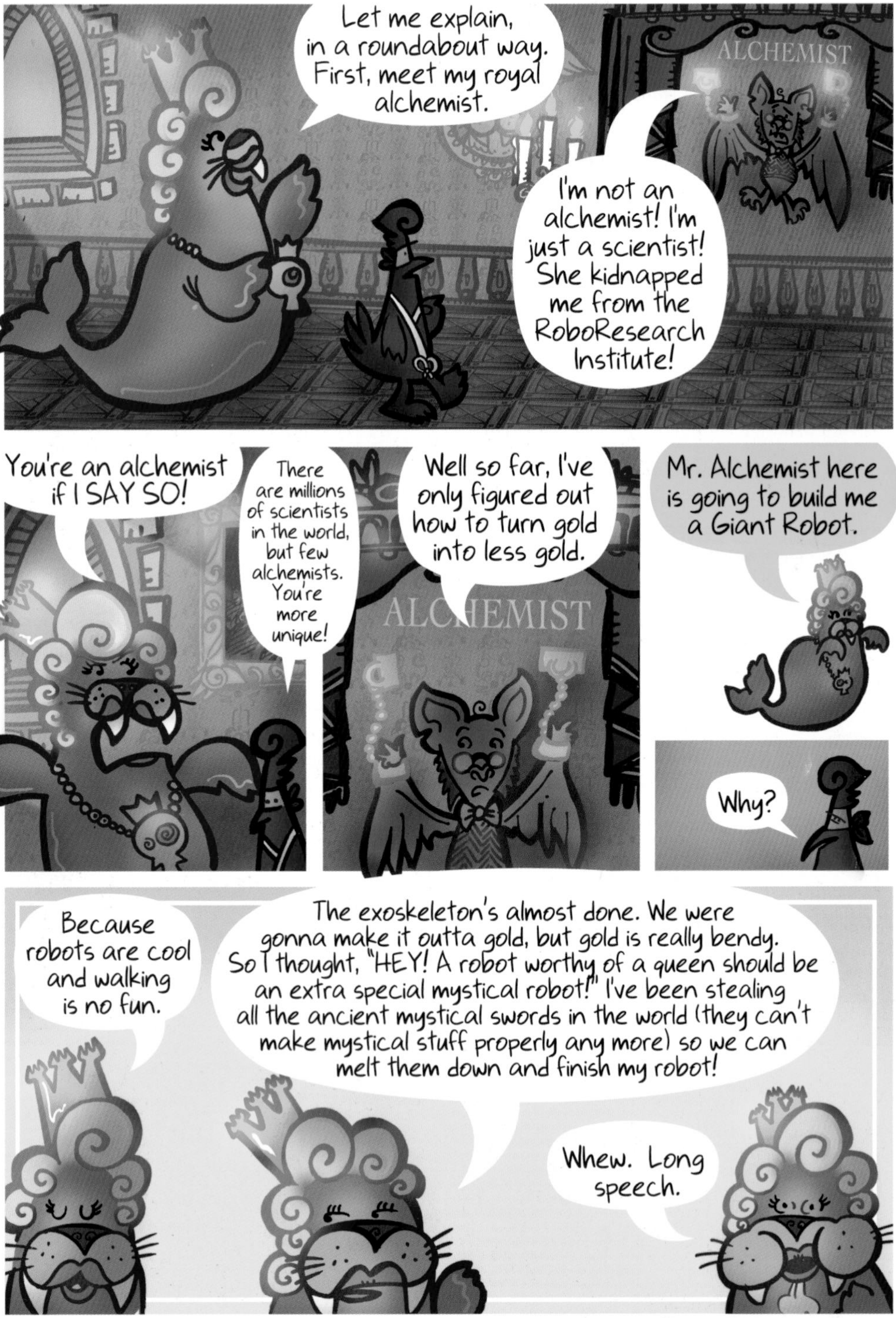
Let me explain, in a roundabout way. First, meet my royal alchemist.
ALCHEMIST
I'm not an alchemist! I'm just a scientist! She kidnapped me from the RoboResearch Institute!
You're an alchemist if I SAY SO!
There are millions of scientists in the world, but few alchemists. You're more unique!
Well so far, I've only figured out how to turn gold into less gold.
ALCHEMIST
Mr. Alchemist here is going to build me a Giant Robot.
Why?
Because robots are cool and walking is no fun.
The exoskeleton's almost done. We were gonna make it outta gold, but gold is really bendy. So I thought, "HEY! A robot worthy of a queen should be an extra special mystical robot!" I've been stealing all the ancient mystical swords in the world (they can't make mystical stuff properly any more) so we can melt them down and finish my robot!
Whew. Long speech.

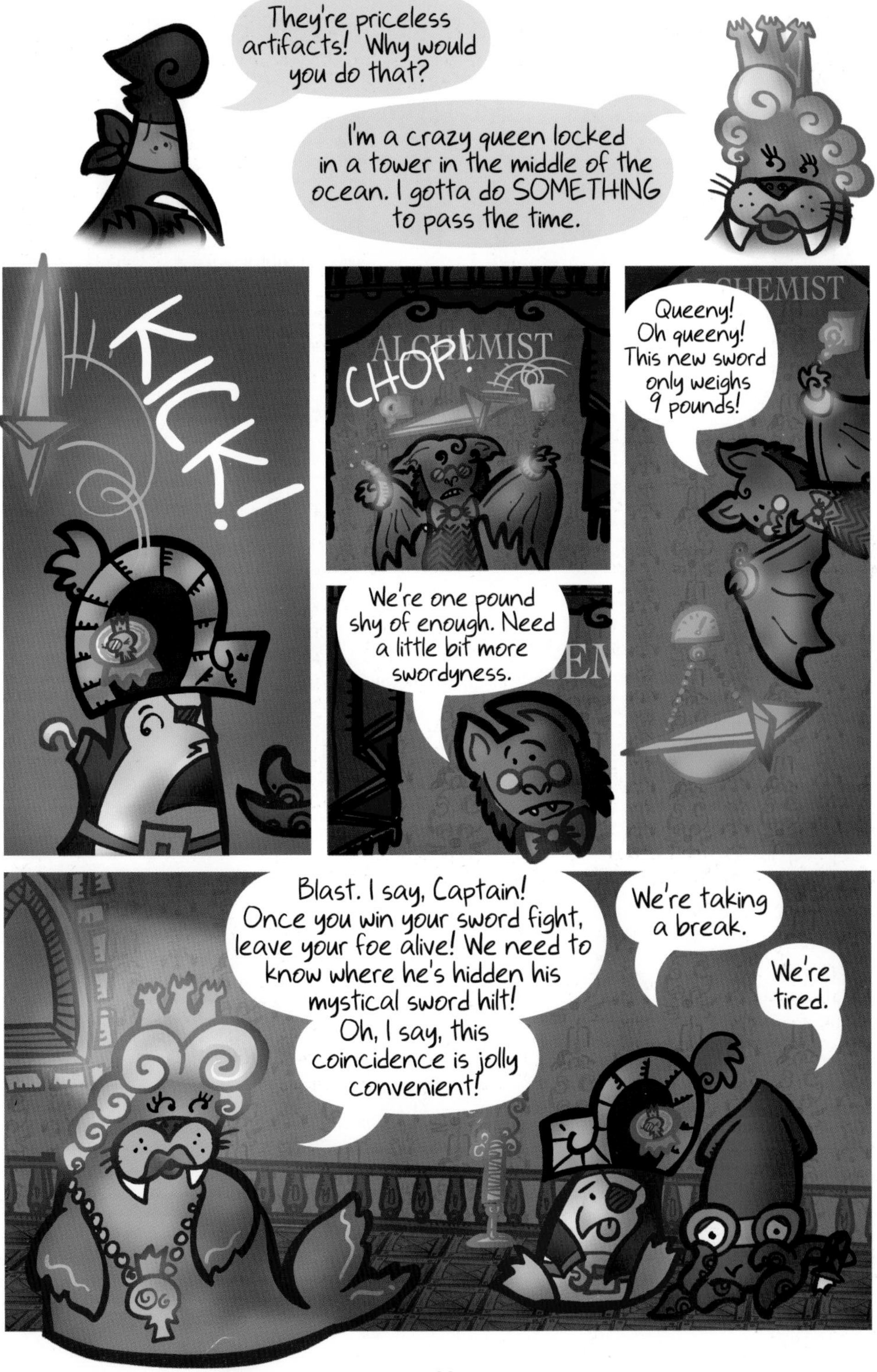
They're priceless artifacts! Why would you do that?
I'm a crazy queen locked in a tower in the middle of the ocean. I gotta do SOMETHING to pass the time.
KICK!
CHOP!
ALCHEMIST
Queeny! Oh queeny! This new sword only weighs 9 pounds!
We're one pound shy of enough. Need a little bit more swordyness.
Blast. I say, Captain! Once you win your sword fight, leave your foe alive! We need to know where he's hidden his mystical sword hilt! Oh, I say, this coincidence is jolly convenient!
We're taking a break.
We're tired.

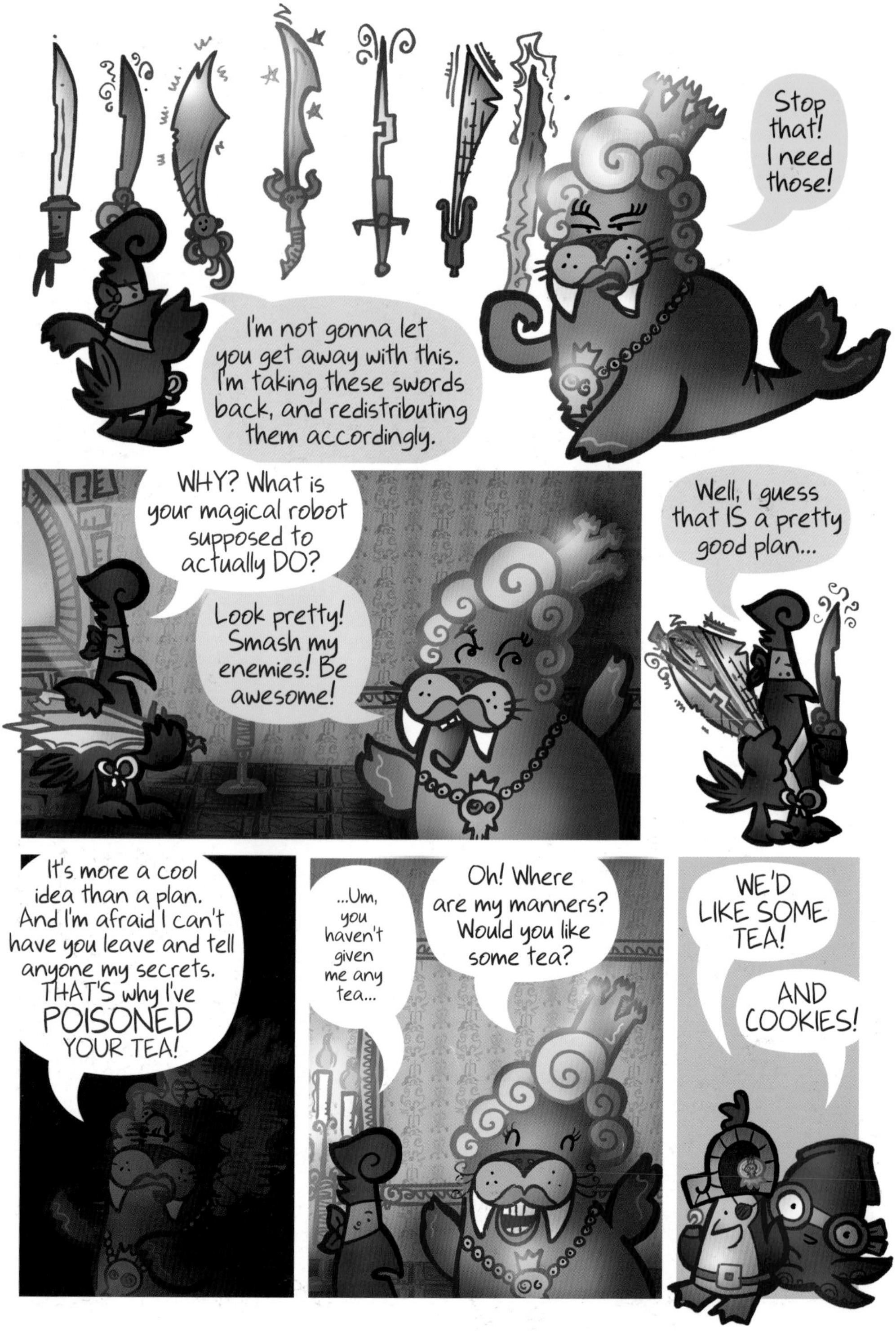
Stop that! I need those!
I'm not gonna let you get away with this. I'm taking these swords back, and redistributing them accordingly.
WHY? What is your magical robot supposed to actually DO?
Look pretty! Smash my enemies! Be awesome!
Well, I guess that IS a pretty good plan...
It's more a cool idea than a plan. And I'm afraid I can't have you leave and tell anyone my secrets. THAT'S why I've POISONED YOUR TEA!
...Um, you haven't given me any tea...
Oh! Where are my manners? Would you like some tea?
WE'D LIKE SOME TEA!
AND COOKIES!

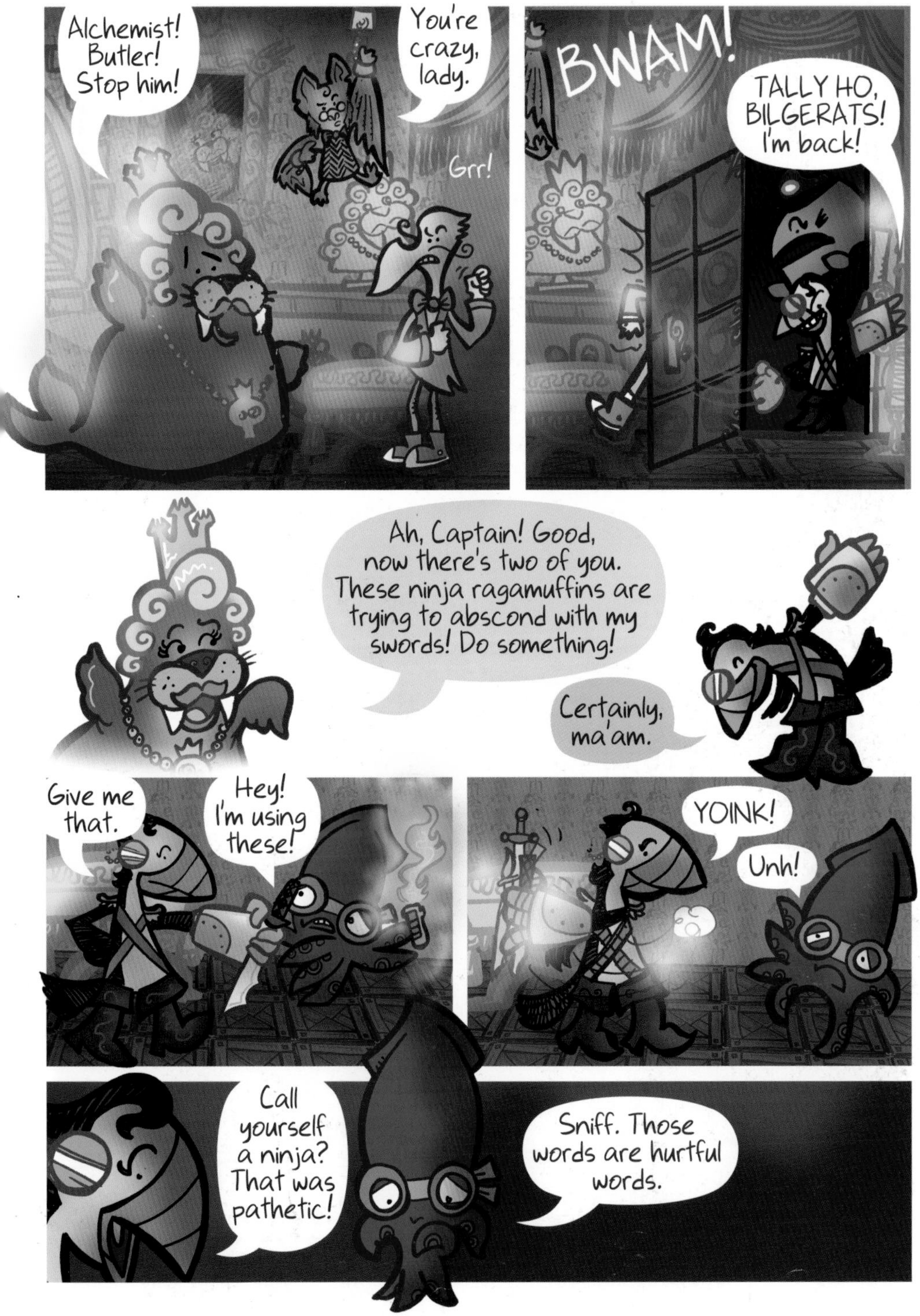

Alchemist! Butler! Stop him!
You're crazy, lady.
Grr!
BWAM!
TALLY HO, BILGERATS! I'm back!
Ah, Captain! Good, now there's two of you. These ninja ragamuffins are trying to abscond with my swords! Do something!
Certainly, ma'am.
Give me that.
Hey! I'm using these!
YOINK!
Unh!
Call yourself a ninja? That was pathetic!
Sniff. Those words are hurtful words.

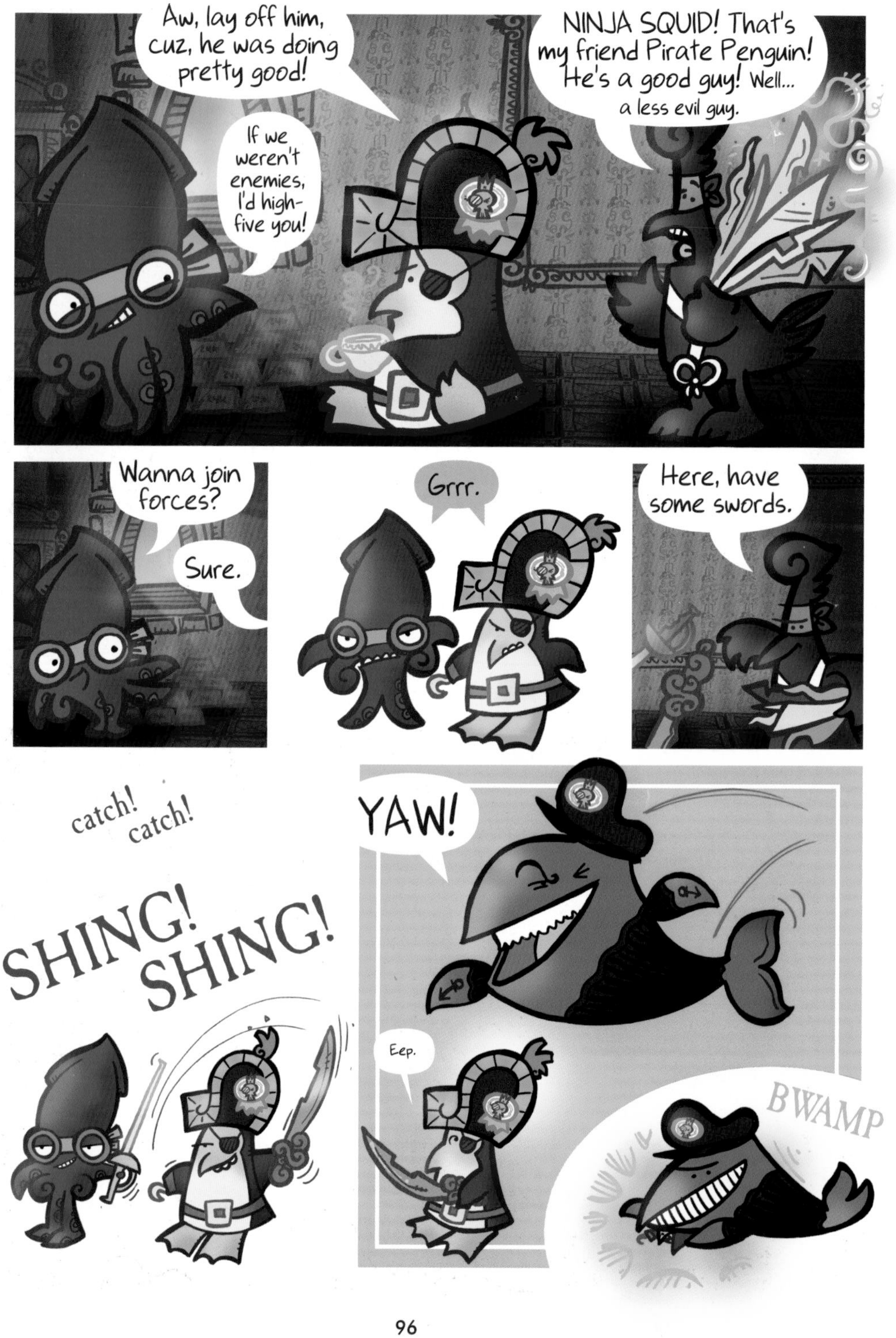

Aw, lay off him, cuz, he was doing pretty good!
If we weren't enemies, I'd high-five you!
NINJA SQUID! That's my friend Pirate Penguin! He's a good guy! Well... a less evil guy.
Wanna join forces?
Sure.
Grrr.
Here, have some swords.
catch!
catch!
SHING!
SHING!
YAW!
Eep.
BWAMP

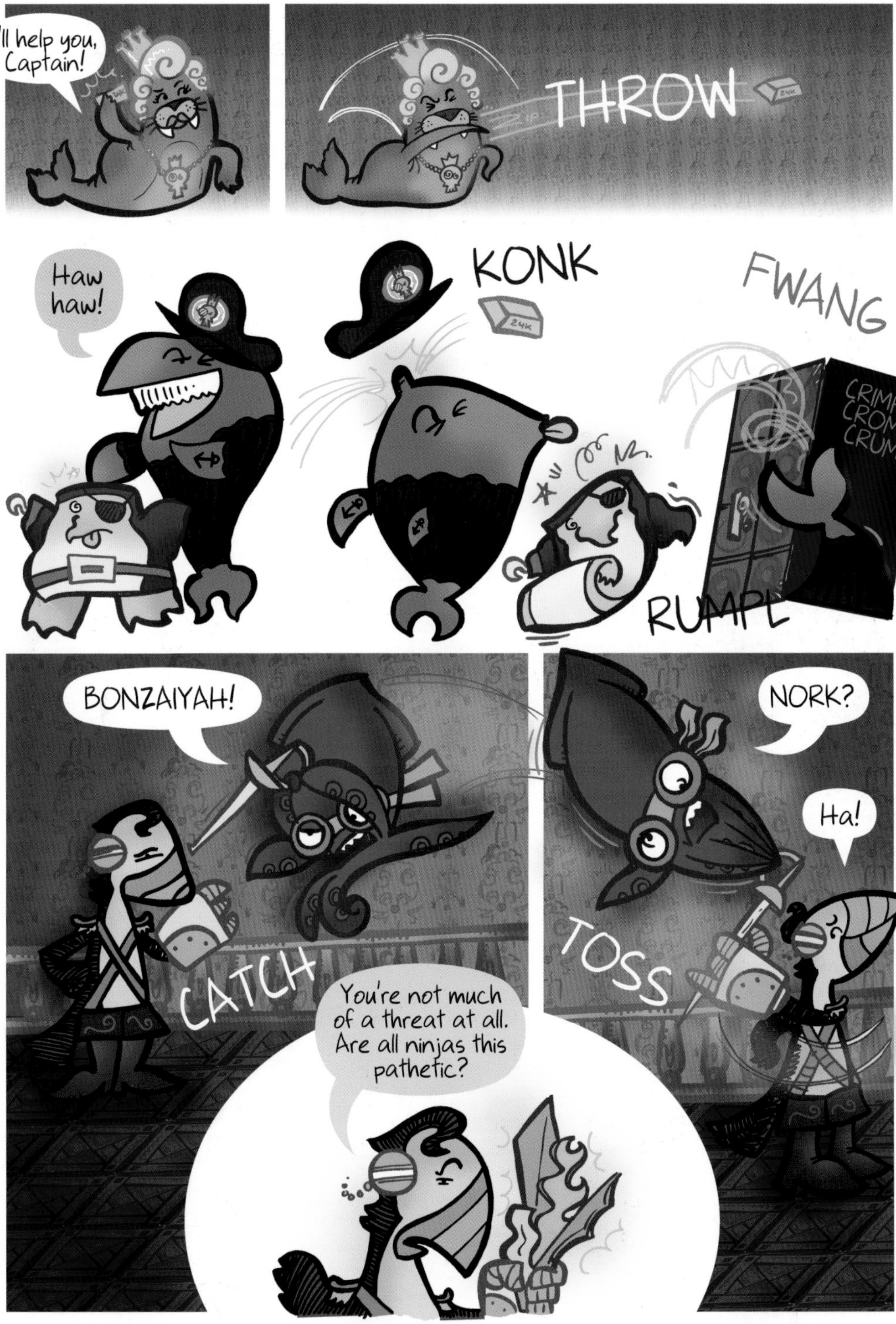
I'll help you, Captain!
THROW
Haw haw!
KONK
FWANG
CRIMP CROMP CRUMP
RUMPL
BONZAIYAH!
CATCH
NORK?
Ha!
TOSS
You're not much of a threat at all. Are all ninjas this pathetic?

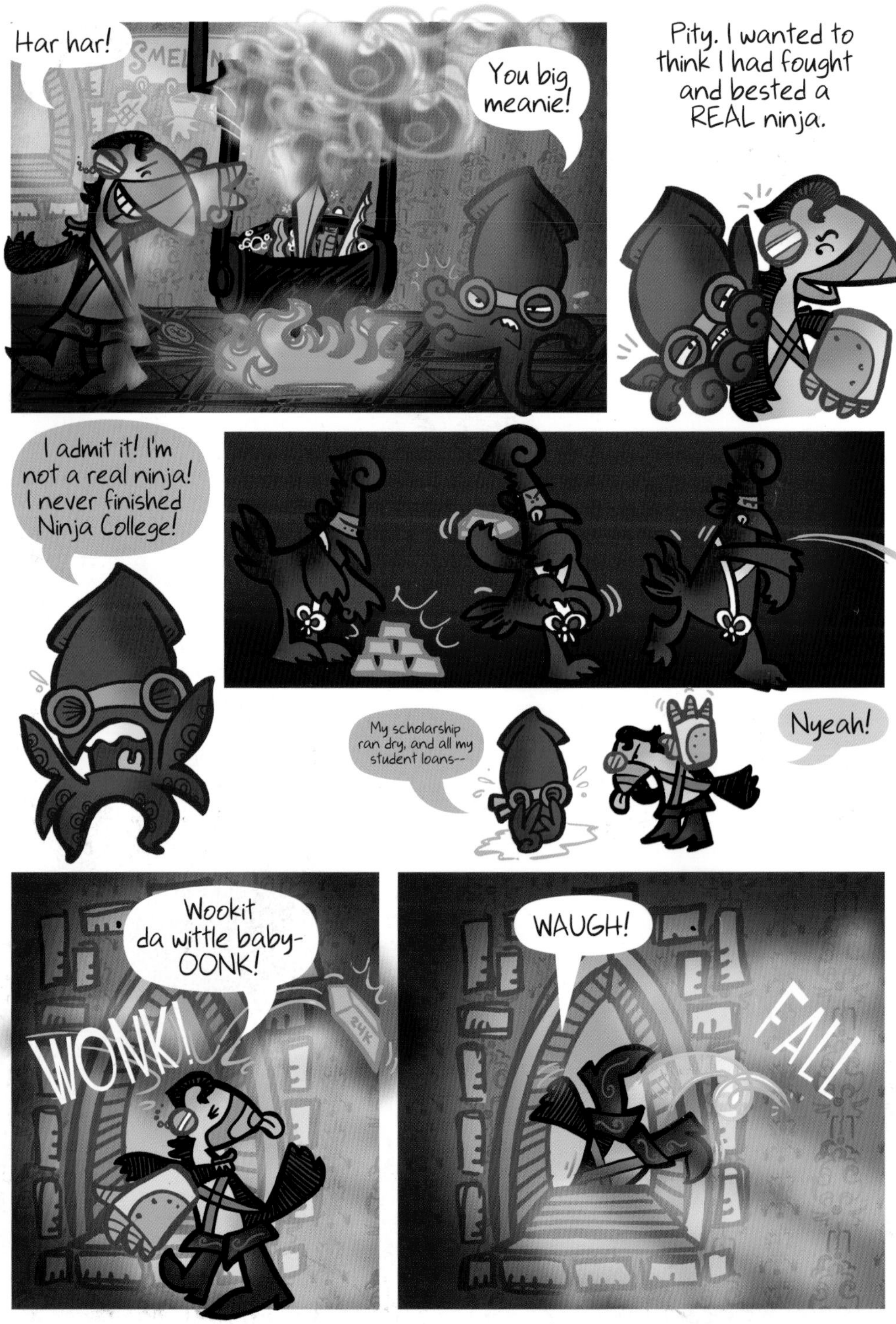

Har har!
You big meanie!
Pity. I wanted to think I had fought and bested a REAL ninja.
I admit it! I'm not a real ninja! I never finished Ninja College!
My scholarship ran dry, and all my student loans--
Nyeah!
Wookit da wittle baby- OONK!
WONK!
WAUGH!
FALL

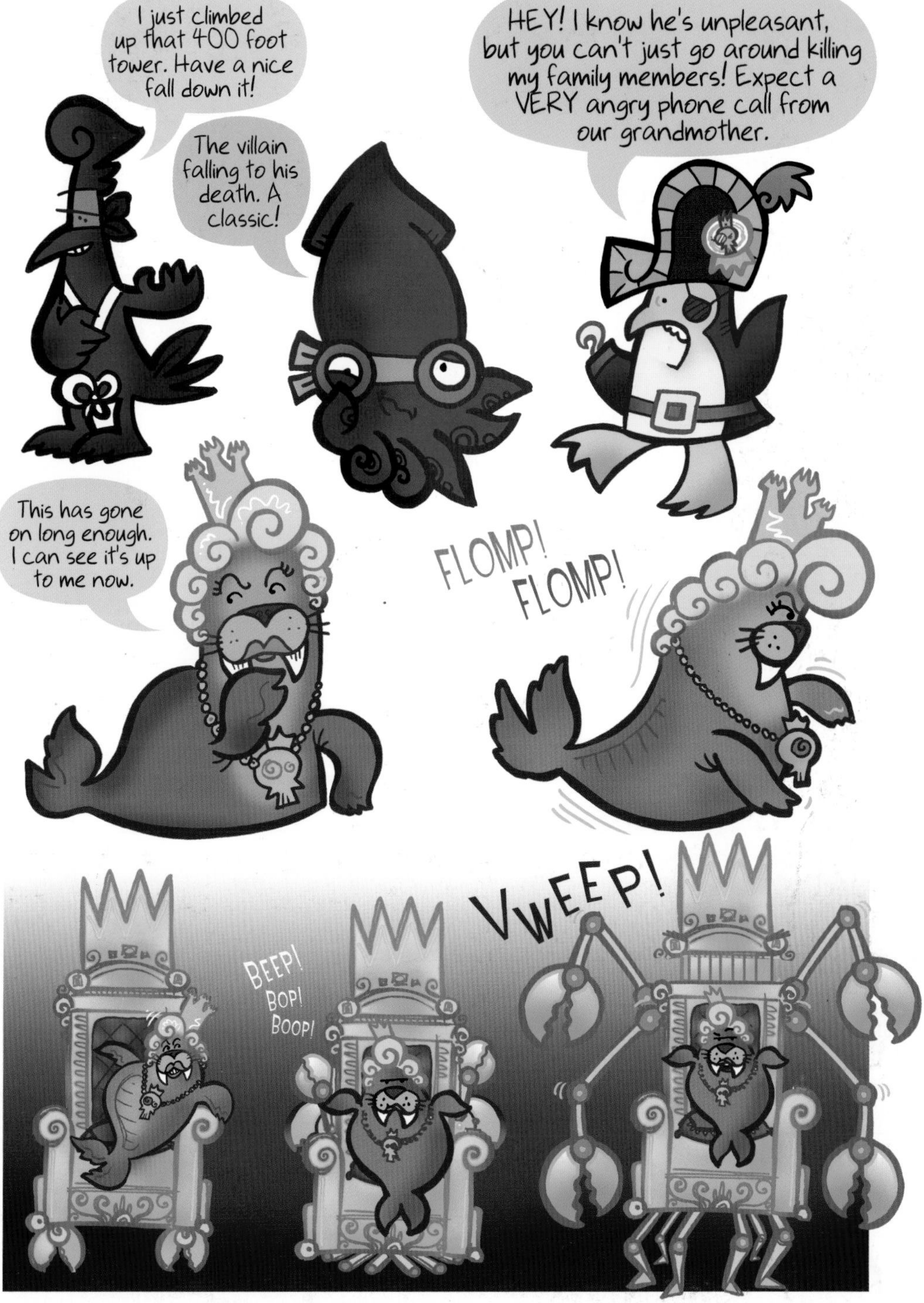
I just climbed up that 400 foot tower. Have a nice fall down it!
The villain falling to his death. A classic!
HEY! I know he's unpleasant, but you can't just go around killing my family members! Expect a VERY angry phone call from our grandmother.
This has gone on long enough. I can see it's up to me now.
FLOMP! FLOMP!
BEEP! BOP! BOOP!
VWEEP!

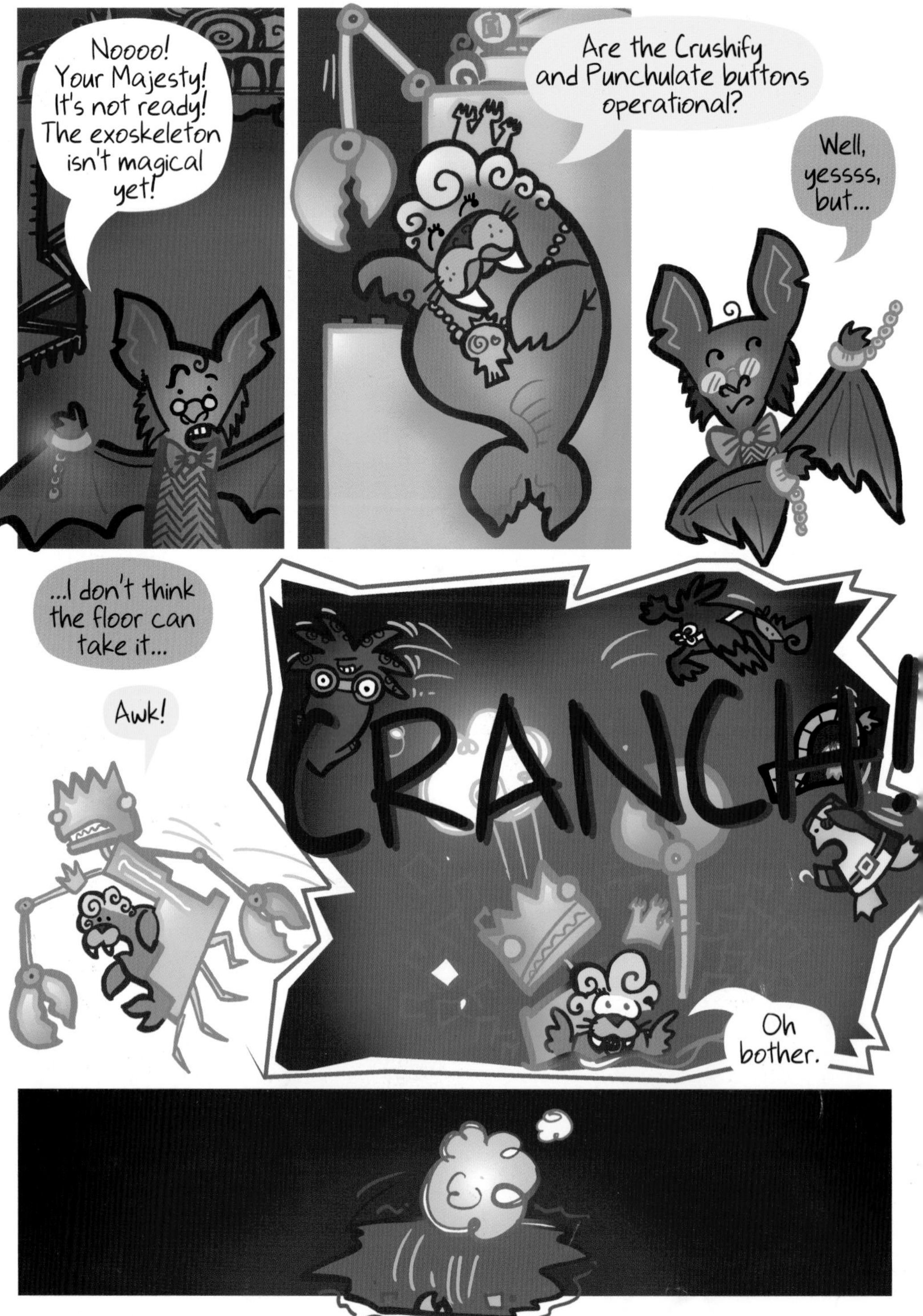
Noooo! Your Majesty! It's not ready! The exoskeleton isn't magical yet!
Are the Crushify and Punchulate buttons operational?
Well, yessss, but...
...I don't think the floor can take it...
Awk!
CRANCH!
Oh bother.

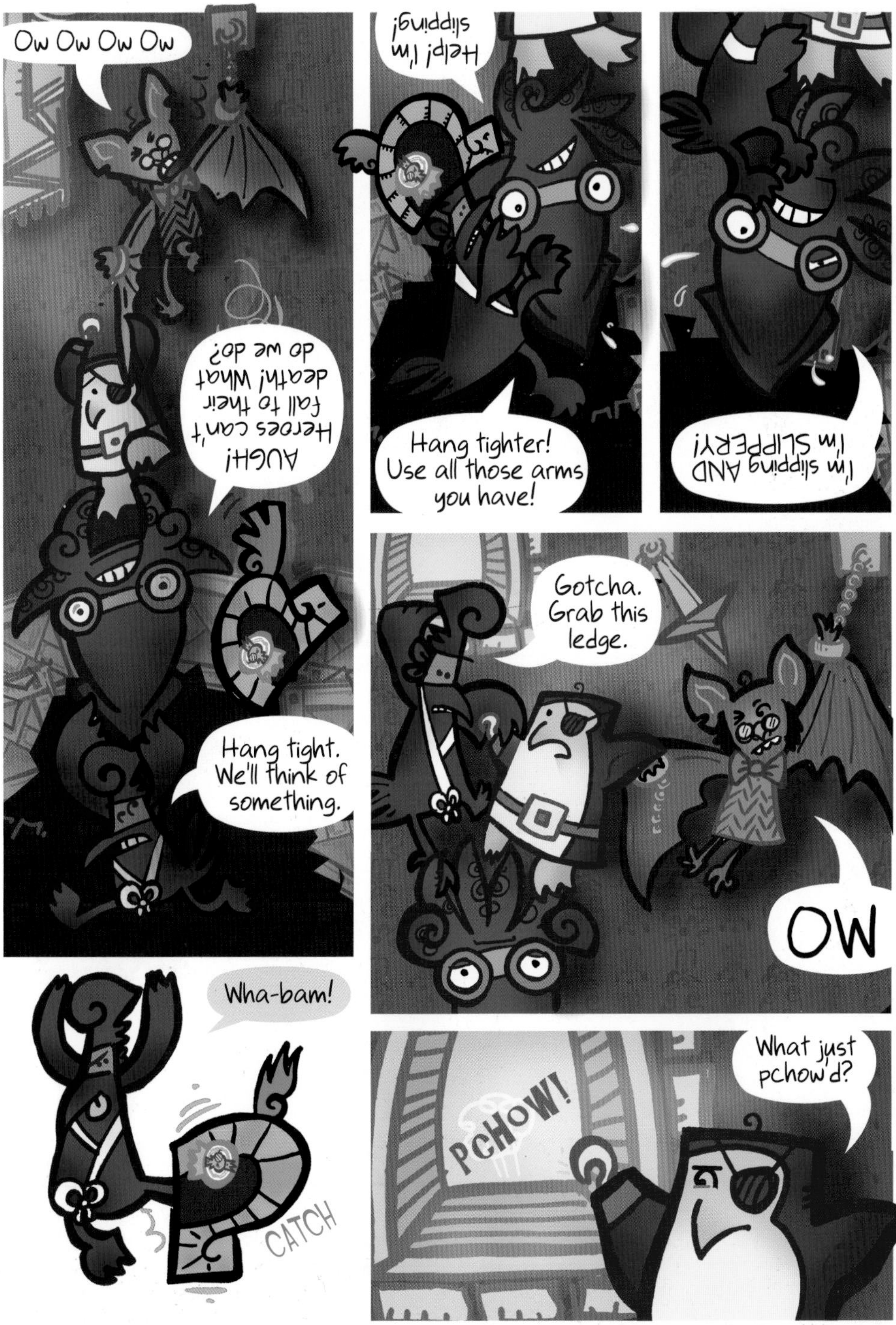

Ow Ow Ow Ow
AUGH! Heroes can't fall to their death! What do we do?
Hang tight. We'll think of something.
Help! I'm slipping!
Hang tighter! Use all those arms you have!
I'm slipping AND I'm SLIPPERY!
Gotcha. Grab this ledge.
OW
Wha-bam!
CATCH
PCHOW!
What just pchow'd?

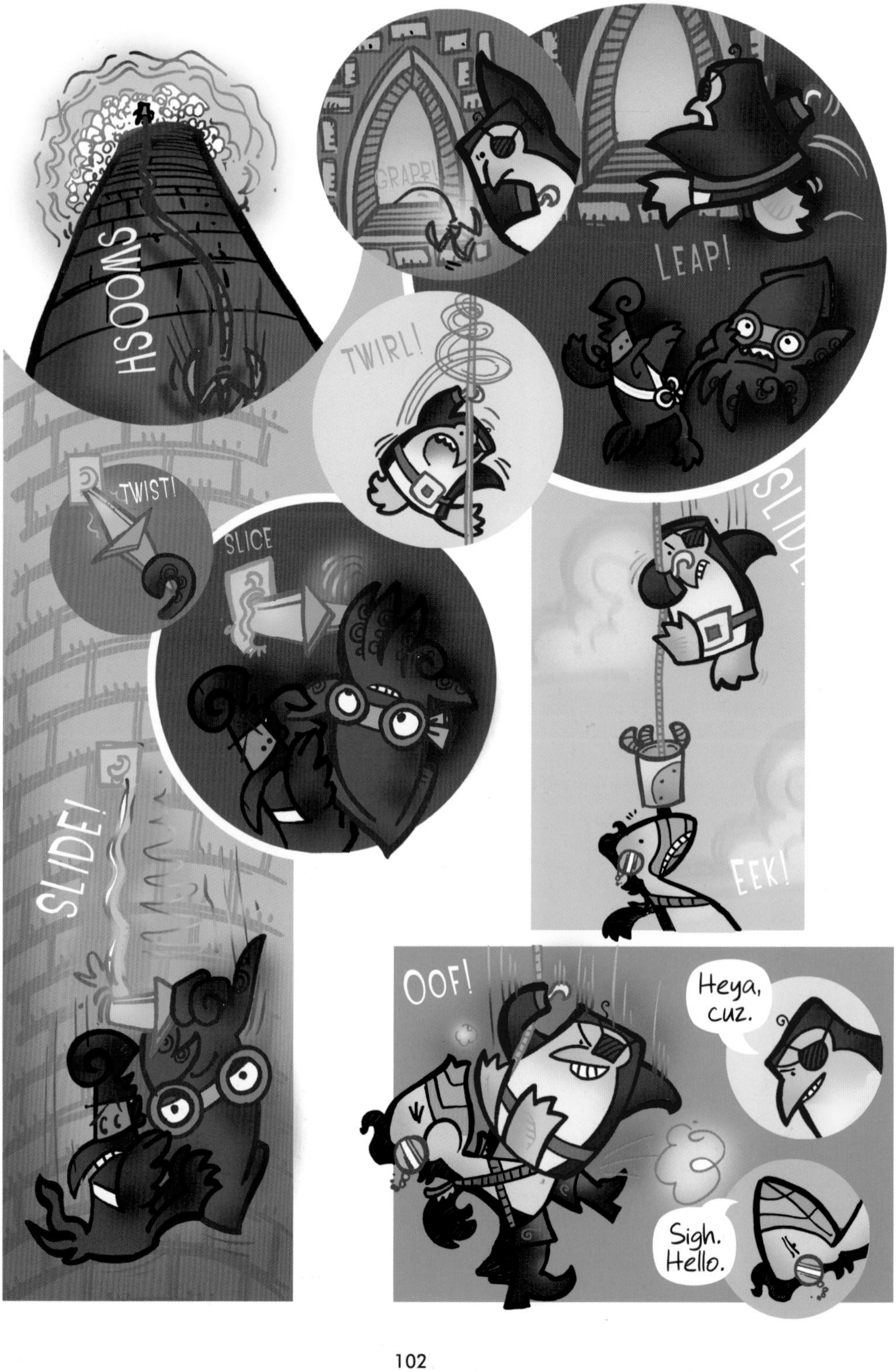
SWOOSH
GRAPP!
LEAP!
TWIRL!
TWIST!
SLICE
SLIDE!
SLIDE!
EEK!
OOF!
Heya, cuz.
Sigh. Hello.

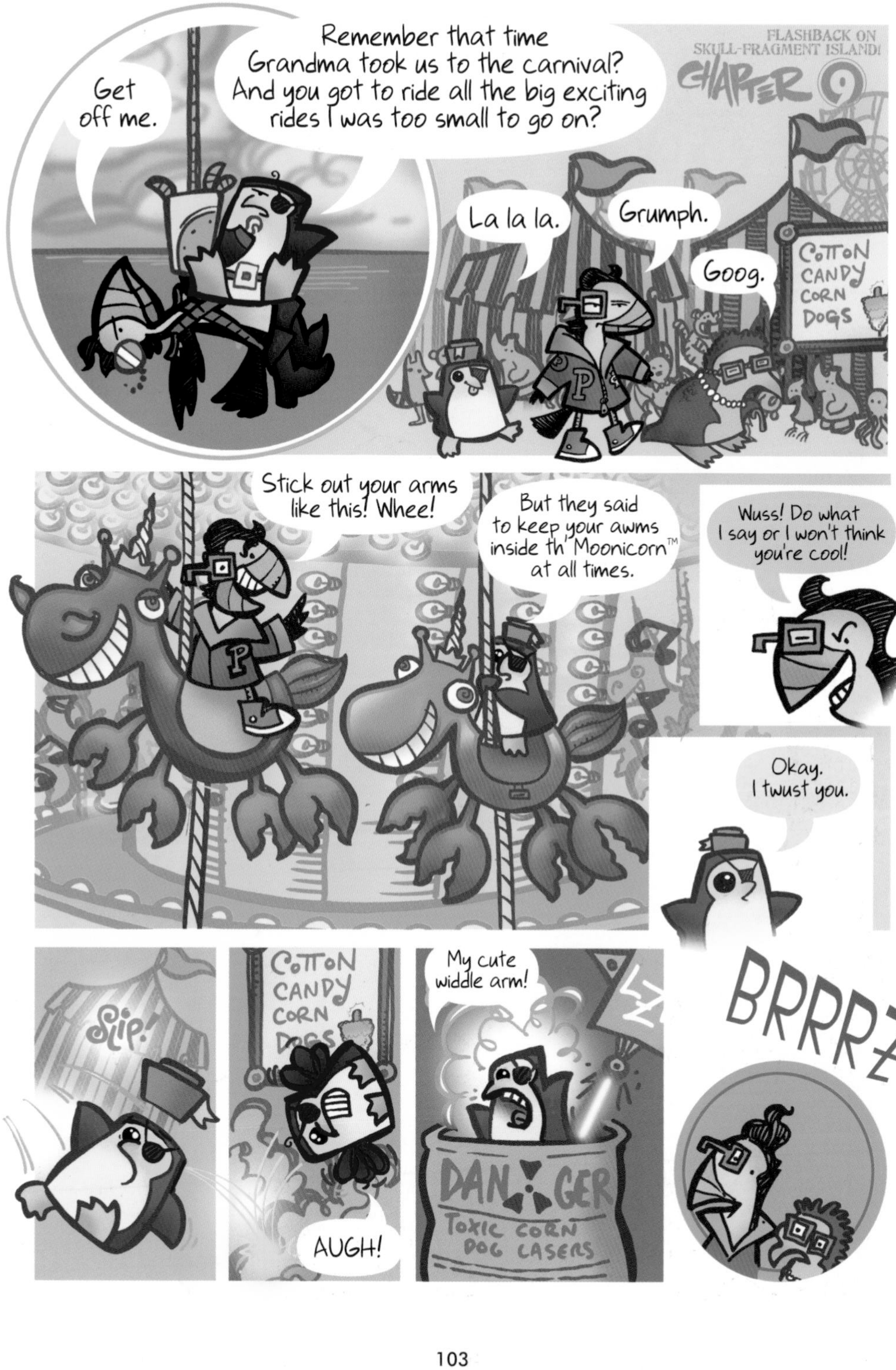

FLASHBACK ON SKULL-FRAGMENT ISLAND!
CHAPTER 9
Get off me.
Remember that time Grandma took us to the carnival? And you got to ride all the big exciting rides I was too small to go on?
La la la.
Grumph.
Goog.
COTTON CANDY CORN DOGS
Stick out your arms like this! Whee!
But they said to keep your awms inside th' Moonicorn™ at all times.
Wuss! Do what I say or I won't think you're cool!
Okay. I twust you.
Slip!
COTTON CANDY CORN DOGS
AUGH!
My cute widdle arm!
DAN GER
TOXIC CORN DOG LASERS
BRRRZ

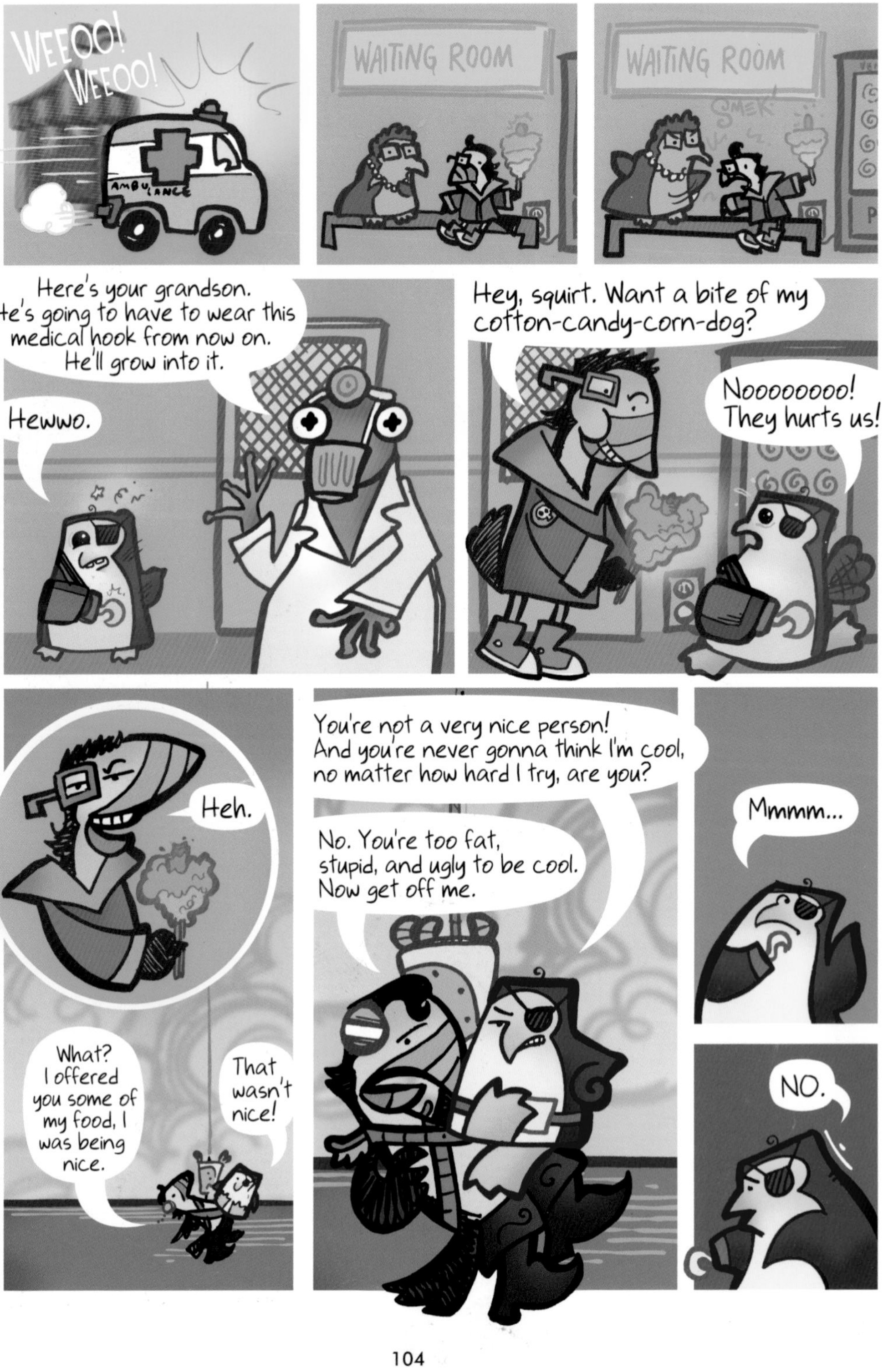
WEEOO! WEEOO!
AMBULANCE
WAITING ROOM
WAITING ROOM
SMEK!
Here's your grandson. He's going to have to wear this medical hook from now on. He'll grow into it.
Hewwo.
Hey, squirt. Want a bite of my cotton-candy-corn-dog?
Noooooooo! They hurts us!
Heh.
What? I offered you some of my food, I was being nice.
That wasn't nice!
You're not a very nice person! And you're never gonna think I'm cool, no matter how hard I try, are you?
No. You're too fat, stupid, and ugly to be cool. Now get off me.
Mmmm...
NO.

Grr!

What

SMEK!

SLAP! SLAP!

SLAP!

FALL

This sword through the wall is like a knife through butter!

FLIP!

SLICE!

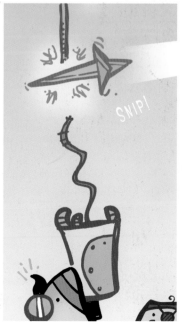

SNIP!

SLAM!

Bleep!

AUGH!

SPLASH!

My beautiful power hand! I'm not supposed to get it wet!

The sword! Where's the sword!?

FLURNCH!

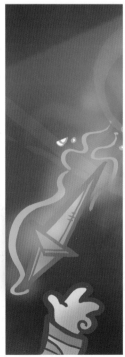

Looky what I found! Am I the King of Atlantis now?

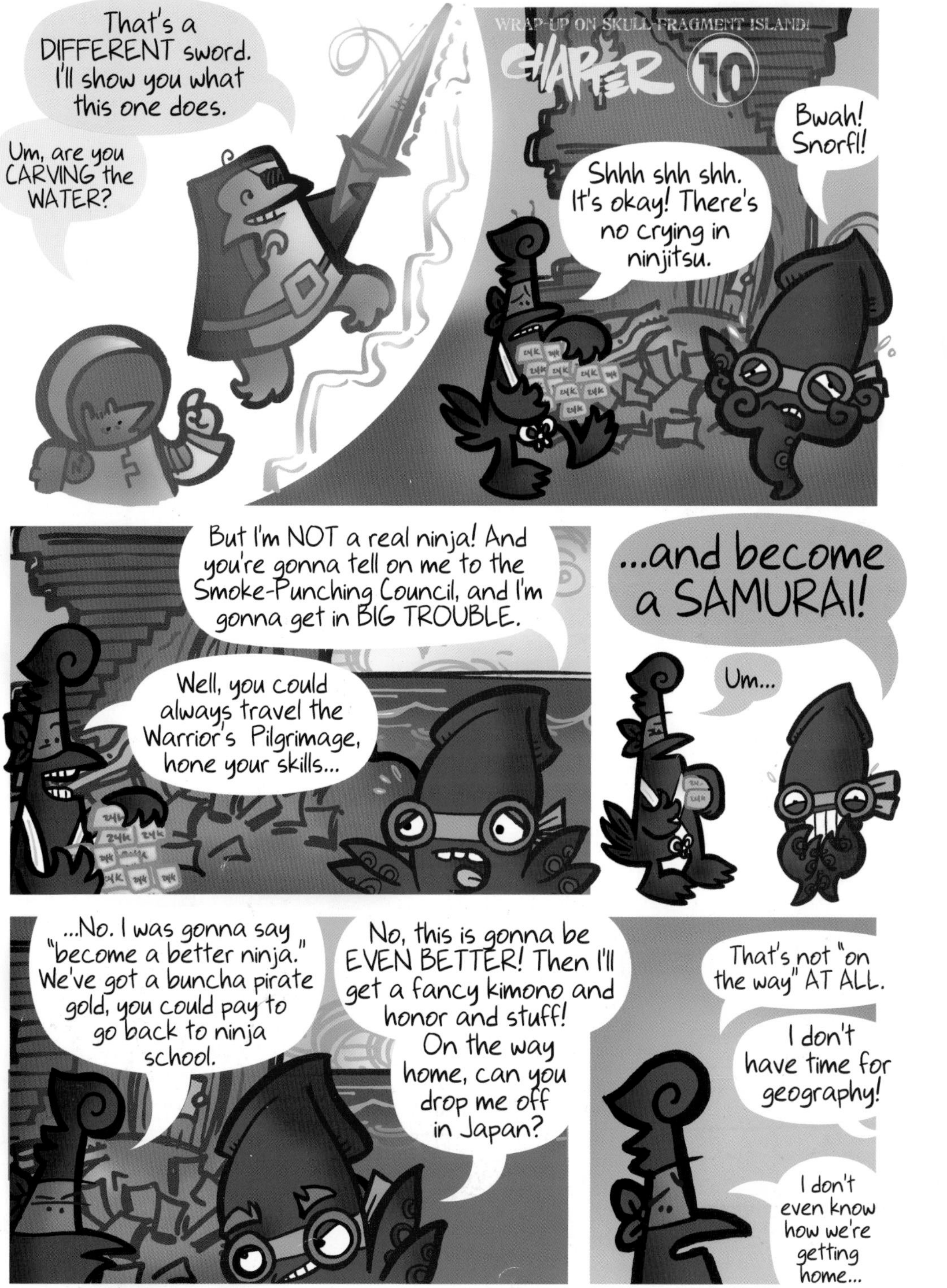
WRAP-UP ON SKULL-FRAGMENT ISLAND!
CHAPTER 10
That's a DIFFERENT sword. I'll show you what this one does.
Um, are you CARVING the WATER?
Bwah! Snorfl!
Shhh shh shh. It's okay! There's no crying in ninjitsu.
But I'm NOT a real ninja! And you're gonna tell on me to the Smoke-Punching Council, and I'm gonna get in BIG TROUBLE.
Well, you could always travel the Warrior's Pilgrimage, hone your skills...
...and become a SAMURAI!
Um...
...No. I was gonna say "become a better ninja." We've got a buncha pirate gold, you could pay to go back to ninja school.
No, this is gonna be EVEN BETTER! Then I'll get a fancy kimono and honor and stuff! On the way home, can you drop me off in Japan?
That's not "on the way" AT ALL.
I don't have time for geography!
I don't even know how we're getting home...

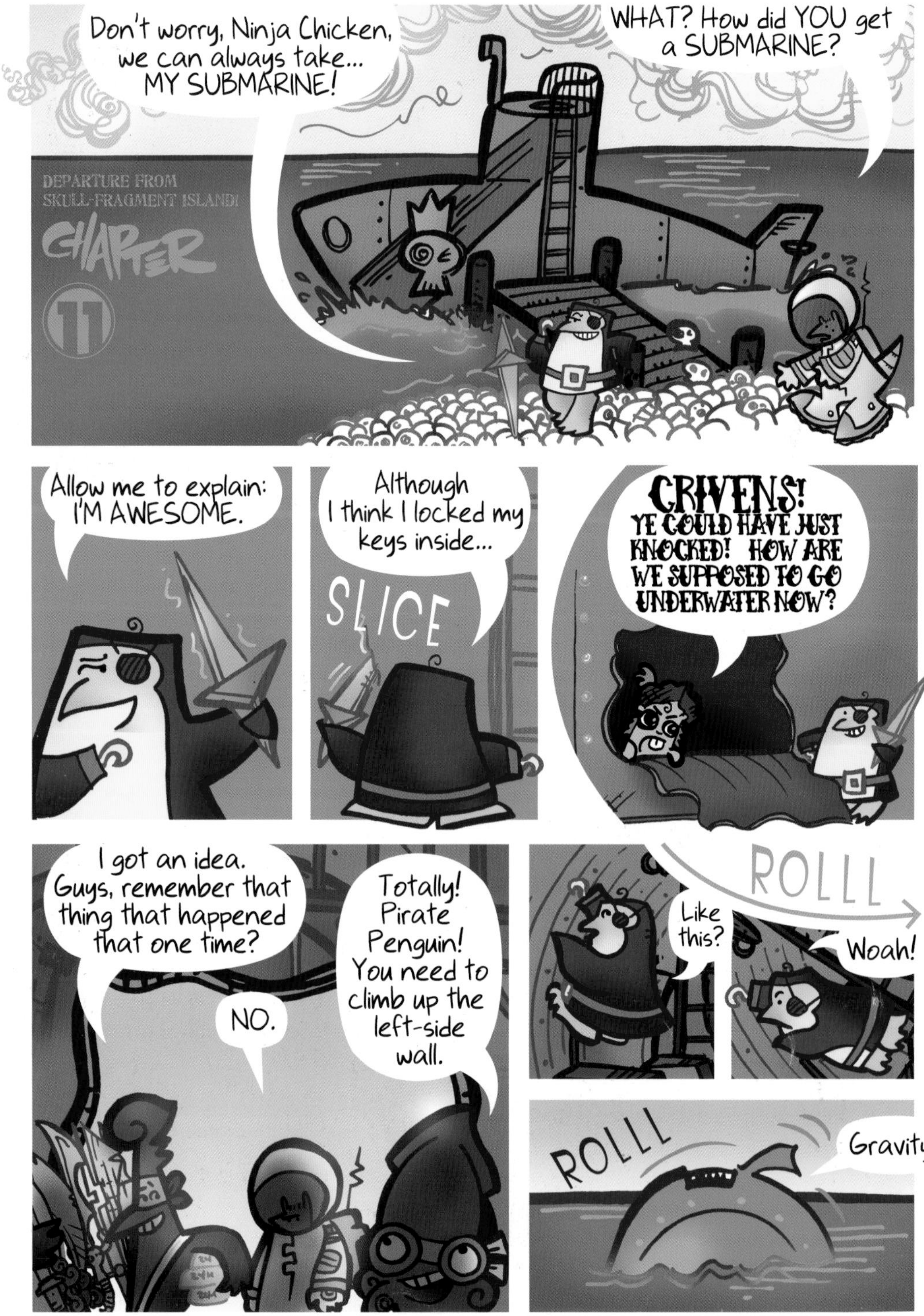
Don't worry, Ninja Chicken, we can always take... MY SUBMARINE!
WHAT? How did YOU get a SUBMARINE?
DEPARTURE FROM SKULL-FRAGMENT ISLAND!
CHAPTER 11
Allow me to explain: I'M AWESOME.
Although I think I locked my keys inside...
SLICE
CRIVENS! YE COULD HAVE JUST KNOCKED! HOW ARE WE SUPPOSED TO GO UNDERWATER NOW?
I got an idea. Guys, remember that thing that happened that one time?
NO.
Totally! Pirate Penguin! You need to climb up the left-side wall.
ROLLL
Like this?
Woah!
ROLLL
Gravity!

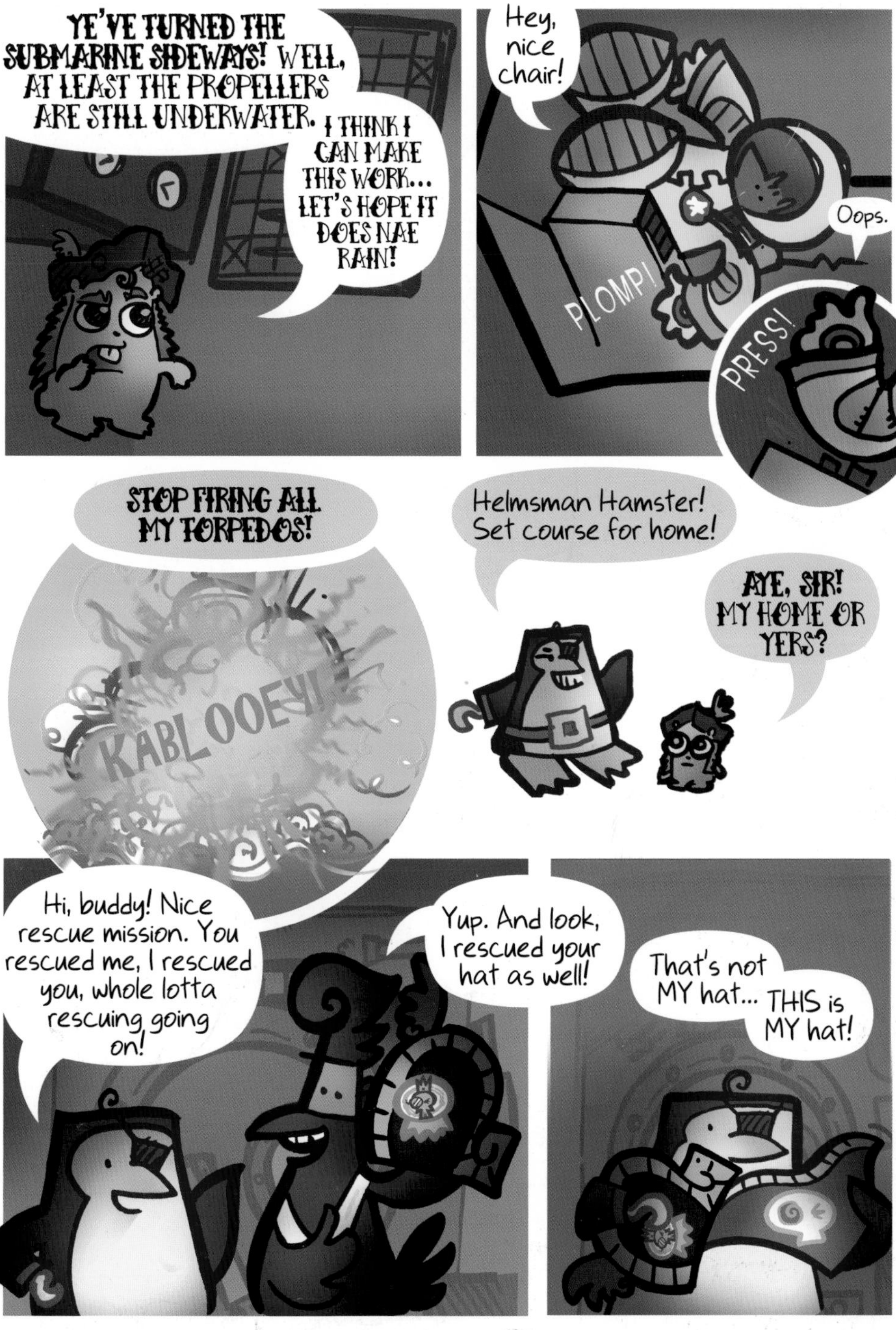
YE'VE TURNED THE SUBMARINE SIDEWAYS! WELL, AT LEAST THE PROPELLERS ARE STILL UNDERWATER.
I THINK I CAN MAKE THIS WORK... LET'S HOPE IT DOES NAE RAIN!
Hey, nice chair!
PLOMP!
Oops.
PRESS!
STOP FIRING ALL MY TORPEDOS!
KABLOOEY!
Helmsman Hamster! Set course for home!
AYE, SIR! MY HOME OR YERS?
Hi, buddy! Nice rescue mission. You rescued me, I rescued you, whole lotta rescuing going on!
Yup. And look, I rescued your hat as well!
That's not MY hat...
THIS is MY hat!

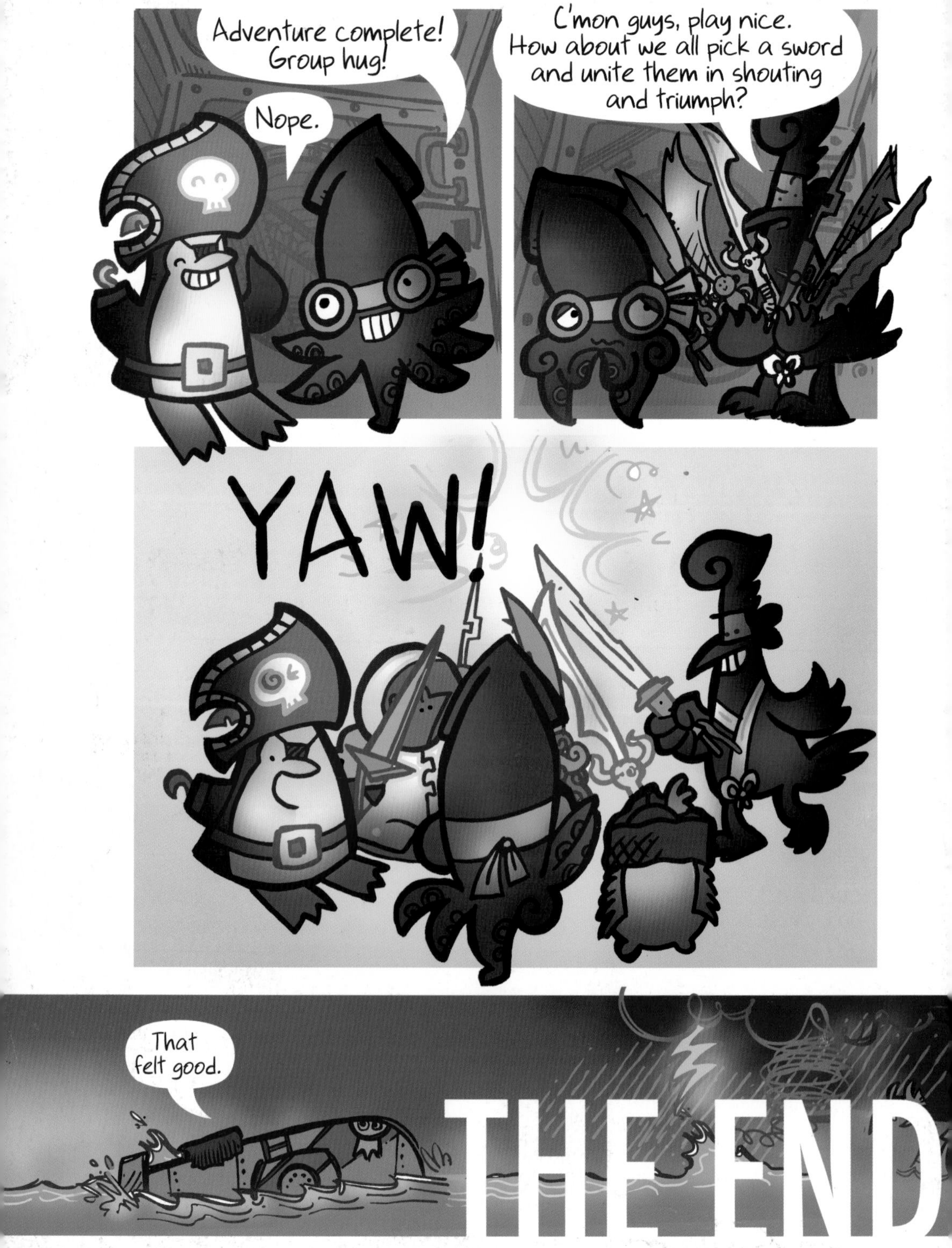
Adventure complete! Group hug!
Nope.
C'mon guys, play nice. How about we all pick a sword and unite them in shouting and triumph?
YAW!
That felt good.
THE END

Epilogue:

On the long voyage home, the main characters found the lost city of Atlantis, and Astronaut Armadillo became its king because he was holding the right magic sword at the time. He was a cruel ruler, and his citizens revolted within hours.

Helmsman Hamster piloted the submarine all the way back to his house, #12 Broccoli Street. It's quite hard to drive a submarine down a street, but he managed it somehow.

Samurai Squid bought a series of "How to Samurai" instructional DVDs from Slothgard Van Damp. He watched Disc One while drinking a cheesy protein blast shake. Discs Two and Three are still in the original package.

The bad guys stayed marooned on their exploded island for a while, until they remembered that the island had wheels, and so they drove it somewhere else. The Queen had a new idea and ordered the Alchemist to design hundreds of smaller pirate robots, so she could use them to steal all the gold in the world. Privateer Puffin was given a new gold robot hand to control them, and also a solid gold hat, which was heavy.

Ninja Chicken eventually delivered most of the magic swords back to their rightful owners, all except for five of them. This was mostly Pirate Penguin's fault. It's a long story. Maybe I'll tell you about it in Book Three!

OUTRODUCTION BY RAY FRIESEN

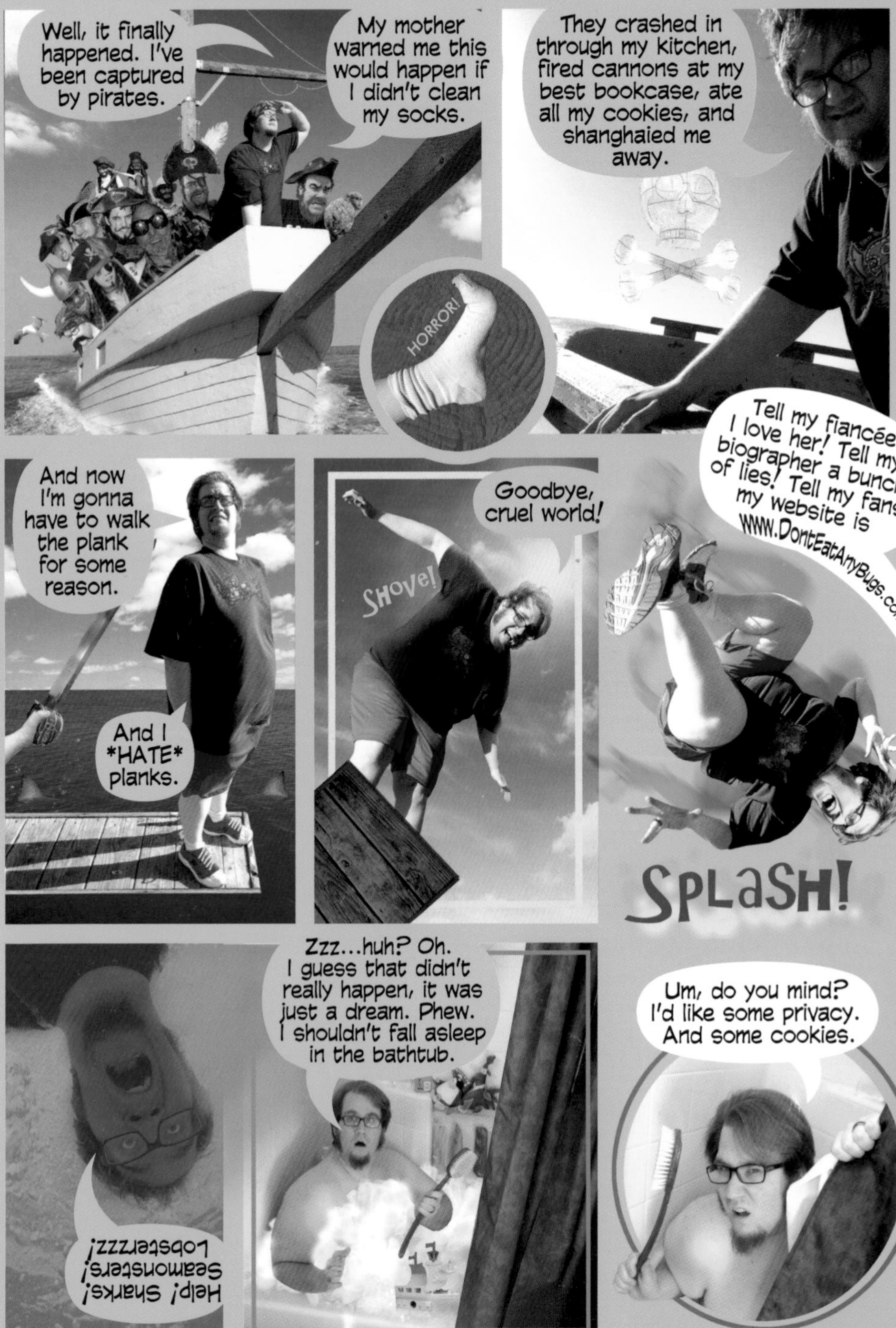

Well, it finally happened. I've been captured by pirates.
My mother warned me this would happen if I didn't clean my socks.
They crashed in through my kitchen, fired cannons at my best bookcase, ate all my cookies, and shanghaied me away.
HORROR!
And now I'm gonna have to walk the plank for some reason.
And I *HATE* planks.
Goodbye, cruel world!
SHOVE!
Tell my fiancée I love her! Tell my biographer a bunch of lies! Tell my fans my website is WWW.DontEatAnyBugs.com
SPLASH!
Help! Sharks! Seamonsters! Lobsterzzz!
Zzz...huh? Oh. I guess that didn't really happen, it was just a dream. Phew. I shouldn't fall asleep in the bathtub.
Um, do you mind? I'd like some privacy. And some cookies.

TABLE OF CONTENTS

BMX

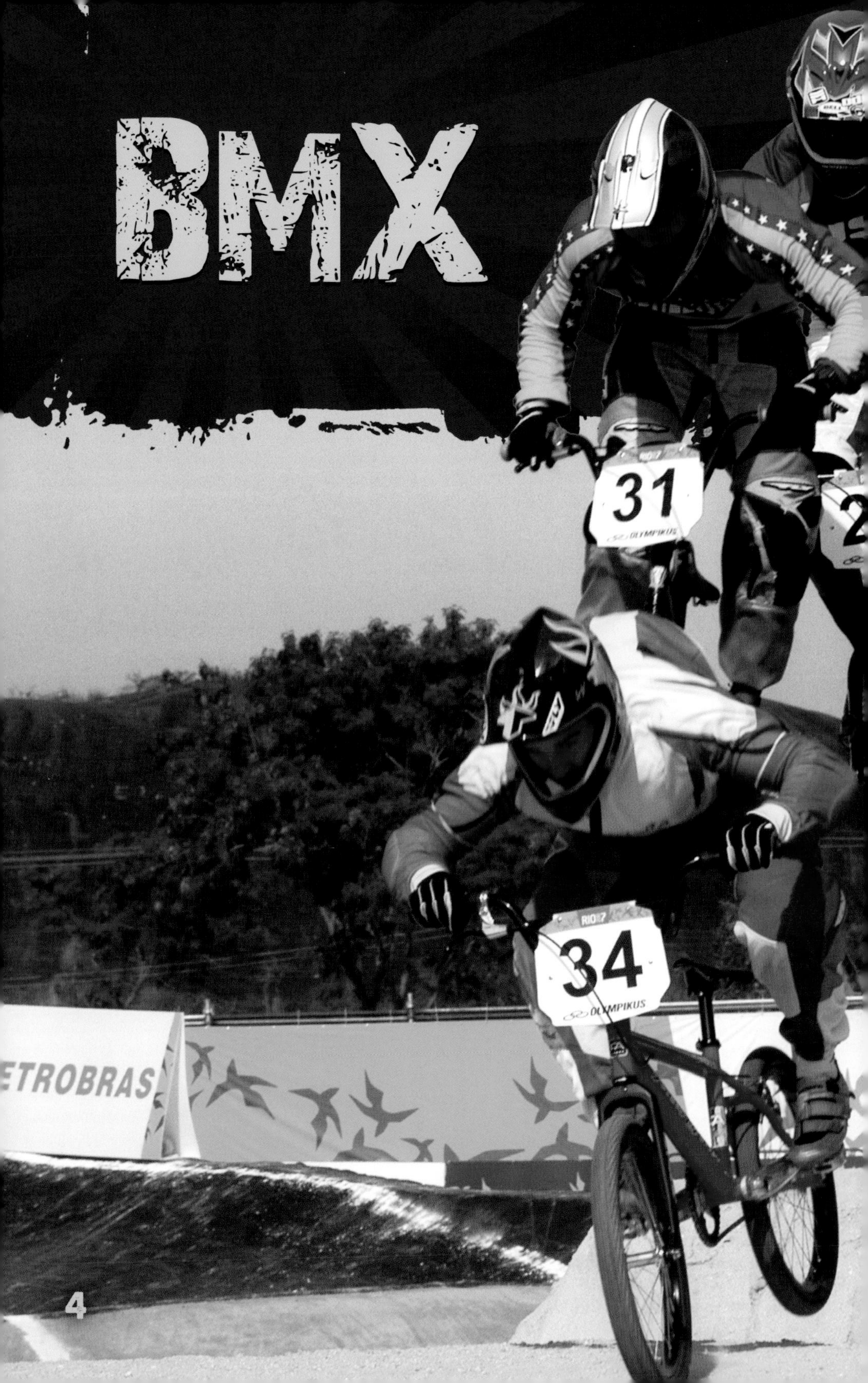
31
OLYMPIKUS
34
OLYMPIKUS
ETROBRAS

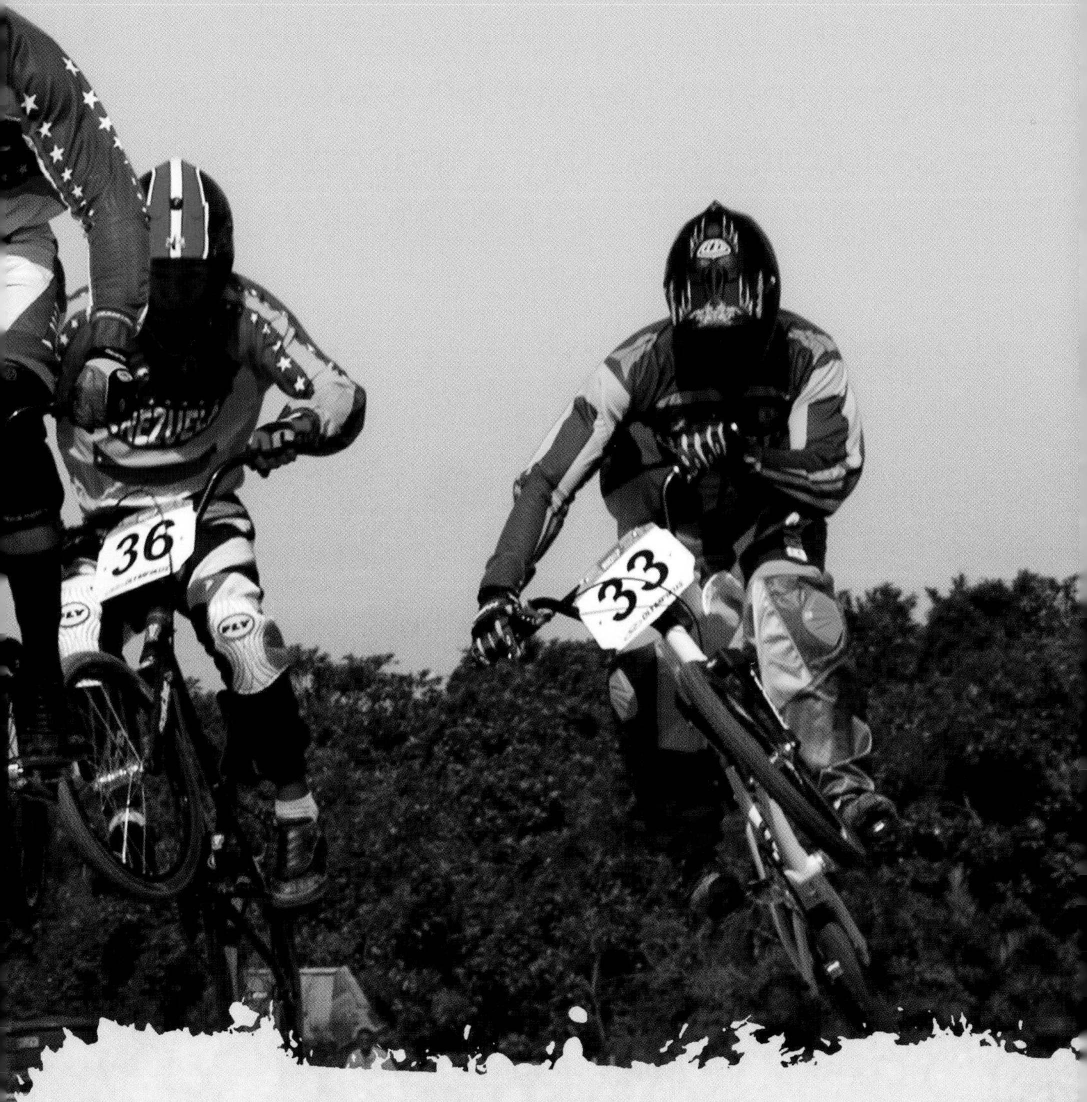
36
33

BMX stands for Bicycle **Motocross**. It is a sport where you race bicycles at extreme speeds on **tracks** often made of dirt.

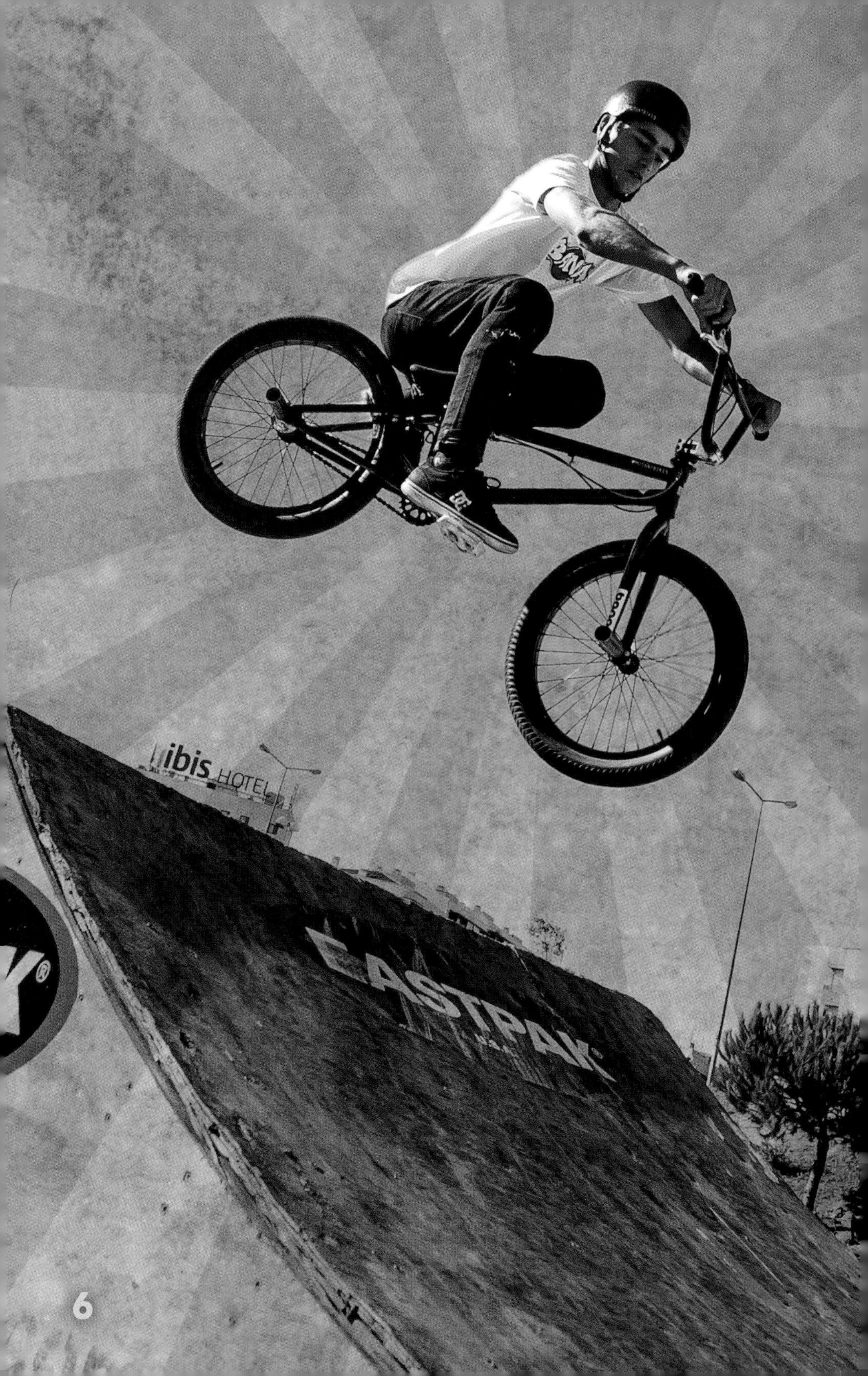
ibis HOTEL

BMX began in the late 1960s in Southern California. It was invented when **motocross**, a form of **off-road** motorcycling, was very popular.

TYPES

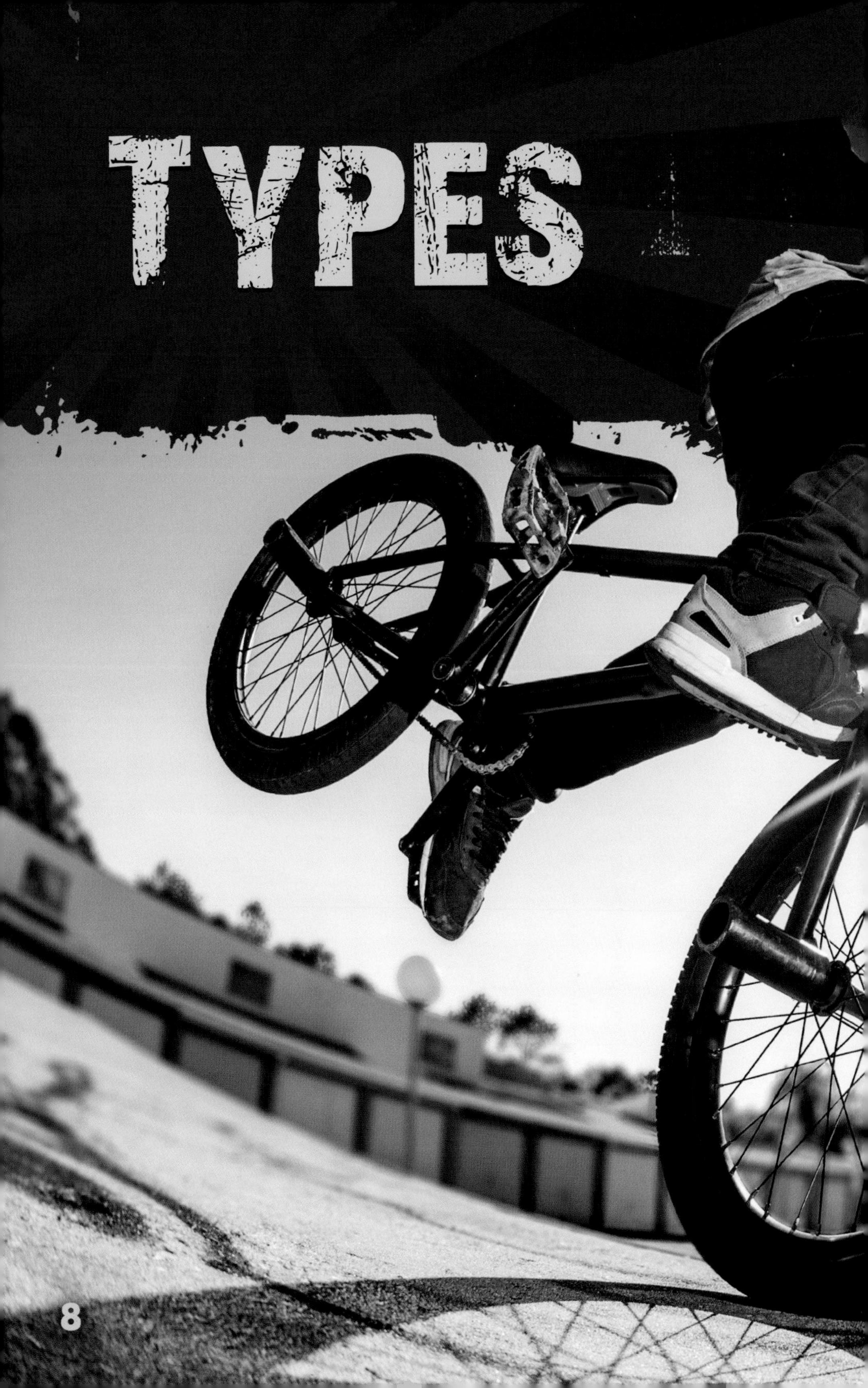

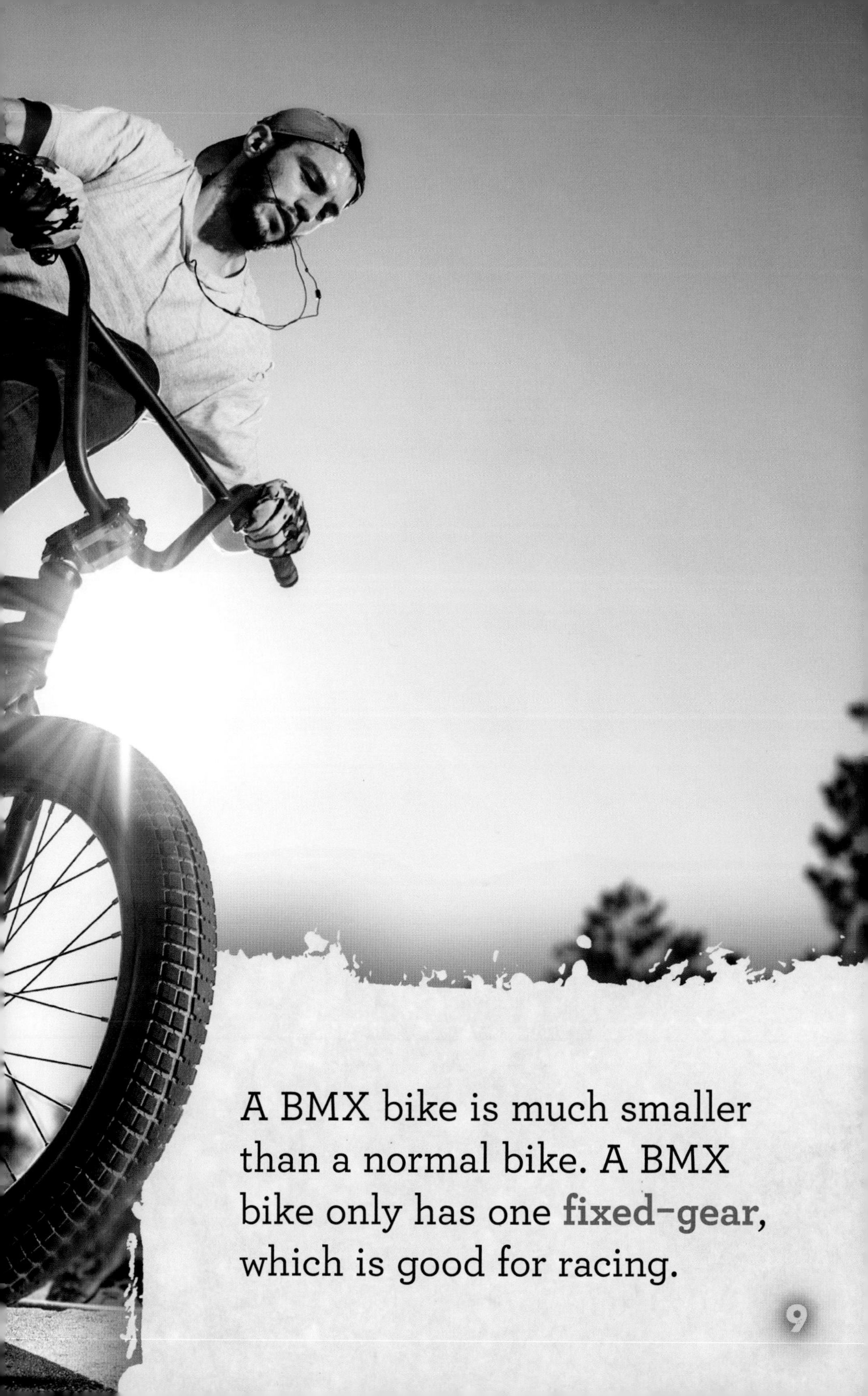

A BMX bike is much smaller than a normal bike. A BMX bike only has one **fixed-gear**, which is good for racing.

There are five types of BMX bikes for different uses. There are race, dirt, park, street, and flatland BMX bikes.

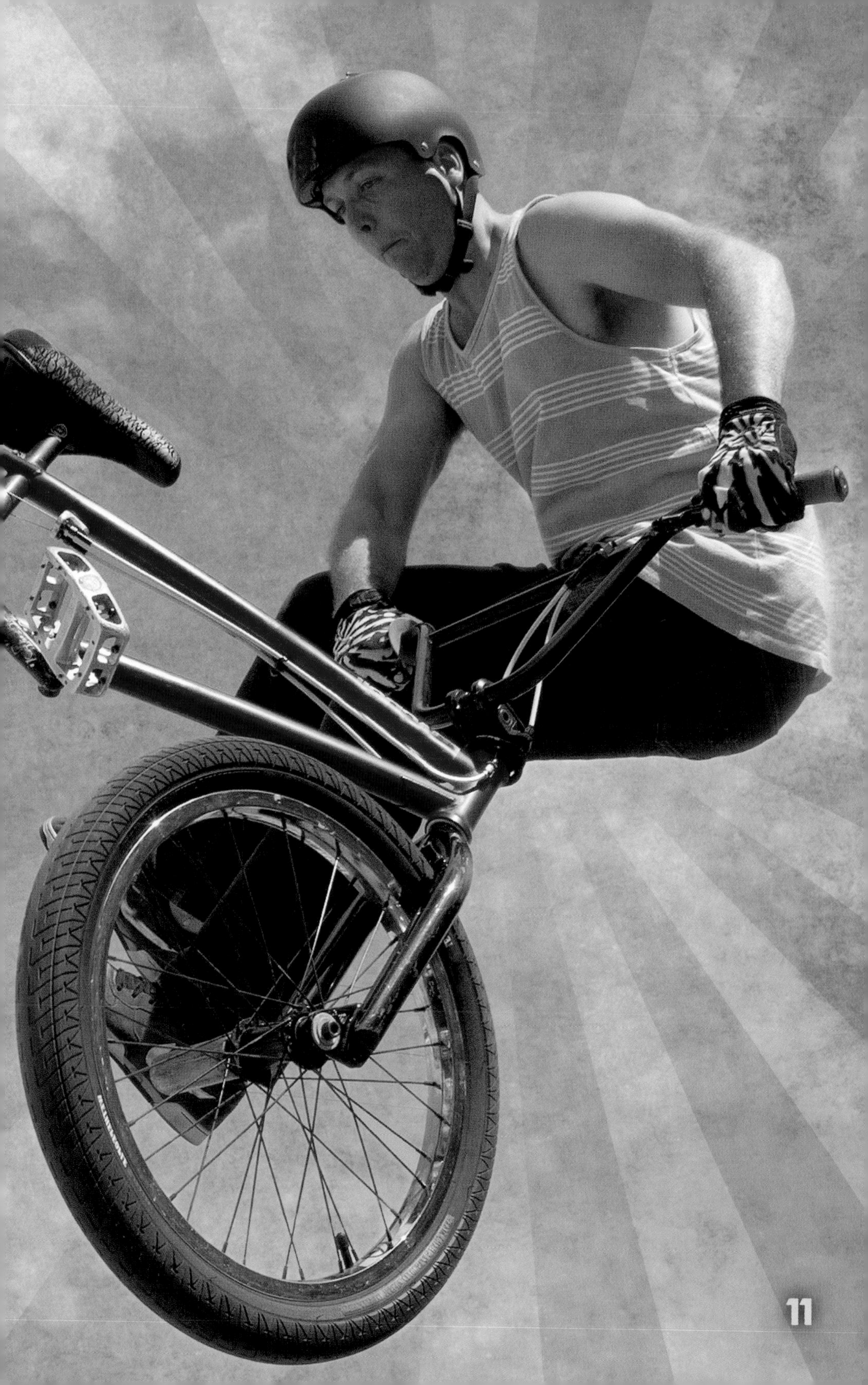

Dirt BMX bikes go **off-road** on dirt and bumpy **paths**. Flatland bikes perform tricks on flat ground and in skate parks.

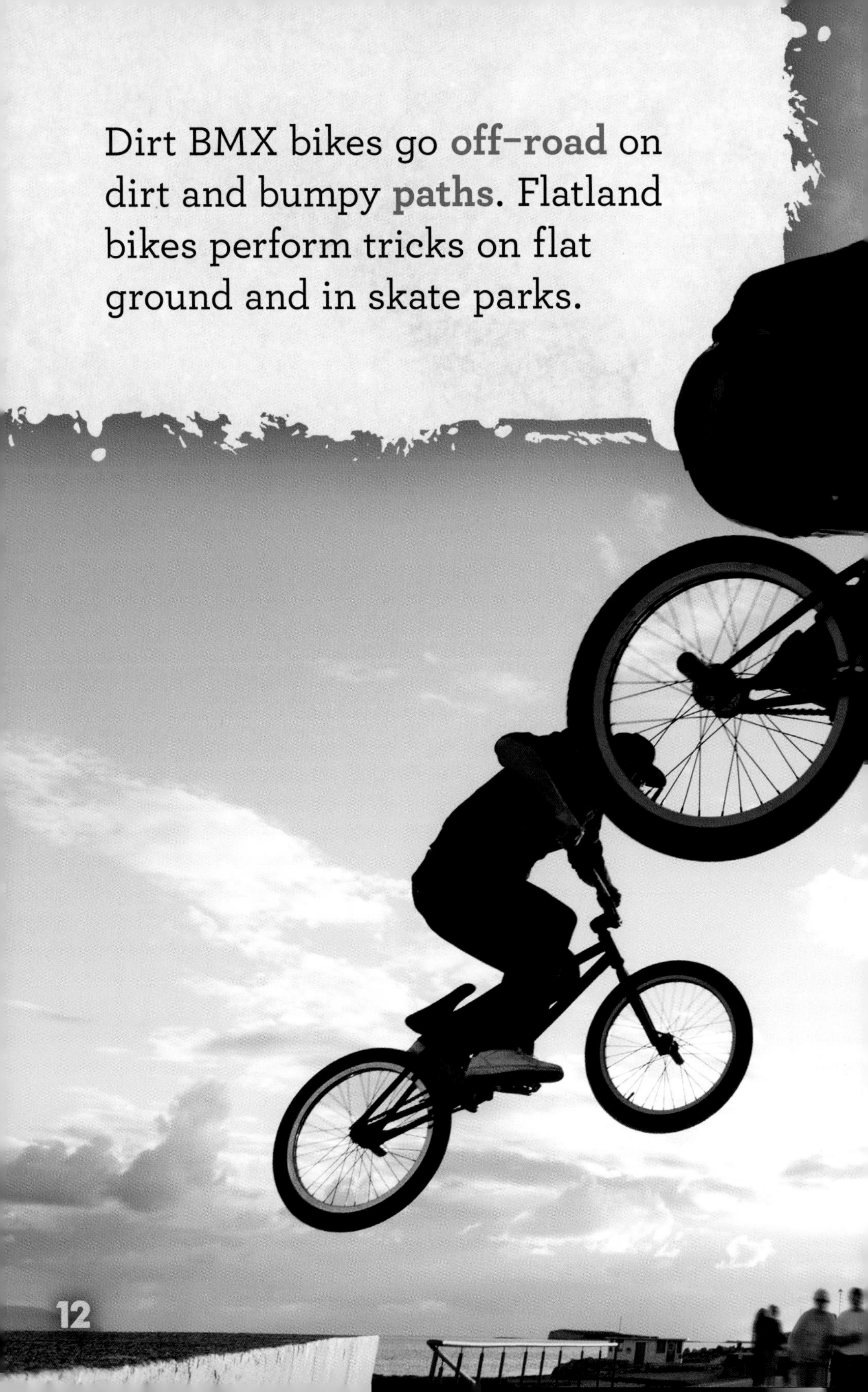

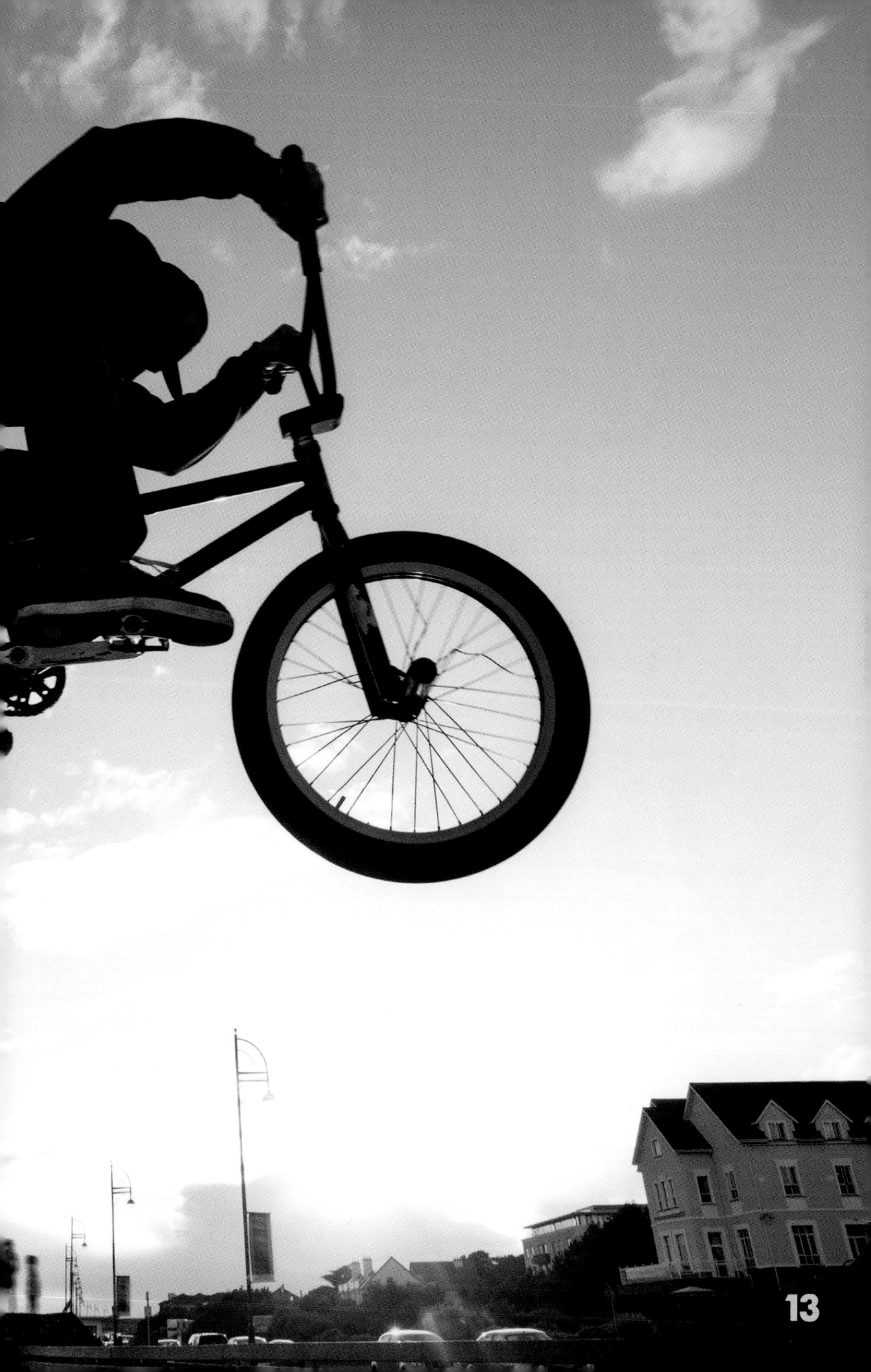

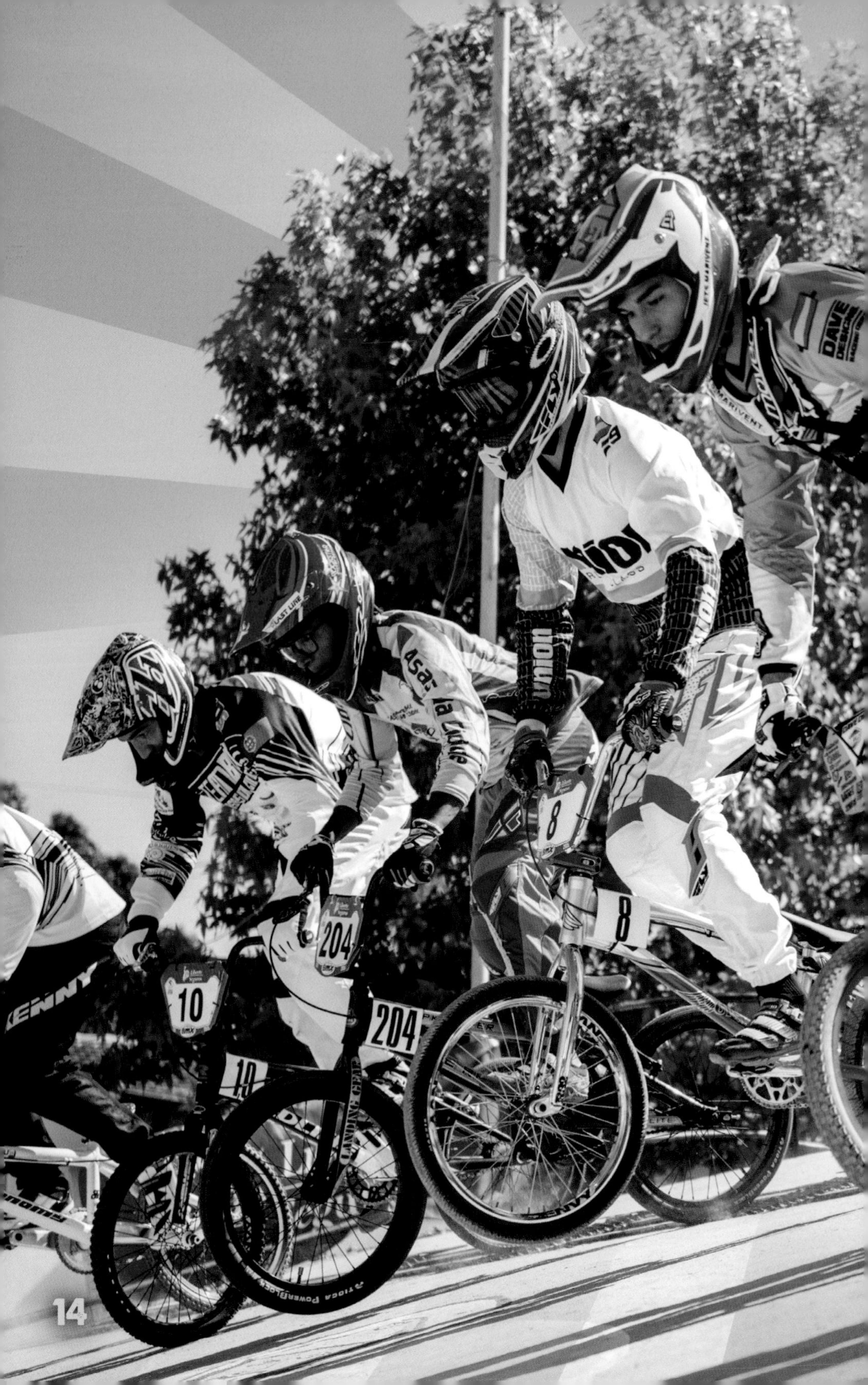
KENNY
10
204
8
LANDING GEAR

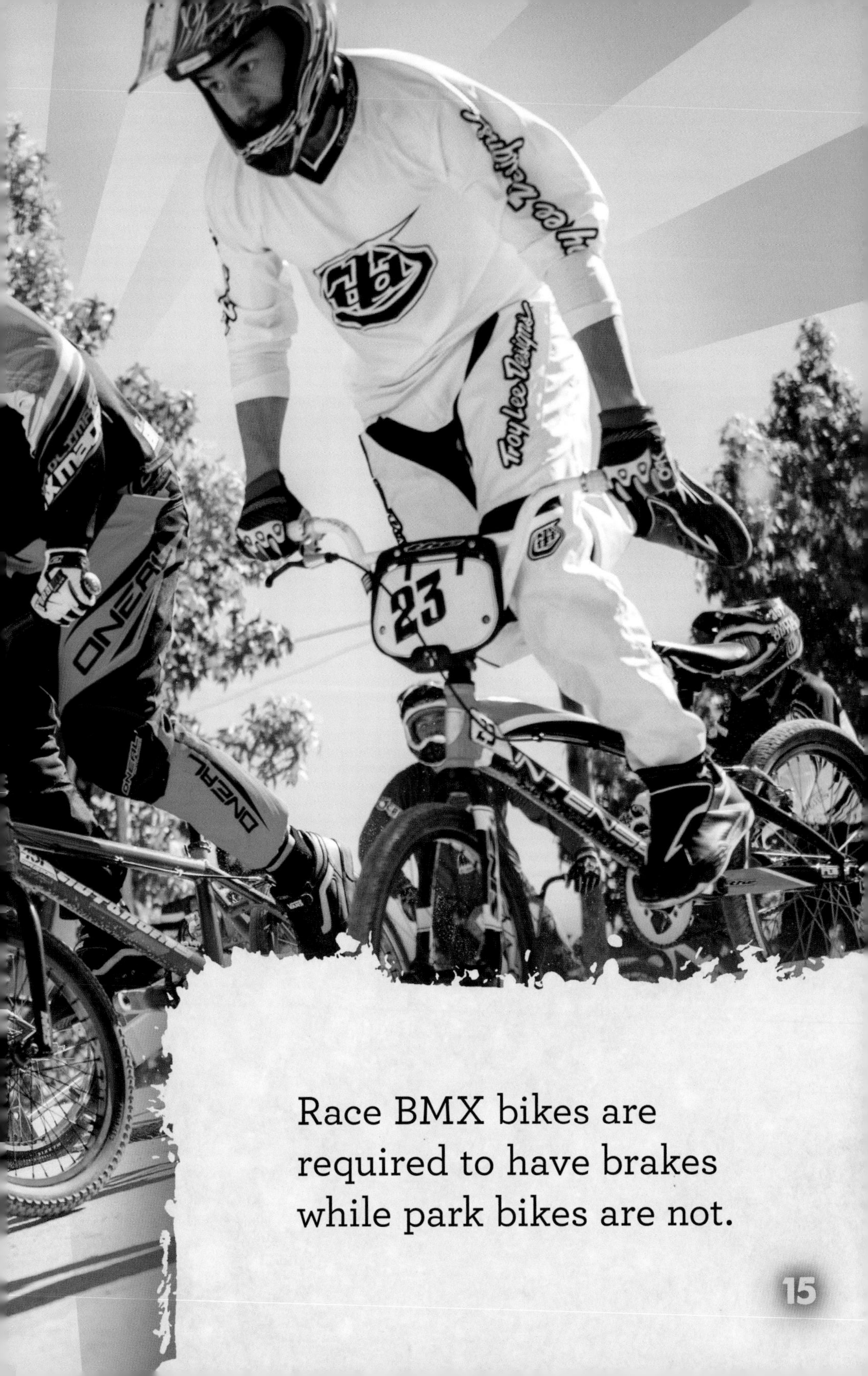
Troy Lee Designs
23
ONEAL

Race BMX bikes are required to have brakes while park bikes are not.

RACES

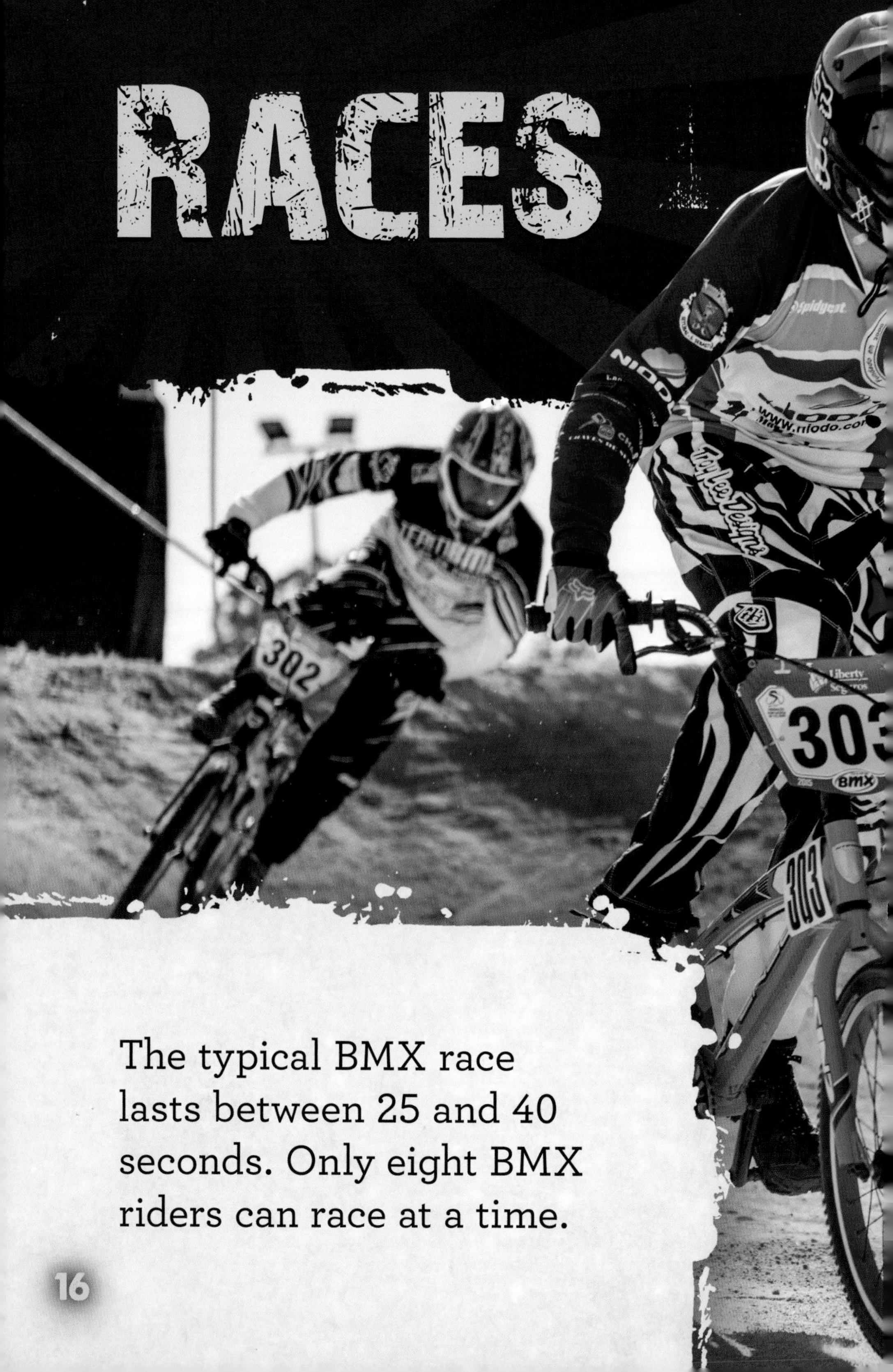
302
303
www.niodo.com
BMX

The typical BMX race lasts between 25 and 40 seconds. Only eight BMX riders can race at a time.

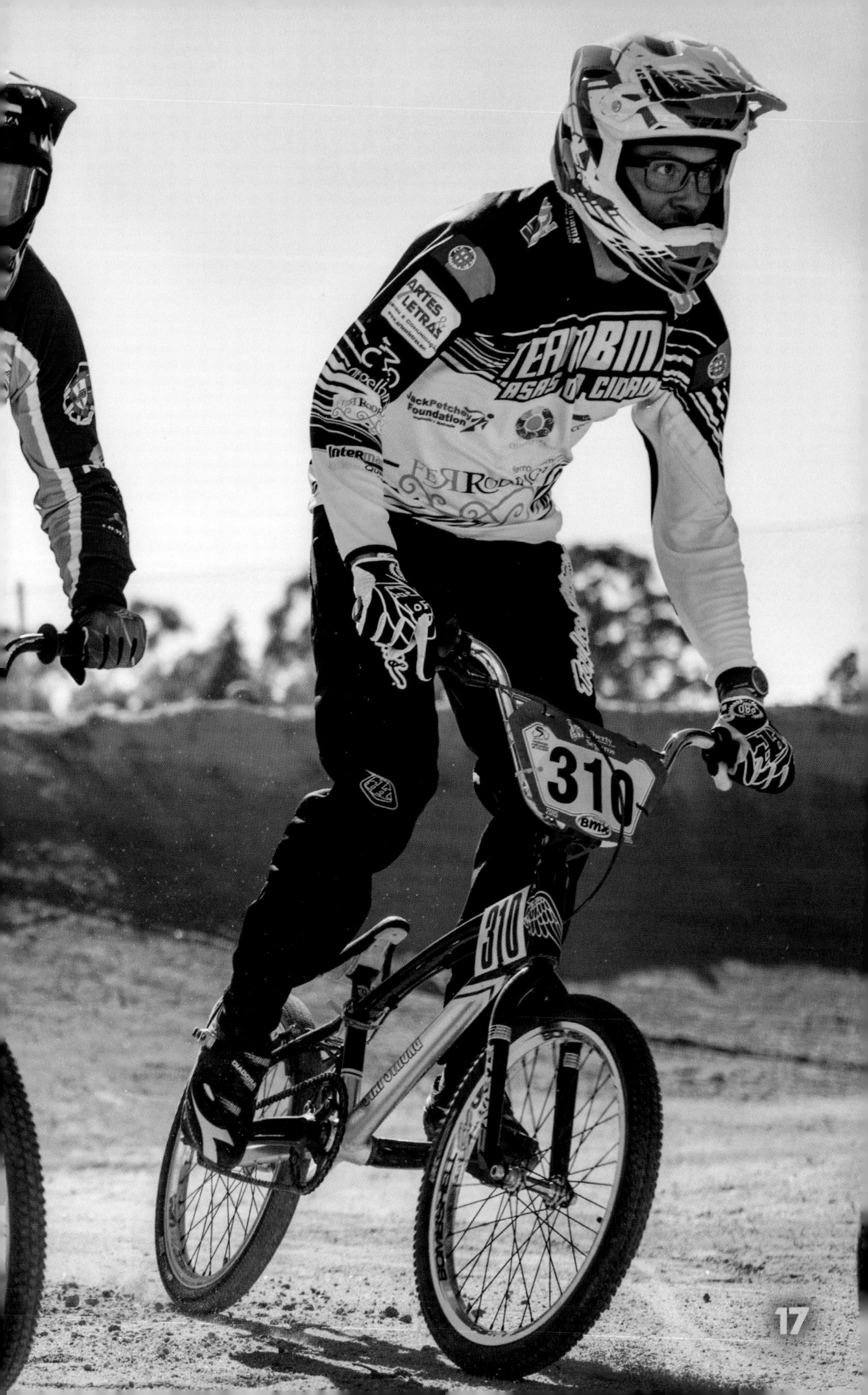
JackPetchey
Foundation
310
310

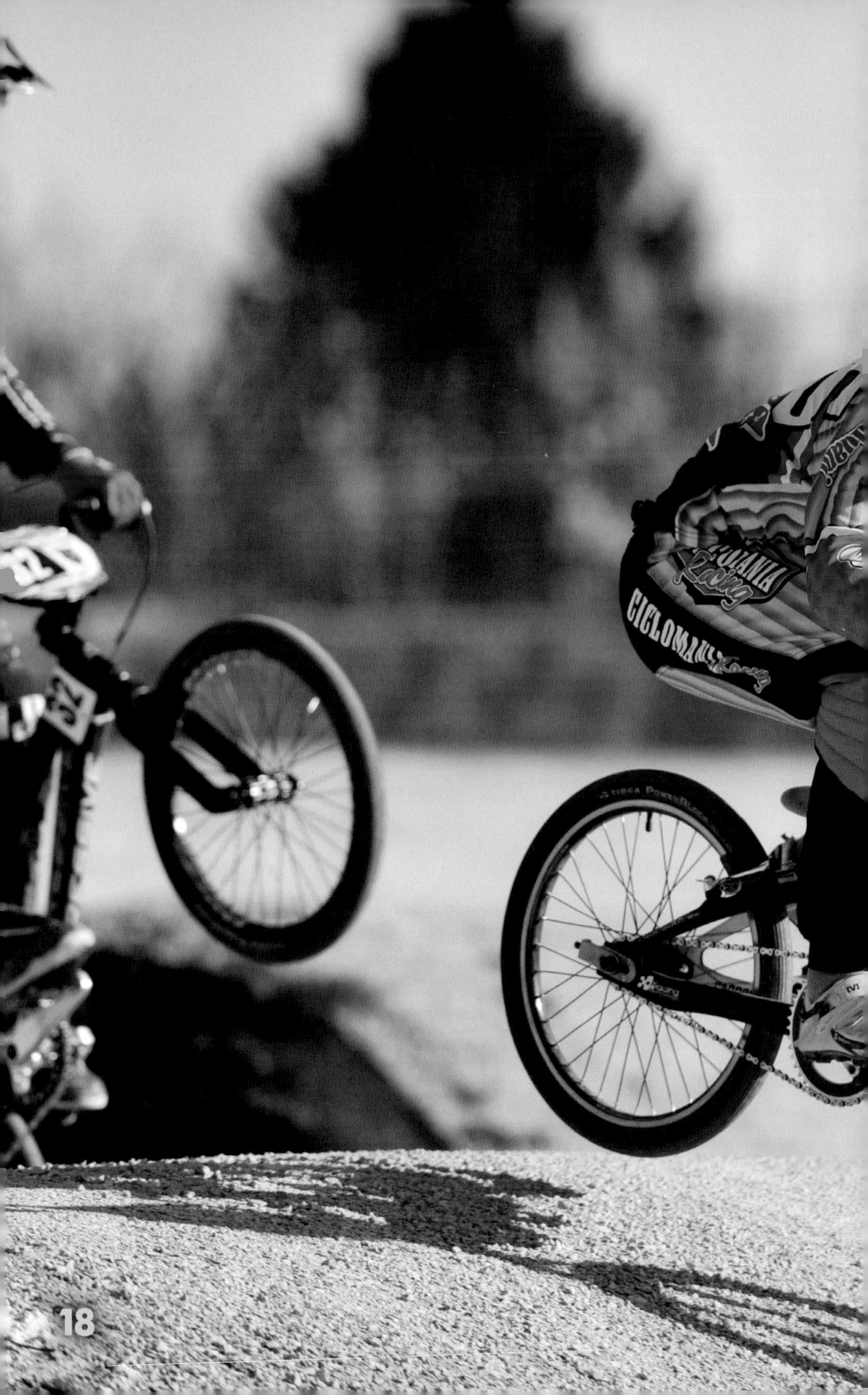
CICLOMANIA Racing

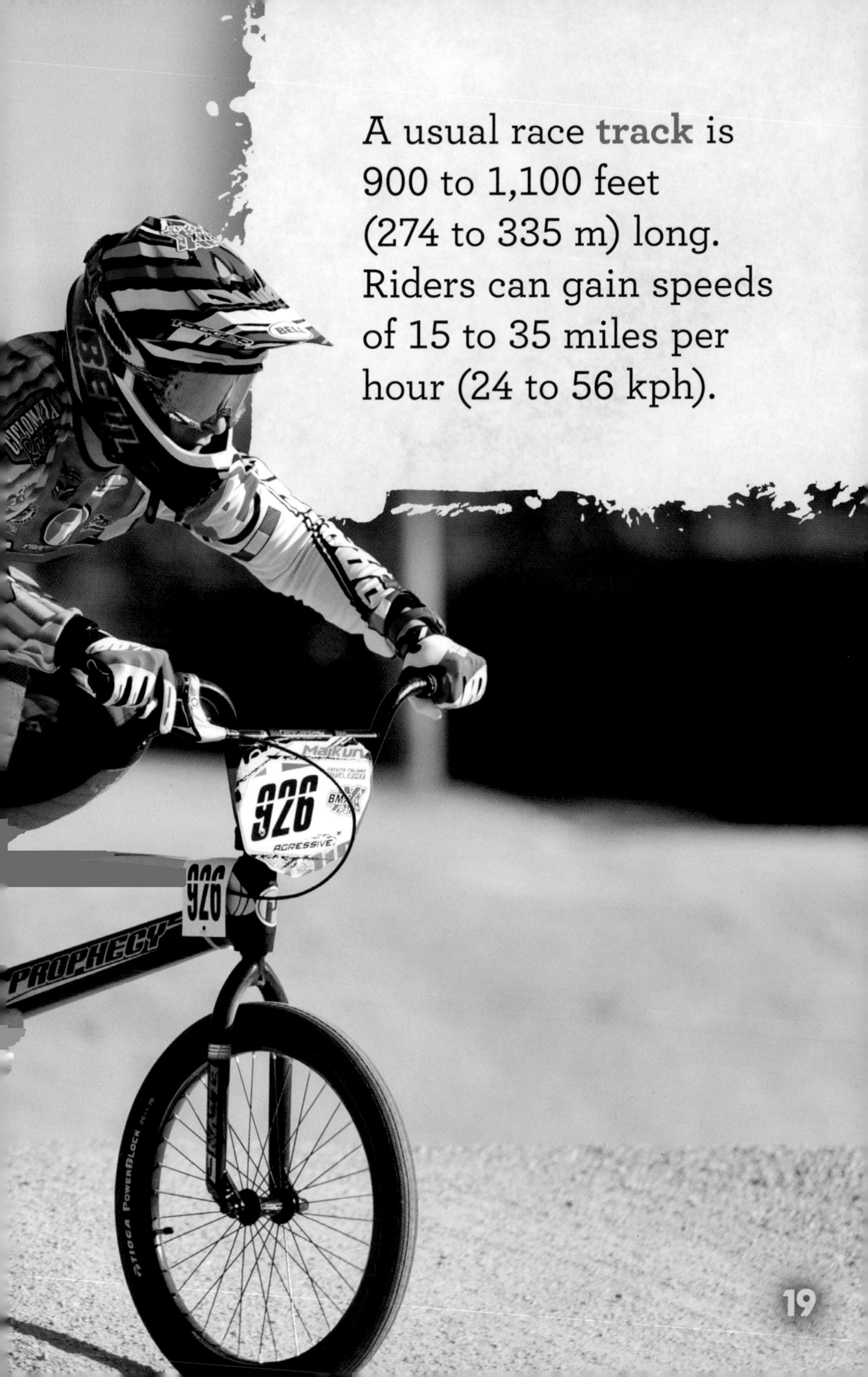
BELL
926
AGRESSIVE
926
PROPHECY

A usual race **track** is 900 to 1,100 feet (274 to 335 m) long. Riders can gain speeds of 15 to 35 miles per hour (24 to 56 kph).

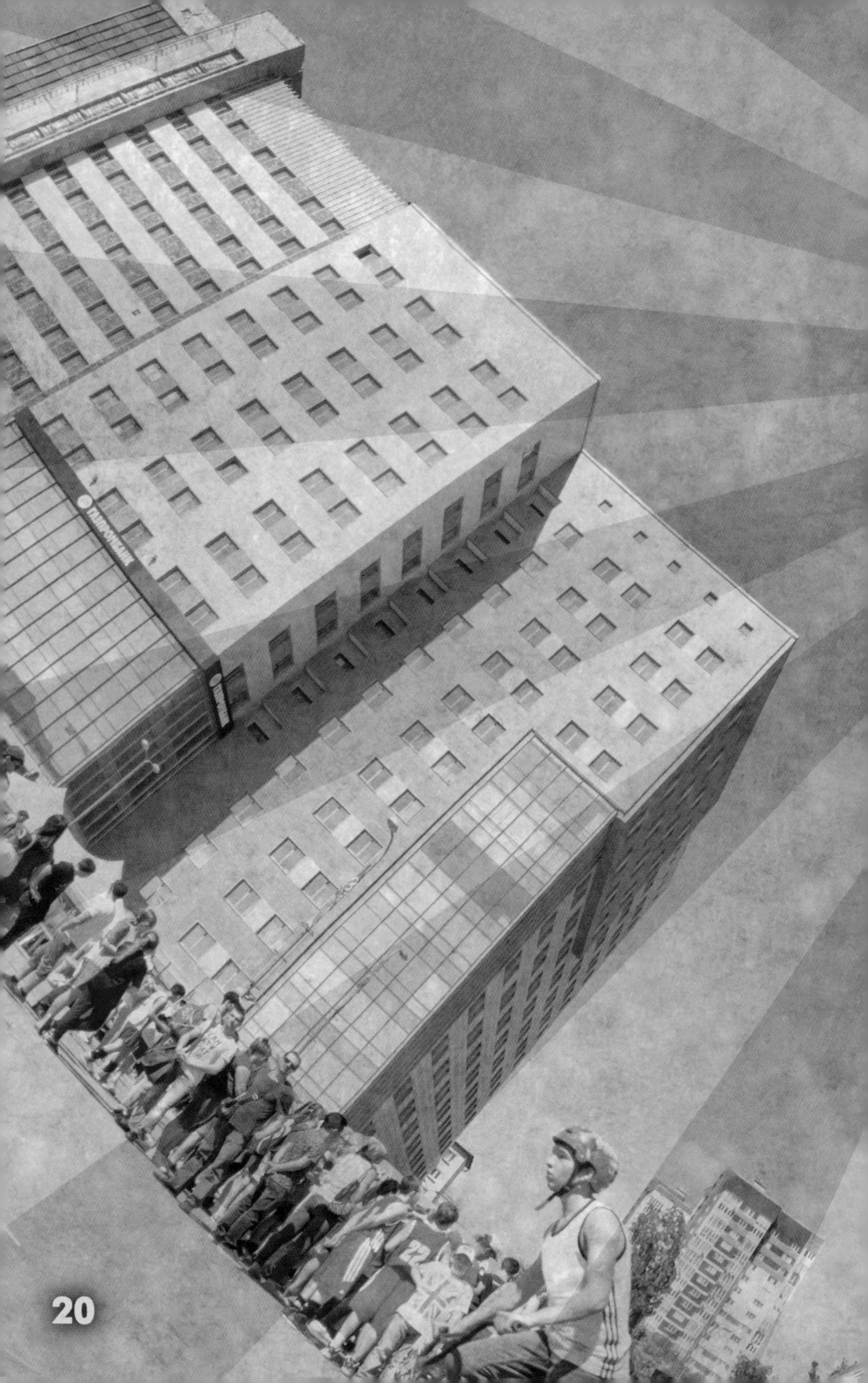

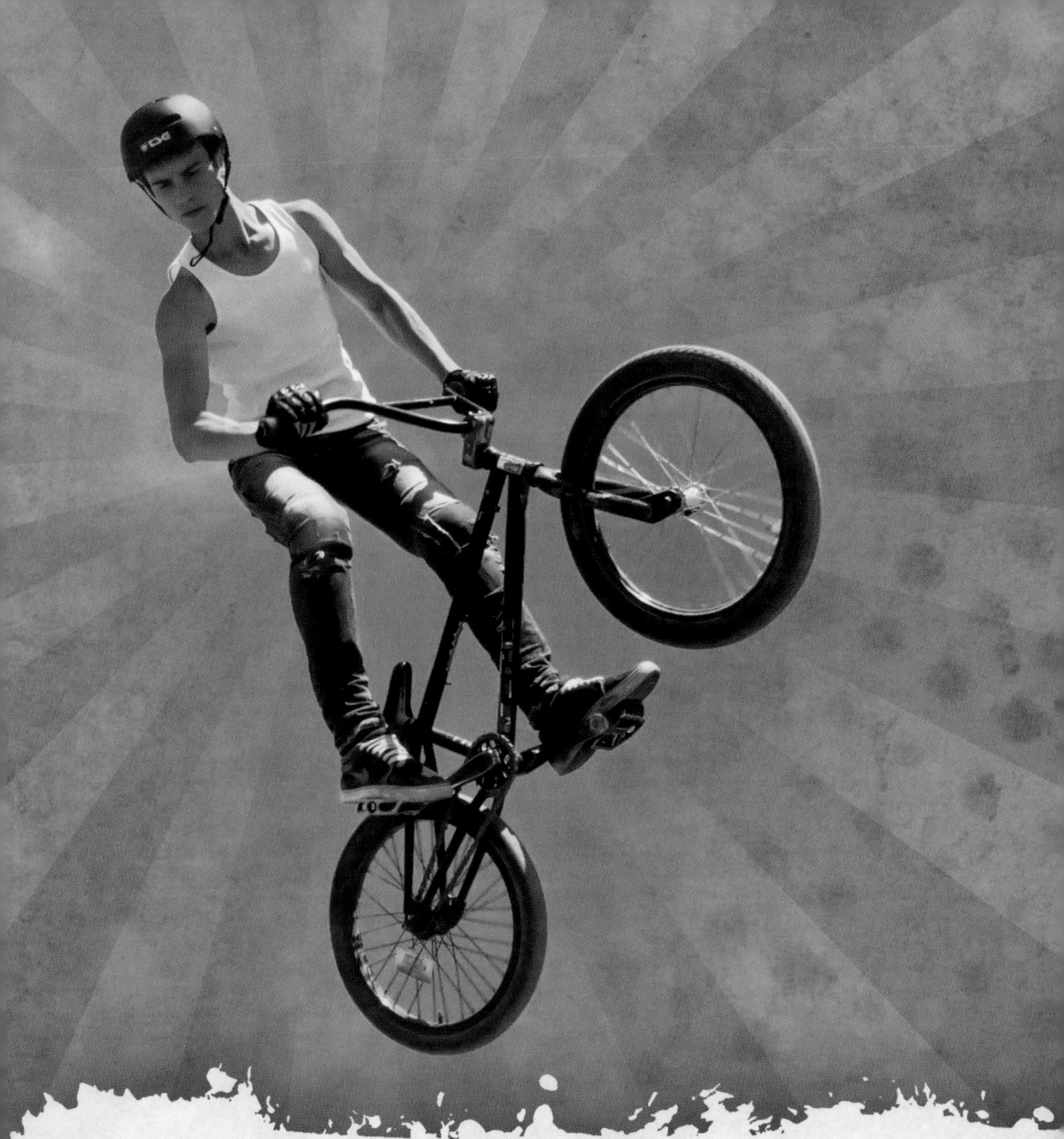

BMX racing made its debut as an **Olympic sport** in the 2008 Beijing Games. And **Freestyle** BMX is now an important event at the Summer X Games every year.

GLOSSARY

fixed-gear – a single speed bicycle used for racing.

freestyle – an extreme sport centered on stunt riding.

motocross – form of off-road racing with motorcycles on enclosed tracks.

off-road – riding a vehicle on difficult roads or tracks, like sand, mud or gravel.

olympic sports – the biggest sporting event in the world that is dived into summer and winter games.

paths – an open area for people, animals, and vehicles to use.

tracks – a course laid out for racing, usually made of dirt.

ONLINE RESOURCES

Booklinks
NONFICTION NETWORK
FREE! ONLINE NONFICTION RESOURCES

To learn more about BMX, please visit abdobooklinks.com. These links are routinely monitored and updated to provide the most current information available.

INDEX